Praise for Carolyn Brown's Honky Tonk series

"Fun, sassy and fast-paced romance... perfect for readers who love escaping into the dreamy and blissful flirtations this romance is sure to bring."

—*RT Reviews*, 4 stars

"Funny, witty, heartfelt and sexy... A great start to what is sure to be a sizzling series!!!!"

—Book Junkie

"*I Love This Bar* rocks... Sexy cowboys, sassy women, and a barrel full of laughter."

—Erotic Horizon

"Guaranteed to leave you countrified and satisfied! This series has pumped up the fun, but will still give you that warm tingly feeling you'd expect from [Carolyn Brown's] happily-ever-after romances."

—Love Romance Passion

"Sometimes humorous, sometimes touching, and Brown's fans will be pleased to reconnect with her trademark cast of quirky characters."

—*Booklist* starred review

"Hot cowboys, sassy women, country music, and good ole fashioned loving will keep you thoroughly entertained and wanting a cowboy of your own."

—Wendy's Minding Spot

Also by Carolyn Brown

MY GIVE A DAMN'S BUSTED

Carolyn Brown

sourcebooks
casablanca

Published by Sourcebooks Casablanca, an imprint of Sourcebooks, Inc.
P.O. Box 4410, Naperville, Illinois 60567-4410
(630) 961-3900
FAX: (630) 961-2168
www.sourcebooks.com

Printed and bound in Canada
WC 10 9 8 7 6 5 4 3 2 1

This is for my brother,
Douglas Gray

Chapter 1

"DAMMIT TO HELL!" LARISSA PUSHED THE CAR DOOR OPEN, crawled up the embankment to the road, popped her hands on her hips, and started stomping toward the son-of-a-bitch who'd put her vintage Mustang nose-down in the ditch.

"Well, shit!" Hank Wells said when an oak tree brought the pickup truck out of a long, greasy slide. He unfastened the seat belt and opened the door to check the damage.

"Are you drunk?" the woman yelled, marching toward him like she was going to tackle him like a football fullback when she reached him.

Well, hells bells, it wasn't his fault that the wreck happened. He hadn't asked that stupid deer to play chicken with the front of his truck. He started toward her at the same speed. "Hell, no, but I could damn sure use a drink."

"Who in the devil taught you to drive? Or do you even have a driver's license? If my car is damaged, you are going to pay for it, and parts for a 1965 Mustang don't come cheap. Can't you drive any better than that?"

He threw up his hands in anger and pointed toward a dead deer on the other side of the road. "The damn thing jumped out in front of me. I broadsided him even though I stomped the brakes all the way to the metal.

What happened to your car isn't my fault, woman, so don't come up here hollerin' at me."

They both came to a halt with a dead buck and ten feet of space between them. The car's radio and the truck's radio were tuned to the same station and the volume turned up loud enough to wake up everyone in Mingus, Texas. A double dose of Jo Dee Messina singing "My Give a Damn's Busted" blared from both vehicles.

She ripped her sunglasses off and gasped. "That's the God's gospel truth. My give a damn *is* busted. I don't care what you say, it is your fault, cowboy. You braked so I had to slam on my brakes or else crawl right up in the bed of that rusty bucket of bolts, so that makes it your fault."

The devil was supposed to be a little sunburned critter with horns, a forked tail, and a pitchfork in his hands. He was not supposed to be wearing snug fitting blue jeans, an open chambray shirt flapping in the hot summer wind, and showing off a broad, muscular chest that was sexy as hell.

If it looks like the devil, smells like the devil, and sounds like the devil, chances are it does not have a halo or wings, Larissa thought.

Well, it damn sure looked like the devil bringing a dose of temptation with lips made for kissing and a chest made to cuddle up against so it had to be the devil. Right?

"Are you hurt?" the cowboy asked gruffly.

"No, are you?" It came out high and squeaky but she was lucky to find any semblance of voice at all. She was afraid to blink for fear he'd turn back into a permanently sunburned man with a forked tail and horns. Another five minutes and she would have been home instead of squaring off with a hunky cowboy on the side of the road with a dead deer between them.

"Hell no, but my dad is going to pitch a shit fit when he sees this truck," he said.

"Your dad? You mean that isn't even your truck?" she asked.

"Yes, I mean no, it is not my truck. Thank god it wasn't my car," he said.

"That's real sweet of you," she said sarcastically as she put her sunglasses back on. If anything they made things worse. His chest looked even more bronzed and sexy with the dark glasses than they did without them. Tingles skipped up and down her spine in spite of the blistering July heat.

"Don't get smart with me, woman. My car is worth a little more than that rusted out piece of shit," he said.

"You hear that song playin' on the radio? Well, honey, that's where I am today. My give-a-damn don't give a damn if you drive a Mercedes or a rusted-out pickup. I just want to know if you've got insurance."

"Hell, I don't know what Dad keeps on the old vehicles. But insurance wouldn't pay for your car. I never touched you. That was your accident," he said.

"But you caused it," she argued.

"It wasn't me. Sue the damned deer."

Larissa's emotions began to let her down. She should be mad as hell that he was the cause of her precious car being tail-up, nose-down in the ditch. But all she wanted to do was kiss his lips.

"Oh, no!" she exclaimed and turned pale. Had the wreck stirred up the dormant genes she'd gotten from her mother? She was thinking like Doreen for the first time in her life! That was scarier than facing a forest fire with a cup of water and no backup plan.

He took a step forward. "What? Are you going to faint or something?"

"No, I'm not going to faint. What do we do now?" She'd give up chocolate before she told a perfect stranger that she'd been thinking about her mother. She didn't even tell her best friends about Doreen. Hell, she didn't tell her enemies about Doreen.

He removed his sunglasses and straw hat and looked at the two vehicles.

He had dark hair and whiskey colored eyes. She forgot all about the deer, the wreck, her mother, and even her fancy car. The late afternoon breeze carried his shaving lotion toward her. That did it! Stetson always made her think about satin sheets, candles, and vintage wine. He looked like the devil in disguise in that open shirt; Stetson made him smell like the devil; his voice was deep and southern and made her insides go all mushy. Lucifer had arrived in the flesh.

Every single thing that the former owners of the Honky Tonk, Daisy and Cathy, had told her they'd experienced the first time they'd seen their future husbands had happened in the past ten minutes—emotional roller coaster, physical attraction, and anger. Larissa Morley was not interested in long-term relationships, so he could take a teaspoon and dig his way back to hell with it. She was not taking the bait.

"That damn deer jumped right out in front of me. I stomped the brakes but hit it anyway. If you hadn't thought right fast, your car would've slammed into my truck. It was pretty damn good defensive driving," he said in a deep Texas drawl that went from harsh to soft.

"Don't try to butter me up, mister. If my car has so much as a scratch on the paint, you will fix it," she said.

Larissa was beginning to understand her mother's taste in men a hell of a lot better. Doreen would have taken time to touch up her makeup and spray on a bit of perfume before she got out of the car. She would have waited for the cowboy to help her up to the top of the ditch and then swooned so he'd catch her. All Larissa could do was keep her mouth shut to keep from drooling.

"I keep telling you that it's the deer's fault. Call the police and we'll both tell them what happened. They'll declare it a no-fault accident. Hell, I didn't even see you in my rearview. I didn't know you were there until I got out of the truck," he said.

"Oh, all right. I'll call Luther to come haul us out of the ditch. He can take you and that truck home. It isn't going anywhere but the body shop or the junk pile. Want him to take it to one of them rather than back to your place?" she asked.

He shook his head slowly. "It'll have to go home. That's Dad's favorite old truck. He may shed tears."

Her voice sounded almost normal when she said, "That's your problem, not mine. I'm calling Luther."

"Does he work for a tow company?" he asked.

"He's the bouncer at the Honky Tonk. He works for an oil company but he's got access to a tow truck," she said.

"Oh," he said flatly.

He put his sunglasses back on so he could really look at the woman. It damn sure wasn't the way he wanted to meet Larissa Morley. She was prettier than the pictures his investigator had taken and a lot smaller. He'd expected someone like Cathy O'Dell: six feet tall and practically bulletproof. But Larissa wasn't anything like Cathy. She was smaller, had thick black hair, lips made for kissing, and a body that filled out those jeans really well.

She eased back down the ditch to turn off the car's engine and retrieve her cell phone. Her purse had turned upside down on the floorboard and the phone had slid under the passenger's seat. She looked like a contortionist as she stretched out across the driver's seat and console and fished around until she finally found it.

Hank went back to the truck and groaned again when he saw the bashed-in door. His phone had been on the dash. It was lying in plain sight right where he'd been sitting and was playing Victoria's ring tone. He put the phone on mute and shoved it in his shirt pocket. The engine had coughed and sputtered sometime after that song about my give a damn being busted. He turned off the engine and tucked the key into his pocket.

She had finished calling Luther when he made it back to the road.

"How long?" Hank asked. Victoria would throw a fit worse than Henry when he found out about his old truck if she thought he'd deliberately not answered her call.

"Ten minutes, tops. Might as well come on up on my porch and wait."

He followed her. "You live here? That's rotten luck. Another two minutes and you'd have pulled into your driveway."

The house was a small frame house with peeling

paint, a wide porch across the front, and a tiny back porch on the east side. Two rocking chairs that had once been white but with chipping paint worse than the house were on one end of the porch. It had the shape of a house built in the thirties when Mingus was an up-and-coming town. Back when it could boast a population of more than the two hundred and eighty-six that lived there nowadays.

"If you'd have hung on a little longer you could have crashed on the east side of my house rather than the west and I'd have made it home. I could have driven with a deer flattened out on the front of my car longer than you did," she said.

"If that deer would've hit your fancy-pants car, it would have totaled the thing, so don't give me a lot of sass."

"I'm a good enough driver I would have missed him to begin with. Go ahead and sit down. I'll bring out some iced tea. You take yours sweet?" She'd be hospitable and take him a glass of tea. She didn't trust herself to revive him without mouth-to-mouth if he passed out on her front lawn. But she wasn't going to invite him into the house even if it was cool inside and blistering hot out on the porch.

"Yes, ma'am, and thank you. I'm Hank Wells, by the way."

"Larissa Morley."

She disappeared into the house and braced herself on the kitchen cabinets. She fanned her face with the back of her hand. The reality of the accident hit her like a wrecking ball going after a wooden outhouse and her legs went all rubbery. Her hands shook as she set two Mason jars on the cabinet and removed an ice tray from the freezer and twisted the ice cubes out of it. She sloshed tea out onto the floor and swore as she cleaned it up.

Hank sat down, leaned forward, and looked down the road at the truck. The oak tree had broken the slide but the door and the whole rear quarter panel was scraped and mangled. It was a small price to pay if it netted him what he'd been trying to find out for months. He'd been trying to figure an angle to meet Larissa ever since she had taken over the Honky Tonk. And one horny old buck out chasing a doe across the road had provided him with the opportunity.

If he'd hit the tree on the driver's side instead of the passenger's, he'd have more than jittery nerves and a sore chest where the seat belt kept him from bouncing around inside the cab of the truck. If she'd have slammed into his truck with her fancy little car she might be dead and he'd have to start all over with the next Honky Tonk owner.

"Knowing your enemies is half the job of winning the war," his mother's voice said so clearly that he looked up to see if she was standing in front of him.

But Victoria wasn't in Mingus and he would have had his head examined for a concussion if she had been. Victoria would never be sitting on the front porch of a house like this, drinking sweet tea while she waited on a tow truck driven by a man named Luther. But then Victoria would have never been in that stinking hot truck. She might have been in the little vintage Mustang. He wondered where Larissa had gotten a car like that. She wasn't old enough to have had it from her youth and she wasn't rich enough to have bought the thing. Another mystery for him to figure out now that he'd met her.

She carried the iced tea to the porch and handed a jar to him. Their fingertips touched and high-voltage electricity passed between them. She wrapped her hot fingers around the icy cold jar and hoped the heat didn't melt the ice and boil the tea. Why had Hank Wells set her nerves on edge, anyway? She saw handsome cowboys six nights a week at the Honky Tonk and all she had to do was nod and they'd have fallen over their boots to dance with her or buy her a drink. The adrenaline rush must still be affecting her. By the time she drank her tea, she'd be back to her old sassy self and he wouldn't look nearly so handsome.

Hank gulped down the cold liquid and stole a couple of long sideways glances toward her. She had straight black hair, brown eyes, high cheekbones, and a full mouth. There was no doubt that there was Indian heritage in her background. She might reach his shoulder, which would put her at about five foot six inches tall. His dad would say that she was built like a red brick outhouse without a brick out of place.

Jessi Colter! That's who she reminded him of! She looked like Jessi back when she was younger. Henry still listened to the old vinyl records on an ancient stereo system. Jessi Colter was one of his favorites and Larissa Morley was a dead ringer for her.

"You sure you're not hurt?" he asked. The anger had died and he was genuinely concerned for her, even if she was a hot little spitfire of a woman.

"Might be sore tomorrow but the car just slid into the ditch. It wasn't much of a crash really," she said.

She couldn't believe she was letting him off the hook that easy. Only minutes before she'd been ready to douse him in honey and throw him to the Texas fire ant population. Now she was being nice? Nothing made a bit of sense.

"I'll have a seat belt burn. We were pretty damn lucky," he said.

"I guess so," she agreed, still trying to make sense of her emotions. At least she was calming down and wouldn't be stroking out because of high blood pressure. That should be a comfort, but it wasn't.

The man that crawled out of the tow truck was as big as a side-by-side refrigerator. He wore bibbed overalls, a white undershirt, work boots, and a layer of dirt and sweat. Hank's belt wouldn't fit around Luther's neck or his biceps, and the scowl on his face looked like he was going to kick ass first and ask questions later. Hank wondered if he should run or sit still. If he was as strong as he looked he could pick Hank up and snap him like a piece of uncooked spaghetti.

Luther shouted as he thundered across the yard. "Are you hurt, Rissa?"

"No, I'm fine. Want some iced tea before you pull us out of the ditch?" she offered.

Luther drew his heavy dark brows together and gave her a once-over. "You sure you're all right? Want me to haul you to the doctor or call Angel to take you just to make sure? Did you bump your head? You look pale to me. There might be something broke inside of you that you can't feel right now. This here's the sorry sucker that made you wreck your fancy car?"

Larissa shook her head. "I'm fine, Luther. If I'm pale

it's because of fear, not pain. My life didn't flash in front of me so it wasn't even a close call. I'll get you some tea. This is Hank Wells and truth is it wasn't really his fault. He can't help it if he can't swerve and miss a deer." She was glad for an excuse to get away from the scalding vibes dancing around between her and Hank. She'd heard that when folks kissed death that they had weird, unexplainable feelings. That was why she'd had such an attraction to Hank. Sure he was a fine looking man, but he definitely was not her type. Tomorrow morning when the adrenaline rush calmed down he probably wouldn't even be good looking.

Luther sat down on the edge of the porch. "I'm Luther. And you are Hank Wells, the man that Rissa thinks can't drive worth a damn?"

"That would be me. She don't have a lot of trouble speaking her mind, does she?"

"Rissa don't mince words. She tells it like she sees it."

"I found that out. Thanks for bringing a tow truck so fast."

Luther looked down the road at the truck, the car, and the dead buck. "Reckon we'd best call the game warden too." He fished a cell phone from his bib pocket and reported the accident.

"Y'all call the police yet?" he asked when he finished telling the game warden where he could find the freshly killed buck.

"Don't reckon there's any need for that. Wasn't nobody's fault but that deer," Hank said.

"Where are you from? Haven't seen you in Mingus before." Luther eyed him carefully.

Larissa returned with a quart jar filled to the brim. "I

don't think there's anything wrong with my Mustang. It'll probably just need a good washing to get the grass and dirt from the bottom. I braked when I saw the deer jump out in front of the truck. I was sliding but it was slow by the time I slipped into the ditch."

Luther nodded and looked at Hank.

"My dad has a spread up north of Palo Pinto. I'm only in this area a little while in the summer. Don't get down this way real often."

Larissa frowned. "Did I butt into a conversation?"

Luther sucked down half the tea before he answered. "I'd just asked him where he was from and he answered. That was the end of the conversation, so you didn't butt into nothing. Thank you for the tea. It's hotter'n hell today. I'll be glad to work at the Tonk tonight just to get to sit down in the cool air conditioning."

"So you work for Lambert Oil and the beer joint?" Hank motioned toward the tow truck with that logo on the side. He knew all about Luther Mason. He just never reckoned on the man being as big as a barn door. The mug shot his investigator had sent showed a big man, not an enormous one.

"Both. Over at Lambert Oil, Angel McElroy is my supervisor. Rissa is my boss at the Honky Tonk," he said. "Lucky I got access to a tow truck or y'all would've had to call J. C. or Elmer to come get you out with a tractor."

"How's things going with Angel and Garrett? I haven't seen them in the Honky Tonk in weeks." Larissa tried to focus on something other than Hank's lips and eyes.

"The official honeymoon was over weeks ago but I'm not sure the real one is ever going to be finished. Someday

I'm going to get what they've got." Luther sighed.

Larissa patted him on the shoulder. "I hope so."

Hank set his empty jar on the porch and stood up. A big diagonal red welt had puffed up on his chest. He flinched when he touched it.

"Hurts like hell, don't it?" Luther said. Hank nodded.

"I've had a couple of those and believe me when that seat belt locks down on a big old boy like me it hurts real bad. There's a lot of meat for it to sink into. It'll be worse tomorrow and it'll take a couple of weeks before it goes away."

Larissa looked at the welts and then her eyes traveled up to Hank's face. His gaze locked with hers and it was several seconds before either could blink.

Luther looked from one to the other. "Y'all know each other?"

Larissa noticed a movement near her rocking chair and was suddenly interested in the black and white tomcat she'd adopted. "Not until thirty minutes ago. That dead deer introduced us."

Luther finished off his tea and chewed on a chunk of ice. "Well, I'm damn sure glad I wasn't the one who introduced you if that's the thanks it gets. Come on, Hank. You can help me pull Rissa's car out of the ditch and make sure it's all right. Then we'll haul you home."

Hank figured Luther was powerful enough to carry the Mustang to Larissa's driveway on his shoulder. But when Luther told him to lock the chain under the car, Hank didn't argue. The winch groaned and the car came up out of the ditch smoothly. Larissa got inside, started the engine, and drove it into the driveway. Luther studied the whole thing three times from tires to chassis down to the sides for paint damage and even the windshield for cracks.

"Don't appear to be anything wrong," Luther said.

"I really think it's all right," Larissa said.

"Well, a damned old buck isn't going to pay up if something is cracked or broken, and we don't want Hank here to think we're making him pay for something that happens later. I reckon you are a stand-up guy, Hank. Do you see anything wrong with this car?" Luther asked.

Hank's tone went icy. "It needs to be washed but it's not hurt. If you find anything wrong within the next thirty days, call me and I'll send you a check."

Larissa glared at him. Warm one minute. Cold the next. Did he have a split personality? "You can bet your sweet ass I will. If my car even hiccups I will be calling you. What is your number?"

"I'll be at the ranch for a month. It's Henry Wells, Palo Pinto, Texas. Look it up."

"Let's get your poor old truck away from the tree and take you home, then," Luther said.

Larissa stood on the porch and watched the wench bring the truck up to the road. Luther deftly moved the tow truck into position and waved when he and Hank crawled into the cab of the tow truck.

She picked up the empty tea jars. Her mother would have already fallen off the porch with a fatal heart attack if she'd known that Larissa served someone who looked like Hank from a Mason jar. Doreen would have taken one look at the man and the flirting would have begun right there. Larissa had seen it happen many times before and the men were usually built about like Hank Wells. He might be a cowboy in a rusted old truck but she could fix that with one trip to the car dealership and an English tailor. In fifteen minutes she would have invited him for dinner in Paris or London, booked a flight to take them there the next day, and maybe even taken him to bed once or twice before then. If not then she would seduce him on the plane and they'd arrive for dinner with healthy appetites. Yes, sir, Doreen did like her boyfriends and Hank was the perfect age.

A pickup came to a screeching halt, squealing tires in front of her house about the time that she opened the front door. "Shit! Not another wreck!" She slammed the door and spun around to see who'd hit what.

"Good god, Merle, you scared the crap out of me. I thought we were in for two wrecks in one day," she yelled.

Merle Avery made a beeline toward the porch, cussing the whole way. "Don't you be telling me that I scared the shit out of you, girl. It's a wonder I didn't have a heart attack. I've got my three score and ten in and am living on borrowed time already and if you ever tell a soul I owned up to that, you won't die in a wreck. I'll put a damn hit out on you. Are you all right?"

Merle had seen seventy come and go a while back but if anyone ever had the guts to utter those words they'd better run fast and far. If she ever caught them they'd be pushing up daisies instead of two-stepping at the Honky Tonk. She and Ruby Lee, the original owner of the Honky Tonk, had blown into Mingus at the same time back in the early sixties. Ruby Lee had built a beer joint and Merle had set about selling western shirt designs overseas. Both of them turned their enterprises into gold mines. Ruby Lee had died eight years before in a motorcycle accident and left the

Honky Tonk to Daisy O'Dell. Since that time Merle had taken every woman who'd owned the beer joint under her wing and befriended them as if they were her own kith and kin.

"I'm fine. It didn't even scratch my car. Come on in. Luther and Hank left part of a pitcher of sweet tea." Larissa held the door for her.

"Tea, hell! Get me a shot of Jack, straight up. I drove over here like a bat out of hell, girl. I burned a hundred miles off those tires and it's a wonder I didn't roll that damn truck. I was doing a hundred miles an hour when I passed the Honky Tonk. Angel called and said Luther had to bring the tow truck because you'd had a wreck. I was afraid I'd have to follow the ambulance to the hospital." Merle flopped down on the sofa. She threw her hand over her forehead dramatically and let out a whoosh of air. "Damn, I ain't been that scared since the day Ruby Lee made me ride on that motorcycle of hers. I told God if he'd just let me live I'd never get on that thing again. He did and I didn't."

Larissa went to the kitchen, pulled down the bottle of Jack Daniels, and poured three fingers in a pint-sized Mason jar. She carried it to Merle and said, "I'm sorry. I didn't think about Angel calling you. It wasn't even much of a wreck. Hank hit a deer and swerved all over the road and I either had to brake hard or smash into the rear end of a truck. That sent me into a slide and I wound up in the ditch. I never figured on anyone even knowing about it."

"Honey, you can't fart in a town this size without everyone in town knowing what you ate for dinner." Merle tossed back the whiskey in two gulps and sat the jar on the coffee table.

"Well, I'm fine and the car isn't hurt. The truck met up with an oak tree but Hank wasn't hurt either, other than he's going to have a seat belt bruise," Larissa said.

"You got to hire some help in that beer joint. If you get hauled off to the hospital, who'd run it?" Merle said. Her straight-out-of-the-bottle black hair had been recently done and piled up on her head. Her jeans were tight and her signature western shirt was open to show a tank top under it. Her boots were scuffed and worn.

"Don't know that I've ever seen you in worn out boots," Larissa said.

"Don't be changin' the subject. I'm old but I'm damn sure not stupid. I was down in the basement working on a new design when Angel called. I grabbed the pair by the back door that I wear when I mow the yard," she explained. "Now about that hired help?"

"I've been thinking about hiring someone because business has picked up so much. I promise I'll think harder, but why would it matter if the joint was shut down if I got hurt?"

She rolled her eyes toward the ceiling and crossed herself. "Girl, you are talkin' blasphemy. That place ain't been shut down since Ruby Lee built it. Where in the hell would I go to shoot pool and have a beer after I've worked all day if the Honky Tonk was closed? I'm protectin' my own interests here," Merle said.

"You could run it as well as I could," Larissa told her.

Merle shook her head emphatically. "Ruby Lee wanted me to go in partners with her and I turned her down. She was my best friend and I said no. You think anyone else could talk me into it, you're crazy. When she died I almost crawled up in that casket with her but at least I still had the Honky Tonk. Daisy was already runnin' it so it wasn't so bad. Then when Daisy left I already knew Cathy so I didn't get worried. Same with you. Cathy fell in love with Travis and got married, but you were already my friend so it wasn't a catastrophic change. Girl, you got to find some help. That's all there is to it. You don't hire someone, I will."

Larissa sat down in a rocking chair and set it to moving with her heel. "How'd you survive Tinker leaving?"

"It was time for Tinker to retire. He's happy as a monkey in a banana factory out there on his property. So it wasn't any big thing when Luther went to work for Cathy," Merle said. "Tinker was tired and ready to retire when Ruby Lee died. If he hadn't felt like he was Daisy's surrogate dad he wouldn't have stayed, but he did and I was glad. I don't like change at my age. By the time he decided to quit, there was Luther. He's big and burly like Tinker and the change wasn't so bad."

Larissa threw up her palms. "Okay, okay, I'll really, really think about hiring someone."

"Well, that's settled. I'm going home to finish my job. Thank god you ain't dead," Merle said bluntly.

"Drive legal," Larissa said.

"I'll drive anyway I damn well please."

"Then be careful so I don't have to bail you out of jail for speeding. It'd be a shame to shut down the Honky Tonk so I could come up to the courthouse and get you out of a cell with a bunch of hardened hookers and drunks."

Merle gave her a dirty look. "You find me a whole cell full of hardened hookers in this whole county and

I'll gladly visit with them in jail. Might even sell a few shirts."

"Get on out of here and thanks for coming to see about me. That means a lot," Larissa said.

When Merle was gone she got a case of nervous giggles. A year before she wouldn't have believed it if someone had told her what she'd be doing on that summer night.

—∿∿—

Henry Wells sighed when he looked up from the backyard and saw his truck being towed into the yard. He headed that way in long strides and held his breath until he saw Hank crawl out of the passenger's side of the tow truck.

When he was close enough they could hear him over the noise of the winch he asked, "What happened?"

"Deer jumped out in front of me and sent me into a sideways slide into an oak tree," Hank said.

"That's my favorite old truck," Henry said.

"I'm sorry, Dad," Hank said.

"You hurt?"

"Just a seat belt bruise."

"Hurt anyone other than the deer?"

"Woman in a Mustang behind me landed in the ditch but her car wasn't hurt and she seemed fine. I told her to call me if there were any problems," Hank said.

The truck hit the ground with a thump and Luther detached all the chains. He took off his leather work glove and extended his hand. "I'm Luther Mason."

Henry shook his hand. "I'm Henry Wells, Hank's dad. What do I owe you, son?"

"Not a dime. Come on down to the beer joint some-time and buy me a beer, and we'll be even up. Got to get home and get cleaned up for my second job. Hope next time I see you it ain't in this kind of way." Luther got back into the truck, turned it around, and left a dust cloud in his wake as he headed back down the lane.

"Nice kid. Big as a barn, ain' he?" Henry said.

Hank pointed at the truck. "I ain't never seen a barn that big. We going to fix it or junk it?"

"I'll work on it in my spare time. Give me something to do other than watch reruns on the television at night after you're gone," Henry said.

"I'll buy you another one," Hank offered.

"I reckon you would and could. Reckon I could buy three to replace it if I wanted to, but I don't. That old truck has some memories in it. Be like tradin' in a grandpa on a stranger. There's trucks around that we can use while I work on that one so don't worry about it. I'm glad you didn't kill nothin' other than a deer. Did you call the game warden?"

"Luther did."

"We better go on in the house and tell Oma what happened and that you wasn't hurt. If she looks out here and sees the truck, she's liable to have a fit."

Hank nodded. "I'll be back in a minute. We should've had Luther take it on out to the barn."

"Boy already brought it home for the price of a beer. That's enough. I'll fire up the tractor and hook onto it. Won't take but a minute to get it down in that barn where we keep the implements. You can tell me all about how it happened while we walk back," Henry said.

"I figured you'd have a cussin' fit," Hank said.

"Guess I'm gettin' too old for fits. They take a lot of a man's energy. I'm just glad you're alive, son. Someday you're goin' to slow down and appreciate livin'," Henry said.

"Maybe." Hank threw an arm over his father's shoulder.

Chapter 2

LARISSA WAS SURPRISED TO LOOK UP AND SEE HANK RIGHT across the bar from her that night. She figured he'd be home in his recliner moaning and groaning about the seat belt burn. His wife would bring him beer and potato chips and maybe even run his bath water that night while the kids played with grandpa. She hadn't been so physically attracted to a man in years. Maybe not ever, and he wasn't even her type. She usually went for someone a lot less rough around the edges. But something about those eyes and the shape of his face, not to mention all those muscles, sent her hormones into overdrive. She hoped he *was* married because the kind of white-hot heat she felt when he was around wasn't healthy. At least if there was a wife at home, he'd be permanently off limits. If he wasn't married and he visited the Honky Tonk every evening for a week she'd be nothing but a blubbering basket case.

"Hello, again. What are you doing back in this part of the county? I figured you'd have gotten enough of Mingus this afternoon," she said.

"Thought I'd come down and see what all the fuss was about. My friends say this is the best place in the state for old music, cold beer, and dancing," he said.

"They're damn right. What can I get you?" Who were his friends and when had they been in the Tonk? Were they the preppies over at the closest table with a bucket of beer and a pitcher of tequila sunrise in front of them? Or were they the cowboys circling the jukebox deciding which songs to play? She decided they were probably the cowboys but then he said he only spent a little while in Palo Pinto County each year so maybe it was the preppies.

"Two bottles of Coors," he said.

She set two bottles of beer in front of him, picked up the ten dollar bill he'd laid on the counter, and made change. She was careful not to touch his hand when she dropped it into his palm. If his touch was as hot as his smoldering eyes she would fall down on all fours and follow him around like a little lost puppy with her tongue hanging out. Her reaction earlier that evening was supposed to have been an adrenaline rush brought on by a near death experience. It should have passed when her nerves settled down. What happened?

Good God Almighty, get a hold of yourself, girl. You've seen good lookin' cowboys before. You've been on every continent in the world. What makes this one so special anyway, other than the fact that you've been too busy for even a long passionate kiss the past six months?

Justin Langley, a Monday night regular at the Honky Tonk, sat down beside Hank. "Hey, Larissa, I need a place to sleep for my eight hours of down time. Can I use my regular trailer space?"

She pulled a chart out from under the counter. "It's empty. I'll write you up for it. Want a beer?"

"Just one to help me sleep," Justin said.

"Comin' up," Larissa told him.

Justin turned to Hank. "Who are you? Ain't seen you in the Honky Tonk before. You just a stranger passing through or did you move to this area?"

Hank stuck out a hand. "Hank Wells. Trailer space?"

Justin shook it. "Justin Langley. I drive a semi and stop in here on Monday nights for a few beers before I turn around and head down to Galveston in the morning. Yep, she's got twenty of them out back of the Honky Tonk. Someday she's going to marry me and we're going to see the world from the cab of my truck. It's just a matter of time. Owners of the Honky Tonk always fall in love with a customer and he's always a cowboy. I'm a cowboy who rides in a truck rather than on a horse's back. She'll come around someday."

Larissa made it back down the bar in time to catch the last remark. "Darlin', I will marry you when angels sell rainbow snow cones in hell. Besides, you've got a girlfriend so stop teasing me."

"And what about this magic charm thing all the women talk about? That one where the owner of the joint ends up married to a cowboy?" Justin asked.

"That's not a charm. It's a curse and it's ending with me," she said with false bravado.

Hank disagreed. The Honky Tonk had to have a charm of some kind. Daisy wouldn't sell the place but gave it away to her cousin. Cathy wouldn't sell either, but gave the Honky Tonk to Larissa Morley. Now she was determined to never leave. What magic did an old weathered building and two jukeboxes have, anyway? Had the wood been passed through a voodoo queen's blessing or something? Had an ancient witch put a curse on the women who ran the place?

"So where you from, Hank?" Justin asked.

Hank forgot about curses and voodoo and answered, "My dad has a spread up around Palo Pinto."

"Cattle or oil?"

"Angus."

"Always thought I'd like a ranch when I settle down. Hey, Larissa, you want to raise Angus when we get married?" he yelled above the jukebox noise.

"Keep dreaming. Listen to what's on the jukebox," she said.

Dancers were out on the floor forming long line dances to "My Give a Damn's Busted" by Jo Dee Messina. Twice in one day she'd heard that song. Was there supposed to be a message in it?

Justin grabbed his chest with both hands. "You are breaking my heart. Is your give a damn really, really busted?"

"Busted all to pieces," she said.

"Is it just busted or plumb broke?" Justin pushed on.

"What difference does it make?" Hank asked.

"If it's just busted we might find parts to fix it. If it's plumb broke we might as well go on home," he said.

"Don't forget your hat," Larissa said.

"Sounds to me like you got some persuading to do," Hank said.

"Ah, Larissa is just playin' hard to get."

Larissa had searched the ends of the earth looking for a place to hang her heart. When it found a home in Mingus she fought it for weeks. When it decided it wanted to own and operate the Honky Tonk, she'd thought about extensive psychotherapy or else an MRI to find out if she had an acute brain tumor. But the heart will have what the heart wants or else it will pine away to nothing. It wanted to live in Mingus and run a beer joint and Larissa gave it what it wanted. Now she owned the Honky Tonk and had been happy as a drunk trapped in a wine cellar.

She made her way from one end of the bar to the other and stopped in front of Hank with renewed purpose to put a vice clamp on the physical attraction. "Need another beer?"

"I'm still workin' on this one. I took the other one to Luther for payment for his help today. How long have you owned this place?" Hank knew exactly how long Larissa Morley had owned and operated the Honky Tonk. His file on her was slim but it was accurate from the day she moved to Mingus. Before that she didn't exist.

"Moved here last winter," she answered.

"Like it?"

"It's home."

"Want to dance?"

"Don't dance with the customers, but thanks."

"Buy you a beer or a drink?" Hank asked.

"Don't do that either. Thanks."

Justin patted him on the shoulder. "Don't feel bad. I've been tryin' to talk her into the same thing since last spring. Women! Can't understand them. Can't live with 'em and it's against the law to shoot 'em. Ever hear of that book that says they are from a different planet than men folks?"

Larissa left them to discuss the impossibility of getting along with women and made her way down the bar, waiting on customers as she went. Monday nights used to be slow until word got out there was a quaint little beer joint just over the border into Palo Pinto County with a jukebox that still played old records at three songs for a quarter. The Internet and blogging had opened up whole new avenues of word-of-mouth advertising and now the place was hopping every night. Sometimes Luther had to turn the customers away at the door to wait on the porch or in the parking lot until a few got tired and left.

"Hey, Larissa, here's our song. All you got to do is tell me that you love me and the next time it won't be so hard." Justin pointed to the jukebox where "Say It Again" by Don Williams was playing.

She shook her head and frowned.

"You really in love with her?" Hank asked.

"Naw, I just like to tease her. I got a girl in south Texas who can shoot the eyes out of a rattlesnake at fifty yards. I wouldn't dare fall in love with another woman. She'd shoot me, throw my carcass out for the coyotes, and never look back. She's one of them country girls that songs are written about and I'm so much in love with her it ain't even funny. We're gettin' married at Christmas time and I'm settlin' down to an office job." Justin picked up his beer and headed to the pool tables.

Hank turned around on the bar stool and watched the dancers fill up the floor in a slow two-step as Merle Haggard sang a slow ballad. He was reminded of Toby Keith's "I Love This Bar." Toby mentioned hookers, lookers, bikers, and preppies in the song. Hank saw women who could be hookers in their tight fitting jeans and low cut blouses; those who were lookers in their high-dollar designer jeans and boots and hundred dollar haircuts; bikers over there at a table with their tattoos and earrings; preppies in their pleated slacks and dress shirts; and more hats and boots than he'd seen in one place since the last time he attended a cattle sale on the Lazy R Ranch up in Palo Pinto, Texas.

The Honky Tonk was a weathered gray building with a wraparound porch with a flashing neon sign atop a three-tiered façade. Inside it was one big room with two pool tables in the right corner, a few tables pushed around the walls with chairs surrounding them, a bar across the entire back side, and two jukeboxes.

Sitting on the stool and taking stock of the place, Hank couldn't figure out why anyone wouldn't sell it for ten times what it was worth. But the previous two owners had turned down million-dollar offers for a piece of Texas dirt and a building not worth a tenth of that. If there wasn't a curse on the place, then what would it take to make Larissa sell?

His heart clinched up in his chest when he looked up and caught her looking at him. Something stirred but he was in the Honky Tonk on a mission and he would not be deterred by a sexual attraction that could be satisfied with one night in a cheap motel. He held up his empty beer bottle and pointed at it. She popped the top on another and brought it to him.

"So you don't dance with customers or let them buy you a drink. If a customer asked you out to dinner would you go?" he asked.

"I work six nights a week. Only day I have off is Sunday." Larissa hadn't been on a real date in six months. Hank Wells rattled her nerves like a marble in a tin can just sitting on the bar stool. She couldn't imagine spending a whole evening with him with no one else around.

Rattled her nerves, hell! Whatever sexy vibes he threw out set them on a roller coaster that took her breath away.

"Then Larissa Morley, will you go to dinner with me next Sunday? I will pick you up at noon. What's your favorite restaurant? Or if you want a home cooked dinner, tell me what your favorite food is and I'll ask Oma to make it for you. It's payment for almost totaling your car today," Hank said. In spite of the job, he would really like to spend more time with her. Getting to know her was part of the job, but she was all the things he liked in a woman. Strong. Independent. Sassy. Funny. Kind. Well, that last one might be up for debate but she had given him a jar of iced tea while they waited on the tow truck.

Her heart wanted to say yes but the little crawling itch on the back of her neck said something wasn't right. He had mesmerizing eyes. He was sexy as the devil in disguise. He made her little heart jump around like a kid in a candy store. But... and there was that little three letter word getting in the way. Until she could look at him and see no buts, and she dang sure didn't mean butts, she wasn't going to succumb to all the heat between them.

"Thanks but no thanks. I've got plans for this Sunday," she said.

Justin poked his head between two customers halfway down the bar. "Hey, Larissa, fix up a bucket of Coors. Me and Julio and Patrick got us a hot game of eight ball going back there."

"You must've lost the first round." She set a galvanized milk bucket on the bar, shoved six bottles of cold Coors down into it, and topped it off with two scoops of ice.

Justin picked up the bucket and carried it back to the tables. "Yep, I did."

Larissa made her way down the bar, filling orders and jars. When she got back to Hank he still had half a bottle of beer so she didn't stop until he spoke.

He nodded toward the jukebox. "Who's that singing?"

"That's the great Emmylou Harris. You didn't grow up on old country music, did you?" she asked.

Maybe that was the wrong thing about him. He didn't belong in the Honky Tonk and was an impostor. The previous Honky Tonk owner, Cathy, used to say that her "bullshit" radar went off when something wasn't the absolute truth and when Larissa had worked as a bartender long enough she'd find her radar. Evidently she'd worked there long enough because it was sending red lights and a whining noise that only she could see. The prickle on her neck and the way he looked at her with a veil over those strange colored eyes had set it off big-time.

"Sure I know Emmylou. I just didn't recognize that song," Hank said.

Merle Avery claimed the stool next to Hank. She was an expert pool shooter and had seen more groups come and go in the beer joint than anyone in the county. She wore snug fitting blue jeans and her designer western shirt had red roses embroidered on the back yoke. She always carried a special case for her custom made cue sticks and never touched the freebie sticks on the wall. That night she set her case on the floor between the bar stools and studied Hank for a full minute.

"Do I have something on my face?" he finally asked.

"No you don't, but I'm old enough that I can stare and not give a damn if it's rude. I'm deciding whether I'm going to like you. Who are you?" she asked Hank.

He hadn't planned on getting the third degree from everyone in the state of Texas when he decided to drop by the Honky Tonk, but he put on his best smile and said, "I'm Hank Wells, ma'am. Who are you?"

"Name is Merle Avery. You one of the new crowd that heard about the place on one of them Internet things?"

"No, ma'am. Just word of mouth. Friend said that the Honky Tonk was the hottest place around on Monday nights. I'm the one who hit the deer this afternoon and sent Larissa into the ditch," Hank said.

She leaned back and started at his boots, let her gaze go up his long legs to the Texas Longhorn bull on his tarnished silver belt buckle, on up to chambray work shirt sleeves that had been rolled up to his elbow, taking time to check out his hands and his neck.

"I heard about that. Larissa said you laid down some rubber tryin' to get that truck stopped and that it was probably totaled, old as it is. Why did you come all the way back down here tonight?"

"That's exactly what happened. And it is probably totaled out but my dad is bound and determined to fix the thing. He's got this affection for it. I think it's a sixty-something model and he's already put two engines in it. I've been hearing a lot about this place. I was close and the chores were done so I came to town for some company and a beer."

"You almost fooled me, Hank Wells. But you are a drugstore cowboy. You ain't the real thing."

Words froze in his throat.

Larissa stopped in front of them. "He's not real?"

"He's the best fake I've ever seen," Merle answered.

"What makes you say that?" Hank asked hoarsely.

"Two things. Your neck is lily white. That means you don't work outside enough to be a real honest-to-god cowboy at your age. And your fingernails. That's dirt up under them but it's not ground in enough. Add that to the fact that you didn't recognize Emmylou and something ain't kosher."

"I don't have to justify myself to you, Miz Avery. But I am not a fake. My father owns the Lazy R Ranch north of Palo Pinto. Henry Wells? Heard of him? I have a job in Dallas and don't spend all my time on the ranch," he drawled. "When I'm at the ranch, I'm a bona fide cowboy whether I look like one or not."

"I knew Henry years ago," Merle said. "Didn't know he had a boy. Don't tell me that truck you wrecked is an old sixties model Ford. Red with white leather interior?"

"It is. How'd you know that? You clairvoyant or something?"

"I've got the memory of an elephant, honey. When you go home you tell Henry that you were down here at the Honky Tonk. He might explain about that truck if he wants you to know. Me, I ain't sayin' another word except I understand why he would never junk it." Merle picked up the beer that Larissa set before her and took a long gulp. "You any good at pool?"

"No ma'am, but I understand there's a couple of guys back there who are," he said.

"Ah, that Julio and Patrick ain't no competition. Julio's Mexican temper and Patrick's Irish one get in the way of either of them bein' good at anything but arguing. Damn, I miss Garrett and Angel," she said.

Hank looked at Larissa with a question in his eyes.

"Angel would be her niece and Garrett is Angel's husband. They're newlyweds and don't come in too often anymore." Larissa barely got the words out when someone ordered two buckets of Miller Lite and a pitcher of hurricanes.

Merle waited for the noise of the blender to stop before she turned to Hank. "I can see by the way you look at Larissa that you are interested. If you want to impress her then you got to work on getting that neck red and them hands dirty. She said when she took over the Honky Tonk that the only way she'd ever look at a man was if he was a real cowboy."

Hank frowned. "And I thought I was pretty damn close to the real thing. Not that I'm interested in impressing Larissa or anyone else in this place. Someone else can have my stool. You have a good evening, ma'am."

"Go haul some hay or drill some wheat and bring a red neck back with you when you come back in here," Merle told him.

He tipped his hat at her and made his way through line dancers doing their routine to "Johnny B. Goode" by Buck Owens. He could still hear the guitar licks when he opened the door to his father's newest pickup truck. He crawled inside and rolled down the window. He'd rather have been driving his own car but one look at it and not just Merle, but everyone in the county, would know he didn't belong in the Honky Tonk. The next singer was Loretta Lynn. He'd recognize that nasal twang anywhere because he'd heard his father and mother argue about it when he was a little boy. His mother hated anything country and his father loved everything country. His mother was a socialite and citified woman who liked

Broadway plays and classical music; his father was a rancher who listened to country music and grew his own food. They'd married on a whim and divorced before the ink was dry on the marriage license. The only thing that connected them was a son conceived on the wedding night in Las Vegas, Nevada.

Hank leaned his head back on the headrest and listened to the country music drifting out through the parking lot. Sweat poured down his neck and when he shut his eyes a visual materialized of Larissa Morley in those skin-tight jeans and that little red knit top that barely touched the top of her jeans. She was a tasty little morsel and he'd be the first to admit she'd gotten under his skin. She wasn't the first woman who'd taken his eye the few times he went slumming, and she wouldn't be the last. He would get over it and her because he had a job to do, and a relationship with the likes of Larissa Morley would blow the hell out of his work.

The next vision that flitted through his mind was Hank introducing a bartender to his mother, Victoria. He imagined the look on her face when he said, "Mother, meet Larissa. She owns a beer joint called the Honky Tonk."

"She would die of an acute cardiac arrest," Hank said aloud as he started up the engine to the truck and drove north toward Palo Pinto. He pushed the button and Merle Haggard's voice filled the truck. He kept time to the beat with his thumb on the steering wheel.

Larissa was so busy behind the bar that she seldom knew when anyone arrived or left at the Honky Tonk, but the minute Hank Wells left his bar stool she knew it. She watched him walk across the floor, meandering around the line dancers and out the door past the Honky Tonk bouncer, Luther.

"Why did that particular man make you pant?" Merle asked.

Larissa shrugged. "Remember that song 'Somebody's Knockin''? It says that she'd heard about the devil but she'd never dreamed that he'd have blue eyes and blue jeans. Well, I never dreamed he'd have whiskey colored eyes. Terri sings that they'll have a heavenly night. I was ready to test that out without asking a single question. Lord, he could be serial killer and I'd still peel them jeans off his firm little hind end and enjoy doing it. I almost said yes when he asked me out to dinner. But something ain't right. I can feel it in my bones, but at the same time I'm kicking myself for not saying yes. Remember how Cathy said that Travis was sex on a stick on her wedding day? I didn't understand such a crazy saying then but I do now. It would probably be best if Hank Wells didn't ever come back in this place. I don't know what the attraction is, but it's damn sure there."

"Last time I saw something like this was when Jarod collided with Daisy," Merle said.

"And they got married and she gave her cousin Cathy the Honky Tonk. Then be damned if Travis didn't kiss Cathy on New Year's Day and, dear God, do you think there's a hex on this place? The owner falls for a cowboy?" Larissa moaned.

"Hell, I hope not. I'm tired of the Honky Tonk changin' bartenders more often than a hooker changes her underpants," Merle said. "Listen to Shelly West singing that song. I'd rather see you drink too much tequila and wind up dancing on the bar, kissing all the cowboys, shooting out the lights, and starting a fight as wind up falling in love."

"Jose Cuervo" played through to the end with the dancers kicking and slapping their fannies in unison. It played twice more and then the dancers hit the bar in a dehydrated frenzy ordering Mason jars of beer and pitchers of margaritas.

Merle wandered over to the jukebox and put some money into the slot. She pushed H5 to play "Somebody's Knockin'" so she could hear all the words again. Larissa was too damn classy a broad to get caught up with a drugstore cowboy even if he was the devil in disguise. At least Cathy and Daisy, the former owners, had each gotten a real, live guar-damn-teed cowboy down to the boots and belt buckles. If Larissa couldn't have the bona fide product, then she needed to kick the devil with his whiskey colored eyes and blue jeans out the front door. If she couldn't do the job then Merle was sure that Luther would be glad to do it for her.

Hank parked the truck in the front yard of the rambling ranch style home with a big porch wrapped around three sides and coon dogs lounging on the front steps. His father, Henry, sat in a wooden rocking chair with wide arms back in the shadows. When he spoke, Hank jumped.

"Didn't mean to startle you. Where you been?"

"That little beer joint down in Mingus that everyone is talking about," Hank said.

"One that plays country music and looks like it came out of an old Western movie set or the brick one up north?" Henry asked.

"The Honky Tonk? You been down there?" Hank asked.

"Lots of times back when Ruby Lee owned the place. Sit a spell."

Hank pulled up a second rocker and eased down into it. "Who was Ruby Lee?"

"A lady that I should've married instead of your .momma, but hindsight is the only thing that's not tainted like rose-colored glasses. Ruby Lee was a hellcat from over in east Texas. Her daddy was a preacher man and he couldn't get the hell preached out of that girl, no sir. When she was legal aged she took off and went to Dallas to her aunt's place and got a job. Worked two jobs. One at an office and the other as a bartender. That's where I met her. I was down there for a cattle sale and she was the bartender at the sale. God, she was pretty and we fell hard. Then her aunt died and left her a wad of cash and she wanted to build a beer joint in Palo Pinto County so we could be close together. My wife wasn't going to own no damned old beer joint and I told her so. Asked her to marry me and move to the ranch with me. She told me to ride that idea straight to hell and kiss the devil right smack on the ass when I got there. She built the Honky Tonk and ran it until she died. I went down there and tried to talk her into giving me a second chance but she wouldn't. I met your mother and married her and never went back. Are they still playing the old songs like they did when Ruby put the joint in? She said she'd never change any of it."

"They were playing Emmylou and Loretta tonight," Hank said.

Henry nodded seriously. "And Merle Haggard, Willie Nelson, and Waylon Jennings. Those are the old stars."

"Why couldn't your wife own a bar?" Hank asked.

"I was too proud. Back in those days everyone would've talked and what other people thought was important. People's opinions and my stubborn pride cost me the love of my life. I cared about your mother in those few weeks we were married but I never got over Ruby Lee. Who's bartending these days? I heard that she left the Honky Tonk to some little old dark-haired woman that she'd kind of adopted like a daughter. Named Daisy O'Dell."

"Daisy married a rancher named Jarod McElroy last fall and gave the Honky Tonk to her cousin Cathy," Hank said.

Henry cocked his head to one side. "How'd you know all that?"

"Don't take long to hear the history when you are sitting on a bar stool in the joint," Hank said.

"What'd Cathy look like? Was she another dark-haired beauty?" Henry asked.

"Tall, blonde. How long has it been since you were down there?"

"More than thirty years. When I asked your momma to marry me I stopped going," Henry said.

"Well, Cathy married an oil engineer in the spring and moved out to the panhandle. She gave the place to Larissa Morley. She's dark-haired and dark-eyed," Hank said.

"Be careful. Them dark-haired ones will steal your heart."

"Why'd you fall for Mother if you liked dark-haired women?" Hank asked.

"Man can love lots of women but only one gets to lay claim to his heart. Your mother was a beauty. Still is and so smart it ain't funny. Don't know why in the hell I'm tellin' you this tonight. Guess it's because you brought up the Honky Tonk. Think I'll go on in to bed. We got hay to put in the barn tomorrow. You going to help or go out and wreck another one of my vehicles tomorrow?"

"Merle says that she knows why you want to fix up the old truck instead of junking it, and she says that my neck ain't red enough so I reckon I better get out in the hay field and get it the right color," Hank said.

"Now Merle is a different story for a different night." Henry's chuckle came from deep in his chest. "I'm sure she remembers that truck. She saw it often enough back in the first days of the Honky Tonk's business. I'll rattle your door for breakfast."

Henry was a tall, lanky man and might have retired seven years before when he reached sixty-five but he loved the ranch too much to put it in anyone's hand but his son's and Hank wasn't ready for it. Maybe that dark-haired beauty down at the Honky Tonk would settle him down. A father could always hope.

"Good night, Dad," Hank said.

"Night, son."

Larissa locked the door behind Luther at two o'clock. It had been a booming night even for a Monday, which was fast turning into their busiest times. When Cathy and Daisy ran the place Monday night was old jukebox night.

The rest of the week they played the newer artists, but the Tonk soon got a reputation for being the new "in" place for vintage country music, so nowadays Larissa only plugged in the new jukebox on Friday and Saturday nights.

She picked up a beer and carried it to the nearest table where she propped her legs up on an extra chair. Bartending was the hardest work she'd ever done but she loved every minute of it. From the music to the customers hustling and hassling her. Like Toby Keith said, she loved the bar with its lookers, hookers, bikers, and preppies.

"But I would like to kiss that Hank fellow just once to see if it would set me on fire. Just thinking about it makes me tingle all over," she said aloud. "Still, something just ain't right. Was it that crazy song playing through my head that made me think about him being the devil? I'm talking to myself out loud. Wonder if Cathy ever did that after she shut the place down?"

She tipped back the bottle and finished off her beer and left by way of the back door. She pushed the button on the remote to roll up the garage door where she parked her vintage 1965 Mustang every night. She wondered on the way home why Hank Wells had asked her to dinner so quickly. Was that what had made her think something wasn't right? Or was there a little suspicious part hiding in her heart saying that Daisy and Cathy found a sexy cowboy when they owned the Honky Tonk and it could happen to her also? Did Larissa want a love in her life? Or did she want to be like the old original owner and go out in a blaze of glory without a man?

Chapter 3

Larissa shared her small two-bedroom home with a stray cat she had inherited when she bought the house. The real estate agent couldn't tell her the cat's name or even if he had lived at the place before the previous owner died. He was black and white and got the name Sylvester because he reminded her of the old cartoon cat. The first time he showed his cocky independence she called him Sylvester Stallone. That got shortened to Stallone which fit him better than the bumbling Sylvester who was always chasing Tweety Bird.

Stallone wasn't worth much when it came to hoeing the garden but he was a fine listener and she could tell him anything. He sat beside the knee-high okra plants and the green beans, moving when she got ahead of him, chasing the occasional butterfly out of the garden, and he didn't disagree with a thing she said. Starting with opening the Honky Tonk the night before, she told him about the whole evening, including Merle fussing because no one could give her any pool competition and the new cowboy who'd set her emotions in a tailspin.

"And then I looked up and there he was. After the wreck I didn't think he'd ever want to even look at me again. Hell, I even thought he was married, but evidently he's not if he's asking me out. There's an aura about him. Not even the English Earl made me go all smushy inside. Did you ever find a little feline beauty that set your ears to twitching? What is the matter with me? God, I'm turning into a crazy old cat lady who plants a garden and talks to tomcats and doesn't have a man in her life." She leaned on the hoe and wiggled her bare toes into the warm soft dirt.

The sun had passed the straight-up stage and was slowly sinking to the west, but the rays were still hot enough to make sweat pour down her neck and wet the band around the bottom of her bra. Her cutoff jean shorts had two damp spots on the seat and there wasn't a dry thread on her faded orange knit tank top. She'd pulled her short hair up into two lopsided dog ears but errant strands kept sneaking out and sticking to her face and neck.

She swatted a mosquito and left a smear of blood on her arm in its wake. "Damn things are big as buzzards in this part of the world and out to suck every drop of my blood. Why can't you chase them the way you do butterflies and birds?" she fussed at Stallone and went back to chopping weeds from her garden.

"Hello, where are you, Larissa?" a deep voice called from the front yard.

She stopped and shaded her eyes with her hand. "Luther?"

"I was driving past and thought I saw you back here. Garden is lookin' good. Got any iced tea?" Luther asked.

"It's in the fridge. Help yourself and make me a glass while you're at it." Larissa propped the hoe against the back of the house. The back porch was little more than a stoop with a tiny roof held up with two scaly porch posts. She sat down on the bottom step and leaned back against a post. She'd just about hock old Stallone for a breeze but a good wind in Texas couldn't be bought, begged, or stolen in July. Truth be told, if it did blow it'd be like the forced air from a furnace and cook the skin right off a person. Still, she could long for a nice cool ocean breeze. It wasn't a cardinal sin to wish for something even if it was like wishing for gelato from that cute little Italian restaurant that she liked so well. She was wondering what in the devil made her think of that place when Luther pushed the back door open.

"I found some cookies on the table and ate two of them." The quart-sized Mason jars looked like shot glasses in his big paws.

She reached up and took one jar from his hand and said, "Janice made them. You should have eaten more so I wouldn't have to work the garden so much to get rid of the calories. I can't leave the danged things alone. So where are you headed?"

"Back to the ranch. I came in to the office to bring a form and pick up a V-belt. Got to work on a rig. Sometimes I make excuses to go to the office just so I can talk to Tessa. Now I understand why Travis always wanted to run the errands that would take him to the old office where Cathy worked. Lord, that woman has gotten under my skin so bad it hurts. I want to ask her to move in with me but I'm scared to death she'll say no and then tell me to get lost," he said.

"I don't think she would say no," Larissa said.

Luther's eyes sparkled. "Really?"

"Only way you're ever going to find out is to ask her. You really ought to marry Tessa."

"I would go to the courthouse with her tomorrow if she'd have me," Luther said.

"Well, honey, she tells me all the time that she gets tired of living all cramped up. She was raised up on a ranch and loves the outdoors much as you do."

"I want all of it. Marriage. Kids. And the whole thing. She's too pretty to want to tie up with something big and ugly as me," he groaned.

Larissa clicked her fingers and Stallone came over to get his ears rubbed. "You got to make her feel special."

"I ain't no good at that romancin' shit," Luther said.

"Most men aren't, but women want that romancin' shit and if they don't get it, nothing happens in the relationship," she said.

Luther narrowed his eyes at Larissa. "Should I take her roses or candy?"

"Flowers and tell her she's beautiful in whatever she's wearing that night," Larissa said.

"She's beautiful all the time," Luther said.

"How many times have you told her that?"

He dropped his head and looked up at her from under heavy dark brows. "Them is hard words to say."

"Learn to say them," Larissa said.

"How'd you get so smart when it comes to women folks?" he asked.

"I'm one of them women folks," she laughed.

"I'll give it a try but every time I get around her I get all tongue-tied and nothing comes out right. We can talk about the rig all day and I can tease, but when it gets time to be serious I'm speechless," he said.

Larissa patted him on the arm. "Say what's in your heart."

"I can put up a rig or flirt with any other woman, but Tessa is special. She gets my hormones to flowing but she's my friend too. I wouldn't ever want to throw that away for a quick romp in the hay," he said.

"Tell her that in those words and hand her one long-stemmed rose. Tell her that she's one of a kind, just like the rose," Larissa advised.

"I'll have to practice sayin' that for a long time before them words would come out of my mouth, but thanks Rissa. I'll ask her out on Sunday. I ain't leavin' you without a bouncer in the beer joint, and besides, she's in there all the time anyway." Luther set his tea jar on the porch and disappeared around the side of the house.

He'd rented the ranch from Jezzy and Leroy when they moved to Hampton, Virginia, a couple of months before. Jezzy had been one of the Honky Tonk regulars when Cathy ran the place. She'd inherited the ranch when her grandmother died and then Angel and her crew found oil on the land and Luther took care of the wells. Leroy's daughter, Sally, married a military man and moved to Virginia and Jezzy and Leroy followed her the next month. Now those were two people who did things their way. They'd been friends since they were kindergarten students in Bugtussle, Oklahoma. Jezzy had her affairs and never married. Leroy married three or four times and had one daughter. They lived together in a purely platonic relationship. Larissa hated to see them move away because she and Jezzy had become really good friends.

But like Merle said, crowds came and went in the Honky Tonk. There were those like Chigger and her crew that had been regulars back in Daisy's time as bartender, then Jezzy and Angel who'd been regulars during Cathy's reign as bartender. Now it was Larissa's turn and her regulars were Julio, Patrick, Justin, and Eddie, the Monday night truck drivers. Betty and Elmer, Janice and Frank, and Linda and J. C.—Mingus citizens who were off to Las Vegas for a week—and Merle, who'd been there since dirt. Larissa figured Merle sat down in a pasture and refused to move so Ruby Lee built the Honky Tonk around her. And Amos who'd been there almost as long as Merle. He'd been in love with Ruby Lee but she refused to marry him. He owned oil companies all over the world and was mega-rich. He was more than seventy and still rode with a motorcycle club and brought the whole biker crew to the Honky Tonk at least once a week. And of course Luther and Tessa, who would eventually figure out they were made for each other.

Stallone came out from under the porch when Luther had gone and rubbed around her sweaty legs leaving cat hair in his wake.

"Do you have a fluffy little lady friend you want me to talk to?" Larissa asked.

Hank poked his head around the corner. "You talkin' to that cat or to me?"

She jumped. There she sat in all her sweating glory. Barefoot. Hair like funky rockers from the nineties. Dirty. Smelling like a bag lady who hadn't seen a shower in a month. She consoled herself by deciding that if Hank Wells was a real cowboy, then he'd seen sweaty, working women before in his life. If he wasn't, then there was something fishy about him anyway.

"He don't give me much sass and he don't carry gossip. Are you stalking me?"

"No, ma'am. I was driving through town and saw you in the garden a while ago. When I came back through I noticed you sitting on the porch. I thought I'd stop by and make sure you hadn't found any hidden bruises."

The telephone in the house rang but she ignored it. "I'm fine. How are you? That seat belt bruise about gone? Want some iced tea or a beer?" she asked.

"Beer sounds good on a hot day like this," he answered.

Sweat stains circled his faded chambray shirt that hung open baring his broad chest. His old truck had both windows rolled down so evidently the air conditioning didn't work. His jeans had hay stuck to the legs and his work boots were scuffed at the toes.

"I been haulin' hay with my dad," he said. "Friend of his down in these parts only needed a few of the little bales so I hauled them down here on the back of the flatbed out there. Air conditioner went out in it years ago but the damned old engine is like the Energizer bunny. It refuses to die."

"Sounds like hot work. Have a seat over on the porch under the shady part. I'll be right back," she said.

She refilled her jar and pulled a cold beer from the refrigerator, popped the cap off, and stood at the kitchen window a few seconds staring at his back. It was thoughtful of him to check on her. A friend would do that and Larissa liked the friends she'd gathered around her in Mingus. There was always room for one more and Hank seemed lonely. Maybe he was looking for friendship too. She picked up her tea and his beer and carried both out to the porch. He'd taken his straw hat off and was fanning with it while Stallone watched warily from the edge of the garden. Her heart skipped two beats and then set about trying to thump

out of her chest when she saw him sitting there with
sweat pouring down the back of his sunburned neck,
black hair flattened against his head, and those light
brown eyes looking up at her.

*When did I begin to like working cowboys? My pref-
erence in men never did include tight jeans, belt buckles,
and straw hats. That's why I figured I was safe from the
Honky Tonk curse.*

He tilted the bottle up and enjoyed a long, wet drink.
"Thank you. This hits the spot."

"Nothing like cold beer on a hot Texas day."

He nodded toward the plot with knee-high corn,
okra, beans, and tomato plants. "So you makin' a
garden?"

"Tryin' to. It's my first attempt. Mingus don't offer a
Gold's Gym so gardening is my exercise, plus I get food
for my efforts that has no preservatives and tastes much
better than store bought," she said.

*God, please shut my mouth. I sound like a commer-
cial for natural fertilizer.*

"My dad makes a garden every year. Hated picking
beans when I was a kid but love the food," he said.

She liked him. Yes, he was sexy as hell but it went
beyond that. He'd picked beans for heaven's sake and
he liked garden fresh food. He'd stopped by just to see if
she was all right. That could easily translate into a good
friend if nothing else.

The phone rang again and no amount of ignoring it
made it hush.

"Guess I'd better get that. Excuse me," she said.
She took her time getting into the kitchen in hopes that
whoever was so persistent would give up but it didn't

work. She'd far rather be out on the porch in the hot steaming sun getting to know Hank better than talking to anyone she knew on the blasted telephone.

She picked up the cordless receiver and walked to the kitchen window where she could look her fill of him as she talked. "Hello," she said impatiently.

"Larissa Morley, please," a masculine voice said.

"This is Larissa. Whatever you are selling, I'm not interested." She started to hang up.

He began talking very fast. "Miss Morley, I'm not a salesman. I'm not trying to give you credit cards or sell you stock in a time-share. This is Wayne Johnston. I work for Radner Incorporated."

"Who?" she said icily.

"Radner Incorporated. We would like to arrange a meeting to discuss buying the Honky Tonk beer joint from you. We have come up with…"

"Hush right there. I'm not selling my business. Get that through your head once and for all and don't call here ever again. I don't give a damn if you offer me a third world country in exchange for the Tonk. It's not for sale," she said.

"But…"

"Not butts or asses. That's the end of the discussion, Mr. Wayne Johnston of Radner Incorporated."

"Miss Morley, you live in a rundown house and work six nights a week in a cheap beer joint. I'm willing to offer you enough money for a much better lifestyle. Why won't you sell it to me?"

"You may squat in a bed of poison ivy and fall backwards in it, Mr. Johnston. How do you know where I live or who I am, and why do you want it so bad? Have you been stalking me? Well, darlin', you can damn sure come around and I'll tell you the same thing to your face. And why doesn't Hayes Radner come see me in person if he wants my business so badly? Is he a sissy that hides behind big business? If he wants my business, tell him to come talk to me in person. Is there gold hiding under my beer joint or something?"

Mr. Johnston's tone turned icy cold. "Mr. Radner is a busy man. No, there isn't oil under the beer joint. Radner Corporation wants it to incorporate it into their amusement park. We will own that town eventually."

"Don't get too damn comfortable if owning Mingus is the thing that's going to write your paycheck. You might find yourself moving from the penthouse to the outhouse. Good-bye and don't harass me again." She slammed the receiver down with enough force that she hoped it gave him a major migraine.

She inhaled deeply several times before she went back out to the porch. Hank had set the empty bottle on the porch step. Stallone slowly inched over toward the porch and sniffed the tip of Hank's boot.

"I think he's trying to decide whether to trust me or not," Hank said.

So am I. My flight mode tells me to run away, but this blasted heat between us creating sparks that are hotter than a barbed wire fence in the middle of hell says to stick around. Slow down, girl. Easy does it. He might turn out to be involved with someone else and only interested in friendship, like Luther.

She sat down and pulled her knees up. "Folks say that you can't fool kids or dogs. I don't know if that includes cats or not."

"My dad has a barn full of cats. When I came out to the ranch as a kid I loved it when there was a bunch of kittens out there. I used to name them. One year they were Sesame Street characters, then they were race car characters from a cartoon I liked. Then I got old enough for a pony and the kittens took a backseat."

"Be careful, Stallone; he's a fickle friend. Man that would turn his back on kittens for a danged old pony can't be trusted," Larissa warned the cat.

"Is that the voice of experience I'm hearing?" Hank grinned.

"It is. We had kittens and when I got my pony I'm afraid I was a fickle friend too." She smiled at the memory of that first pony her grandfather brought home.

The cat stuck his tail straight up and strutted back to the garden where he laid down and eyed Hank from a distance.

Hank smiled. "Looks like he's the one who's fickle. He was warming up to me until he heard about the pony. I won't tell him that you'd trade him in for a horse if you got the chance."

She giggled. "He hasn't got a thing to worry about. I'm past the love of horses stage in my life. It only lasted a few weeks anyway. First time the critter bucked me off into a mud puddle, I was finished with him. Cats don't treat you like that."

"I'm glad to see you laugh. You looked like you could chew up railroad spikes and spit out staples when you came out after that phone call. I hope it wasn't bad news."

"Not at all. A telemarketer trying to buy something that's not for sale and never will be." The smile vanished and her tone turned from toasty warm to frigid.

Hank cocked his head to one side. "That's strange. Most telemarketers are trying to sell, not buy."

"Some fool from Dallas has been trying to buy the Honky Tonk for a couple of years now. Guess he thought since ownership has changed he'd have a chance at it. Idiot doesn't realize that I'd have less reason to sell than any of the previous three owners. But that's not important. I told him no and now it's over. Sorry sucker thought he could sweet-talk me into a deal by offering me a fortune. Radner Corporation ought to fire his sorry ass. If that's the best they've got then they ain't got much."

"Why would you have less reason to sell it?" he asked. His conscience was yelling at him to fess up and be honest with the woman but he shoved it away.

"Ruby Lee built it and she wouldn't sell it because it was her baby. She wouldn't have sold it to God for a front row seat in heaven. Daisy wouldn't because she didn't give a damn about the money. Cathy wouldn't because she didn't need the money. I won't because it's where my heart found a home. That whole bunch of Radners, be it two or fifty, can kiss my naturally born stubborn ass."

"I see." Hank chuckled. "Well, I reckon I'd better get the truck on back or Dad will be sending out the militia. I'm surprised that he even let me drive another one of his vehicles after that deer accident. He's got a soft spot for every one of his old trucks." So much for sweet-talking her or befriending her into selling the Honky Tonk. He'd have to find out more about her and see if there was anything in the world that would make her give it up.

"I understand completely. I got a soft spot for my beer joint," she said. "Come back if you're in these parts. Me and Stallone don't venture out very far in the daytime. I've always got cold beer and iced tea. But if you ever preach any nonsense to Stallone that involves trading him in for a horse, I'll…" she hesitated.

"You will what?" His eyes twinkled.

"You don't even want to know," she said.

Patsy Cline was singing and the dance floor was filled with two-steppers when Luther shut the doors behind Hank that night at the Honky Tonk.

"Evenin', Hank," Luther said.

"Looks like business is hopping. I was lucky to get in, wasn't I?" Hank said.

"Yes, those behind you will have to wait until someone leaves. We're at max capacity. She really don't dance with customers. She ain't just bein' mean to you. Thought I'd clear that up," Luther said.

"That's good." Hank waved as he cut around the edges of the hardwood dance floor. Tammy Wynette was singing "Your Good Girl's Gonna Go Bad" when he claimed the last empty bar stool. Was Larissa a good girl or a bad girl? Hank would gladly help her *go bad* if she gave him half a chance. He'd tried to keep the job in perspective but he kept seeing her in those cutoff jean shorts every time he blinked.

Merle gave him a long look. "So you came back? Why didn't you bring Henry?"

Hank came back to the present with a jerk. He wondered when she had sat down beside him. Or had she been there the whole time and he sat down beside her? Larissa had definitely gotten under his skin. "He was tired. He hasn't got the stamina to put up hay all day and dance all night anymore," he answered.

Merle smiled and leaned around him. "Old age, gravity, and time gets us whether we like it or not. Tessa, this here is the son of an old friend of mine and Ruby Lee's. Remember, I told you all about her. Well, this is Hank Wells, his son. I didn't even know he had a son until last night."

Tessa smiled brightly. "So do you dance, cowboy?"

"Afraid I've got two left feet," he said.

"Too bad, but everyone has one fault. Guess yours is that you haven't got rhythm. See that big old bouncer back there? Big as he is, he's light on his feet when I can talk him into a dance, which is what I'm about to do. Do you shoot pool?"

He shook his head.

"Guess you're just eye candy, then." Tessa hopped off the stool and motioned to Luther to dance with her to an old Bill Anderson tune.

Tessa was a brunette with green eyes that were even bigger through the lenses of her black-rimmed glasses. She had rounded hips that were slightly larger than the top half of her body. But there were no sparks when she touched his arm as she was leaving. Not a single hot vibe shot through his veins like it did when Larissa handed him a beer and touched his fingertips.

"Evenin', Hank," Larissa said. The attraction she had for the man heated up her insides until they were little more than a conglomerate of aching desires. "What can I get you?"

"Larissa." He nodded. His mouth went so dry that he craved a beer worse than if he'd been dancing for an hour. *How about a romp in the hay? Or at least a long, lingering taste of those lips?*

He roped in his wayward thoughts and said, "Coors, please."

She set a bottle on a paper coaster in front of him. He handed her a bill and deliberately let it fall so they'd both grab at the same time. When their skin touched it was as if fire had jumped from hell and scorched his palm. It wasn't fair to be attracted to the only woman that he should not look at once much less twice with lust in his heart and soul. She owned a beer joint. She lived in a sorry looking house that wasn't as big as his closet in Dallas. She was *the job*. So why in the hell did he want to take her to bed?

"Sorry about that," he said hoarsely. Things weren't supposed to happen this way. Who was Larissa Morley and why in the devil wasn't there any more information on her? Hells bells, his people could find everything on Luther and Merle and even Larissa's friends Betty, Janice, and Linda and their husbands. He had pages and pages on all of them, from where they were born to what their finances looked like. But prior to Larissa coming to Mingus there was nothing. And to top it all off he liked the woman. She was hardworking and a hoot to sit and talk to. He could spend a whole week just talking about gardening or cats on her back porch.

She shoved her hand in her pocket to let it cool off. "Did you get the hay all baled and in the barn?"

"The little square bales went to the barn. The big round ones are drying in the field. You ever done any baling?" he asked.

"You asking me to take on another job?"

"Maybe. You interested?"

"Could be. I like learning new things," she said.

Merle shook her head emphatically. "Rissa, do not let this cowboy coerce you into baling hay. Girl, that's the hottest, dirtiest work in the world."

Larissa smiled slyly. "It's okay, Merle. I baled hay one time in my life and I know how hard the work is. Tell you what, Hank. I'll bale hay for you but you have to work for me if I do."

"Doing what?" He wiggled his eyebrows.

She wiggled her own dark brows. "Something really sexy. You interested?"

"I might be."

"I need someone to help me paint my house."

He groaned. "I hate to paint. Dad made me paint a barn one summer for punishment."

"What'd you do?"

"What did you do to have to bale hay?" he asked right back.

"Touché, Mr. Wells. Someday I might tell you but tonight I've got work to do. So are you going to help me paint or not?"

"How many days for how much painting?" he asked.

"Hour for hour. I'll drive a hay truck or use a pair of hooks and stack the hay but you have to help me paint an hour for every hour I help you get the hay from the field to the barn."

Merle threw up her hands in disgust. "You are both crazy. I'm going to go find someone to whip at eight ball."

"I really hate to paint," Hank said.

"I really hate to sweat," Larissa said.

He inhaled deeply and let it all out in a whoosh. "You got lots of beer at your house? Painting is a hell of a hot job."

She grinned. "Do you have lots of beer at your ranch? Haying is a hell of a hot job too."

He stuck his hand over the bar. "Starting tomorrow at noon when the dew is dried?"

She hesitated so long that he was pulling it back when she reached out and shook with him. Neither was prepared for the blistering fire that glued them to each other. When he let go she quickly made an excuse to grab a cold bottle of beer to put out the burn in her palm.

Chapter 4

BETTY, LINDA, AND JANICE WERE ON LARISSA'S BACK PORCH when she opened the door to let Stallone in the house that morning just before noon. She still had sleep in her eyes and a nightshirt that barely reached her knees. She yawned and motioned them to come in even though they didn't wait for an invitation and plowed right inside. Betty had a short mop of gray curls and enough wrinkles to prove that she was past sixty-five. Janice had a deal with Miss Clairol that kept her hair dyed a muted shade of blond but the wrinkles around her eyes proved she could run Betty a close race on age. Linda was a couple of years younger and had salt-and-pepper hair she wore in a chin-length bob. All three of them wore jeans, T-shirts, sandals, and a worried expression.

"So when did y'all get back from Vegas? And why the long faces? Did you lose your shirts at the slots or your husbands to those fancy dancers?" she asked.

Betty started a pot of coffee.

Linda set a platter of cookies on the table.

Janice got down the cups and saucers.

"We got back yesterday. Linda probably gained twenty pounds and Betty got drunk off her ass and it's a damn good thing that she's too old to get pregnant because Las Vegas always makes Elmer horny. I came home with fifty more dollars than I left with so I'm the lucky one," Janice said.

Betty pushed the button on the coffee pot and sat down at the table. "Long faces don't have anything to do with Las Vegas. Last night we all three got a phone call from Wayne Johnston, the henchman from that Hayes Radner company. He's getting serious now, Larissa. He says that Hayes will own Mingus before it's all said and done and we'll lose our chance to make big bucks. His offers only stand for one week. Elmer is all fired up about selling and retiring out west with our kids."

Janice sat down in one of the four chairs surrounding the table. In the thirties houses were built about the same around Mingus. Good sized living room that opened right into an equally large kitchen. Two bedrooms off to the side separated by a bathroom in a short hallway. Larissa's kitchen cabinets had so many coats of white paint on them that the doors did not shut all the way. The brown and yellow linoleum on the floor should've been replaced back when Moby Dick was a minnow.

Larissa had plans to remodel the whole interior eventually. She wondered if Hank Wells was any good at interior carpentry work. Did he hate it as much as painting? Could she barter for his services? What could she entice him with for that kind of work? Her hands went clammy when she thought about just how she could pay him.

"So?" Betty said.

Larissa blinked away enough naughty thoughts to earn her a backseat in hell on a barbed wire fence for eternity. "It'll have to be an all-or-nothing deal. If one person in Mingus holds out, he can't put in an amusement park, can he? He's teasing us with big money to get us all worked up and ready to sell. But when it comes time to put our name on the line it won't be much more than market value. Anything else doesn't make a bit of business sense."

Betty stood up, leaned on the cabinet, and waited for the coffee to drip. "I figured that out but Elmer is flipping back and forth. One hour he says he'd never sell his great-grandparent's home; the next he's saying that when we are dead and gone our kids will sell it and won't get a tenth of what the Radners are offering if we sell first."

"Well I ain't sellin'," Linda said. "And I own a whole block of Main Street. If he wants to build a park around my land that's fine and dandy. I may put in a hog farm on my lots if he does. Let the city slickers get some real good country aroma."

"What's J. C. say about that?" Larissa asked.

"He don't give a shit what I do. It was my momma's land and before that it belonged to her daddy. J. C. says he wouldn't move for half the money in Fort Knox. He's a damned old pack rat and he's too lazy to pack it all up. That's the real story. Truth is I don't give a damn why he won't sell because I don't want to leave Mingus. It's home."

Janice ate a cookie while she waited on the coffee. "Frank says that he was born in that house we live in and he reckons it'll do to die in. We're three couples and one beer joint owner. Think we can sway everyone else to sit tight and refuse to sell?"

"I reckon we can have us a town meeting and ask everyone to attend," Larissa said.

Betty poured coffee and the women gathered around the table. "Sounds like a good idea to me. Why don't we invite Hayes Radner to come to the meeting? That way he can see that we don't intend to do business with him and he can get his sorry ass on up the road to the next town he wants to raze and take over."

Larissa nodded. "I had a call too and I put him going but I think a town meeting would be just the thing. It would show those people that money don't always get its way. How about a month from now? We can put up fliers down at the Smokestack and around town, maybe even get someone to write it up in the newspaper. I'll take care of all that and we can have the meeting at the Honky Tonk. There's plenty of room and it's empty in the daytime," Larissa said.

Janice figured days in her head. "Today is the fifteenth. How about Saturday, July 31. That'll give us a couple of weeks and a few days past that. If you drag it out a whole month, the community will lose interest. If we hit 'em hard and fast and keep talking it up we can fire everyone in town up real good. We ought to have it at the City Hall. There's a big oak tree where we can string up him and his henchman, Mr. Johnson, if things get out of hand."

"Can't get enough people in there. The religious folks will just have to suck it up and repent later for going into a beer joint. We can put a little note at the bottom of the fliers that the bar will not be open during the meeting. And if things get out of hand I'll just poison the bastard's punch. Ain't no use in dirtying up a good rope," Larissa said.

Linda dipped a cookie into her coffee and got it to her mouth just before it fell apart. "That ought to give us enough time to get everyone all worked up. I reckon

I can light a fire under the ladies' asses in my Sunday school class. J. C. can talk it up to all the folks in the feed store and down at the Smokestack when he goes for coffee. Give them men something new to fuss about other than politics and Monday night football."

Larissa stood up and pushed her chair under the table. "I'll get on the computer and make fliers and start getting the word out to all the customers at the Honky Tonk over the Internet. You'd be surprised how many have asked me to be their friend on Facebook. But right now, I've got a new friend and we've made an agreement. I have to haul hay today for him to help me paint this house. Maybe I'll invite him to our meeting too. He's new to these parts but he's pretty impressive. He might help put old Hayes' nose out of joint. Y'all put Stallone out before you leave. I'll see you tonight, right?"

"Hauling hay? Are you crazy, girl? Don't that beer joint make enough money that you don't have to take on a second job?" Janice asked.

"Y'all ever hear of Henry Wells?" Larissa asked.

"Hell, yeah. He's got the biggest spread in the county. Up north of Palo Pinto. Back when Ruby Lee first built the Honky Tonk, he used to come in pretty often. He was one smooth dancer. If I hadn't already branded Elmer, I might've gone for him," Betty said.

"Did you know his son Hank?"

All three shook their heads.

"I heard Henry got married to a rich bitch and it didn't last until the honeymoon was over but I didn't know about a son," Linda said.

"Well, me and his son made a deal. He stopped by to see if I was all right after our little wreck incident and I think we're going to be pretty good friends. He's been by the Honky Tonk a couple of times and I'm going to haul hay and he's going to help paint my house."

"Is he pretty?" Janice asked.

Larissa placed one hand over her heart and fanned her face with the other. "But even better, he's a good old hardworking cowboy. He don't care about impressing a girl with flattery or fancy duds. He's just plain old Hank and I like that."

"Then get on out of here and go get all hot and sweaty with the man. Wish I was thirty-five years younger and I'd go with you, but gravity got my boobs and ass years ago," Betty said.

Larissa could hear them giggling as she backed the car out of the carport.

———

Hank had parked the hay hauling truck and was on his way into the house for dinner when he noticed a puff of dust following a vehicle on the way down the lane. When Larissa stepped out of her car he lost his ability to talk and was very glad for sunglasses so she couldn't see his eyes. She wore faded jeans, work boots worn down at the heels, a chambray shirt opened to show a skin-tight red tank top underneath, and a bandana wrapped around her forehead.

"You ready to haul some hay?" She was surprised that her voice came out normal. He looked like something from one of those old Marlboro cigarette commercials. All he needed was a horse instead of a flatbed truck. The burning embers blazing between them had nothing to do with the hot Texas summer wind. He had trouble shutting up that niggling voice that said he had no right to feel like he did when he hadn't been honest with her.

"I'm going to have some lunch. Have you eaten?" His words sounded stilted and formal.

She smiled and his heart thumped against his chest. "No, I haven't had lunch."

"Well, come on inside and set up to the table with us. Can't have you working all afternoon on an empty stomach." He motioned for her to walk beside him.

She was careful not to let her hand brush against his and kept her eyes away from him. *Friendship, girl. That's all you're interested in. Toss some ice water on those hormones.*

"Where *did* you get that Mustang? I've never seen one that old in such good shape," Hank asked.

"My grandfather left it to me. Sometimes I wish I had the nerve to sell the damned thing. My grandfather bought it brand new back in '65. I inherited it when he died."

"Why would you ever want to sell something like that?"

"I said sometimes. There are days when I'd like a small truck. Someday I might buy one anyway. There's lots of room in the garage out behind the Honky Tonk. I could have both. So do you like my Mustang?"

Not as much as I like you, he thought.

He said, "Of course I like it. It's a classic. You ever want to sell it, call me. I'd be interested in buying it."

They reached the door and he opened it for her. She stepped inside to wonderful odors coming from the kitchen. "Mmmm, something smells good."

"Oma made potato soup and quesadillas today."

"Sounds wonderful. I had four chocolate chip cookies for breakfast. I expect they'll disappear before the afternoon is half gone and I'll be plumb faint with hunger."

He opened the door into the house and stood to one side. "We'll keep you fed good if you'll help haul hay. Hey Oma and Dad, we got a guest. Set another plate," he called out.

"You sure this is all right?" Larissa whispered.

Henry met them at the dining room door that opened off the foyer. "Come right on in here. Hank said he'd made a deal with you. I can't imagine a little slip of a thing like you haulin' hay. Did you grow up on a ranch?"

Larissa was in awe. Henry was taller than Hank by three or four inches, had a beautiful mop of thick gray hair, and the bluest eyes she'd ever seen on a man. He reminded her vaguely of the actor Sam Elliott, and his voice was just as deep and southern. If he ever came to the Honky Tonk, she'd have to arm Luther with a two-by-four just to keep the women, young and old alike, from attacking him.

"Yes, sir, I did. Not a big operation like this but I did live out in the country."

Henry led the way to a dining room table big enough to seat twelve people. A tall, thin woman who'd been blond at one time carried a big pan of soup straight from the stove and set it on a trivet in the middle of the table.

"I'm Oma, chief cook, bottle washer, diaper changer when Hank was a baby, and housekeeper around this place. You remind me of Ruby Lee," she said bluntly.

Henry grinned. "She does, don't she?"

"Was Ruby Lee part Indian?" Larissa asked.

"No, she just had dark hair and was about your size," Oma said. "Well, y'all better get busy on this food. Hay won't bring itself to the barn and you got to eat for the energy to do the work."

"I need to wash up before I eat. Y'all go on ahead," Hank said.

Henry seated Larissa. "Help yourself. Oma will bring in the quesadillas soon as that last fryin' gets done. Tell me about the Honky Tonk. Did you make any changes?"

She ladled soup into her bowl and had a bite before she answered. "The only thing I changed was that we have old jukebox three nights a week now. We plug it up Monday, Tuesday, and Wednesday."

Henry's heavy white eyebrows drew down into one long length of hair across his forehead. "Old jukebox? You still got one like Ruby Lee put in there? I didn't know them old dinosaurs were still in existence."

Larissa shook her head. "Not like it. The exact same one. We still let the customers have three plays for a quarter."

Henry filled his bowl to the rim and started eating. "I'll be damned. Just goes to show that bein' old don't mean wore completely out, but those records should have worn out years ago."

Larissa nodded. "I'm sure several have over the years, but there's a closet full of replacements. Ruby Lee must've bought every one she could get her hands on because when one gets scratched up and skips the maintenance man replaces it. He says that the Honky Tonk jukebox is the oldest one in the state that he keeps up. The customers love the old thing. I could've sold it a thousand times in the past few months, but it ain't for sale and never will be, just like the Honky Tonk won't ever be for sale."

Oma set a platter piled high with flour tortillas folded over melted cheese, picante, and chopped chicken. "These go right well with potato chowder. You sure you ain't related to Ruby Lee in some way? You even talk like her. Full of sass and vinegar and not afraid to speak up."

Larissa looked up at her with a question on her face.

"Even that expression is like her. What do you think, Henry?" Oma asked.

"She's a ringer in some ways but I think she looks more like Jessi Colter back in her younger days," Henry answered.

"Me too," Hank said from the doorway. He crossed the floor in a few easy strides and sat down beside Larissa.

"Can I have your recipes for both of these? I'm teaching myself to cook," Larissa changed the subject.

Oma smiled. "I'll write them down. Come on around and I'll teach you what I know."

"Better plan on staying forty or fifty years if you plan on learning all Oma knows," Henry said.

"It would take longer than that for Oma to teach her everything she knows," Hank added.

Henry nodded in agreement. "You got that right, son. Now tell me what happens on the nights when you don't have the old jukebox plugged in? Did you go to live music like they got on up the road at Trio's?"

Larissa took a sip of iced tea and said, "Hell, no! We don't have live music. Who needs that stuff when we got all the old stars and the new ones at the touch of a fingertip? When Ruby Lee was killed she left the Honky Tonk to Daisy O'Dell. Daisy had worked there seven years and she was kind of like a daughter to Ruby. I understand they only fought once and that was when Daisy wanted to put in a new jukebox so the customers could listen to the new country music. They made an agreement that they'd only use it on weekends but it slowly worked its way into other days. Seems like nowadays the customers rather have the old stuff as the new. It's making a big comeback. They call it vintage music these days."

Shut up, Larissa! You are doing it again. Talking too much and too fast because you are nervous. So slow down and hush. Push food into your mouth. It's impolite to talk with a mouth full so that will take care of it.

"So you never did know Ruby Lee?" Henry asked.

She shook her head.

"That woman was full of spit and vinegar and wouldn't have backed down from a grizzly with a toothache. I swear she could tell a person to go to hell on a silver poker and he'd not only go out and buy the poker but he'd look forward to the damn trip. She was a lot like you. She would have made a deal with a man to haul hay just to get him to paint a house like you've done. No wonder you remind Oma of her. I understand that my boy has to help you paint your house in Mingus in order for you to help us in the hay field. Sounds like he's gettin' the easy part of the deal," Henry said.

"It needs scraping. I don't think it's seen a coat of paint since the original was put on in the thirties. It looks like warmed over sin on Sunday morning right now, so he's not getting off one bit easy," she said.

Hank groaned.

Larissa spun around and pointed a long slim index finger at him. "You saw the place so don't you go backin' out of our deal. Besides, you're the one who brought up the idea of me helping haul hay so put on your big boy undershorts and suck it up. "

"I didn't say a word," he protested.

"I heard that groan and so did Henry and Oma. I expect you know how to scrape a house or am I going to have to teach you how to use a scraper?"

"Never done it before but I got a feelin' I'm about to learn. So tell me, Miss Sassy Drawers, do you have any idea how to haul hay?" he asked.

"I could outdo you any day of the week," she smarted off.

It started as a chuckle and built up into a full-fledged guffaw that had Henry dabbing at his eyes with the dinner napkin. "I want pictures of him scraping and painting your house, Miss Larissa. You take 'em and I'll pay double for them. Only time I ever knew him to paint anything was when he had to paint a barn one summer."

"And why did he have to paint a barn?" Larissa asked.

"Decided to go to town in one of my vehicles without asking me if it was all right. Then he didn't come home until almost daylight and he had beer on his breath," Henry said.

"How old was he?"

"Fourteen and he didn't even have a permit much less a driver's license," Henry answered.

"Damn! Don't go dragging out all those old stories," Hank protested.

"I had to haul hay all day and half the night for sassing," Larissa said.

"Tell me more," Hank said.

"Tit for tat. You tell me something and I'll return the favor, maybe," Larissa said. "I'll get you those pictures,

Henry, and they won't cost you a dime. I'll even blow them up and frame them so you can put them on the mantle above the fireplace. You do have a fireplace, don't you?"

Henry continued to laugh. "I do back in the den but if I didn't, I'd have one put in just to put a picture of my son painting a house in Mingus."

"Does your daddy want a picture of you haulin' hay? Where do I send it? I bet he'd get a big kick out of seeing his little girl all sweaty in the hay field," Hank asked Larissa.

"Don't think he would, but Mother might think it was a hoot. Take your camera with you and I'll send her one over the net. I told her I was learning new things. She won't believe a picture though. She'll say I fixed it on the computer just to shock the hell out of her."

"Where does she live?" Hank pried.

"Which day of the week? Last week she was in Rome, this week in Paris, and next week in London. I'd have to check her schedule to be sure," Larissa said.

"Sure she is," Hank muttered.

She flared up at him. "You doubt my word?"

Maybe they couldn't be friends after all. Friends believed friends even when they weren't telling the whole truth or when they were beating around the bush.

"You even got a temper like Ruby Lee. Must be the Honky Tonk that makes its women so sassy but I like you, Larissa Morley. You can sit up to my table any day you want to drop by the ranch," Henry said.

"Thank you, Henry. You can sit up to my bar and I'll even give you the first beer of the evening free any night you want to come by the Tonk. Did anyone

ever tell you that your son can be exasperating?"
Larissa said.

Oma pulled up a chair and joined them. "You don't
have to tell me and Henry that. We already know it."

Hank threw up his palms defensively. "I'm sitting
right here and I didn't doubt you. I suppose it's possible
that your mother has been to Rome and Paris since there
is a Rome, Georgia, and a Paris, Texas. You were just
kidding, right?"

"Would you believe that she goes into town once a
month and they've got a computer at the library where she
checks out books and checks for emails from me? And
that I grew up in a double-wide trailer with eight brothers
all older than me who work in the coal mines?" she asked.

"And where would that be—in Rome or Paris?"
Hank asked.

Larissa giggled. "In Hickory Holler, Tennessee, right
next to Loretta Lynn's old home place. Momma works
at her dude ranch."

"What's your momma's name?"

"Why are you so interested and why would you
believe that rather my original story?" That itchy crawly
feeling on her neck was back.

Hank chuckled. "Hey, we're just joshing and I'm just
making conversation."

"You going to look my mother up or something?"

"Is she as beautiful as you? I might look her up myself.
I ain't never been to Hickory Holler, Tennessee."

"Mother is absolutely stunning. Why, when she puts
on her best jeans and western shirt, she's the belle of
any barn dance," Larissa teased. If Hank wanted to joke
around he'd met his match.

"I bet she is, darlin'," Henry said. "She got a feller? I might be interested in going to one of them barn dances and talkin' her into a two-step or two."

"Mother always has a feller," Larissa said honestly.

Hank clamped his mouth shut. Her mother sounded like a hooker. Even with a name, he'd never find her in the backwoods hills of Tennessee. That story sounded much more probable than a mother who jet-setted around the world.

───∿∿───

Larissa drove the hay truck on the first trip. Sweat flowed from her forehead to her neck and on down into her bra. What in the hell was she thinking when she agreed to this deal? If she drank on the job, she'd bet that Hank had drugged her drink before he started talking about hay.

When she had a full load backed into the barn she grabbed a set of hooks and began to stack it as Hank threw it off. It was twice as hot inside the barn as it had been out in the field. What little breeze blew out there was shut off in the barn. The hooks felt like they'd been wiped down with Vaseline by the time she'd hauled four bales off the truck.

"Here, you might need these." Hank threw her a pair of brown cotton work gloves.

"Thanks. I should've remembered to bring gloves." She put them on and kept working.

When they finished unloading, she swiped the moisture from her forehead with the back of her hand and hopped up on the back of the truck and waited.

He wiped sweat from his brow. "What are you doing?"

"It's my turn to load and yours to drive. I'm not a pansy. I've hauled hay before," she said.

"For sassing in Tennessee, right? Did you live on a farm?"

"You think coal can't grow under the ground and hay on the top? We didn't call it a farm or a ranch or a plantation. It was just home."

Hank shook his head. "I can't let you load and me do nothing but drive the truck. It just flat out ain't right even if it is the fair thing. You drive and then help me unload. Dad would scalp me with a butter knife if I sat in a truck and let you sling bales."

She narrowed her eyes. "You still have to help me scrape the house. I'm not as nice as you. I won't give you the easy job just because you let me off the hook."

He grinned.

Her pulse did a fast two-step.

He put his hands on her waist to help her from the back of the flatbed truck and she gave a little hop. When she was firmly on the ground he didn't move his hands. She looked up to see his eyes go soft. They were even sexier with that bedroom look. Then his lips found hers and the whole hay barn heated up to seven times hell's temperature, which wasn't supposed to be possible.

The sheer passion in the lingering kiss made her knees go weak and her blood pressure shoot out the tin roof toward the wispy white clouds in the summer blue sky. When Cathy and Travis got married they danced their first dance to "Can't Help Falling in Love" by Elvis. The tune ran through her mind as Hank broke the kiss and started another.

Larissa refused to fall in love with anyone, especially Hank Wells, a man she knew next to nothing about. But her feet wouldn't move in that direction and her body kept leaning in as the next kiss deepened.

Elvis' voice in her head said that only fools rush in. Larissa was not a fool. She finally pulled back only to have him hug her tightly.

"What was that?" she asked.

"A damn fine little making out session. Now let's go finish bringing in the hay. It'll take at least a week to get it all in so I reckon I'm going to owe you a week of painting," he whispered into her hair.

Good God, a week to work with him on this and another of painting. My nerves will be a quivering bowl of jelly by the time we get both jobs done if he kisses me every day.

When the Honky Tonk opened that evening Larissa's fanny was dragging so bad it was a wonder it didn't get splinters from the wood dance floor. Hopefully her body would adjust to the hard work and each day would be less tiring. If not, she fully well intended to make Hank pay up when they started working on her house.

Linda, Janice, and Betty were among the first in the joint and ordered a bucket of beers to take to their table. Their husbands, J. C, Elmer, and Frank, had claimed both pool tables. Elmer and Frank were cueing up for a game on the back one and J. C. had Merle cornered at the front one.

"So how did the hay business go?" Betty asked. She wore creased jeans, boots, and a red sleeveless western shirt that evening. Her gray hair had been brushed back and held with a bright red headband.

"We'll be hauling hay every day for a week, which means he owes me seven days of painting. He's going to scrape and paint until his little fingers bleed when it's my turn because I'm so tired I could fall down in a heap and sleep for a week," she said.

"What's he look like? He must be hotter'n one of them guys on the front of Betty's romance books to make you go to the hay field two days in a row, much less a whole week," Janice said.

Hank sat down at the end of the bar. "Whose fingers are going to bleed and who's on the front of a romance book? Please set me up with a quart of Coors tonight. Not the light stuff either."

"Hank, meet my friends Janice, Betty, and Linda," Larissa made introductions.

"Pleased to meet you, ladies. Y'all from here in Mingus?" He knew all of them, had pictures of them in the files along with where they lived and how much money they made on last year's tax return.

"Yes, we are. You interested in painting more than one house?" Linda winked.

"No, ma'am. If Larissa hadn't been such good help today I wouldn't even be painting hers. But she sure knows her way around a hay barn. Truth is I didn't believe her when she said she had hauled hay but she handled those hooks like a pro. Y'all ever been to her house in Tennessee?"

Linda shook her head. "You from Tennessee, girl? We all thought you was from up north."

A smile turned up one side of Larissa's mouth. "I'm from lots of places but one of them had hay in the field and it's like riding a bicycle. Once you've worked in it all day, you are a pro."

"Come on, girls; we got to keep beer in our men's hands or they'll be whinin' to go home before midnight," Janice said.

Betty waved a hand over her face when she was far enough away that Hank couldn't see her. Linda rolled her eyes and Janice pretended to wilt. Larissa's half-smile turned into a full-fledged grin. They'd only seen the outside of the package. Once they saw how sweet and kind Hank was, they'd be trying to marry her off to the man.

Larissa put the Mason jar of beer in front of Hank and made change for his five dollar bill.

"So are they friends of your mother's?" Hank asked.

"Hell no! My mother has never met those three but she might when she comes to visit me next fall," Larissa said.

"From Tennessee?" Hank asked.

"If her flight takes her through Nashville. Why are you so interested in where I came from anyway? It's not important."

"I like you and I'm just making conversation," he said.

Hank felt like he was butting his head against a brick wall. His intentions were to glean information about the bartender, but the more he dug the less he knew, and the more he was around her the more he liked her. And he had absolutely no right to like her or lead her on.

It hadn't taken ten minutes in the beer joint that first night for the customers to bring up the fact that a man by the last name of Radner was trying to buy up the town and that Larissa wasn't selling. They said the last owner had turned down a million and a half for the old beer joint and Larissa was even more stubborn. Add that to the day when he'd been sitting on her porch and the icing was on the cake; Larissa wouldn't sell her beer joint until angels opened a brothel in a holiness church.

Why? Hank wondered as he sipped the beer and watched Larissa go from customer to customer, filling jars, packing buckets, and making blenders full of mixed drinks. She'd said it was because she had found a home. Why didn't she have a home before and why wasn't there a scrap of intel on her? Was she in the witness protection program? Was that why she wouldn't even think about selling her beer joint? It made more sense than anything else. She'd witnessed something back in Tennessee and Mingus, Texas, was the perfect place to hide. Now she'd inherited the Honky Tonk and it wasn't that she wouldn't sell out but rather that she couldn't.

Chapter 5

"Excuse me, ma'am, but could I talk to you after closing time?" the lady asked Larissa when she reached the part of the bar where she waited.

"Who are you?" Larissa asked in a tone so cold that it would have frozen the hair from the devil's ears. The woman wasn't a day over twenty, had red hair cut in a short, over-the-ears, no-nonsense style, and green eyes. She wore a denim miniskirt, a hot pink tank top stretched over boobs that were bigger than her hips, and cowboy boots with sharp toes and a walking heel.

"Sharlene Waverly," she answered.

"Did Hayes Radner send you in here?" Larissa asked.

Hank was two stools down and leaned forward to listen when he heard the Radner name. The ice in Larissa's voice could have brought on a snowstorm right there in the middle of July.

"No, but I know who he is by reputation," Sharlene said. "He's from Dallas and richer than Midas."

Hank leaned back but strained to catch every word.

Sharlene went on, "I know that he's trying to buy all the land in Mingus for an amusement park, that you have a town meeting scheduled, and it's looking like Mr. Radner is going to hit a brick wall. I might incorporate that into my story, but it's not the headline. I work for the *Dallas Morning News* and I want to do a feature on the Honky Tonk. The headline will be *Party and Pick Out a Part'ner*."

Larissa frowned. "What?"

"You are the fourth person to own the Honky Tonk. Ruby Lee gave it to Daisy and it took a while but she found her soul mate right here in the beer joint. Then she gave it to Cathy who also found love here. I want to follow your life for a few months and see if you are the third. Plus there's the Walker triplets, Angel and Garrett, and numerous others who've met and fallen in love in this place. Is it blessed?" Sharlene asked.

"More like cursed," Larissa chuckled.

"Whatever it is, I'd like to shadow you for a while. Would that be possible?" Sharlene asked.

Larissa thought about it a few seconds before saying, "You know how to pull a handle and fill up a Mason jar with beer?"

"No, but I could learn."

"How often are you going to shadow me?"

"Until I get the story. I'm working on my own on this one trying to show the boss I've got enough initiative to work my way out of obits. I get off work on Friday at five. I could work Friday and Saturday nights," Sharlene offered.

"It's going to be a dud," Larissa said.

"A what?"

"You ever light firecrackers on the Fourth of July?" Sharlene nodded.

"Ever light one that just fizzed and died?"

She nodded again.

"That's a dud. You can shadow me and help behind the bar but you won't get a story. Hayes Radner can buy the whole damn state of Texas but he's not getting my beer joint. Put that in your article and tell him to take the day-old newspaper to the outhouse and wipe his ass with it," Larissa said.

"When do I start?" Sharlene asked.

"Right now. Come on back here and get a handle in your hands."

Hank tipped up his beer and drank deeply. When he set it down Larissa was in front of him. It was beginning to look like nothing could shake that woman out of Mingus or the Honky Tonk, but he didn't give up easily. There just might be a way if he dug hard enough and long enough.

"Another one?" she asked.

"No, I think I'll have a Grey Goose martini," he said.

"Never pictured you for a martini man," she said.

"It's my mixed drink of choice. You were pretty vocal about Hayes Radner. Ever seen him?"

"No I have not, but I'm sending one of our fliers for our town meeting to his Dallas business address with a note to come out and show his face or stop pestering us. He's the biggest sissy I've ever heard about. I bet he doesn't even have a set. Anyone with balls would come in here and talk to me in person. We'd just love to have him attend the meeting and figure out once and for all that he's not buying Mingus for a damned amusement park," she said.

"Well, I think I'll go on home and get a good night's sleep. We'll be starting to paint your house bright and early, right?" Hank said.

The smile on Larissa's face was warm and sweet, erasing the bitter expression that she'd had when she spoke about Hayes Radner. "If you knock on my door before eleven o'clock I'll shoot you. I don't go home until two thirty and I'm not pleasant without eight hours of sleep. So come between eleven and noon and we'll work all afternoon. Kind of like the hay baling hours."

"But I kept working half the night after you left," he said.

"And I'll keep working until two in the morning after you leave."

"Fair is fair. I'll be there between eleven and noon." He waved. Whew! She did get riled easy when Hayes Radner's name came up. He wondered what she'd do if old Hayes walked into that meeting with a briefcase full of real money. Would the sight of that many hundred dollar bills make her backpedal all the way to the bank?

She watched him until the door closed behind him. They'd worked every day for a week in the hay fields and there'd been a couple of near-miss kisses, but every time there was a split second hesitation. As if he wasn't sure he wanted to open Pandora's Box again, which made Larissa even more wary. She could never remember being so attracted to a man and so afraid to wade right into the water to see how deep it really was.

Sharlene set four pints on a tray. "Is that the one?"

"One what?"

"The lucky cowboy who gets to take you out of the Honky Tonk?"

"I told you that your article is going to be a dud. I'm getting free work and you are going to get nothing. Hank is my friend. I helped him haul hay. He's going to help me paint my house. He is a sexy thing but that much heat would burn out in a hurry. He's not for me." Larissa laughed. "So are you married, attached to a significant other, or what's your story?"

"None of the above. I'm just a hardworking girl from Corn, Oklahoma, who'd love to carve out a place at the *Dallas Morning News* with an office and a view," she answered.

"And you think the Honky Tonk is going to give you that kind of edge?" Larissa asked.

"Never know. It's worth a try. Women buy magazines with articles on how to find their soul mate. Why shouldn't they pin my article on their refrigerator door and then rush to the Honky Tonk every night? It's easier than some of those things I see in magazines and it'll stir up some business."

Larissa refilled the peanuts and pretzel bowls. "I'm full to capacity several nights a week already. I'm not sure I want to stir up any more business."

"That song that's playin' is the story of my life," Sharlene said.

"How's that?" Larissa asked.

"Jason Boland is true country. Not any of this bubblegum rock mixed up in alternative country. Listen to what he's singing about. Cheap bourbon whiskey and pearl snap shirts are the things that stay the same. That's me. I'm as pure country as Strait, Jones, and Williams," she said.

"Then what in the hell are you doing in the newspaper business? Girl, you should be workin' behind the bar all the time. You want a full-time job?" Larissa said.

"Maybe someday but right now I got this hankering to write. Always wanted to do romance novels but that's even harder to break into than newspaper. Here they come. Three line dances and they're thirsty. Get ready," she said.

Larissa made drinks by the pitchers and singles and Sharlene worked the beer end of the bar. Shadowing her for a story might not be so bad if Sharlene was really willing to work her two busiest nights. But by closing she might decide that shadowing a bartender was even harder work than writing an article about an old beer joint and go on to her next idea for a story that would put her in a corner office with a view.

"Hey, hey, who you got workin' for you?" Amos claimed a bar stool between two of his biker friends. They were all harmless folks in spite of their tats and pierced skin. For the most part they'd been professional white-collar workers and their only rebel streak was riding Harleys and blowing off a little steam on the weekends.

The previous fall Amos had put an office trailer behind the Honky Tonk with twenty travel trailer hookups back behind that. He moved the trailer at the beginning of the summer, putting the office in a renovated house not far from the post office and city hall. Larissa had leased the acres that the trailer hookups were on and rented them out to travelers and truck drivers.

"Get ready for some serious business, Sharlene. Trouble just arrived and his name is Amos. This is Sharlene, my new weekend help who thinks she's going to find a story by working for me." She smiled at the three bikers in their black leather 'do rags and vests. "What're you boys drinkin' tonight?"

"I want a Coors in a bottle and what are you talking about, a story?" Amos asked.

"Momma wants one of them fancy martinis you make and I need a bucket of Miller," Will said.

"And my table wants two buckets of Bud," Barron said. "Who'd you say your new help is?"

"I got the martini. Buckets are under the counter there. Six to a bucket. Two scoops of ice," Larissa told Sharlene. "And guys, her name is Sharlene Waverly and she's a reporter from the *Dallas Morning News*. Remember, everything you say can and will be printed for your wives and girlfriends to see."

Amos chuckled. "I see. She's going to write a story about the Honky Tonk now that it's getting to be a popular place. So where's the midnight cowboy who's been hangin' around the past couple of weeks?"

"Pleased to meet all y'all. The cowboy has gone home. I asked if he was the lucky one that she'd leave the Honky Tonk over and she says not." Sharlene talked as she worked.

"I've heard that story before," Amos said.

"Want to talk about it?" Sharlene asked.

"Oh, no, you're not getting me to tell tales that might end up in print." Amos picked up his beer and carried it to the pool tables to watch a game between Merle and Julio.

"This your first time to bartend?" Barron asked Sharlene.

"It sure is."

Larissa spun around. "You are twenty-one, aren't you?"

"Twenty-five last birthday, July 21, two days ago."

Larissa set a martini on the bar. "What have you been doing the last seven years since you got out of high school?"

"Joined the army and that lasted four years. Did two stints in Iraq, came home, and went to college.

Got enough of that in two years so I stopped when I had the associate's degree and went to work. Did some bookkeeping, a little of this and a little of that. Past six months I've been writing obits and doing whatever grunt work no one else wants to do."

"How'd you hear about the Honky Tonk?" Will asked.

"Some friends in the office came over here to party and told me all about it and the magic spell it weaves on lovers. Get ready for the rush again, Larissa. They've danced through four fast ones and they're spittin' dust."

"You got the lingo down pretty good. You sure you haven't worked in a bar?" Larissa asked.

"No, ma'am, but I got to admit I'm already in love with it," Sharlene said.

"Tell me that at two in the mornin' when your feet are dead tired."

The customers had thinned out by quitting time to half a dozen diehards. Luther unplugged the jukebox and told them the place was closing in five minutes. They didn't even grumble as they dragged their tired feet out the door. He set his red and white cooler on the bar, tossed four Dr Pepper cans into the trash, and put the two full ones back in the refrigerator for the next night.

"Busy night when I can't polish off a six-pack," he said as he reached behind the cash register and picked up his check.

"I'm Sharlene. Who are you?" She wiped down the bar one final time.

"Luther. Did Rissa hire you?"

"On weekends so I can watch her. I'm a newspaper person who's trying to break into the lifestyle section."

Luther chuckled and shook his head. "See you tomorrow night, Rissa."

"Be safe." She waved.

"Clean up?" Sharlene asked.

"Not tonight. It'll wait until an hour before opening tomorrow night."

"Where's the nearest and cheapest motel? I'm not driving all the way back to Dallas tonight as tired as I am."

Larissa was a pretty damned good judge of character and Sharlene hadn't sent off her "bullshit" radar one time that night. "I'll make a deal with you. Through that door is an apartment that the bartender slash owner always lived in. When Cathy moved she took the bedroom furniture with her. She did leave the living room and kitchen intact as well as towels in the bathroom in case I ever wanted to crash there. Sofa makes out into a bed. You clean up the place tomorrow in time for opening and you can sleep there. Long as you work for me on Friday and Saturday nights you can have the place for the cleanup."

"It's a deal," Sharlene said.

"Get a beer and we'll prop our feet up for a few minutes. Cathy taught me that back when I first worked for her."

Sharlene drew up a pint jar of Coors Light and carried it to a table where she pulled out a chair and propped her boots on it just like Larissa had done. "Ah! Lord, that tastes good."

"You like beer?"

"Yes, ma'am, and I'm the one spittin' dust right now." Sharlene tipped up the jar and took a long drink.

"How'd you end up in the army?"

"I grew up in a little bitty town in Mennonite country up in Oklahoma. Corn's not much bigger than Mingus. Five kids and our parents lived in a two-bedroom house out in the country. I had four older brothers. It was get mean or get whupped. I got mean and didn't know what I wanted to do with my life so when I graduated I joined up. Do I need a key to get into that apartment?"

"No, but come mornin' you might want to make a trip down to Stephenville to stock the refrigerator if you're going to spend a couple of days a week back there," Larissa said.

"I'm going to get my bag and call it a night then. I could sleep standing up in a broom closet right now," Sharlene said.

"See you at eight tomorrow evening," Larissa said.

"You always this trusting? I could take everything in that cash register plus a trunk full of high-dollar liquor."

"Yep, you can. But I'm as mean as you are and you'd best run fast, long, and hard if you do." Larissa set her empty bottle on the table. "Lock up behind me. There's a key to the back door of the apartment on the kitchen table so you can go and come as you please for groceries or whatever."

"Thanks, Larissa," Sharlene said.

"You are very welcome. You're going to earn every word you don't get to write."

The next morning Larissa opened the back door to let Stallone in the house and blinked a dozen times before she believed her eyes. Hank was sitting on the porch, his back against a post and one knee drawn up. He wore faded overalls and a white gauze tank top, scuffed up boots, and a dusty old misshapen straw hat.

"Mornin'," he said.

"How long you been sittin' there?"

"About fifteen minutes. I'd have started scrapin' but I was afraid I'd wake you up. I didn't want to work with an old bear all day so me and Stallone have been having a Mexican standoff." He nodded toward the black and white cat sitting at the edge of the garden with his ears laid back and giving Hank a dirty look.

"Come on inside and have a cup of coffee while I get dressed."

He leaned against the inside doorjamb while she made coffee. The house was old and in need of multiple repairs. He wondered how much she'd paid for it and how much it would take to buy it from her. His claim to fame had always been that he could read people but Larissa Morley stopped him in his tracks. Her movements and even the short red silk pajamas covered with a fancy kimono robe screamed money. But no one with money would be living in a seventy-year-old house in Mingus, Texas.

"Why'd you ever move here?" he asked.

"You want the truth?"

"I'm a big boy. I think I can handle it," he said.

"I'd been hunting for myself in all the wrong places and couldn't find peace or happiness so one day I quite literally pulled down a map of the United States, shut my eyes, turned around three times, and put a tack in the map. Then I moved to Mingus and that is the gospel, pure unadulterated, one hundred proof damn truth."

"You are crazy," he said.

"Probably. But I'm happy."

She brushed past him on the way to the bedroom. She looked up into his eyes but he blinked and looked away. The moment passed even though a flash of heat flickered between them. She wanted the kiss and felt cheated when he let the opportunity pass.

His jaw gritted in anger. He wanted to hold her, to kiss her, and even more, but he couldn't, not until he knew who she was and why she was so attached to the Honky Tonk. Was he making the same mistake his father had made? Did it really matter if she owned a Honky Tonk? Did it matter that she'd found her niche in Mingus, Texas? What did it matter to Hank Wells?

She hurriedly threw on a pair of cutoff jean shorts, cowboy boots that she'd used in the hay field, and a bright red tank top, then smeared sunblock on her face, arms, and legs and brushed her hair up into a lopsided ponytail. When she went back into the kitchen he'd already poured two cups of coffee and was sitting at the table.

"What color are you going to paint the house?" he asked.

"Turquoise."

He jerked his head around so fast that his neck popped. "What?"

Larissa smiled. "I love the islands. Folks down there aren't afraid of color. So I bought turquoise paint and the trim is going to be hot pink. It'll be bright and make me laugh."

"This is not the islands. When and what islands did you visit?" he asked.

"There's lots of books in the library and I like the ones with pictures," she said. "My mind is made up and the paint already custom mixed. I only bought one gallon of lemon yellow though. Don't you think that's enough for the porch posts and front steps?"

He swallowed hard. The woman baffled him more than he thought possible.

"And if there's any left I'm going to use it to paint my kitchen chairs. One of each color and then I'll buy some purple for the fourth chair."

"You don't strike me as that kind of woman," he said.

She shoved a bagel into the toaster and got out the cream cheese. "What kind of woman am I?"

"Classy. I could picture you in a little café in Paris having coffee and watching the people."

Her breath caught in her chest and it ached until she remembered to exhale. "Boy, I've got you fooled. What in the hell would make you think something like that?"

"The way you carry yourself and hold your head. You've either been around people who were classy or else you come from money somewhere up the line. Did you lose your shirt with bad investments?"

"Sorry to pop your sweet little bubble but I didn't lose jack shit on any investments," she said. "Want something to eat before we start? I figured we'd work until about three and take a lunch break down at the Smokestack. You fed me so I'll feed you but I don't have Oma living in my house to cook for us."

"Better give me a couple of those bagels. Got any espresso hiding in the house to go with them?" Hank said.

"Sorry, plain old coffee is the fanciest thing I'm offering. No lox or caviar for the bagels either. This is not the Café de la Paix. I might rustle up some plum jam that Linda brought over last week."

He snarled his nose. "With cream cheese?"

"Don't knock it until you've tried it," she said.

"You eat it that way?"

She didn't answer but scooped up a tablespoon of plum jam and topped off the bagel with cream cheese spread over the top. She shoved it toward his mouth and he opened it on impulse. "Bite," she said.

He obeyed.

"Not bad."

She motioned toward the toaster where his had popped up. "Help yourself."

Biting into the bagel where his mouth had been caused her insides to go all mushy and a blush to warm up her neck. Sharing anything with him brought on thoughts of sharing more—like her bed.

He smeared cream cheese on two bagel halves, put them on a paper plate from a stack on top of the microwave, and carried it to the table. "Tell me that you aren't serious about the colors for the house. And when did you have breakfast at the Café de la Paix?"

"Like I said, I read a lot. You ever had breakfast there?"

"Yes, I have. I love Paris. Love the laid-back way you go to the café for coffee and end up sitting at a table on the sidewalk for hours watching the people and talking to the locals," he said.

She nodded. "Sounds like fun. Someday maybe I'll have breakfast there. And yes, I am very serious about the colors and the chairs too. I think I'll leave the table its natural color since it's still in good shape. But the chairs are all mismatched so they'll look cute in different colors. I got them at four different garage sales. I made several purchases in surrounding towns when I first

bought the house. Found my bed over in Gordon, the
dresser in Mineral Wells, and the rocker in Palo Pinto.
My dishes are all mismatched. My house is a picture
of life. It's not perfect and it's all mixed up but stuck
together with contentment and love."

"A philosopher?"

"No, just a hippy born thirty years too late. Want
another bagel before we go to work?" she asked.

"No, I believe this will hold me," he said.

"I got everything all ready on the front porch.
Ladders, scrapers, paintbrushes, and pans. Linda loaned
them all to me. Bless her heart. Saved me a fortune in
buying all that stuff that I'd just have to store in the
garden shed later."

He followed her out the front door. "Didn't take you
long to make friends in Mingus, did it?"

"Never thought about it. Linda lives on the next corner
and Betty and Janice are her friends. We just kind of got
to know each other. Then I got to know Cathy when I
went hunting a martini and some company one night and
met the regulars at the Honky Tonk and everything fell
into place. Convinced me I was where I needed to be."

He picked up a ladder and carried it out in the yard.
"I'll do the high places. You can do however high you
can reach. And honey, when you get this house painted
to look like a Bahama Mama hut, they may run you out
of Mingus."

"Or else folks will stand in line to hire us to paint
every house in town like it." She grinned.

He grimaced. She had about as much finesse as a
trailer trash hooker. It must have been that earthy char-
acteristic that had attracted him. Most men liked that

kind of woman but only for a night or two and they left the money on the nightstand.

He tried to make sense of his feelings as he scraped peeling paint from two-inch Cape Cod siding. She kept up with him on a lower level, the hot July sun beating down on them with a breeze that felt like it was flowing straight from a bake oven.

"Lord, I could use a gelato from the Daphne Inn," she mumbled.

"In a plastic cup because they say that a cone interferes with the pureness of the flavor?" he asked.

"You've been there too? Just what do you do in Dallas when you are there? Rob banks or are you a famous thief?" She really did crave a gelato in a plastic cup and a long sit on a bench near the fountain. If she'd been living in her previous life and had met Hank when he was a Dallas head honcho, they would have probably gotten along splendidly.

"No, I'm just a businessman whose business takes him to Paris and Italy occasionally." That nagging voice started again telling him to be honest and tell her that he spent time in Europe every year just because he loved the old country. But to make that admission would mean he'd have to tell her more and more and finally she'd pour a bucket of that hideous paint on his head in a fit of anger.

"How long do you think it'll take to get this all done?" she asked.

"This is Saturday. If we work hard, we might have the scraping finished by the middle of the week. The rest of the week we can paint." He was glad to change the subject.

"Tomorrow?" she asked.

"Is Sunday. Ranchers take that day off for a day of rest. We didn't haul hay on that day."

"Okay." She drug out the two syllables to make five or six.

"So I thought maybe I'd pick you up about ten in the morning and we'd go fishing out at the lake. I'll have Oma make us a picnic," he suggested.

"Is that a date?" She smiled.

"Do you want it to be a date?"

"If it's a date do I get a kiss at the end of the day?" she teased.

"Do you want a kiss at the end of the day?"

"Yes, I do," she said.

"Why?"

"To see if it will knock my socks off like the first one did or if that was just a fluke," she said.

"And if it was?"

"Then I'll stop thinking about it."

"You don't have any trouble speaking your mind, do you?"

She shaded her eyes with the back of her hand. "Not a bit. That bother you?"

He smiled down at her. "It wouldn't do any good if it did. So at the end of our date when we have a second kiss are you going to be honest and tell me if it knocks your socks off or are you going to fake it to keep from hurting my feelings?"

"Honey, I don't fake a damn thing."

His mind fell into a deep gutter.

———•~~~•———

At three she wiped the sweat from her brow and said, "If I don't put food in my body soon you are going to have to call the undertaker." She went into the house, got her car keys, and tossed them to him. "I'm too weak to drive. You'll have to do it. Just remember she's my special baby and if you are mean to her, you'll never drive her again."

"Yes, ma'am." He held the door for her.

The Smokestack is the only business in Thurber, Texas, population from five to eight depending on who a person talks to that day. The restaurant is in an old warehouse building with the walls covered with antiques and pictures of days when Thurber was a thriving town.

Larissa led the way to a booth toward the east end of the restaurant. She slid into one side and Hank did the same on the other. She held up two fingers when the waitress looked up and nodded when she mouthed "pie."

"So what are you cooking today?" Hank asked.

"Chicken fried steak, mashed potatoes with gravy, salad with garlic bread on the side, hot rolls, and coconut cream pie. Sweet iced tea. Speak now if you don't like ranch dressing or sugar in your tea and I'll tell the waitress to make a couple of changes."

He shook his head. "Both are fine. That all they serve in here? It's quaint, but it's not the Brasserie Bofinger on the Rue de la Bastille, is it?"

"Nope, but I don't expect you'd get a Texas-sized chicken fried steak there, would you? Or that you'd go there in paint-stained overalls either," she smarted off. She leaned across the table and whispered, "As far as what else they have or serve in here, I have no idea. I've never seen a menu."

He frowned. "Why?"

"Because I came here first with Cathy and Amos and they never ordered from a menu. The chicken fried steak is so good I can't imagine ordering anything else. I've got another confession. I've never been fishing."

His smile erased the frown. "Are you serious?"

"Do I need to go buy any equipment?"

He shook his head. "No, Dad keeps enough fishing stuff out at the ranch for an army to use. He loves to fish on Sunday afternoon."

"Is he going with us?"

"No. He's going to Whitesboro to a gospel singing. Would you rather go to that?"

She shook her head. "I hear singing every night. I'd rather go fishin'."

The waitress brought iced tea and salads. Hank downed half his tea before he came up for air. "That's almost as good as Oma's."

"What do you do when you aren't at the ranch? I remember you said once that you didn't live there all the time." She sipped at her tea.

"I work in an office in Dallas. Love the ranch in the summertime so I spend as much time as I can in this area."

"Even better than the Café de la Paix?" she asked.

"Now that's a hard question. Which one do you like best?" he asked right back.

"Like you say, it's a hard question. I don't get over to Paris nearly as often as I did back before I inherited the Honky Tonk," she said. But her thoughts went to that café while she looked out the window at heat waves rising up from the concrete parking lot.

"I never know when you are joking or telling the truth," he said.

"Keep 'em guessing." She giggled.

A man in a three-piece suit that was definitely tailor-made, a red polka-dot power tie, and shoes with tassels stopped beside their booth. Hank's face changed drastically when he looked up.

Larissa watched his expressions after she gave the man a quick glance.

"Hello. What brings you to this area?" Hank asked. The look on his face said to answer the question and get the hell out of Thurber.

"Had some business in Abilene. Love their cheeseburgers here so I stopped for lunch. Who's this pretty lady?"

"Larissa, meet W. J. He works in the same firm I do in Dallas. This is Larissa, the lady I told you about that owns and operates the Honky Tonk," Hank said. His eyes were shifty and trying to relay a message for W. J.

"Right pleased to meet you, Larissa," W. J. said. "Well, I'll be on my way. Got to get back to the firm by closing time to finish off some reports. Anything you want me to tell the boss lady?"

"Just that I'll be back the first Monday in September." Hank's smile was forced.

"With good news?" W. J. asked.

"Never know. The boss lady will have to be patient." A stone statue had more expression than Hank did.

"That ain't going to happen in this lifetime." W. J. walked away.

Larissa watched his face and wished she could read him better. "It was very nice to meet you," she called out.

"My pleasure to finally meet you, Miss Morley," W. J. called back and disappeared out into the heat.

Hank mentally patted himself on the back for getting through that meeting without stumbling all over his nerve endings and emotions. Damn the luck anyway. Who would have thought his assistant would be in the Smokestack at three o'clock in the afternoon on a Saturday.

"Who is the bitchy boss lady that has no patience?" Larissa started on her salad.

"My mother," he said.

She almost choked. "I'm sorry."

"Don't be. Mother can be bitchy when she doesn't get her way, and once she's decided she wants something, she's not pleasant until she gets it," Hank said. His jaws and eyes had relaxed and he was almost normal again.

Larissa swallowed hard. "Sounds like my mother."

But your mother is backwoods trailer trash and mine is a multi-millionaire entrepreneur with a grudge against my father.

"What's your mother's name?" she asked.

"Victoria. And yours?"

"Doreen, and she has red hair just like the little girl in the movies."

"Well, now that's a surprise. I pictured her with black hair and brown eyes," Hank said as he ate his salad.

"That's my father. He was Indian. Mother is pure Irish. Red hair, green eyes. Think Sharlene only taller. Think someone who doesn't look much older than Sharlene too."

"Oh, come on. If she's your mother she has to be fifty," he said.

"Yes, she is and if you ever meet her and say that, you will have a red dot between your eyes within a week."

Hank cocked his head to one side. "What?"

"Think sniper and a red laser dot. Think hit man and big bucks. So is your mother tall and dark-haired like you?" she asked.

"Was your father a sniper in the war or something and he's got this vendetta against anyone who thinks your mother looks fifty? And my mother is a tall blonde with blue eyes. They say I look just like my father did at my age."

Larissa finished off her salad and swiped the remaining salad dressing up with the last bit of garlic bread. "Don't remember my father. He left before I was a year old. Mother would simply put out a hit on you and no one would ever know that Hank Wells died because he thought she was fifty and not thirty. They'd think he was in the wrong place at the wrong time and got hit by a shell probably meant to kill a deer. You do know they kill them with guns instead of cars sometimes, don't you?"

"It was a truck, not a car, thank god," he said.

Doreen Morley. He wrote that name on his memory. As soon as he got home he'd make a call to have her investigated. Information was vital in his line of business. Come morning he'd know if Doreen Morley still lived in the same trailer, if she was a pole dancer in a nude bar, or if she was a Sunday school teacher in a religious commune. Yes, sir, Hank Wells was about to find out exactly where Larissa Morley came from and what she'd done in the past thirty years.

Victoria Wells. Larissa said the name six times so she wouldn't forget it. One phone call and tomorrow she'd know everything about the woman. She'd know if the woman inherited her business or if she'd built it from scratch and exactly what kind of business it was, why she and Henry weren't married anymore, and what it was that she wanted so badly that she was bitchy these days. And her investigator would find out what it was that made Larissa wary of the best looking cowboy she'd ever seen.

Chapter 6

Jo Dee Messina was singing "My Give a Damn's Busted" when Luther opened the doors that evening and started checking IDs.

Sharlene's cowboy boots were tapping out the rhythm on the floor as she waited for the first rush to the bar. The dark green halter top was the same color as her eyes and flipped out over the top of a denim miniskirt that showed off muscular legs.

"This is my song," she said when Larissa joined her behind the bar.

"Why?" Larissa had barely had time to take a shower and wash the dried paint chips from her dark hair. She had run a hair dryer through it a few times, flipped it back with a wide red headband that matched her tank top, and hoped it didn't look too bad. She wore capri length jeans and red boots.

"Because it is. Describes my last boyfriend to a T. He filled my head with lies and twisted my heart until it snapped, just like the song. Be careful of that cowboy who's flirting with you. He might do the same thing," Sharlene warned.

Larissa topped off the pretzel and peanut bowls and set two blenders on the back workstation. "I thought you were interested in a big story about me and the cowboy falling in love so you could have the office with a view."

"Something ain't right about this one. Might be that he will break your give a damn. I'm not in a hurry with my story. I want it to be real when I write it, not contrived. Besides, I like it here at the Tonk. I don't care if it takes a couple of years to write your story."

"Two buckets of Coors and a pitcher of tequila sunrise," a customer said. She was a twenty-something woman with black hair that hung to her waist. She wore denim shorts and a halter top that covered enough to keep her out of jail but wouldn't flag a freight train.

Sharlene had the buckets filled at the same time Larissa set the pitcher on a tray with six empty pint jars.

The woman handed Sharlene a fifty dollar bill and waited for change. "So when did Larissa hire you to help?"

"Last night," Larissa answered.

"Where's Julio tonight?"

"He usually comes in about nine on Saturday nights. Should be here before long," Larissa answered.

"Then I'll make do until he gets here." She motioned for two of her friends to help carry the buckets and tray back to their table.

"Is she a hooker?" Sharlene whispered.

"No, honey, she's a Chigger."

"What's that?"

Larissa laughed. "Chigger is a woman who came to the Honky Tonk for at least seven years, maybe more, every single weekend. Way I heard it is that she said sex was too damn much fun to charge money for it."

"Was Chigger her real name?" Sharlene asked.

Larissa set out the ingredients to fill an order for two pitchers of pina coladas. "No, it was something like Willa but everyone called her Chigger."

"Why?"

"She said she was like a real chigger, that she could put an itch on a man that was unbearable until she took him to bed," Larissa said. "Hey, I forgot to ask. How'd you like the apartment?"

"It's great. Wish I had something that nice in Dallas. I made a grocery store run this morning after I cleaned up the beer joint. Picked up some staples that'll last several weeks."

Larissa filled a bucket with Coors and added two scoops of ice. "That sounds good. So it's going to take a while for you to get this story written?"

"However long it takes you to find a husband."

"Then you'd best load up enough to last more than a few weeks," Larissa said with a laugh.

A prickly sensation on her neck said that Hank was in the joint. It grew hotter and hotter the closer he got to the bar. By the time he was on a bar stool she wanted to shovel a scoop of ice down the back of her tank top.

"Martini," he drawled when she looked at him.

Her mouth felt like she'd crossed the Sahara without a drop of water.

"Could I get two pitchers of margaritas and a pitcher of Coors?" The woman who'd cornered Julio the minute he arrived poked her head between Hank and the woman sitting next to him.

"I can make margaritas," Sharlene said.

The woman shoved between Hank and the customer next to him, pressing every part of her scantily covered body as close to him as she could. "Whew! Where'd you come from, darlin'?"

Larissa set the martini in front of Hank.

"I would've pictured you as a beer man, not a sissy martini man."

"Looks can be deceiving." He grinned.

She leaned in close to whisper seductively. "I can think of places to put that drink that would be a hell of a lot more fun than a Mason jar."

"Crystal glass?" he asked in fake innocence.

"We'll start with that sitting between my boobs and go on to other places," she flirted.

Larissa fought the urge to reach across the bar and snatch all that long black hair out by the roots. Did Hank always draw women to him like flies on a fresh cow patty?

Of course he does. With those muscles, that drawl, and those damn sexy eyes, you are crazy to think you'd be the only one interested in him.

"Here's your order," Sharlene said. "You find that rancher who likes to dance?"

"I did but I'd trade him in on this package." She gave Hank a long, sideways wink.

"His wife would jerk those hair extensions off and choke you to death with them. Then she'd feed your eyeballs to the feral cats that come up from the woods at night. I wouldn't mess with him if I was you," Sharlene said.

The woman cut her eyes around at Hank. "Shame on you! You should wear a wedding ring."

"Against my religion," he said.

"Religious man don't belong in a beer joint." She huffed off toward the table where her friends waited with the hired hands from Garret's ranch.

Larissa giggled and then it turned into full-fledged laughter. "How'd you know those were extensions?"

"When I left Iraq the second time I decided I wanted an inside job working with women. Didn't care if I ever dealt with a man again. So I started a six-month course in cosmetology. Figured out the first six weeks that working with bitchy women wasn't a bit better than working with arrogant men so I quit and went to find something else," Sharlene said.

"I'm not married. Never have been," Hank said. Sharlene grinned. "Thank you, Sharlene Waverly, for saving me from having to drink a martini from a chigger's belly button."

That set Larissa off on another fit of giggles. Sharlene was good behind the bar, had a sense of humor, and worked her butt off. She wondered if she might change the woman's mind about the newspaper business and put her to work full time.

"What's that supposed to mean?" Hank asked.

Larissa wiped her eyes with a bar rag. "I'll tell you about Chigger tomorrow. I don't have time tonight. Here they come again, Sharlene. I swear three line dances and they're so thirsty they'd lap up warm beer from a pig trough."

"Four and we'd have to learn how to sink an IV," Sharlene said.

Sara Evans was singing "Suds in the Bucket." Sharlene did a couple of wiggles as she drew up a pitcher of Miller. "I love this song. It's the story of my life. Soon as I finished high school I left the suds in the bucket and didn't look back."

"Ever been back?" Hank asked.

"Oh, yeah. Ten days into boot camp I thought I'd made the biggest mistake of my life but my name on the line said they owned my ass four years. So I sucked it up but yes, I went home. My momma damn sure learned a lot in those years."

"It happens," Hank said.

"Sounds like you walked a while in my boots. You been in the army?" Sharlene asked.

"Oh, no! Not me," Hank said.

Sharlene pointed to the jukebox. "Oh, listen! Don't you just love country songs? They tell the whole story. You don't know how many times we used the title of this song over there. 'Did I Shave My Legs For This?' was our theme song!"

Hank breathed a sigh of relief that she'd gone off on another tangent and stopped asking him questions.

Larissa could have strangled her. She didn't care if the women in Iraq never shaved their legs. She wanted to know what he'd done if he hadn't gone to the military and she had the distinct feeling that he was about to say more when Sharlene butted in. Damn! Damn! Damn!

"You sure you don't dance with the customers?" Hank asked.

A slow two-stepping song by George Strait put several dancers on the floor. Larissa remembered the first days when she came to the Honky Tonk and had no idea how to do the country dances. She wanted to dance with Hank so badly that her heart hurt from the yearning.

"Not when we are this busy. Maybe later," she said.

"Then I'll stick around. When you get ready for a dance, you let me know. I'm going over and watch Merle and Patrick shoot pool." He carried his martini with him.

"What's that about not dancing?" Sharlene asked.

"It was a rule back in Ruby Lee's day. I may change it tonight. You seein' someone you want to do a little two-steppin' with?" Larissa said.

"Not me, but if you're ever goin' to make up your mind about that chunk of sex in cowboy boots you'd best dance with him," Sharlene said.

"Why?"

"What better way to get right up close and personal? What other rules did Ruby have?"

"No letting the customers buy you a drink and no men in the apartment."

Sharlene fanned her face with her hand. "Whew! Did she hate men or what?"

"No, I think she loved them, maybe too much. They tell me she was a hellcat, a preacher's daughter. I heard that she didn't put a bar in close to her old stomping grounds because she was afraid her daddy would stand in the parking lot and preach her customers out of hell and into heaven. Oh, I do like this song," Larissa said.

The first notes of a lonesome piano started "To Make Me Feel Your Love" by Garth Brooks.

"Go dance with him. You ain't goin' to get nothing any slower than that tonight. The crowd's been playin' fast stuff," Sharlene said. "Besides, how you goin' to know if he's the one or not if you don't give him a chance?"

Larissa looked across the bar. Hank had leaned against the wall and was staring right at her. She nodded and he met her in the middle of the floor. She wrapped her arms around his neck and he looped his around her waist. They barely moved around the edge of the floor but she understood what Sharlene meant as two hearts, only physical inches apart, beat in perfect unison while they listened to Garth sing one of the greatest love songs of his career.

Hank buried his face in her hair and sang with Garth about the winds of change blowing wild and free but that she hadn't seen nothing like him. He sang that he would go to the ends of the earth for her to make her feel his love.

When the song started playing the second time she looked up at him and he nodded toward Julio and the chigger-woman in the middle of the dance floor. "I saw him poke the same buttons four times. Folks better get ready to slow dance for about fifteen minutes."

She laid her cheek on his chest and shut her eyes. The lyrics said the storms were raging on a rollin' sea on the highway of regret, that he could make her happy, that he could make her dreams come true.

That's what I want. Someone to love me so much that he'd play this song four times in a row and two-step with me all four times.

The third time the song started she took a step backwards but Hank didn't let go. He enjoyed keeping Larissa in his arms longer than it took to kiss her that one time in the hay barn. Like Garth said, he could hold her for a million years to make her feel his love if only things were different.

She opened her eyes to see Julio and his woman dancing right next to them. He winked and grinned. Larissa nodded slightly and looked up at Hank. He kissed her on the forehead when the song started the fourth time and kept dancing.

"If you're going to hang for a calf, you might as well hang for a full-grown Angus bull," he said.

"What?"

"If you are going to break the rules for one dance, then make it worthwhile."

"Would you go hungry and go crawling down the avenue for me?" she asked right after Garth sang those words.

"I would," he said. *God, please don't let her ask me if I'd do her wrong like Garth says in the next part of the song.*

At the end of the last song he bent her backwards and brushed a kiss across her lips. "Thank you for the dance and for breaking the rule with me. I'm honored."

"You should be," she said breathlessly.

He stood her back up and kept dancing to another Garth tune called "The Dance."

"One more?" Hank asked Larissa.

"Dance or kiss?"

"Either or both," he said.

She nodded. "What about this song? Who played it and is it going to last through four times?"

"I played it but only once."

"Are you telling me something?" Larissa asked.

"I'm shouting it from the rooftops, lady. All you have to do is listen. You are beautiful and our lives are better left to chance. And whatever pain is in the future, I'm glad for this moment with you, Larissa Morley. And I wouldn't have missed this dance with you for anything the future has to offer."

"You are a romantic," she whispered.

He was as good a dancer as he was kisser. If that silly feeling in her heart would shut up and quit saying that the other shoe was about to drop she could have easily been the third princess in the fairy tale that Sharlene wanted to write.

Hank whispered the words in her ear as Garth sang them, telling her that if he'd known how things would fall, he might have changed it all and that he was glad he didn't know how it all would end because he could have missed the pain but he would have had to miss the dance.

When the music stopped he stepped back and bowed slightly.

One word seared its brand into her heart.

That was "Amen."

Chapter 7

A FEW WHITE PUFFY CLOUDS FLIRTED WITH EACH OTHER across the summer blue sky. The lake water made very little noise as it slapped against the grassy knoll where they'd thrown out their quilt. A bird with a long neck and legs lit a few feet away and tried to convince them that it was big and mean enough to send them packing but finally gave up and took to the air. A couple of frogs had a contest going to see who had the deepest voice. A few crickets were singing out of tune. The mosquitoes were lazy and had stayed home, but a fly or two had braved the heat and tried to suck up a drop of beer occasionally.

Larissa kicked off her sandals and lazed back on a patchwork quilt and watched the red bobble out in the water. She wore cutoff denim shorts and a white eyelet lace halter top tied around her neck. She'd pulled her hair up into a ponytail but it kept sneaking down to stick to her sweaty neck. Hank's faded jeans had holes in the knees and his unbuttoned chambray shirt gave her peeks of his broad chest. His sandals were with hers at the edge of the quilt. She was glad that she'd worn dark sunglasses so that she could check out that Longhorn belt buckle whenever she wanted.

A portable CD player kept George Strait's fifty number one songs going while they sipped icy beer from longneck bottles. Hank stretched out on his back and kept an eye on his fishing line. He'd propped both their poles in the metal vee of a device he'd brought along.

"So this is fishin'," she said.

"Fun, ain't it?"

"I could get used to it on Sunday after a busy week in the Honky Tonk."

"So how is Sharlene working out?"

"After two nights I wish she'd quit the newspaper and come to work for me exclusively. We hit it off from the beginning. That don't happen nearly enough in today's crazy world."

"You and I have hit it off pretty good after you got over being mad at me for hitting a deer and making you slide into a ditch," he said.

She smiled. "We did, didn't we?"

"Where do you think this will go?" he asked.

Nowhere! It can go nowhere because of who I really am and who I work for. But today I'm an old dirt farmer with a red neck and a love for country music and I'm going to enjoy being just that. I'll worry about tomorrow when it gets here, he thought, answering the question for himself.

Larissa shrugged. "Depends on whether we catch fish and whether you know how to clean them if we do. If you can get them into the right sized pieces, I'll call Linda and ask her how to fry them."

"You never cooked fish?" Hank asked.

She shook her head. "Love fried catfish or grilled trout or that—" she almost said the fish they served at the little Italian restaurant right near the Vatican, "but I wouldn't have any idea how to cook them."

He scooted over next to her, slipped an arm under her, and drew her close to his side. "I wasn't talking about fish when I asked that question, Larissa."

"I know what you were talking about and I don't have an answer. What do you think?"

He kissed her on the forehead. "Right now I just want this day."

"Then that's what we'll have. One day at a time."

He shut his eyes. If only he was Henry Wells' son every month of the year and not just the one month he had vacation time.

That idea brought him up short. He'd never wanted to live on the ranch indefinitely until that moment. He'd always looked forward to his month in Palo Pinto but he'd always been more than ready to go home when it was finished. The past week he'd dreamed of Larissa every night and they were always on the ranch, not in Dallas.

Two detectives had spent most of the night and the morning and had come up with absolutely nothing on Doreen Morley, which suggested to him that the woman flew so low under the radar that no one knew jack shit about her. It also fully supported his theory that her mother was probably trailer trash. She must've worked for some rich people before she landed in Mingus, Texas, to know so much about France and Italy.

One day at a time, she thought. That's all anyone got anyway. No one on the face of the earth had the promise of any more than that, be it the Queen of England or the lowliest, homeless hobo in Harlem. One day was all any of them got and Larissa was going to enjoy her day in the sunshine.

She'd called her investigator immediately after Hank left the beer joint the night before, apologized for calling so late and told him what she wanted. An hour before Hank picked her up that morning she'd heard back from him. There was no Victoria Wells anywhere in the world that had the right age, credentials, and a son by the name of Hank. There were no Victoria Wells listed in the business directories in Dallas. There was an interesting article or two on Henry and his ranch. He raised prime Angus, had an interest in a couple of oil companies, and could buy Fort Knox out of his petty cash drawer.

Evidently Hank's mother was a small business owner who didn't make the Forbes list and he'd divided his time between her and Henry. She'd asked her investigator to find out all he could about the Radners and he'd sent sheets of information but said they were a very private bunch of folks and there were no pictures floating around. She'd give half her inheritance, which was enough to buy half the state of Texas, to see a picture of Hayes Radner. She imagined him to be a short, fat little fellow with a rim of thin hair around a bald head. Maybe little nondescript piggy eyes behind black plastic glasses. To prove that she was right would give her a hell of a lot of satisfaction.

"Penny for your thoughts," Hank said.

"I was thinking about Hayes Radner," she said.

"What about him?" Hank's heart sank. Of all the people in the world, he did not want to talk about Hayes right then.

"Daisy and Cathy saw him once but I haven't. They knew the enemy. I don't. I can't find a single picture of him on the Internet or in a magazine, yet he has enough money to buy a whole town for an amusement park? Is he a ghost or a descendent of Howard Hughes? I called Cathy and asked about him but she couldn't remember much. It was raining the night he stopped by the Honky Tonk and talked to them. She said couldn't remember any details except that he was cocky as a Banty rooster and had a driver that he ordered around like a puppy dog."

Hank chuckled. "Maybe he and his family like privacy. Maybe they aren't glory hounds who live and breathe for front page tabloid coverage. What makes you think he's the enemy?"

"I'm the third owner of the Honky Tonk since Ruby died and he's approached all of us to buy the beer joint either in person or by phone. He sent people to buy it for him and they were very adamant. It appears that he gets what he wants and doesn't give up. Neither do I. He only thought he hit a brick wall with Daisy and Cathy."

Hank sat up quickly and grabbed his fishing pole. "Damn it. Just got a teaser. The bobble went under and I thought for sure I had a fish on the line." Damn the job he had to do. She was going to cuss, rant, and throw things when she found out who he worked for in Dallas.

"Looks like we might be depending on Long John Silver's for our fish tonight," she teased.

He fell back on the quilt. "Might be too hot for them to bite."

"Oh, they're always biting at Long John's. Never been in there and heard the waitress say that they didn't have any fish because it was too hot for them to take the bait."

Hank rolled over on his side and propped up on an elbow. "You are beautiful, Larissa Morley. Your eyes sparkle when you are teasing."

"Thank you." She got that much out before he leaned forward and kissed her hard and passionately.

A movement at her foot caused her to jerk away from him and grab her fishing pole, which was inching out toward the edge of the water.

"What?" He frowned.

"I got a fish," she yelled.

He grinned but didn't move. "Well, bring the sucker on in and we'll cheat Long John's out of a profit today."

When she picked up the rod, it bent into an arch and the line was tight. "What do I do?" she gasped.

He looked up and was on his feet in one swift motion. He wrapped his arms around her waist and covered her small hands with his larger ones. "We'll give him some line and tire him out. Like this." He released the lock on the reel and let it play out until the line was taut but not ready to break and the rod was straight. "Now let him swim around a little and then reel in a few inches at a time." He couldn't remember when he'd had so much fun as he'd had that summer. All the expensive vacations he'd had in the past didn't compare to hauling hay, scraping a house, and now fishing with Larissa.

"I feel like I'm on one of those boats and fishing for whales or marlin or something that hangs on the wall," she said.

She looked at the thin fishing line moving rapidly away from her instead of getting closer. That's the way it was with her and Hank. She was right there beside him and when he kissed her the line was tight and the rod bent into a rainbow arc but in a few minutes she was moving away from him.

Hank reeled the fish back in a few feet and locked the reel, letting it relax before repeating the process several more times. Finally, she could see something coming toward the bank just under the water's surface. "Hot damn! We're going to catch it, Hank! We're really catching a fish. Can you believe it and it's a big one?"

He backed up and let her finish the job alone. "You've played it out. Bring it on in."

The turtle was as big as a dinner plate and when it was on the bank, she sat down with a thud and sighed. "All that work and it's a turtle. Shit!"

His laughter echoed off the water and bounced off the willow trees with their feathery leaves blowing in the Texas summer wind. When he caught his breath, he said, "Darlin', that's life."

"Ain't it the truth," she fussed. "Get it off the hook and turn the critter loose unless you or Oma know how to make turtle soup. I can't bear the thought of cracking its shell to get at the meat."

Hank set the turtle free to paddle back out into the lake. "So when did you eat turtle soup?"

"Mother and I had it in… it doesn't matter. We ate it together. She loved it and I hated it. Couldn't get past the idea. Same with squirrel and venison. It might be wonderful vittles but I'd rather buy my meat in plastic covered packages at the supermarket."

To Hank she'd just proven that she came from a poor background where her relatives were hunters and ate wild game. That would be the reason she hung on so tightly to her beer joint and why she wanted to paint her house such ungodly colors.

"Want another beer? It's hotter'n seven kinds of hell out here, especially after using up all that energy to pull in a damned old turtle," she said.

He raised a rakish eyebrow. "You're hot?"

She opened the cooler and took out two beers. "That's what I just said."

His eyes twinkled. "Really, really hot?"

Her eyes widened until white showed around the dark brown pupils. "Are we talking about the weather?"

"How hot are you?" he asked as he scooped her up in his arms.

The beers rattled together when she dropped them on the quilt. "What are you doing?" she gasped.

He waded out into the water. "Cooling you off."

She kicked her legs and squirmed. "Put me down. You wouldn't dare. I didn't bring anymore clothes. You didn't say a word about swimming."

He laughed and tossed her as far as he could. "Don't ever dare me, darlin'."

She came up spitting and spewing. Her feet barely touched bottom and whatever was on the bottom oozed between her toes. She'd swam in every ocean in the world, in pools small enough to barely qualify as a swimming place and those so big a dozen elephants could hide in them. But she'd never been thrown out into a Texas lake in her clothing.

Hank arose like a merman off to her left, water sluicing off him in sheets, his dark hair wet and his eyes sparkling. Heat that had nothing to do with the weather radiated off them as their gazes locked.

She reached up and untied her halter top, peeled it from her wet body, and slung it at the bushes along the side of the bank. After that she removed her shorts and underpants and hurled them to hang in the bush with her top. Naked in lake water was even more exhilarating than a hot tub in a bikini.

"Your turn," she told Hank.

His shirt landed on the bush next to hers. His shorts missed and wound up near the pallet. His boxer shorts covered her underpants.

"Ever been skinny-dippin'?" she asked.

He shook his head.

"Well, then we're skinny-dippin' virgins," she giggled.

He walked toward her without taking his eyes from hers. George Strait's voice came from the bank singing a song about how much better the world would be if the whole world was a honky tonk and revolved around an old jukebox. He said if you were looking for love or someone to heal that broken heart, you'd be in luck if the whole world was a honky tonk.

"Ain't it the truth." She nodded toward the CD player.

"Yes, ma'am." He drew her into his arms.

The whole lake's temperature rose by several degrees when their bodies melted together under the water. When wet skin touched wet skin and he pushed dripping hair from her face so he could kiss her lips, she thought she'd faint from desire. His mouth made love to hers while minnows nibbled at their toes.

"Wow!" she whispered when the kiss ended.

"I agree." He hugged her tightly and then fell backwards with her into the water. "You ever made love under water?"

"Not yet," she said.

He picked her up and carried her to the edge of the lake not far from where their clothing hung drying in the summer sun. He gently laid her in the shallow water with her head cradled in his arm on the grassy bank. The water felt like warm silk as it washed over her body. His calloused hands were filled with heat as they touched her. His lips sent passion surging through her every nerve. She arched against him and began a journey of her own, running her hands over his body, her fingertips becoming conduits for even more passion.

"Have I told you today that you are beautiful, Larissa Morley?" he whispered between kisses.

"I think so but I'm not complaining. Darlin', this is a sensation like nothing I've ever felt."

He lowered his face to hers again. "Me too."

"Is that a snake?" She gasped and pointed before their lips touched.

"Yeah, it's a big old lazy water moccasin, but he won't bother us if we leave him alone."

"Are you sure? He looks pretty wicked."

"I'm very sure. Look, he's crawling away in the opposite direction. He's not interested in us," Hank assured her.

Larissa smiled and buried her face in his neck, tasting the musty lake water with every kiss. Who would have ever thought that unpurified water could make her senses reel with passion?

His hands slid up her inner thighs. "Your skin is so smooth."

"It's the water."

"No, it's you. You feel like satin sheets."

"Who needs a bed with satin sheets when there's a lake with a soft sandy bottom?"

When he moved on top of her, she groaned and wrapped her arms around him. The slow rhythm in the water was the most sensuous sex she'd ever known. She wished it would last forever, but if it did the whole lake would begin to boil.

"God, this is good," she murmured.

"Your first skinny-dipping sex?" he asked.

She opened her eyes to find him smiling. "Is it yours?"

He nodded. "But honey, if you are willing, it won't be my last."

The rhythm increased and she dug her nails into his back and whispered, "Hank, please, now."

He collapsed on top of her in the water, weightless with no need to roll to one side. Yes, indeed he would surely like to give that another try. But he couldn't see making love to another woman in water without seeing Larissa's sweet face every time he did. And that brought on instant acute stabs of guilt. He should have been up-front and honest with her and their relationship should have never, ever gone this far under the subterfuge.

Larissa felt the afterglow dim. "What's wrong?"

"Nothing. Not one thing," he said as he picked her up and carried her out of the water.

She shivered.

He laid her on the quilt and pulled the side around them to form a cocoon. "You feel good in or out of water, sweetheart."

She ran her fingers over his naked back, letting them trail below his waist to his hips. "So do you."

He buried his face in the softness of her neck and brushed soft kisses along her cheekbone to her lips where he settled in for long, lingering kisses that had them both panting. She moaned when he made his way down to her toes telling her with every kiss how lovely that part of her body was. By the time he made his way back up she was a quivering mass of pent up emotions ready to explode.

When he finally stretched out on top of her, her mind was void of everything but Hank Wells. If someone had asked her about Hayes Radner she would have asked, "Who?" If they'd asked her directions to the Honky Tonk she would have wondered what they were talking about.

"This feels so right, darlin'," he whispered as he began a rhythm as slow and sweet as the George Strait song on the CD player.

As luck would have it Strait was singing a soft ballad called "The Man in Love with You," when they both whispered the other's name and collapsed in the fiery emotional fireworks show spitting out beautiful colors all around them.

He rolled to one side, taking her with him and burying his face in her still wet hair. "Hot damn!"

"Hell yeah!" she said breathlessly. "I believe act two was as good as the first act."

"I heard bells and whistles."

"I saw fire."

He nuzzled his face deeper into her neck. "Want a beer or a nap?"

She snuggled down into his arms. "Nap, then beer, then round three."

"Darlin', after that, round three might have to wait. I'm whupped."

She shut her eyes and let the tender rainbow called afterglow wrap her up in its warmth as she drifted off to dream of Hank Wells and his sexy eyes.

When she awoke a Texas sunset was flashing its bright colors in the lake water and Hank was laying out a picnic supper on the edge of the quilt that wasn't covering her naked body.

"Mmmm," she said sleepily.

"Your clothes are dry and only a little bit stiff from the lake water. I laid them over there beside you but I have no objection if you'd like to eat in the nude," he said.

"Or take another swim before I put them on?" she said.

Her eyes were still dreamy and flying at half-mast. Her hair went every which way, some in her face, the rest all clumped together in dried straight strands. He'd sucked off every drop of lipstick with his kisses and the rest of her makeup had been washed away when he tossed her out into the water.

"You are beautiful."

"And you are a wonderful liar. I look like hell but right now I don't give a damn. I'm hungry and I'm happy."

"Then bring your happy little hungry naked self over here and have some chicken and potato salad," he said.

Suddenly she was conscious of being barely covered with the quilt and blushed. She grabbed her clothing, turned her back, and hurriedly dressed. The underpants were still slightly damp as well as the waistband of the jean shorts. She saw dried mud on her toenails and checked her hands before she picked up a dill pickle and a piece of fried chicken.

He handed her a paper plate and a plastic fork. "Oma thinks of everything. There's even wet wipes if you get greasy fingers."

"Was she like a mother to you when you visited there?" Larissa wanted the subject to go anywhere but to the sex they'd had.

"No, more like a grandmother. She's older than Dad by five or six years. She raised her kids on the ranch. Her husband was the foreman for years until he died. Dad was raised up with her kids but he's older by a dozen years than her two sons."

"So she'd know all about your mother?"

Hank smiled and shook his head. "I'm not sure anyone would know all about Mother. She's a powerhouse of a woman. I can't even begin to imagine her ever married to my dad. He's so laid-back and calm and she wakes up in a frenzy every morning."

"What kind of work do you do for her? This is some good food. What's in this potato salad?"

"You'd have to ask Oma that question. I just eat it. I don't ask how she makes it. Basically, I'm the make-it-run-smoothly man in the office. If Mother wants something I set the wheels in motion for her to have it."

"What kind of business is it?"

"That's hard to say. My grandfather started it as an oil equipment company. Then when the oil boom fizzled he diversified into a dozen other avenues. Tourism is the new thing Mother is into. She sunk a fortune into Texas tourism."

"I guess she'd probably know Hayes Radner then. He wants to turn Mingus into an amusement park. Maybe I'll go visit her and she can introduce me to him," Larissa said.

Hank had to swallow three times before the bite of potato salad would go down. "Better call ahead and make an appointment."

"Naw, I wouldn't do that. I'll just wait until our town meeting. He'll show up. Egotistical as he is, he won't be able to stay away. Besides, just look at all the people he can tempt to sell at one time. I'm actually doing the man a big favor by bringing them together in one place. 'Course he doesn't realize that most of them are not selling. The ones who might are outlying folks who don't have a single square inch of town property."

"Did I tell you that I woke up after our nap with round three on my mind?" He had a wicked gleam in his eye.

"Okay, point taken. You are tired of hearing about Hayes Radner. Truth is I'm tired of talking about him. But honey, round three is going to have to wait until later."

His dark eyebrows shot up. "Why?"

"Because it's getting dark and all kinds of things come out to bite me in the dark. Like mosquitoes, spiders, and even that ugly snake that almost kept us from making wild passionate love in the water."

"Does that mean we have to go home after we eat?" he asked.

"It means that we can watch the moon come up and talk all night but I'm not taking off all my clothes to provide a buffet for the bugs and critters."

He picked up a brownie from a plastic container and held it out for her to have the first bite. "Oma makes them from scratch with real butter and imported vanilla."

"Mmmm." Larissa made appreciative noises as she chewed.

"You are like this brownie."

"Hey, now, I'm brown from my part Cherokee father but I'm not that dark," she said.

"I'm not talking color. I mean that you are made from scratch. Real ingredients, not fake," he said. "What is it that song says about being American made? From your sexy brown eyes to your silky hair, you are made from scratch American. It even mentions your tight blue jeans and when it comes to lovin' if I'm remembering the song right. Oak Ridge Boys, wasn't it?"

She nodded. "I'd never listened to much country before moving to Mingus. Now I'm their biggest fan."

"You should be. You run a honky tonk and listen to it six hours a night. What did you listen to?" Maybe that was the chink in her tight fitting armor that would lead him to her secrets.

"Mostly classical," she said.

"You? Classical?" He gasped then laughed. "You almost had me believing that. I bet you cut your teeth on Loretta Lynn and Waylon Jennings just like I did when I was at the ranch."

She just smiled.

He scooted next to her and wrapped his arms around her, pulling her down to the wrinkled quilt for a series of long, lingering kisses. "I think maybe you got dressed too soon," he said.

"Well, we can sure fix that problem, can't we? But you said you were too tired for act three," she teased as she nibbled his earlobe.

"I'll do my best, fair sexy maiden. That little nap and chocolate has revived me," he whispered in her ear.

"So you think I'm sexy?" she asked breathlessly.

"Darlin', only a sexy woman could wrangle three acts out of a one act play," he said.

The third time was slow and easy. The snake was forgotten. The mosquitoes couldn't penetrate the cocoon of a quilt that was wrapped around them. Time stood still and the moon and stars smiled down on them as they forgot every problem and enjoyed each other's bodies.

Afterwards Hank held her for a long time and wished again that things were different. Even the sloshing noise of the gentle lake waves blending with the crickets and tree frogs couldn't completely erase that niggling little voice that kept telling him he was playing with pure fire and about to get burned.

Chapter 8

On Monday morning Larissa awoke to lightning jumping through her bedroom window in micro-flashes like an old Brownie camera flashbulb. Thunder rumbling in its wake reminded her of the story her nanny used to tell her about it being nothing but a wagon load of potatoes tumbling out.

"Yeah, right, Jenny Walker." Larissa covered her head with a pillow and talked to her deceased nanny. "It sounds like the apocalypse, not a ten pound bag of potatoes."

The rain did not start with a few small drops making pinging noises against the cellar door right outside her bedroom window. It hit with the force of a fireman's hose and she burrowed down deeper into the bed. She covered her head with a pillow to block the noise and the lightning, but it didn't work. Light crept in the sides and the thunder was loud enough to wake a deaf person.

She could barely hear the ring tone on her cell phone and it was on the fourth and final rendition of "Redneck Woman" when she reached out and groped toward the nightstand for it.

"Hello," she grumbled.

"Well aren't you in a grumpy mood this morning," her mother said.

"It's storming and raining and we were going to scrape and paint my house today," Larissa said without changing her tone.

"Stop whining and go home where you belong or better yet leave the whole mess behind and join me here. You don't have to paint and scrape a shanty or work at a beer joint, Larissa," Doreen said.

Larissa threw the pillow to the side and sat up. "I am home. Where are you?"

"No, you are not at home. You will never be at home in that dingy place. You are on another one of your soul-searching larks. Sometimes you remind me so much of your father that it's scary. He had visions of grandeur too. Only his was stepping up in the world, not down." Doreen's tone was icy.

"Maybe that's because I've got half his genes. Where is the worthless sumbitch, by the way?" Larissa asked.

Doreen's brittle laugh cracked around the edges. "Stop trying to find him, Larissa. He made his choice back before you even knew who he was."

"Why?" Larissa asked.

"I've told you the story so many times it's worn out. Because he loved the check my father offered him more than he loved either of us. I didn't call to argue with you, darling. I've got to be in Dallas for a charity event the first week in September. Think you could get away for a weekend?"

It was on the tip of Larissa's tongue to say no but she sighed and said, "It's a possibility if it's on a Friday or Saturday night."

"It is. Saturday night. Think you could get away on Friday and we'll do some shopping and visiting? I'll be at the Hyatt Regency while I'm there. I'll book a room for you. I have to leave on Sunday afternoon but it would be wonderful to have you all to myself for three days." Doreen's tone warmed as she made plans.

"That might be doable," Larissa said. "I'll have Sharlene trained well enough by then and Luther will be there," she mused aloud.

"Honey, I don't care if you hire Mickey Mouse and Minnie to run that horrid place. Just promise me you won't back out," Doreen said.

"Mother, it's not horrid. Come on down here and visit. You might find a place to hang your hat and stop roaming the world." Larissa yawned.

"I'm bringing someone for you to meet. I'm ready to quit roaming and settle down."

Larissa threw herself backwards on the bed. "Dear God."

"You *will* be surprised," Doreen said.

"I'm sure I will. Can he vote and buy beer?"

"That's not very nice but the answer is yes to both. And that's all I'm telling you about him. You can form your own opinion when you see him. He's asked me to marry him and I'm considering it but I want you to meet him first," Doreen said.

"Where'd you get him? Club Med? And why does my opinion matter?" Larissa remembered other men her mother had brought home. If any of them proposed Larissa wasn't privy to the fact. What made this one different?

"You're not getting another bit of information, darlin'. That way I know you'll come to Dallas and not make a last-minute excuse. Your curiosity will win the fight. I know you. And you are my daughter so your opinion matters," Doreen said. "September tenth, Hyatt Regency. I'll meet you in the lobby at three."

"I'll be there. Will Boy Wonder be with you?"

"Depends on when he can fly in. You will definitely meet him at the charity event."

Larissa rolled her eyes. "I can hardly wait."

"Don't be sarcastic," Doreen snapped.

Larissa threw back the sheet and padded to the door barefoot. "Someone is ringing my doorbell. Please tell me it's you."

"Sorry to disappoint. I'll see you in a few weeks and we'll be talking in between. Love you, kid," Doreen said.

"Love you back," Larissa said as she flipped the phone shut and swung open the door.

"I wasn't expecting that kind of welcome," Hank said.

"I wasn't talking to you. We can't scrape and paint today," she said.

He held up a dripping plastic bag in one hand and a movie in the other. "And we can't do much at the ranch either. Thought maybe we'd watch a movie and have a late lunch together."

"Well come on in. What'd you bring?" she asked.

He could hardly take his eyes from her standing there in an oversized T-shirt that stopped mid-thigh, her hair tousled, and her brown eyes still droopy with sleep. He did manage to find his voice and say, "An old movie and the stuff to make potato chowder."

"Did you bring Oma's recipe?"

"I did. And all the ingredients."

"Cook or watch the movie first?" She helped him unload the groceries on the kitchen cabinet.

"Cook and watch the movie while we eat," he said. His hormones threw in a trip to the bedroom in between but he didn't voice it out loud.

"What do we do first?" she asked.

"How about this?" He slipped his arm around her waist and hugged her tightly to his chest. "Or this?" He tilted her chin up for a long, hard kiss.

"Whew!" She gasped when he released her. "If that's a start, the finish would probably blow my head off."

He kissed the top of her head and ran a hand up under the shirt to rub her back. "Want to see?"

"I'll take a rain check," she said. "I'm so hungry I'd pass out in the middle of the sex if it's as hot as your kisses."

"Okay, then. We start by frying up a pound of bacon. Where's a skillet?" He stepped back, picked up the package of bacon, and turned the knob on her electric stove.

"That was too easy," she said.

"I'm willing to wait. You're like that old commercial for Heinz ketchup. You are worth waiting for," he said.

She pulled a skillet from the bottom cabinet and set it on the burner. "I'll throw on some clothes. How'd you get into the house without getting soaked?"

"Umbrella. It's on the porch." He peeled bacon off in long strips. "You don't have to put on clothes for my benefit. I think you look fine just like you are."

"I think I'll at least add a pair of shorts to the outfit, just in case Linda and the ladies come by for coffee later. Might take a lot of explaining if I'm running around like this with you in the house."

He raised a dark eyebrow. "You don't want anyone to know that we are…"

"Are what?" she asked.

"That we've been…"

"Been what?" she asked again.

He chuckled. "Words don't work, do they? What are we?"

"Two grown consenting adults."

He popped her on the fanny. "Go put on your shorts and get presentable."

"Two. Grown. Consenting. Adults." She said each word distinctly. "That means you don't tell me what to do."

He threw up his greasy hands. "Hey, I was teasing. You always grumpy in the morning?"

She shot him a look and shut the door to her bedroom. Yes, she was grumpy. She'd been awakened by her mother. She'd tried to find her father as well as her niche in life for seven years and to be reminded of failure didn't make her all smiles and giggles. Add to that a kiss that made her knees weak and sent her thoughts plummeting from kitchen to bedroom and romping around in bed for the rest of the day with Hank. Then his complete acceptance to wait and not kiss her a hundred more times before declaring that he couldn't possibly wait to make love to her. It was enough to make an angel grumpy and Larissa did not have a halo.

Hank whistled while the bacon cooked. So Larissa had a burr in her saddle in the mornings. She could never match his mother in that department. One look from Victoria before mid-morning would scald the paint off a brand new pickup truck. Employees learned quickly to leave her alone until she'd had a pot of coffee and at least four doughnuts. Sugar and caffeine was what kept her fueled and ready to wheel and deal.

Larissa pulled on a pair of flannel pajama bottoms and put on a bra. Maybe later she'd take it off, but right then it seemed like a suit of armor against her own emotions. She brushed her hair, flicked a bit of blush on her cheeks, and added a hint of lip gloss to her full lips.

She opened the door into the kitchen to the smell of coffee and bacon. "I'm sorry I was an old bear. I need coffee and sunshine."

He handed her a steaming cup of coffee. "This will get you going."

She took a sip or two then set the cup aside. "I'll peel potatoes while you do that."

"Wow! Not even half a cup and you are civil? That wouldn't even take the evil gleam from my mother's eyes," he teased.

"Honey, *you* would take the evil gleam from my mother's eyes," she muttered.

He heard every word. "And what is that supposed to mean?"

"It means she's coming to Dallas in a few weeks for me to meet her new main man," she said honestly.

Hank laid out the last few pieces of bacon to drain on paper towels. "So she's not married?"

Larissa giggled. "Not since I was a tiny baby."

"So what's the big deal about her bringing a new man?" His attention went on alert as he remembered his mission. For several days he'd forgotten why he was spending so much time in Mingus. While he'd been busy trying to dig up anything and everything on Larissa, he'd started to really like the woman. He didn't care when it was just heat between them. That could be remedied in a hurry, but now that Larissa was his friend, he'd almost forgotten his original mission. It didn't matter because friend and lover would come to a screeching halt when she had the meeting at the Honky Tonk and found out that Hank was not on her side of the argument.

Larissa shrugged. "Mother has maintained her beauty. She's fifty but she looks my age. We easily pass for sisters. Once a lady, not a man, mind you, who'd I'd suspect of flirting, but a woman my age, asked if I was the older sister. She draws young men to her like flies on waffle syrup. The last one was younger than me. He had no idea I was her daughter."

He raised a skeptical eyebrow. "And this woman lives in Tennessee and works at Loretta Lynn's dude ranch?"

She laughed. "Mother lives wherever the wind takes her. The part about Loretta Lynn's ranch was a joke. She wouldn't mess up her Jimmy Choos by getting out of her limousine at a dude ranch. Not unless she spotted a hunky man, then she'd go to the nearest western wear store and arrive in proper style."

He filed the information away. He'd been looking in the wrong places. Doreen Morley must be amongst the rich and shameless instead of the poor and shameful. "She must be wealthy for that kind of lifestyle."

"Wealth is relative. Do you consider yourself wealthy? You've sat in Paris cafés and eaten in Italian restaurants. Are you rich? How much water do I put on these potatoes?"

"Barely enough to cover them. Soon as they are cooked we poor it all off and add milk." He read from the recipe. "While they are boiling, we crumble up all this bacon and chop an onion and the parsley. Is your mother just coming to Dallas to see you? Why doesn't she come here and stay with you?"

Larissa laughed. "My house wouldn't hold her luggage. No, seriously, she's got a charity function of some kind. I expect she'll spend a few days at the home place up in Perry, Oklahoma, while she's here. Especially if she wants to impress Boyfriend Number Umpteen."

"Are you bitter?" He carefully added the name of the town where the home place was located to his list of things to pass on.

She shrugged. "I wasn't. Indifferent most of my life. Not bitter, though. Mother is charming, fun, and a hoot to be around. We have a great time but she's my friend, not my mother. My nanny was my mother figure. She died seven years ago. That's when I decided to find myself."

"Did you?" he asked.

"Find myself?"

He nodded as he crumbled bacon into a bowl.

"Oh, yeah. I went here and there and even over yonder and Larissa wasn't there so I really did pull down a map in the library at our house and I really did stick a pin in Mingus, Texas. I thought I'd gone to the end of the world, made a left-hand turn, and felt hell's scorching fires when I found Mingus. But I found Larissa Morley here. You ever go on a journey hunting yourself?"

He swallowed hard. "I never lost myself."

"Oh, you are lost, honey. If you are living in two places and one of them has a mother like mine, then you are definitely lost. Try my trick. Get one of those thumbtacks with a big plastic head and blindfold yourself. Turn around three times and stick it in a map. See where it takes you," she said.

"Maybe I'll try that sometime. Right now I'm pretty content with where I am." His heart clinched up. He wasn't content. He was miserable. Larissa Morley had him twisted around her finger and he dreaded the day she found out that he was working for the other side.

The smell of the onion caused tears to drip from her cheeks. Hank busied himself at the stove so he wouldn't see her cry. After the meeting concerning the sale of Mingus, which he'd already decided was not about to come to pass, she would really cry and the thought pierced his heart.

"Hey, hey, anybody home?" Linda called from the living room. She, Betty, and Janice paraded into the kitchen. They stopped dead when they saw Hank at the stove and Larissa crying.

She held up the onion and giggled. "Come on in. Hank has the coffee ready. We're making that damn good potato soup stuff I was telling y'all about. You can eat with us soon as it's done. Stop giving Hank drop-dead looks, Janice. I'm crying because of the onions."

A part of Larissa was glad for the intrusion because it stopped the questions and conversation about her mother. The other part wished they'd make excuses and leave so she could have Hank all alone that rainy day.

"I'll make a pitcher of tea," Linda said.

"I'll check the pantry and see if there's anything to stir up a dessert," Betty said.

Janice went to the cabinet and took down a plastic bowl. "I'll make a pan of biscuits to go with the soup. Bring out the flour and shortening while you are in the pantry, Betty."

Hank raised an eyebrow.

Larissa smiled. "They are as much at home in my kitchen as in their own. Got to admit they're a hell of a lot better at cooking."

Janice patted her on the shoulder. "Aw, honey, when you get another thirty or thirty-five years on you, you'll be better than us. Look how far you've come in the past six months. Lord, first time you tried to make a biscuit I figured we'd have to go up to the sheriff's office and register the thing as a concealed weapon. If you'd have flung that thing at a man, it would have killed him dead on the spot."

Hank stole glances at the three women. They were all somewhere between sixty and seventy. Was that why Larissa liked them so well? They'd become surrogate mothers.

Betty brought out flour, sugar, shortening, cinnamon, and everything else they needed and set it all on the cabinet. "Hey, how does snicker doodles made up in bars sound? That's faster than waiting for cookies."

Hank poured the boiling water off the potatoes and added milk. "I feel like a chef. Let's put a fancy restaurant in downtown Mingus. Anyone know of a place I could buy?"

"I own a chunk of what used to be downtown Mingus but not even Hayes Radner who thinks he's God could buy it from me. And honey, I'm too damned old to be working in a restaurant," Linda said as she mixed butter and sugar together. "I'm close to retirement and when I can talk J. C. into it we're going to travel."

"Where to?" Hank wished he had a notebook with him. Larissa made mush of his brain most days and he had trouble at night remembering what he was supposed to put on the list for the investigators to check out.

"I haven't decided. If I leave it up to J. C. it'll be to Galveston for a night and maybe a day and then drive back home so fast that he won't even stop for a dollar burger and a pee break. He doesn't like to be away from his bed or his remote. I had to keep him liquored up in Vegas to be able to stay there a week and there were dancing girls and roulette wheels. That should tell you how much traveling we'll really do but it's a nice dream." She laughed.

"You should see the exotic places like France and Italy. Maybe England or even Sweden," he said slyly. "How about you, Betty? You want to travel farther than Galveston?"

"Hell, no. I don't want to leave Mingus. Elmer is thinking that we ought to sell out and move to be closer to the kids but he's going to be sleeping with one mad she-coon if he does. Hell, he might be sleeping with his old coon dog if he sells my house. I'm not leaving Mingus. This is home and I'm happy here. I love the whole bunch of them but if I lived close they'd drive me stark raving mad. If he wants to go worry with them, then power to him. He can go by himself and I'll stay right here. "

Janice threw up her flour covered hands. "Don't look at me. Frank wouldn't sell his chunk of dirt if God wanted to buy it for a new church house. Besides, I wouldn't know what in the hell I'd do without my friends. I'd be lost and miserable. If Elmer gets a wild hair up his ass, you can live with me, Betty. Hayes Radner might as well scratch his ass with a length of barbed wire as come around wanting our place."

He didn't need to remember any of the conversation. If the rest of Mingus felt the same way there would never be an amusement park there. The Radner Corporation would have to move on down the highway and find another piece of property.

"Hank brought a movie to watch when we finish our mid-afternoon brunch," Larissa said.

"You changing the subject. Lord, girl, you're the one who's been on the soapbox and preached the hardest about this thing. I figured you'd throw them onions down and begin to oratin' like a holiness preacher on the last night of a revival," Linda said.

"I'm just tired of it. I want to eat good soup, scarf down about six of those biscuits and some cookies, and watch a funny movie. I'll be glad when it's over. I'm not selling. You three aren't. We'll hope the rest of Mingus doesn't. But with what we all own, he'd be getting only a little portion of what he needs and wants. So he might as well cut off a piece of barbed wire and bare his butt."

Betty giggled. "What movie you got? That new one with Sandra Bullock?"

"Hank's brought in *The Best Little Whorehouse in Texas*. Y'all ever seen it?" Larissa asked.

Janice clapped her hands and flour mushroomed over the table. "Love it. Haven't seen it since it came out in the movie theater more than twenty years ago. Remember when we left the husbands at home and went down to Stephenville to see it?"

"I would never forget that movie," Betty said. "I came home and thought about turning one of my empty buildings into a whorehouse. Figured we were far enough from Palo Pinto and the sheriff that I could get away with it for a while."

"Why didn't you?" Larissa asked.

"Figured Elmer would spend all my profit on the hookers and then I'd have to kill him and spend the rest of my life in prison. Besides, the sheriff up in Palo Pinto wasn't nearly as good lookin' as Burt. Hey, why don't you put in a chicken ranch and Hank can run for sheriff. Can you sing like Dolly?"

Larissa shook her head. "Not me. My singing turns the hot water cold in the shower."

Hank chuckled at the thought of running for sheriff of Palo Pinto County. Somehow he couldn't picture himself in that role even though in another lifetime he could easily see Larissa running an old-time brothel.

"I'm ready for the onions so I can brown them in the bacon drippings," he said.

She carried them across the room in a small bowl and handed them to him, their hungry eyes locking in the foot of space separating them. Hank's conscience drove a railroad spike through his heart. He could not make love with Larissa again, not until after the town meeting. How could he live with himself?

After the meeting, she'd never speak to him again. That brought on pain worse than his conscience inflicted. How had he fallen for the woman? He'd come to the ranch with one stone in his hand to kill two birds. He'd spend a month with his father away from three-piece suits and high-dollar deals. He'd sip a beer in the evenings on the front porch, enjoy Oma's spoiling, and all those things that drew him back to an easier way of life year after year. And he'd also do a little undercover work for the firm if he could get a foot inside the door with Larissa Morley.

"Get a room," Linda giggled.

Larissa blinked and laughed with her. "Hard not to stare at something that looks like Hank, ain't it?"

"Darlin' if I was thirty years younger I'd do more than stare," Betty said.

Hank blushed.

Larissa laughed harder.

The biscuits and cookies went into the oven at the same time. When the soup was finished they were ready to serve right along with it. Larissa sliced Colby cheese and added a few sweet pickles to a saucer for a relish plate and Linda set the table. Hank drug an extra straight back chair from the living room and all five of them crowded around the small table. He felt like Judas at the last supper. He wouldn't be a bit surprised if he dug out the change in his pocket that there wouldn't be thirty pieces of silver.

"So how long you stayin' up at your dad's ranch and what do you do in Dallas? Damn this is good. I've got to write off the recipe before we leave. Elmer will love it. I might make a pot full for supper. Hand me one of those biscuits, Linda," Betty said.

Larissa looked at Hank, suddenly realizing she didn't know much of anything about what he did in Dallas. "What do you do in the big city? I bet you don't wear cowboy boots and western cut suits."

Hank bit the inside of his lip to keep from laughing. "No, I wear three-piece suits and dress shoes. I work in a big firm that diversified years ago into many areas. I have a doctorate degree in business finance."

"Well, Dr. Wells, it's hard for me to picture you all decked out like that," Larissa said.

"It's harder to picture myself as sheriff of Palo Pinto County," he said, trying to change the subject.

"A doctorate degree, huh? Wait 'til I tell J. C. that Larissa's got a fancy executive scraping her house and making potato soup in her kitchen. He won't believe a word of it," Linda said. "Pass me the cheese, Betty."

"When I come to Palo Pinto, I'm a cowboy just like my dad," Hank said.

"Well, it'll make a hell of a good story," Linda said.

When they finished the mid-afternoon lunch, Betty cut and stacked snicker doodles onto a platter while the rest of the crew put leftovers away and washed the dishes. She set them on a foldout tray in the living room so they could nibble while they watched the movie. The clock said it was five minutes past two. The movie would be over by four and she'd easily have time to make a pot of that delicious soup for supper.

"Everyone get a comfortable seat and we'll put the movie in." Larissa wiped her hands dry on a terry dish towel.

Linda claimed the rocking chair. Betty and Linda sat on the sofa. That left the loveseat for Larissa and Hank.

Betty ran a hand over the dark green micro-fiber couch arm. "I still can't believe you found these two pieces at a garage sale. They're practically brand new."

"It's a good story so I'll tell it while Hank gets the movie ready. They came from Abilene and I spent almost as much on the U-Haul truck to get them up here as I did the furniture. It was an estate sale and a husband and wife team was getting rid of everything. It was his grandmother's stuff and he'd made the stupid mistake of telling his wife about an affair that morning. I made a ridiculous offer for these two pieces plus the rocking chair and she sold them to me for fifty dollars," she said.

"Vengeance was hers that day," Linda said.

"Yep, it was and he couldn't say a word. I lost out on a gorgeous lamp but he made that sale and it went for five times what I paid for the furniture."

"You ladies ready?" Hank asked.

They all nodded and he pushed the button on the remote control. The next two hours the rain came down in buckets and they watched the madam of the Chicken Ranch, Miss Mona, and her sheriff boyfriend try to save her brothel from a TV muckraker. Hank did not see himself as the sheriff but took the place of the muckraker. The Chicken Ranch was a symbol of Mingus, Texas. Miss Mona, of course, was Larissa. When the story ended he made an excuse, left the movie in the DVD player, and headed north with "what ifs" playing in his mind the whole way home.

Chapter 9

ON TUESDAY IT RAINED.

Larissa waited for Hank to call or come by but he didn't. She rationalized that it might not be raining in the northern part of the county. He and his dad only had a few more days before he went back to Dallas.

On Wednesday it cleared off.

Hank called to tell her that he wouldn't be by that day either because the house would still be wet, making it impossible to scrape or paint.

"So I guess I'll see you tomorrow?" she asked.

"At noon. We got to get the rest of that place scraped and painted so it'll be done before I leave," he said.

"Which is when?"

"Right after the meeting on Saturday. I promised I'd be back in the Dallas office by Monday morning. I'm flying to Paris on Tuesday and I need to get everything together," he said.

"Aha, the cowboy turns professor. That sounds like a good plot for a thick romance book," she said. "Want some romance before we start scraping?"

"I reckon if we're going to get this house painted turquoise before I leave then we'd best get busy," he drawled. "I'll be there tomorrow. Will you be cooking at the Smokehouse for us?"

"Not tomorrow. I've got a surprise," she said.

It was evident from the minute he showed up the

next day that something wasn't right. She couldn't put her finger on it but her gut said that something had changed drastically in his life. Had she done something to offend him the day they had dinner with the ladies?

"So tell me, are you tired of the ranch and ready to get back into the fast life?" she asked when they'd finished scraping in the middle of the afternoon.

"Honestly?" he asked.

"Is there any other answer? We've joked. We've made love but we are friends, Hank. What's on your mind? What happened since I saw you last other than rain?"

"Always before I've been so ready to go back to my friends, my condo, and my lifestyle in Dallas. This year I'm not. My dad is getting older and slower. I feel like I'm needed on the ranch more than in the office," he said.

"So stay," she said. "Surprise is that we are having dinner today over at Linda's place. She made pot roast and invited us to come over and eat leftovers. They all had hairdo appointments in Abilene but I know where the key is. We just have to heat up a plate in the microwave. She even made pecan pie."

"That sounds wonderful." He smiled but it did not reach his eyes.

Linda's house was close enough that they walked. Twice his hand brushed hers and he made an excuse to distance himself from her. Both times she wondered if he was battling a difficult life decision or if he was sorry about their skinny-dipping that Sunday.

Larissa turned over a rock in the flower bed and brought up a key. The house still smelled like roast and yeast bread and she was starving. "You really should put in a café with these women, Hank. You'd run the Smokestack some serious competition."

He didn't have the heart to tell her that in three days none of them would even be speaking to him, much less wanting to go into business with him. She helped her plate and stuck it in the microwave for a couple of minutes. He'd barely gotten his loaded when she pulled hers out and carried it to the table.

"Go on and eat. You don't have to wait for me. I ate breakfast. You probably had a cup of coffee and a cookie," he said.

"It was a chunk of leftover snicker doodle dipped in coffee." She cut a piece of roast and moaned when she put it in her mouth. "This is soooo good."

He removed his plate from the microwave and joined her. He'd worked up an appetite in spite of the conflicting emotions and the roast was seasoned just right. Linda could easily run a café.

"Are we going to start painting today?" he asked.

"I've got more than three hours before I have to take a shower and go to the Honky Tonk. I'm anxious to get started. Way I figure it is with both of us working we can get a lot done in three hours. The house isn't very big. We should have it done by quittin' time on Friday if we keep after it. Want to start earlier tomorrow? I'll give up some sleep to get it finished before you leave."

He buttered a hot roll. "I'll be here at nine."

"I'll be up and ready then. Are you going to miss me when you go back to Dallas?" She held her breath waiting on the answer.

He looked across the table and his eyes went all soft and dreamy like they'd been on Sunday when they were making love. "I'll always miss you, Larissa. This has been an incredible month. I'm glad that crazy deer introduced us."

She smiled.

He didn't ask her if she'd miss him. He already knew the answer. Once the cat was out of the bag she'd never want to set eyes on him again.

"I cannot believe you are really going to paint this house turquoise. I thought you were joking with me like you do all the time," Hank snarled when he opened the first can of paint.

"I told you I love the islands. If I hadn't found myself in Mingus I might have gone back there. I love the bright colors, the siestas, and the laid-back lifestyle."

"How long were you there?" He remembered her talking about the islands before and he'd brushed it off as fantasy.

"Six months. In a turquoise house with hot pink trim. It was about this size only it did not have air conditioning. It was right on the beach though. Want to go there with me sometime?" she asked.

"Just tell me what time to meet you at the airport. We'll have to get a red-eye on Sunday morning and fly back on Monday." He slapped the first brush load onto the siding and grinned. The Chicken Ranch didn't have a thing on Larissa Morley.

"I've got Sharlene helping me now. I could manage a long weekend."

"Tell you what, you give me a couple of weeks back at the Dallas grindstone and call me anytime you want.

I bet I can get away for any long weekend that you can," he said.

She smiled brightly. He wasn't upset with her after all.

She started painting. "Will we go skinny-dippin' in the saltwater?"

He kept his eyes on the bright colored paint and didn't look at her. "If you want to skinny-dip, we'll hang our clothes on the bushes and dive right in."

"Gawd Almighty, what are you doing?" Amos parked his motorcycle in the driveway and shook his head.

Hank was glad for the distraction. He'd been amazed that Amos hadn't recognized him and had been nervous as hell around him those first few times he'd been in the Honky Tonk. But lately he'd begun to fit into the Hank Wells cowboy skin better and better.

"I know. It looks like shit, don't it?" Hank said.

"That's enough from both of you. When it's all done it'll be beautiful. Hell, everyone in Mingus might be painting their houses to look like Bahama homes," she said. "Beer is in the fridge if you are thirsty."

"Thirsty, hell! I need a dose of Pepto after looking at that color. I cannot believe you went to all the trouble to scrape the old paint off if you were going to put that shit on your house," Amos said.

"That's what I told her," Hank said.

"Looks like I'm outnumbered today but you'll both rue the day you made fun of my pretty house," she said.

Amos grinned. "I'm thirsty enough to shut up right now. Has Linda and the ladies seen this?"

Larissa shook her head. "I'm surprising them."

"You sure are, darlin'." Hank laughed.

Chapter 10

LARISSA WAS WORKING ON THE WEST SIDE WHEN HANK parked his pickup in the driveway the next morning. If her mother was really as wealthy as the picture Larissa had painted the last time she talked about her, the woman was going to have a cardiac arrest when she removed her fancy sunglasses and the color blinded her.

"I'm around here," Larissa called. "Your brush and paint bucket are on the front porch."

"Coffee?" He rounded the end of the porch and stopped. She had a bandana around her forehead and wore paint splotched cut-off jeans and a bright pink tank top. She was barefoot and sweat glistened on her lightly toasted skin. She was a hippy, born forty years too late, and desire flooded his body.

"In the pot. Heat it in the microwave." She didn't look at him. Didn't need to. He still looked like the devil in tight blue jeans, still smelled like him with Stetson shaving lotion, and his voice hadn't changed a bit. She hadn't found out a thing about Hank Wells except that he was Henry's son by a woman named Victoria. That's all her investigators could find out. Hank was thirty-two years old and had been born in Dallas.

Her mother might seduce him and play with him like a cat with a mouse for a few weeks, but she'd die if she thought Larissa was really falling for the guy. When Larissa got ready for a permanent commitment and a trip down the aisle wearing the traditional white dress, it had better be with someone other than a cowboy, no matter how sexy he was. She continued to slap paint on the house, liking it better with each section.

"I stole one of Linda's cookies too," Hank said.

"Help yourself," she said.

He sipped the coffee and waited until she finished spreading out the brush load of paint. He'd wrestled with his conscience all night and was ready to cowboy-up and do the right thing. He'd tell her exactly what he'd been up to from day one. That would end his painting days as well as any relationship they had or ever could have had. It just flat out wasn't right for her to walk into the Honky Tonk on Saturday and find out he was working for the other side.

"I'd like to…" He had to come clean or his heart was going to explode with guilt.

A blaring car horn stopped him from saying anything more. Larissa leaned out around the house and Hank frowned.

Sharlene crawled out of a hot pink Volkswagen bug. "Hey, y'all need another hand? I'm damn good at paintin'. I love the color. It's gorgeous. Reminds me of pictures of an exotic island."

"I don't turn down help," Larissa called back. "You got any old clothes? If not, you can wear some of mine."

"I brought old cut-offs and shirts to clean the apartment this weekend. Mind if I change in your house?"

Hank sighed. Maybe he'd have time to tell her while Sharlene changed.

"Not a bit. Here, Hank, take this brush and I'll show her where things are. I need to take a bathroom break anyway," Larissa said.

Sharlene grabbed a duffle bag from the backseat of her car and followed Larissa into the house. "Nice place you got here. It's about the size of the house I grew up in up outside of Corn."

"Your house was this small and you had four brothers?" Larissa's eyes widened.

"Yep, two sets of bunk beds in the bedroom off the kitchen. Momma and Daddy had the bedroom off the living room. By the time I came along they'd enclosed the back porch into a laundry room so when I outgrew the crib in their room, they put a twin-size bed out by the washer and dryer. That was my room. It worked and we weren't inside kids anyway," Sharlene explained.

"My bedroom is off the kitchen. You can change in there," Larissa said.

"I got a favor to ask," Sharlene yelled through the door as she peeled her miniskirt down over her legs and kicked off her boots.

"And that would be?" Larissa poured half a cup of coffee and dipped a snicker doodle in it.

"They cut back my hours at the newspaper. Last to arrive; first to get the pink slip boot and all. Anyway, I'm only working three days a week. Mind if I use the apartment more than two nights a week?"

"Honey, you can live there and I'll pay you to help me in the bar. Can you do your work from the apartment and send it in?"

She opened the door and stepped out into the kitchen in shorts that had dried paint on them and a shirt that was two sizes too big.

"Probably," she said.

Larissa pointed at the cookies and coffee.

"Thanks. I *am* hungry. Didn't take time for breakfast. When I got the news I just went back to my place and drove straight up here."

"Is your placed rented through tomorrow?"

"Yep, rent is due on Monday."

"Move into the Honky Tonk. We'll talk about wages later. Right now we've got a house to paint and I'll pay you for that too. Hank is going back to his Dallas job after the meeting tomorrow and he can only help today and tomorrow. With another paintbrush we might get it finished."

"Can I paint the Honky Tonk like this?" Sharlene asked.

"Hell, no!" Larissa laughed. "Where did you get that shirt and what did you paint last?"

"It's my brother's cast off. I figured it would be good and floppy to wear for cleaning the place. I got a friend who'll help me move on Sunday. My living room stuff is early redneck attic, so I'll leave it behind. My bedroom furniture doesn't have two pieces that match but they'll fit in the apartment right fine. And the last thing I painted was an old VW bug for a friend. He wanted it to look like an old hippy wagon. Daisies, peace symbols, and the whole nine yards. Then he took it to a body shop and had a shiny clear finish put on it. Damn, it was pretty. Let's go get this house done. What color is the trim going to be? I've got a right steady hand. Want me to start on it while y'all do the flat work?"

Larissa smiled and started out the front door.

Sharlene grabbed two cookies and followed her. "I know I talk too much but it's me. I tried to stop it in the army but I either talk or bust. I get mean when I hold everything in."

"I like a person who's upfront and honest. Talk all you want. What did you do in the army?"

Sharlene suddenly clammed up. "I have to use an old line if I tell you. It goes like this, 'I'd tell you but then I'd have to kill you.'"

Larissa laughed. "Someday you'll tell me because we are best friends and you are an honest soul."

That comment shot a hole through Hank's already guilty heart but he couldn't blurt out what was on his mind with Sharlene there. She'd probably stay all day. At least he still had one more day before the meeting. And he vowed he'd do what was right before that meeting started.

"What color is the trim?" Sharlene asked.

Larissa pointed. "Hot pink. That can right there."

"Ah, man, you sure I can't do the Honky Tonk up like this? It would stand out like a beacon in the night to every hotheaded, lusty cowboy and good-time cowgirl in the whole state," Sharlene said.

"How much did you pay her to be on your side?" Hank drawled.

Sharlene opened the can and dipped a small brush into it. "She didn't pay me anything. I like these colors."

"You wouldn't really paint the Honky Tonk like this, would you? It's got an old-time ambience that is its trademark." Hank kept painting but stole glances at Larissa working beside him. Why couldn't he have met her in different circumstances?

His mother's voice came to haunt him as continued to work. "Life is not fair."

But this time I want it to be fair more than anything else in the world. I'd give anything to be able to stay

*on the ranch and have a long lasting relationship with
Larissa. I would like to be Hank Wells, the cowboy,
forever. I don't want to go home to Dallas. My heart
aches to stay in Palo Pinto or even in this Bahama-style
house. Hell, I'd even put a thatch roof on it if I could
wake up with Larissa by my side every morning.*

"What are you thinking about?" Larissa asked.

"Why?"

"Your forehead was all wrinkled up in a frown."

"I'm not ready to go back to Dallas," he said.

"Then don't. Henry would be tickled for you to come
to the ranch permanently."

"I know. It's been his dream since I was a little boy."

"Then stay." Her heart floated somewhere up around
the wispy white clouds drifting over a blue summer sky.

"It's complicated," he said.

She nodded. "You're talking to the poster child for
complicated. I understand." But she didn't understand
at all. She wanted to grab him by the hand and take him
to the bedroom. But lust wasn't reason enough to change
a person's lifestyle.

"You won't be that far away. You can always drop
by the Honky Tonk," Sharlene said from the front porch
where she painted window frames. "Are the porch posts
going to be pink too?"

"No, yellow," Larissa said.

"Man, it's just not fair. If you ever sell it can I buy it?
I'll hock my twenty-year-old bug and my tomcat. Oh, I
forgot, can I bring a cat to the apartment? I promise he's
litter trained and he's a good boy."

"No problem," Larissa said.

"What's his name?" Hank asked.

"I found him when he was a little kitten last year. Someone threw him in the dumpster. He barely had his eyes open and I couldn't leave him there even if I wasn't supposed to have him in my apartment. So I snuck him up in my purse and bottle fed him for a month before he was ready for real food. He's been to the vet and he's a good boy. Oh, you asked about his name, not how I came about having a cat, didn't you? I couldn't decide on whether to name him Willie, Waylon, or Merle, so I just named him all three. I call him Waylon most of the time, though."

Hank rolled his eyes at Larissa.

She grinned.

"I'm glad I don't call him Merle now that I'm going to be staying in Mingus because it might offend Merle Avery and she's so sweet."

"Merle?" Larissa chuckled.

"She's a barracuda," Hank said.

"Well, she's been sweet to me. I'll bring Waylon on Sunday when I officially move in. Damn, I'm so excited I could dance a jig in a fresh filled pig trough," Sharlene said.

Hank grimaced. She might not be so excited come Saturday when her boss was throwing things and cussing a royal blue streak. He wasn't sure Texas was big enough to house him and Larissa both after that meeting. If not, she could sell her crazy house to Sharlene and move on back to Perry, Oklahoma, or wherever her imagination took her on her next lark.

He worked up a mad spell as he painted. She'd lied to him about her mother living in Tennessee and that sent him on a wild goose chase for information. She'd lied to him about being from Perry, Oklahoma. There wasn't a Larissa Morley on any records up there. Not pictured in a high school annual, not a single newspaper article about a Larissa Morley winning an award at school, and not on the rolls at Oklahoma State University, either.

She probably was affiliated with the witness protection program and made up stories to suit her fancy on a day-to-day basis. Today she was the daughter of a woman who worked at a dude ranch. Tomorrow she was the daughter of a wealthy socialite who had a craving for young men. Next week her father might be an ambassador to a foreign country.

He fed the anger but couldn't hold on to it. Not with her standing right beside him looking like Daisy Duke in those cute little cut-offs showing off shapely legs. Besides, what right did he have to be mad at her for subterfuge?

I haven't been honest. If I had from the time I hit the deer, then today wouldn't even be happening and I wouldn't have a nagging conscience eating at my heart like an acid bath. So what right do I have to be angry with her?

"You're frowning again," Larissa said.

"You sure about hiring someone who thinks this place is pretty?"

Larissa nodded. "Definitely. She's a gift."

"What's a gift?" Sharlene asked. "This house? You got a sugar daddy hiding in the wings? Did Amos buy this place?"

What began as a faint giggle grew into a full-fledged infectious guffaw that had both Larissa and Hank roaring. When they got control, Larissa wiped her eyes with the tail of her tank top, giving Hank a shot of her flat stomach, belly button, and the rim of her bra.

His mouth went dry at the memories at the lake. Could that have been less than a week before? It felt more like a month or a year.

"Amos is my friend, not my sugar daddy," Larissa said.

"Well, what was so damn funny?" Sharlene asked.

"My mother likes very young men. It just hit me that I *should* take Amos to the charity benefit in a couple of weeks. The visual was so funny…" She got another case of giggles.

Sharlene looked at Hank. "Why was it funny to you?"

"I love to hear Larissa laugh like that. It's like a baby's belly laugh. Uninhibited and with I-don't-give-a-damn attitude," he said honestly.

Larissa stopped laughing and patted him on the arm with her free hand. "That's the best compliment I've ever had. Mother says my laugh sounds like a ruptured hippo."

One touch of her paint smeared hand and he was ready to put down the brushes and take her back to the lake. He could wash all those paint splotches away in the lake water and enjoy every minute of it.

"Daddy always says my laugh is like screeching hyenas," Sharlene said. "Guess us Honky Tonk women aren't so feminine, are we? Tell me about Cathy and Daisy. Were they wilting flowers or wild women?"

"You ought to write a book," Larissa said.

"I'd like to write a book. It's been my dream my whole life. I might forget all about the article for the newspaper and write a real novel. Now tell me about Daisy while we work. Maybe I'll call the character based after her Rose or another flower name," she said.

"And what will you call Cathy?" Hank asked.

"I'll think of something. Damn, that's a good idea, Larissa. I think I'll call the character I build on you something like… I'll have to do some research and see what name means 'wild and free,'" she said.

"So you see her as wild and free?" Hank asked. He and Larissa both reached the corner at the same time.

"Of course," Sharlene said. "Mind if I put on some music? I've got my portable CD player in the car."

Larissa poked her head around the side and raised her voice. "Long as it's not rap."

"Waylon would leave me if I played that stuff," Sharlene said.

In a few minutes music from Highway 101 was drifting around the house. It was an older CD recorded back when Paulette Carlson was still singing with them. She sang "Honky Tonk Heart" and said their song of love was almost ended.

Hank could relate to that part of the song. His and Larissa's short-lived romance was getting close to the good-bye kiss. He'd found her in the Honky Tonk and he'd leave her there among her real friends and acquaintances, never to hold her or see her again.

There was too much of Henry Wells in him and too little of Victoria. She wouldn't blink at doing whatever it took to get what she wanted while leaving a wide path of destruction in her wake. Henry still regretted and remembered an unwise choice made more than thirty years before.

"When we get to the other corner we'll call it lunchtime," Larissa said.

He blinked the past away and nodded. "We eating at Linda's today?"

"No, at Betty's. After which, they are coming over for the first viewing. I have to let them see it before it's finished because several people have already called and told them about the color. Linda thinks they're lying. Betty thinks it's a hoot."

"And Janice?"

"She's waiting to pass judgment."

"What're we having today?"

"Elmer smoked a turkey and Betty's making chocolate cake for dessert."

"What is this? Feed Hank until he gets fat? It takes me a month of daily gym trips to get off what Oma puts on me every summer. And now these girls are adding to it. I'll be until Christmas getting back in shape." He managed a weak chuckle.

"Darlin', there ain't one thing wrong with your shape and I should know after that skinny-dippin' trip. Linda says to get to a man's heart you got to go through his stomach. They want you to stick around and they're trying to entice you," Larissa whispered so that Sharlene wouldn't hear.

———

Betty opened the door with a flourish. "Hey, hey, you are here and right on time."

"I brought one more mouth to feed. She came hunting for work so I gave her a paintbrush and promised her I wouldn't let her starve," Larissa said.

"Come on in here, Sharlene. We're glad to have you. Is she pullin' our leg about painting that house turquoise? We didn't get home until after dark last night so we couldn't see anything but that it was darker than white."

"Don't forget your sunglasses," Sharlene said.

"Dinner is buffet style on the kitchen bar. Y'all help yourselves and find a place to sit around the dining room table," Betty said.

"Are you serious?" Linda asked Sharlene.

"I love it. I'd paint the Honky Tonk just like it if she'd let me, and I wouldn't charge her a dime to do it. Reckon they'd let me paint The Mule Lip or the Boar's Nest like that?"

"You'd best not even suggest it," Elmer said. "Those folks would rather let their places rust and rot as paint them up like hooker hotels."

"Elmer!" Betty air slapped his arm.

"Well, he's speaking the truth. Man, this is some good turkey. Did you smoke it with hickory or pecan?" Hank asked.

"Pear. We had to cut down an old pear tree to make room for a barn and I dried the wood for smoking," Elmer said.

The two men joined ranks and sat together. Talk went from smoking meat, to hay, to cattle and the weather.

The five women sat at the other end of the table. Talk went from recipes, to the Honky Tonk, to paint colors, and finally to Sharlene's new apartment.

"So you need anything?" Betty asked.

"It's got a lovely living room outfit and a refrigerator, stove, washer, and dryer. I've got a bedroom suite of sorts and all the basics. I don't have a kitchen table but it can wait," she said.

"Cathy liked that little table and chairs so she took it with her," Larissa said.

"I've got one out in the shed. Bought a new one last year but the old one was still in pretty good shape. I just got tired of a glass top. You want it, it's yours," Linda said.

"Thank you and I'll be tickled to get it," Sharlene told her.

The conversation got around to her cat Waylon and Larissa listened with one ear and did sneak-peeks at Hank. Something was definitely wrong and it went deeper than him having to go back to Dallas. Her "bullshit" radar was humming.

"Oh my God. This is worse than I imagined!" Betty said when she saw the house.

Sharlene peeked around from the west end where she was painting around the windows on that side. "Hi, y'all. I told you to wear sunglasses. Ain't it beautiful? Only someone as wild as Larissa would have the nerve to do this. I love it."

"It's bright," Linda said.

Janice popped her hands on her hips and studied it for several minutes. "I like it. If I squint I can imagine the porch posts in yellow. That's what is going to really set it off. What do they call that stuff in the antique stores? Shabby something?"

"Shabby chic," Linda said.

"Any of y'all want me to do your house next? I'll be looking for a second job before long if they cut back staff at the paper again," Sharlene asked.

"Hell, no!" they said in perfect unison.

Larissa poked Hank on the arm. "They love it."

"Sounds like it," he said.

"It's like a fancy ball gown. You can appreciate the style without being able to wear it yourself. Can you see Merle in something Angelina Jolie would wear on the red carpet?"

He shrugged. "I get your point."

"We'll see y'all at the Honky Tonk tonight," Betty said. "We've got a meeting at the church this afternoon."

"Sure you don't want Sharlene to come up with a color scheme for your house?" Larissa teased.

"I'm very sure and you might be wishing you hadn't painted like this when folks start walking in your front door thinking you have a beauty stop or a sell flowers in there," she said.

Larissa laughed and waved at the ladies as they piled back into Betty's club cab truck and drove toward the church on down the road. At five o'clock she and Hank finished the painting. She was very glad she'd bought a good grade of outside paint that was guaranteed to cover in one coat.

"I like this much less than hauling hay." She carried the paint supplies to the backyard to wash them under a garden hose.

"I'll stop when I get the back side done and then I'll finish up the trim tomorrow. It's slower going than slapping paint on the siding," Sharlene said.

Hank grabbed Larissa around the waist and pulled her to him. They were both sweaty and smeared with paint but he didn't care. He couldn't come clean but he had to have one more kiss to remember what might have been. He tilted her chin up and kissed her hard, tasting her sweet lips.

"Whew! That is definitely hotter than the weather," she said when he broke away.

"You are some lady, Larissa Morley," he whispered into her hair. "Good-bye."

He turned and walked away before she could say anything else.

"See you tonight at the Honky Tonk?" she called out.

He didn't look back but crawled into his truck and slowly drove away.

"What was that all about?" Sharlene asked. "I thought the way he looked at you all day that he was the cowboy who was going to ride up on a white stallion and take you away from the Honky Tonk. I thought he was your Honky Tonk Dream."

"I have no idea. He's got a lot on his mind. Maybe he's wrestling with a decision." Larissa touched her lips.

"To see if he stays or goes?" Sharlene put her hot pink brush under the running water.

"Who knows? They say women are hard to understand. Quantum physics is nothing compared to understanding the male species."

"A-blessed-men, sister," Sharlene said.

Chapter 11

THE HONKY TONK PARKING LOT WAS FULL WHEN BETTY, Janice, and Linda arrived for the town meeting. They thought they were getting there early but the parking lot was full and Linda had to circle around three times before she found a space to pull into.

"Looks like everyone and their cousin came out for this, even if it is in a beer joint. There's Ella Ruth's pickup truck. She'll be on her knees for a week askin' God to forgive her for going into a beer joint even if it is to save her town. Y'all reckon we'll put the Radner bunch on the run?" she asked as she parked.

Janice nodded. "It'll be worth calluses on Ella Ruth's knees if we send the Radners home with their tail between their legs and howlin' at the moon."

Linda waved the smoke away from her face as they weaved between the vehicles on the way to the front door. "Betty, if you don't give them cancer sticks up they're goin' to kill you, girl."

"Ah, you're just wantin' one and can't have it. We all got to die. Might as well go out with our vice in our hand and a smile on our face." Betty tossed the butt on the parking lot and ground out the last embers with the heel of her boot. "Okay, girls, let's go kick some ass. Not just for us but for Larissa. For some reason that Radner bunch wants her beer joint more than anything else."

"Wonder why? Boiled down it ain't nothin' but a wood building with a concrete parking lot. Why would they be so hot to own it?" Linda asked.

"It's the gateway to paradise." Janice laughed.

Linda laughed. "Well, let's go on inside and join forces to put the big Dallas corporation out of town. We don't need their money and the grandkids couldn't come home to an amusement park for Thanksgiving dinner, now could they?"

Sharlene and Larissa had cleaned the place, set up a table on one end to use as a podium, and arranged chairs in two rows. The rest of the folks would have to stand, but it shouldn't be a long meeting. A show of hands, a short speech from Larissa, and if Hayes Radner showed his sorry face, a few minutes for him to give his sales pitch and then the Radners could go back to the big city and let the Mingus citizens alone. Cookies and lemonade was set up on the bar.

A small group of women led by Ella Ruth made a beeline for Janice, Betty, and Linda when they came into the joint. "We were hoping y'all would get here soon. We ain't never been in a beer joint and it's kind of scary."

"Lightning ain't hit it in all the years it's been here so I reckon you're safe in the middle of the afternoon. It ain't nothin' but a building, not so different from a church. 'Cept you get happy in church for a different reason," Janice said.

"Well, we're glad y'all are here. We couldn't never come back when they were servin' liquor and beer and such. God don't cotton to such things and you better watch your mouth, Janice. What you said is pretty close to blasphemy," Ella Ruth Jackson said with a sniff.

Janice sucked up a lungful of air to argue but Betty poked her in the ribs and shook her head.

"You got a mind to sell your land?" Betty asked.

"Lands no. That was my granddaddy's land. It'll go to my kids or my grandkids the way it's supposed to. Besides, I've got property butted up to the downtown part. You think I want an amusement park out my back door? Can you imagine the noise and the traffic?" Ella Ruth answered.

"Grandkids would love it," Linda said.

"Yes they would but that would be a couple of times a year. I'd have to live with the thing all the rest of the time. No thank you. I will not sell one square inch," Ella Ruth declared.

"Y'all feel the same?" Janice asked the rest of the group.

They all nodded as they ate cookies and sipped cold lemonade from paper cups. "You changed your mind yet?" Ella Ruth asked Larissa when she walked past the group.

"Hell no!"

"Don't go gettin' all up in arms with me. I just asked a question." Ella Ruth puffed up.

Larissa patted her on the shoulder. "Sorry, Miz Jackson. I'm just nervous."

Sharlene joined the group. "We should've made a big bowl of fresh fruit and put a package of those wipe-and-go things beside it."

Larissa asked, "Why would we want fruit? We've got cookies and lemonade."

Sharlene pretended to grab a handful and throw it at the podium, then grabbed an invisible wet toilette and wiped at her hands.

Larissa giggled nervously. "We missed a good opportunity. Only trouble is if he comes in here offering half of Fort Knox and I oppose, they might throw the fruit at me."

"Well…" Sharlene smiled wickedly. "I suppose Hank could have supper off your body then."

"Oh, dear, the way these young people talk. Why in my day we would have never thought such things much less said them out loud," Ella Ruth said.

"Yes, but it does sound awfully naughty and I remember when you were the wildest thing in Mingus," Wanda said.

"Hush, now." Ella Ruth blushed.

Sharlene grabbed Larissa's arm and pulled her away. "Wouldn't you like to be just a little naughty to take the edge off your nerves before this meeting?"

"Oh, hush. He hasn't even showed up or called. He might have gone on back to Dallas," Larissa said. The day before had been a whirlwind of yellow and pink paint but she and Sharlene had finished the trim work. Then they'd had a record night at the Honky Tonk with people waiting in the parking lot to get through the doors. She should think about adding an addition to the Tonk to accommodate more people. It didn't look like the popularity of the Honky Tonk was a passing phase after all.

She took her place behind the table and clapped her hands. The room went silent as everyone looked to her.

She took a deep breath and began. "First of all, thank you for attending. I'm not going to give you a long-winded speech about why you should or should not sell your property to the Radner group for an amusement park. I figure you've all pretty much made up your minds before you came. But I would like to take a poll. How many people here are definitely not interested in selling your property?"

More than half the hands in the place went up.

"Okay now, how many are interested but not sure?" she asked.

Half of what was left went up.

"One more showing. How many would sell today if Hayes Radner offered you enough money?"

Six hands were raised.

The door opened and three people squeezed inside the Honky Tonk. A woman in a black power suit, blond hair cut chin length, and a leather briefcase. One of the two men had a bald head and looked vaguely familiar to Larissa. She frowned as she tried to remember where she'd seen him but it quickly turned to a grin when she looked beyond him and saw Hank.

His black hair was feathered back and she imagined she could smell Stetson all the way across the room. She smiled and he bent his head ever so slightly.

"Okay, then," she said. "This place is packed and I don't know some of you folks, so if Hayes Radner is here, we'll give him the floor to make his offers." She left her spot and sat down in a chair on the front row with Betty on one side and Sharlene on the other.

The three people who'd walked in at the last minute made their way to the front. The woman and man stood behind the table and Hank propped a hip at the front of the table.

Larissa looked up at him. "What are you doing?"

He looked straight ahead. If he looked into her brown eyes he wouldn't be able to utter a single word. "Hello, everyone. Some of you know me because you are regulars in the Honky Tonk. Some of you I've never met. I'd like to introduce myself, my mother, and our assistant. The man behind me is Wayne Johnston. He's the one who's been making most of the calls in an effort to buy your land. My mother, Victoria Radner, has had her heart set on owning this place for several years and has investors ready to put their money into an amusement park. I am Henry Hayes Radner Wells," he said.

Larissa shot up like a bottle rocket. "You are who?"

Hank's face was hardened steel. "You heard me. And I'm here to say that my mother and Wayne will still buy whatever land any of you are willing to sell at ten percent over today's market price for land with the hopes that it will have the domino effect and others will sell if you do."

"But we thought you were going to pay millions," an older lady said from the back of the room.

Victoria stood up and spoke. "We have made our offer. We would have paid ten times what it was worth to have the Honky Tonk, but the rest of the land will be bought at ten percent over market. That's quite an offer in today's repressed market. I will be more than glad to have Wayne draw up intent to sell papers today. Are you sure you won't sell me this godforsaken place, Miz Morley?"

Larissa shot icy daggers at the woman. Larissa had seen her type before—every time Doreen came home to

Perry from one of her trips. "It will be a cold day in hell, madam, when I sell this beer joint to anyone. Why are you so dead set on having it anyway? It could easily be outside your amusement park."

"Personal reasons. I will burn it to the ground and concrete the whole area for a parking lot for my amusement park," Victoria said coldly.

"Well, for personal reasons I would burn it before I sold it to you," Larissa said.

"Must be the place. Makes bitches out of everyone who owns it," Victoria said.

"That's enough, Mother," Hank said.

Larissa turned on him. "This is between me and your mother. You keep your two cents in your pocket. Now…" she spun back around to face Victoria. "You don't know me and you didn't know Daisy or Cathy. I don't know about Ruby Lee, but I can vouch the rest of us are loud-mouthed and brassy. But we are not bitches. You are in my place of business so you'd do well to watch your tongue."

"If you have business to discuss with my mother, feel free to come forward. I'm leaving now." Hank was exasperated. It all made sense now. Owning the Honky Tonk would be a slap in Henry's face.

Shock and anger hit Larissa in slow motion. "You bastard," she whispered to Hank.

"Don't call my son that!" Victoria fired up for a second round. She didn't care if it was an audience or that she'd lost her frosty business shell. She was in the wretched Honky Tonk, the place Ruby Lee owned.

Larissa glared at her. "I guess it's not appropriate since you and his father were married. I take it back, Hank. You are a son-of-a-bitch and that's irrefutable."

"I'm not interested in ten percent above market. I'll keep my land," Delores Wilson said. "Come on, Mavis. Let's go home."

"I'm sorry," Hank said softly. He longed to reach out and touch Larissa, to hold her and apologize with more than two words. She hadn't asked for any of this. He should have listened to his heart and now it was too late.

"Sorry?" Larissa raised her voice. "You have deceived me and all you've got to say is sorry!"

"I'm going home, Mother. You and Wayne can take care of this," he said. "A word outside, please, Larissa."

"Oh, you'll get a word, all right." She marched resolutely to the door without looking back to see if he was following.

Victoria turned to Wayne. "This was a big waste of my time. What in the hell is going on here and why is my son going outside with that woman?"

"That's Larissa Morley and I guess they've gotten acquainted over the last month," he said.

"Well, he can damn sure get unacquainted. When it matters the most, he is too much like his father." She looked around the Honky Tonk. "What is it about this shabby place that draws men? It's nothing but a shack with a neon sign. Let's go home and start looking for another place for our investors to put their money."

"I reckon that would be a good idea, ma'am," Luther said.

Victoria shot looks at the big man that would have frozen anyone. "Who are you?"

Luther didn't flinch at the icy glare. "I'm the bouncer in this place and I reckon you and your son have stirred up enough trouble in town for a lifetime.

You got your answer once and for all. Don't be comin' around no more."

"What happened to Tinker?" Victoria asked.

"Retired. He wouldn't like you any better than I do."

"That would make us even. I didn't like him either." Victoria huffed as she picked up her briefcase and headed for the door with Wayne Johnston behind her like a pet pig on a leash.

"What'd Tinker ever do to you?" Luther asked.

"That is none of your business." She threw over her shoulder.

Larissa stomped all the way to the garage behind the beer joint. So he wanted a word? Well, she'd give him enough words to burn the hair out of his ears for the next twenty years. If he wanted just one word she'd have to hyphenate it because all she could think of in a single word was *drop-dead*.

"Stop! Talk to me, Larissa," he raised his voice.

"You don't get to tell me what to do," she yelled and kept going until they were behind the garage. Then she turned around, popped her hands on her hips, and shot poisonous darts from her brown eyes. How could she have been so deceived? Hank was Hayes. She should have seen it from the beginning. Henry should have told her. She should have asked him for more details when she was out there hauling hay. A million thoughts tumbled through her mind and all she could get a hold on was the one that said she'd been such a fool to fall for him.

"Larissa, I wanted to tell you who I really am but it all got out of hand and…"

He paused and looked at her so bewildered that she might have felt sorry for him if she hadn't been so mad.

"…and what, Hank? Or is it Hayes now that you are wearing a custom tailored suit and dress shoes instead of jeans and boots? Was any of it real or was it all just a game to see if you could find out something about me that you could use to make me sell the Honky Tonk? And why in the hell is it so important that you have it?" Her tone was pure ice without a drop of warmth in it.

"I couldn't tell you because it *was* real. You're right. I wanted to get to know you so I could find out if you had a weakness. Neither Daisy nor Cathy did but there was that possibility and Mother has been trying to buy the Honky Tonk for years. Every scheme she could come up with and every owner was a new challenge. It's her one obsession. It was *my job* and I didn't intend to fall for you but I did and I couldn't tell you," he said.

She looked up at black clouds rolling in from the southwest. An omen for sure that she'd made bad decisions and the storm they would bring would be disastrous. "Go away. I'm too mad to talk."

"Can I call you and we can discuss it more later when you aren't mad?" he whispered.

"No," she said bluntly.

"I'll give you a couple of days to think and try anyway," he said.

"Just leave. Don't call and don't ever show your face in my beer joint again. Good-bye, Hank or Hayes, whoever the hell you are. I don't even know you." She turned to watch the storm. She couldn't watch him leave. She couldn't let him stay. All of it hurt too damn bad to bear.

"You knew Hank better than anyone ever has," he said. Walking away from her without holding her in his arms, burying his face in her hair, and tasting her lips was the hardest thing he'd ever done.

When she was sure he was gone, she slid down the back of the garage and hid her face in her hands. Cars and trucks left the parking lot but she didn't hear them. Everything was obliterated by one sentence that played over and over again: "I'm Henry Hayes Radner Wells."

The gaping hole in her chest where her heart had been that morning was a yawning abyss filled to the brim with pain. She'd never felt so alone in her life. Sharlene sat down beside her and threw an arm around her shoulders. She didn't say a single word, which Larissa appreciated more than all the speeches in the universe.

Larissa wanted to cry. She wanted to cuss, rant, and rave like a lunatic, throw things, kick holes in the garage, yank up mesquite trees by the roots and throw them all the way to Dallas at the almighty Radner Corporation. But none of it would come out; it stayed inside and ate at her soul like fiery acid.

Hank got into his black BMW and laid his head on the steering wheel. He'd made the biggest mistake of his life. He should have told her before the meeting and then left the whole thing to his mother and Wayne. He'd handled it in the most juvenile, stupid way possible and he felt like the fool that he was.

He looked up when he felt a presence in the open window. Hoping to see Larissa, even if she was still angry, he turned his head to find Luther's big round face not ten inches from him.

"That was one dim-witted stunt," Luther said.

Hank nodded. "Yes, it was."

"Rissa has been my friend since the first time I set foot in this place. I thought you were a stand-up man. I was wrong. You get this one on the house. You show up here again, I will wipe this parking lot up with your sorry hide. Understood?" Luther said seriously.

"I didn't mean to hurt her, Luther. I didn't plan on the deer hitting my truck. I damn sure didn't plan on falling for her," he admitted.

"Sometimes it's too late to do what you should've done from the beginning. Guess you've learned a tough lesson. Still don't give you any right to come sniffing around, though, so go on back to Dallas and let her heal. You done her dirty. I shouldn't give you another chance but I believe you."

When Luther moved Merle was right behind him. "I knew it. You are just a drugstore cowboy. She deserves the real McCoy. What are you going to do about this, Hank or whoever the hell you are?"

"There's not much I can do. I goofed. I'll take my pride and my mistakes and leave her alone. Take care of her," he said hoarsely and hit the button to roll the window up.

Merle shook her head from side to side and scanned the parking lot for Larissa. As Hank pulled out of the parking lot, she headed toward the garage. She found Larissa with her head in her hands and Sharlene sitting beside her.

Sharlene touched her fingers to her lips. Merle sat down on the other side, took Larissa's hand in hers, and waited.

Thoughts darted through Larissa's mind like feisty children on a school playground at recess—with no intention of slowing down or staying put long enough for her to get a handle on them. One second she was angry, the next sad. But when it boiled down to the kernel of the matter, she was bewildered.

What right do you have to be mad at him other than he made a complete fool out of you? You weren't up-front and honest with him either. But my dishonesty wouldn't have hurt him like his did me. So he's Hank Wells in Palo Pinto County and he's Hayes Radner in Dallas. Two people. That's what I am. I like Larissa Morley and she's happy here in Mingus. So happy that I'd almost forgot about that other one.

Crying was a sign of weakness and she would not be weak. She'd found her niche in life in a peaceful community and in the Honky Tonk. She would not let one crazy day or one cowboy destroy all that she'd discovered. She *was* Larissa Morley all the time now. He *was* Hayes Radner for the next eleven months. Those two people didn't know each other and wouldn't like each other if they did.

It was over.

She raised her head, swallowed twice, and said, "Let's go drink a beer and get ready to open up the Honky Tonk tonight. We're going to have a record number tonight. The saints will be joining the sinners just to talk about Hank Wells turning out to be Hayes Radner."

"That's my girl," Merle said.

The Honky Tonk parking lot was empty and the beer joint as quiet as a tomb when the three women trooped inside. Merle and Larissa sat on bar stools and Sharlene popped the tops off three beers. She tipped hers up and gulped down a third of it before she came up for air with a healthy burp.

Words exploded from Sharlene's mouth like a bull let loose from a chute at a rodeo. "God Almighty that shocked the shit right out of me. Who'd have thought Hank was Hayes. Guess Hank was named for his dad, Henry, and got tagged with the nickname. I thought for sure he would be the cowboy that would carry you off on a big white horse. All goes to show what I know. I'd do better to write fiction. Maybe I will start that book, Larissa. This is horrible. Can I do anything to make it better?"

Larissa shook her head.

"Well, I told you he wasn't a real cowboy. I was about to amend my decision there toward the end and think my first impression wasn't right but I won't doubt myself no more," Merle said.

"Thank you both for your support." Larissa tilted the bottle up but had trouble swallowing even the smallest sip of beer. Her cell phone rang and she flipped it open.

"Hello," she said.

"Larissa, I can't think of anything but how sorry I am," Hank said.

"Wait a minute," she said.

"Hank?" Sharlene mouthed.

Larissa nodded and motioned toward the cash register. "Hand me a dollar bill."

Hank yelled into the phone. "Larissa, are you there?"

"I said for you to wait a minute," she said coldly.

She fed the money into the jukebox and hit the right buttons. Jo Dee Messina's voice came through singing "My Give a Damn's Busted."

"Listen to every word and then hang up. I don't want to hear anything you've got to say. Don't call. Don't come around. I don't ever want to see or hear from you again." She laid the phone down on the top of the jukebox and went back to her beer.

When the song ended she waited a few seconds before going back to the jukebox and picking up the phone again. "I guess he got the message. He's gone."

"That song is perfect," Sharlene said.

"There's a country song for every mood or problem in the world," Merle said. "Like George Strait and Alan Jackson sing about in that one about murder being committed on music row. George says that nobody wants to listen to them old drinkin' and cheatin' songs. Well, if they would, they'd hear life being sung. I got to go home, girls. Y'all need me, you call. I'll be back here in a little bit. You want me to put out a contract on him?" Merle finished off her beer.

"No, he ain't worth it," Larissa lied with tears flowing down her cheeks.

"Go ahead and cry. Get it out and over with," Merle said.

"He's not worth it," Larissa repeated even though she didn't believe a word of it.

Hank Wells was worth it but Hayes Radner had taken over her cowboy. She'd fallen for Hank Wells who was trustworthy and decent. He was kind and sweet. Hayes Radner was a different man. What she knew about him, she didn't like.

Chapter 12

LARISSA PEEKED OUT THE FISH-EYE IN THE HOTEL DOOR, SIGHED, and opened it. She'd hoped for half an hour to get ready for her mother but she was there and she had no choice.

She slung open the door and stood to one side. "Hello, Mother."

Doreen flowed into the room with the grace of a seasoned ballerina. She stopped to air kiss Larissa on the cheek and kept going until she reached the overstuffed recliner beside the window. She sat down, crossed one leg over the other, and smiled. "You look like hell. Only a man can make a woman look so horrid. What's his name?"

"And you look like your usual young, lovely self." Larissa picked up a bottle of expensive water from the top of the entertainment system, twisted the top off, and downed half of it. Her mother's red hair was short this time and framed her perfectly oval face in springy curls. Crow's feet were beginning to play around her eyes. Was that bit of flesh under her chin a wee bit saggy? Oh, dear, was Doreen going to look her age?

"Don't be bitchy with me because you've got man problems, darlin'," Doreen said in her sweetest Southern accent.

Larissa blushed at her unkind thoughts. "Sorry, Mother. How was your trip?"

Doreen's smile was brilliant. "Lovely. And I can't wait until you meet Rupert, but we'll save conversation about him until later. Please tell me you've given up this crazy notion of living in a pigsty and you've gone back to Perry where you belong."

"Can't. It would be a lie and besides, I like my pigsty. The mud is warm and the food trough is always full," Larissa answered.

Doreen sighed.

"I painted my house turquoise with hot pink and yellow trim. It reminds me of those in the islands," Larissa said. "I brought a picture of it and the Honky Tonk."

"I'm not sure I can stand to look at them. Why would you turn your back on everything? It doesn't make sense. How can you do what you are doing when you could have a decent lifestyle? You know how we always loved that little café on the Rue de la Bastille and all those other nice places."

Larissa remembered talking with Hank about that very café. They would have been good together in their *other* lives. She as the rich heiress to her grandfather's fortune and Hank as his mother's son. But those lives had been left behind when they'd become Hank and Larissa.

She shrugged. "It makes perfect sense to me. I'm starving. I worked last night and had a piece of cold pizza for breakfast at noon. Let's have lunch at that little café downstairs and then go shop until dark," Larissa said.

"Now that sounds like a plan. I've asked Rupert to meet us for a late dinner at the Five Sixty in Reunion Tower. You're going to like him—I promise," Doreen said.

Larissa finished off the water, made sure she had a

room card, and held the door for her mother. "I didn't bring a thing for the fundraiser. Is it very formal?"

"Black tie. Tux. I'd say long, slinky, and black. My friend has a son I'm dying for you to meet. He's handsome, educated, and would be a fine catch. We'll shop for something for you to wear to dinner tonight too," Doreen said.

Larissa pushed the down elevator button. "I'm not interested in anyone. I've just come out of a bad relationship."

Doreen shivered. "What better way to get over it than to meet someone new. You look more like your father every day, Larissa."

"And where is my father?" Larissa asked as they stepped into the glass elevator that moved slowly to the ground floor.

Doreen brushed imaginary lint from her silk pant outfit. It was the same shade of emerald green as her eyes and sported a diamond brooch with a center stone that glittered in the light flowing through the spotless elevator glass. "We'll talk about your father over lunch."

Larissa jerked her head around to look at her mother. The door opened and several people waited to get on the elevator but she couldn't move.

"Seriously?" she asked.

"I expect it's time. I'd rather have this conversation over a table as in an elevator with people watching and listening," Doreen said softly.

"Yes, ma'am," Larissa said.

She and her mother moved out and to the right to the café where they were seated immediately at a corner table. Larissa looked over the menu the waitress brought and waited for her mother to begin.

"I'm having the southwest salad without croutons and a glass of white wine." Doreen handed the waitress the menu.

"Chicken fried steak with all the trimmings. Same wine as Mother ordered," Larissa said.

"This is your mother?" the waitress asked.

"Yes, ma'am, it is. She had me when she was barely two years old. It was a miracle," Larissa said.

"Y'all are teasing me," the waitress laughed. "You aren't even kin. Just good friends out for a weekend of fun. No way you two are related."

"You are right," Larissa said. Biologically they were mother and daughter. Doreen had birthed her at the age of twenty and then left her in the care of her grandparents and a nanny for the rest of her life. They really were more like friends than close kin folks.

"Okay, you've bugged me for years about your father. I guess it's time I came clean. I lied. Now let's have dinner and forget all about it."

Larissa shot her a look. "That's not nearly enough. Talk, Mother."

"That looked just like him," Doreen laughed.

"And?"

Doreen sighed. "Okay, I never married your father. It was a college fling and I really didn't want to have you but my mother caught me upchucking in the bathroom too many mornings. I told her not to worry; I wasn't going to ruin the family name, that I was going to take care of it as soon as I found a doctor."

Larissa's face turned ashen.

"Oh, don't look so shocked. I didn't do it but I might have if Mother and Father hadn't ganged up on me. According to them that would have been covering one big mistake with another. There might be a time when I wanted children and an abortion could have long-term effects as in problems having another child. So I went to Italy to study for a year and when I came home it was with you in tow. The story was that Daddy paid the father off and we'd gotten a divorce. It was an easy one to stick to when you started asking questions. I figured either he or Mother would tell you when you got older."

Larissa shook her head. "Go on."

"You look like him. You didn't get a blessed thing from me. Not my hair or eyes or build. He had jet-black hair, brown eyes, and was lean and trim. Never had to watch how many beers he drank or how much he ate. Worked out in the gym all the time and played ball. Listened to that horrid country music."

"His name?" Larissa asked.

"Can't we just leave it alone at that?"

"No, Mother, I want to know his name."

The waitress set their food before them. "Enjoy your meal. Shall I get you another glass of wine?"

"No, I'm fine," Doreen said.

"Maybe a glass of water with lemon," Larissa said.

Doreen forked a small bite of tomato into her mouth. She hadn't spoken that man's name in almost thirty years. The only time she ever thought about him was when she made a trip to Perry to see her family.

"His name was Lawrence Morleo. Nickname Larry. We called him Morley most of the time. I named you

Larissa so there would be a little of him in you. Your middle name was for my grandmother but you know that."

"Morleo isn't Indian. It sounds Hispanic." Hells bells, no wonder she could never locate the man. She'd been looking for Morley instead of Morleo.

"It is. His father was about a quarter Mexican or maybe even less but the Morleo name had come on down through that line. His mother was the Indian. He came to OSU on an athletic scholarship. We had a fling. I went to Italy. I suppose he went home. I never saw him again."

"Lawrence Morleo. Spell it?"

Doreen did very slowly. "So now what? Are you going to hate me? I didn't put his name on the birth certificate because I didn't want you to know. What are you going to do?"

"Find him, eventually. But today we are going to eat this good food, go shopping, meet Rupert, shop some more tomorrow, and go to a fundraiser tomorrow evening. Life goes on and you don't have to know what or if I find out anything." Larissa was suddenly even hungrier and dipped heavily into the mashed potatoes.

"Thank you. I don't want to know. I don't want Rupert to know either so keep whatever you find to yourself. Thank you for not hating me and for understanding," Doreen said.

"I didn't say that. I don't understand any of it but I don't hate you. Eat your salad, Mother. We've got to find me something all fancy for tomorrow night," Larissa said.

Doreen smiled brightly. "You'll look fabulous and my friend's son is going to drool when he sees you."

Larissa put up a hand. "Not interested. Especially if he's a moron who drools. God, Mother, I live in a small town but there's lots of men folks who'd be happy to take me out and not a one of them drools."

Doreen's giggle was high pitched. "I didn't mean that he was mentally challenged."

"If he's so damned fine and good looking, then why isn't he a notch on your bedpost?" Larissa asked.

"Because he's been too young for me until now. Because his mother is one of my best friends and that would make a mess. And besides, I'm in love with Rupert," Doreen said.

"For real?" Larissa could hardly believe her ears.

"I think so."

"And what does Rupert do? Is he a trainer at a gym or a lifeguard at a five-star hotel pool?" Larissa asked sarcastically.

Doreen giggled. "I won't even fight with you over that barb. I might have deserved it. But I'm not telling you a thing about Rupert. I'll let it be a surprise."

"How about this?" Doreen held up a black slinky dress with spaghetti straps and a drooping neckline.

Larissa held up a bright red satin with rhinestone straps and a sparkly spray at the hemline.

Doreen snarled and wiggled the black one.

Larissa shook her head and picked up a coffee colored silk with side slits up to her panty line.

Doreen rolled her eyes and held up a leopard print silk with black satin straps.

Larissa carried it to the dressing room. It fit her like

it had been custom-made instead of an off-the-rack and she liked the side slit lined in the same black satin as the straps. Add a pair of strappy high heeled sandals and a little black satin evening bag and she'd be ready. She stepped out of the dressing room and Doreen clapped her hands.

"Please let me buy that for you. It's perfect with your skin color and eyes. It doesn't look ready-made and it doesn't need a single alteration. Black high heeled sandals, a black purse, my big diamond necklace…"

"No! Not that necklace. No jewelry. The dress can carry itself," Larissa protested.

"Just a slim bracelet. You've got to have jewelry or everyone will think you are poor," Doreen said.

"No jewelry. We'll compromise. I won't wear cowboy boots and a denim miniskirt if you'll concede to no jewels," Larissa said. She really did like the dress even if the zeroes behind the five staggered her.

Doreen shivered all the way from her red hair to her toes. "You wouldn't dare."

"I might even paint freckles on my nose with an eyebrow pencil."

"You win. No jewels. But I intend to go in an emerald green silk that I had made in Paris and, darlin', I'm going to sparkle more than the crystal chandelier."

"I'm sure you will and that will be you."

"Take it off and we'll go find shoes and a cute little purse. Can it have a bit of flash on the strap?"

Larissa shot her another look.

"Okay, okay. Plain Jane, it is. Do you realize that you are thirty years old? You always said you were going to have this big family. Your biological clock is ticking,

girl. You should be elegant at affairs like this so you'll
be noticed," Doreen said.

"Are you telling me you are ready to be a grandmother?" Larissa teased.

Doreen smiled. "Now wouldn't that be funny. I didn't
even want to be a mother and now you're talking about
a possibility I'd be a grandmother. No one would ever
believe that, would they? But I think I might be ready
to be a grandmother. My biological clock is messed
up. I'm ready for children when it's too late to think
about them. I'd like grandchildren. I think I inherited my
mother's genes after all."

"What?" Larissa turned away from the mirror.

"Looking back I'm not so sure that Mother was
ready for parenting when she had me. I had a nanny and
Mother plunged into social work. In those days it would
have been a big black sin to say you didn't want children
after marriage and God help the wayward woman who
had a child without a husband. When you were born she
was ready to be a parent."

Larissa cocked her head to one side. "Then why did
she hire a nanny for me?"

"Because that's the way things were done. I'm not
sure that I wouldn't hire a temporary nanny when and
if my grandchildren ever came to visit me. It would be
fun to play with them. I damn sure wouldn't want to be
responsible for every mundane little thing."

Larissa was glad she and her mother hadn't had the
talk when she was sixteen or even twenty-one. It would
have devastated her to learn that she'd been an unwanted
child at that age. She spun around one more time to
check the back of the dress in the three-way mirror. "Is

Rupert old enough to be a grandfather? That might even be funnier. Meet my children's grandfather, Rupert, who is younger than I am. We might even wind up with one of those I'm-my-own-grandpa things before it was over."

Doreen cocked her head to one side. "So is there a man in your life that might father a granddaughter for me? It might be fun to shop for a little girl's Christmas gifts in Paris or London."

"Like you did mine?"

"Your presents made me happy."

"Did I ever make you happy?" Larissa asked.

"Yes, you did. I loved coming home and seeing you but it was more like watching a much younger sister grow up. At least you made me happy up until you got this harebrained idea about living in a pigsty and running a common beer joint. I didn't want to be around and do all the mother things with you. Nanny could make cupcakes for the school parties and hold your head up when you upchucked. But I liked buying pretty things for you."

Why am I not furious with her? Is it because we never did form that kind of bond and that I had a loving support group at home without her? Would I be like her if I ever did have a child? Larissa thought as she returned to the dressing room, took the dress off, and put on her jeans and boots. She looked at the woman's reflection in the mirror as she brushed her hair. When she found Lawrence Morleo would he recognize her as his daughter? Would he tell her to get lost? "What the eyes don't see, the heart doesn't grieve," her grandfather had told her when she was a teenager and plagued him about her father.

She applied a touch of lip gloss, carefully put the

dress on the hanger, and started to the front with it when she saw the red satin dress on a mannequin.

"That's the one!" she pointed.

"Red?" Doreen frowned.

"I love it. Do you have this in my size?" she asked the clerk.

"That's the only one left and let me see." She checked the tag and smiled. "It is your size. Would you like to try it on?"

"No, just please put this one back and I'll take it," Larissa said.

The sales clerk took it to the desk, along with Doreen's credit card, and returned in a few minutes with it zipped away in a plastic bag.

"Now it's on to Neiman's to find something for you to wear to dinner tonight," Doreen said.

"I'd rather go to American Eagle and buy a new pair of jeans," Larissa said.

"Tonight is even more important to me than tomorrow's fancy dress," Doreen said. "And you will look pretty, not dowdy."

"Up beside you I will always be dowdy," Larissa said.

Doreen looked at her diamond encrusted watch. "Sixty seconds, starting now."

"Okay, okay! I'll stop whining." Larissa giggled. The rule had been when her mother came home that she couldn't whine or pout, not while she was there or when she left. If she had to put on a long face then Doreen only allowed it for sixty seconds.

Larissa showered, powdered, perfumed, and dried her

hair. Then she put on new silk underpants and a bra from Victoria's Secret, a short slip dress in red silk, applied a bit of makeup, and had just picked up her evening purse when her mother knocked on the door.

"You look stunning," Doreen said.

Larissa smiled. "And so do you."

Her mother wore a mint green silk dress with a see-through jacket, a square cut emerald necklace, and matching ring and shoes that had been dyed to match the dress.

Larissa asked, "Does the restaurant have a sign on the door that says, 'No Shirt, No Shoes, No Service'? If it doesn't I might go barefoot. Those shoes aren't the most comfortable things in the world."

Doreen laughed nervously. "I don't think so but you'd better wear shoes just in case. Besides, a little beauty is worth a little pain."

"You mean this isn't a beer, bait, minnows, and hamburger joint all in one?" Larissa asked.

"You've been away from civilization too long. Why don't you sell that beer joint or burn it down and move to Italy with me?" Doreen asked.

Larissa put on a pair of red sandals with a spike heel. She towered above her mother when they walked out of the hotel room. "Is that where you intend to settle down?"

"Yes, it is. Do you want the Perry property? I'll sign the whole place over to you. You can sell it or give it to a charity as an orphanage. I don't really care. I don't want it," she said.

"I'd never sell that place. It was my home," Larissa said.

"I thought you liked the warm mud where you live now. That it was your home," Doreen argued.

Larissa threw an arm around her shoulder. "You really are nervous."

"It shows that much?"

"Your voice changes when you are nervous. It's deeper, got more gravel in it. I've only heard it a few times in my life."

"That's because I've lived exactly the way I wanted. Mother and Father took care of you. That was the agreement. If I didn't get an abortion, they'd see to it the baby was raised and given everything he or she needed or wanted and I could live however or wherever my whims took me. Did you ever need anything that your grandfather didn't provide?"

Larissa thought about that on the ride down to the ground floor. "No, they took care of me and Nanny was a good mother role model."

"I have no regrets," Doreen said.

"Good. I wouldn't want you to ride a guilt trip. They're too expensive and cause too much pain," Larissa told her.

"Father thought you were the best toy in the whole world. After Mother died, he doted on you even more. I gave birth to you but they were your parents," she said.

"Are you trying to convince me or you?" Larissa said.

"Nostalgia. I thought about Larry today and that brought on Mother and Father and even Nanny. As long as you don't hate me, then I have no regrets," she said again.

Larissa put her arm around her mother's shoulder. "Mother, I could never hate you."

Doreen smiled.

They rode the elevator up to the Reunion Tower and were met by a hostess who led them to their reserved table. A gray-haired gentleman stood when they approached. His sparkling blue eyes were set in a round face and he sported a silver goatee and mustache. He was taller than Doreen but not much more than Larissa. He wore his suit with ease and the diamond in the gold ring on his right hand said he wasn't a hotel lifeguard.

"Darling, you look beautiful tonight," he said with an Italian accent in his deep voice.

"Thank you. Rupert, I want you to meet my daughter, Ruth. Honey, this is Rupert."

Larissa flinched. No one called her Ruth anymore. She hadn't been called that for the past seven years and it sounded strange and stilted. She'd brought a new name to her new surroundings almost a year before and she liked it a hell of a lot better.

Rupert pulled out chair for Doreen and then seated Larissa. "I've heard a lot about you and your rebellious streak. I was expecting someone who looked like Doreen. You are just as lovely, in a much different way."

"Thank you. I wasn't expecting someone like you either," Larissa said.

"My hair turned silver early in life. Your mother and I are the same age. She just didn't age and I did," he said.

"I think your hair is beautiful. It's all right to tell a man he has beautiful hair, isn't it? Or is that a social blunder?" Larissa asked.

"A charmer. That she gets from you." Rupert smiled at Doreen.

"She has always been painfully honest," Doreen said.

"I can live with that. So are you coming to Italy to live with us?" Rupert asked.

"No, sir. I own and operate a beer joint in Mingus, Texas. It's home."

"We'll have lots of convincing to do, won't we?" Rupert looked at Doreen and winked.

"Once she sets her mind, she doesn't budge," Doreen answered.

"And you run a pub?" Rupert asked.

"No, I run a plain old American beer joint. You ever watch American films?" Larissa asked.

Rupert nodded. "When I have time."

"Ever see *Roadhouse*?"

He rubbed his goatee. "With that actor who died last year? And the one who looks like a worn out old cowboy? Yes, I did see that film. I rather liked it except where the old fellow died."

"Patrick Swayze and Sam Elliot. Picture the bar that they were working at in that small town. Now make it less fancy and strip it of all the paint," she said.

Rupert looked across the table at her in amazement.

"What?" Doreen looked from one to the other.

"I'll rent the movie and we'll watch it tonight after supper in our room. Neither of us could ever describe it," he said.

"Is it bad? I don't want to see it if she's living in squalor."

Larissa reached across the table and patted Doreen's hand. "Watch it, Mother. You'll see what a Honky Tonk is and it's a damn good movie."

The waitress brought the wine list and menus. Rupert ordered the wine for all of them and prime rib for himself. Doreen decided on a small rib-eye steak. Larissa was tempted to ask the waitress if they had red beans and okra but it was a special night so she ordered chicken kiev.

Rupert handed the waitress his menu and asked Larissa, "So tell me how you came to live in a small Texas town and why you own a Honky Tonk when you could live anywhere and you wouldn't have to work at anything? Being a barmaid has to be hard work and time consuming."

"It is and I love it. How did I get there? I pulled down a map, shut my eyes, turned around three times, and stuck a pin in Mingus, Texas. I'd been searching for myself for seven years. I found what I was looking for in Mingus," Larissa answered.

Rupert touched Doreen's hand. "She is a rebel, my love."

"I can tell by the look on your face that you've found your Mingus, Texas." Larissa touched Doreen's other hand.

Doreen smiled. "I have. If your mud makes you this happy, then who am I to argue?"

It was a good night. The food was good. The view was spectacular. The company was wonderful. But Larissa was glad to be back in her room when it was over. Glad to be able to stretch out on the king-sized bed and think about a man out there named Lawrence Morleo who had no idea he had a daughter.

But when she went to sleep it wasn't her biological father who haunted her dreams but a dark-haired cowboy with his shirt blowing in the wind.

Chapter 13

LARISSA DREW THE CURTAINS BACK IN HER HOTEL ROOM AND looked out over Dallas. Lightning zigzagged through the sky. Thunder followed closely on its heels, adding the drumbeat to the tinkling cymbals that the rain produced.

"Nature's country music," she mumbled. She missed the Honky Tonk. Luther would have opened the doors five minutes ago and Sharlene would have everything shining behind the bar. That girl was one of those miracles sent to the Honky Tonk by angels. Well, maybe not real angels. Larissa doubted if the heavenly kind would send someone with Sharlene's bent toward cussing but maybe from honky tonk angels. Her middle name was organization. Her bubbly personality and quick wit made all the regulars love her.

Larissa had been ready for half an hour. She'd paced the floor for fifteen minutes, wishing she had the nerve to call Hank since she was in his town. But she couldn't reopen that can of worms no matter how much her heart ached for him.

She wondered where he was that rainy night in Dallas. Was he working late in his office? How far was he from her right then? Was he watching the gray clouds drop buckets of water on the town from the window in his corner office? Had they found another small town to buy for their amusement park?

Her cell phone rang.

"Hello." She picked up her purse and started for the door.

"Larissa, it's Hank. Do you have time to talk a few minutes?"

She stopped mid-step. She'd been expecting to hear her mother's voice, not Hank's. The old adage about thinking about the devil and he will appear came to mind as she sunk into the recliner beside the window.

"Are you there?" he asked.

"I'm here. Why are you calling?" she asked.

"Can we meet and talk?"

"Hell, no!" she said.

"I'll meet you anywhere. Honky Tonk. Your front porch. The lake. The Dairy Queen in Stephenville. I just want to talk, to explain now that there's been some time. I need closure if nothing else," he said.

"I can't think about that tonight, Hank. I'm about to leave and, honey, you don't deserve closure," she said.

"Are you leaving Mingus? Where are you going? Will you have the same cell phone?" His voice sounded frantic.

"No, of course not. I wouldn't leave Mingus for half the dirt in Texas. I've got plans that aren't a bit of your business and I have to leave now."

"Is it another man? Have you found someone else?" he pressured.

"Like I said, it's really none of your business, is it?"

"Can I call again?"

"Give it a week," she said.

"Okay, one week from today then. Good-bye."

She flipped the phone shut. Closure? She needed it more than he did but a meet and talk wouldn't bring her a bit of closure. It would just make her want him more. She shut her eyes and remembered the day at the lake and how his body felt next to hers in the cool lake water. The afterglow when they'd made love and the sweetness of sleeping in his arms, wrapped up in a blanket like they were in a cocoon. She wouldn't have admitted it to Sharlene for a chunk of the moon but she had begun to wonder if the curse of the Honky Tonk had fallen on her and Hank Wells was the cowboy who would take her away from the beer joint. But most of all she missed her friend, Hank. The man who teased and laughed with her while they baled hay, while they painted her house, and who bickered and argued with her.

She shook her head to clear the memory. Then she carefully tucked an errant strand of black hair back into the French twist that the hotel beautician had styled that afternoon.

She'd think about it for a week and then decide if she could see him. If not, she'd put it off again. It wasn't as if she were sitting around in her pajamas, eating chocolate, and setting herself up for the boys in the white jackets to come take her away. She had a life in Mingus and at the Honky Tonk even if her heart was shattered. And she would go on living her life among her friends. Betty, Linda, and Janice came over several afternoons a week for a cup of coffee and to catch up on the local gossip. Sharlene was fast becoming her best friend at the Honky Tonk. They'd commiserated together when Hank, aka Hayes, left after the meeting with Sharlene calling him every name she could think of and then starting on the creative ones that combined swear words in ways Larissa had never heard before.

"I thought you were Mennonite," Larissa had said.

"Didn't you ever hear about the preacher's daughter being the wildest kid in the whole town? Well, Corn, Oklahoma, got its little ears scorched pretty often when I got mad," she'd answered.

Larissa laughed at the memory. Sharlene was probably more like Ruby Lee than Daisy, Cathy, or Larissa. Had Hank been Larissa's knight-in-shining-pickup-truck, would Sharlene have been the last woman to inherit the Honky Tonk?

Well, I'll be hanged. I'd never thought of giving it to Sharlene until this minute.

Her phone rang again.

She half expected to hear Hank's voice again since he'd found that she would answer the phone and not let it go to her voice message, which was Jo Dee Messina playing fifteen seconds of "My Give a Damn's Busted."

"Hello," she said.

"The limo is waiting. We will meet you in the lobby," Doreen said.

She picked up her purse and checked her reflection one more time in the mirror. "I'm on my way."

Rupert and Doreen waited, arms looped together, not far from the elevator doors. Dashing was the only word Larissa could think to describe him and it sounded so British. He looked too masculine in his black tux to call him gorgeous and handsome just didn't cut it. Every woman in the place was going to be more jealous of Doreen than they'd ever been when she showed up to affairs with a muscle-bound gigolo on her arm. Rupert's black tuxedo fit him the way only custom-made can, his bow tie was perfect, his silver hair and goatee trimmed, and his smile genuine. Larissa liked him and hoped that her mother had truly found a place to hang her heart.

Doreen was her normal stunning self. She wore flowing midnight blue silk dress that complimented her red hair and flawless complexion. A long stole was draped over her arms and she carried a tiny little purse splashed with shiny clear stones that picked up the light when she moved.

Larissa gave her the once-over and stopped at her ring finger on the left hand. "What is that? It looks like you peeled up an ice rink."

"We didn't want to spring it on you yesterday. We really are engaged. We'll be married in Italy next month and we're hoping you can get away for a while. Darling, you look wonderful. I'm glad you didn't let me talk you into the leopard print dress. Red becomes you. I'm envious," Doreen said nervously.

"You'd look good in a gunny sack tied at the waist with baling wire," Larissa said. "And I wouldn't miss your wedding for anything. But it'll be a fly-in, fly-out. I've got a beer joint to run, remember. I don't leave for long times. Maybe three days. That's max. And congratulations to you both." She hugged them in a three-way embrace.

Doreen beamed.

"Thank you, Ruth," Rupert said.

"That's Larissa, please. I never did like that Ruth name."

"Then Larissa it is," Rupert said.

The limo waited under an awning so they were able to get inside without getting wet. Lightning still danced around in the sky teasing high buildings and putting artificial lighting to shame. Thunder beat out a rumbling rhythm but the inside of the limo was cozy.

"Anyone want a glass of wine while we ride?" Rupert asked.

Larissa shook her head.

Doreen nodded.

Rupert poured from a bottle of Doreen's favorite and held the glass out to her. She sipped it and looked up at with adoration in her eyes. "You never forget a single detail, do you?"

"It's easy to remember the things that make you smile so beautifully," he said.

With someone that attentive, that handsome, and without a doubt very wealthy, she could see her mother was ready to give up the young men.

"How far is it to the hoo-rah?" she asked.

"Ten minutes if the traffic is good," Doreen said.

"And what's the benefit for? The Dallas Cowboy's Cheerleader's uniforms?"

"Honest and funny," Rupert said.

"It's for the arts. We're raising money for scholarships to an art school in Dallas. I didn't ask for particulars. It's a party," Doreen said.

So I'm going to a party to raise money for an art scholarship. Ain't that a hoot? Sharlene will love this story. Headline: Honky Tonk Owner Gets Arty. *Wonder if that sounds like I'm marrying a man named Arty? That ought to set the Women's Club at Janice, Linda, and Betty's church to wagging their tongues. Arty? Yuck! That sounds like an old man with a bald head and hair in his ears.*

The traffic was light and they arrived at a mansion on the outskirts of Dallas by the time Doreen had finished her wine. They were greeted at the door by a man in a black suit who held out a silver tray for the invitation. Doreen produced it from her purse and laid it on top of several others.

Every eye in the place gravitated toward them when they walked into the ballroom. The gorgeous redhead in midnight blue and the dark-haired beauty in shiny red satin acting as bookends for the dashing Rupert.

A woman rushed over to Doreen's side. "I'm so glad you came, darlin'. You don't get down here to Texas nearly enough. And who are these pretty people you've brought with you? God, don't tell me this is Ruth. It is, isn't it? She's simply gorgeous, Doreen, and she looks exactly like her father. I'd forgotten all about him until this moment. Oh my, I wasn't supposed to ever mention him, was I?"

"It's all right. Ruth and I've had a talk about her father. This is Rupert Jovani, my fiancé, and this *is* my daughter, Ruth, all grown up now. And this is Martha, our resident artist tonight," Doreen said.

"Good Lord. I can't believe you turned into such a lovely woman. Last time I saw you, you were a long-legged kid that I didn't think would ever grow into those teeth and eyes. I'm one of your mother's dear friends. Come on in and enjoy yourselves. Eat, drink, visit, and then get ready to write a big healthy check to support my cause." Martha laughed and she made her way across the room to another couple who'd just arrived.

"Is she your age?" Larissa whispered.

"Two years younger," Doreen answered.

Larissa took another look at the woman. She was almost as wide as she was tall and her hair was black and worn long and straight. The flowing pant set was decorated with glistening rhinestones but the whole picture was one of a grandmother playing dress up more than a socialite giving a high-dollar charity party.

"She paints world renowned oils that are too expensive for me to own," Doreen said.

"You've got to be kidding me. Too expensive for you?" Larissa looked again.

"Don't ever judge a book by the cover. It'll fool you every time. She may look like a dowdy fish wife but she's got a reputation in the art world," Doreen whispered.

"So where's her son that you wanted me to meet and is he built like her?" Larissa asked.

"She doesn't have children. Says her career doesn't allow snotty noses and colic. She's donated one of the paintings for a silent auction tonight. It's displayed over there behind that bunch of people. It's my other friend's son I wanted you to meet. She has a career," Doreen explained.

"Is the painting too expensive for you?" Larissa looked at Rupert.

"Nothing is too expensive for me if Doreen wants it," he said.

Doreen snuggled up close to him. "If you buy that horrid thing, it's hanging in your study. I don't like it."

"There's the real answer, then," Rupert said. "So I'm off the hook and my checkbook can stop worrying."

"I like this man, Mother. Let's keep him."

"Oh, I plan on it. And now we circulate," Doreen said.

Larissa headed toward the display. A big man left after writing a bid in the book standing on a podium to one side of the painting. It reminded Larissa of the stand they'd had

at the funeral home for guests to sign at her grandparents'
and her Nanny's funerals. When she took the big man's
place and looked at the painting, it made perfect sense.
The canvas looked as if someone had died and sprayed
bright red blood all over it. The only thing left to do was
bury the tacky looking mess and everyone who witnessed
the death of the ugly thing could sign the book.

She looked at the bids and sucked air. She looked up at
the canvas and couldn't see anything but chaos in the work.
Lopsided splotches of color that resembled a piecework
quilt made by a dyslexic manic depressive who finished it
and then drizzled a pint of blood on it. She tilted her head
to one side and squinted. Maybe it was a jig-saw puzzle put
together all wrong. She turned to other side and squeezed
her eyes shut tighter until everything was one big blur. Now
it made perfect sense. It was a page from a kindergartner's
coloring book and he'd had a McDonald's Happy Meal
for dinner while he was coloring it. The ketchup packet got
caught between his lunch pail and the desk and squirted
irregular lines all over the page. Larissa could almost
make out the form of one of those new kids' toys called a
transformer if she shut one eye completely.

A blond-haired man with wire rimmed glasses who'd
taken up residence beside her said, "Exciting, isn't it?"

"Are you looking at the painting?" Larissa had been
so engrossed in trying to figure out how that could be art
she hadn't even realized anyone was still around.

He nodded.

"Well, I suppose you could call it exciting. There's
lots of color."

His eyes glassed over as if he were a Puritan who'd
been transported ahead in time straight into a bar with

pole dancing girls. "Yes, the color is fabulous. The light is perfect. I can picture it above my sofa in my loft apartment. I've put a bid on it. Would you like to see it in a place of honor when it's mine? By the way, I'm Thomas Whitfield, the third. Most folks call me Whit."

"I'm glad to meet you, Whit, but I'm not from Dallas. I live in Mingus, up in Palo Pinto County and own and operate a beer joint called the Honky Tonk," she said.

When he got a hold of his jaw and brought it back up to clamp tightly shut, he turned heel and left her standing there surrounded by a dozen other people.

"But I thought someone said you were Doreen Lawson's daughter?" A thirty-something lady joined them. She had blond hair, a long face with a nose that was slightly too big, and dark eyes. She was taller than Larissa and heavier but wore her black sheath dress with a draping neckline very well.

Larissa reached out and took a flute of white wine from a waiter's tray. "I *am* that."

"You don't look a thing like her. Are you her daughter or the child of that Italian fellow she's with tonight?"

"No, Rupert isn't my father but Doreen Lawson is definitely my mother."

The woman looped her arm through Larissa's and led her away from the painting. "Hideous, isn't it? My name is Julia. I put the first bid on it so Aunt Martha wouldn't disown me but thank God I was outbid quickly. I'd rather hang a velvet Elvis in my living room as that thing. Come sit with me and we'll scope out the good looking Texans. If it don't wear a Western cut tux, I don't even give it a second glance. And cowboy boots are a plus."

"You should make a trip to Mingus if you like cowboys. First drink at the Honky Tonk is free for getting me away from that thing. It's like a gory movie. You don't want to look at all that carnage but you can't blink," Larissa said.

Julia giggled. "You got it, honey. I've heard of the Honky Tonk. I've got some friends who've been up there. They say it's vintage. Maybe I'll collect that beer sometime. I could have kissed you when you told Whit that you owned a beer joint. The look on his face was priceless."

Larissa sat down on a newly vacated sofa. "You don't like him?"

Julia sat beside her. "Oh, I'll probably end up married to the man. Mother wants me to marry him and his dad thinks it's a wonderful idea. But I'd have to train him and I don't know if I've got the patience. I'd much rather have Hayes Radner. Have you heard of him?"

Larissa inhaled. "Couple of times."

"Now there's a man a woman wouldn't have to train. He's like a brand new house. Turn the key and start living." Julia fanned her face with her hand. "And turn on the air conditioner because it will be some damn hot living."

Larissa raised an eyebrow. "Oh, really?"

Julia went on. "Good looking. Dresses just right. Rich. And honey, if I ever get him into bed I just know he'll make my little old toenails curl up and sing."

"What will they sing?" Larissa asked.

"That song that they always sing when the bride is walking down the aisle." Julia laughed again.

"Well, good luck."

Whit picked two glasses of wine from the waiter's tray and carefully carried them to the sofa where Julia and

Larissa sat. "Julia, darlin', I noticed you didn't have a drink and I brought you one. Did you make a bid on the painting? It's really not fair if you get it because Martha can paint you something anytime. She's your aunt, after all."

Julia took the wine and sipped it. "You outbid me, you rascal. I suppose you'll donate it to the new art department if you win the bid?"

"I hadn't planned on it but that is a lovely idea," he said. "There's my mother and father, at last. I'll be back in a minute. I've got to tell them I've already entered a bid so they won't bid against me."

"Why'd you do that?" Larissa asked.

"If I do marry him, I damn sure don't want that thing staring at me every day. It was self preservation," Julia whispered behind her hand.

A tall dark-haired man stopped in front of them and touched Julia's shoulder. "Hi, darlin'. I thought you might be here."

Larissa looked up into the bluest eyes she'd ever seen. His hair was so black it was blue when the lights from the chandelier hit it and his jaw square. Exactly the kind of man who'd appealed to her in the pre-Hank Wells' days.

"And who is your gorgeous friend?"

"This is Doreen's daughter, Ruth."

Larissa extended her hand. "I prefer Larissa. It's my first name and the one I use these days."

He brought her finger tips to his lips and brushed a kiss across them without blinking, his full attention riveted on her face. "Then Larissa it is. I'm Tyler Green."

She withdrew her hand. "Pleased to meet you, Tyler."

That warm, oozy feeling in the pit of her stomach wasn't there. He was pretty. He was a true knight-in-shining-western-cut suit and high-dollar boots, but he did nothing to excite Larissa. She was reminded of Jo Dee Messina's song, "My Give a Damn's Busted." Had Hank broke her give-a-damn so badly it couldn't be repaired? Was there no man on the face of the great green earth who could make her melt into a puddle at his feet?

"I'm going for food. Want to join me?" Tyler asked.

Larissa shook her head. "No, thank you. I'm not a bit hungry and Julia and I still have some catching up to do."

"Then maybe later," Tyler said.

"He's a player," Julia said when he was out of hearing distance.

Larissa smiled. "Well, I don't reckon he's going to play me, not tonight. How about you?"

Julia winked. "Honey, I'd let him play me like a piano. He's my second choice, behind Hayes Radner. I betcha I could keep him tied up in the bedroom so well that he wouldn't even look at another woman if he'd give me a chance."

"Okay, ladies and gentlemen," Martha said loud and clear into a cordless microphone.

The room went silent and everyone got ready for her fundraising speech.

"Instead of begging you for money we're going to have an auction. Don't get your hopes up. I'm only giving away one of my paintings tonight," she said.

Julia whispered, "Thank God."

"We're going to have a slave auction. Men on this side of the room. Women on that side." She pointed and couples began to separate.

Larissa and Julia sat still while the other women gathered around them.

"We are going to auction off the men to the highest bidder. Let's see how much you girls want the man who brought you. We'll start with Doreen Lawson's date, Rupert. Doreen, you got your checkbook ready?"

Doreen waved it in the air.

"Okay, here's a fine specimen of an Italian and you all know what they say about Italian men." Martha wiggled both eyebrows. "Who's going to start the bidding at a thousand dollars?"

Doreen raised her checkbook.

"Two thousand," Julia shouted.

"What are you doing?"

"Raising money for Aunt Martha's charity. It's all tax deductible. How much did your mother plan on donating tonight?"

"I have no idea," Larissa said.

"Three?" Martha asked.

Doreen nodded.

"Four," a voice from the back said.

"Ten," Doreen said.

"Well, it looks like Doreen either knows something we don't or else she's planning on finding out," Martha said. "Do I hear eleven?"

Larissa looked at Julia.

Julia shook her head. "That's all I'm donating and I'm really going to buy Tyler."

"Then ten it is. Doreen, you get to take him home. I'll expect a full report tomorrow morning at our brunch," Martha laughed.

"Next we have one of our own country boys. Tyler Green. Step up here and let the ladies see what you've got," Martha said.

Tyler took center stage beside Martha right under the chandelier. He removed his coat and tie to a few bump and grind movements, turned around to show everyone his backside, and shot a grin toward Larissa over his shoulder.

"Do I hear a thousand?" Martha said.

"Yes," a tall brunette said from behind the sofa.

"Two?"

Another woman held up a hand.

"Three?"

The brunette nodded.

"Four?"

A third woman got in on the bidding.

"Five. Remember it comes off your taxes and goes for a good cause," Martha said.

The first woman nodded.

"Six?"

A few seconds passed.

"Now's your chance," Larissa told Julia.

Woman number two giggled and raised a hand.

"Seven. Remember whoever buys him gets to keep him until ten o'clock tomorrow morning. Do I hear seven or does Susanne take him home?"

"Seven," the brunette said.

"Eleven thousand, three hundred and four dollars," Julia said. "That's all there is in my checkbook but I suppose he's worth it."

"Darlin', that's just all there is in your checkbook until you call the bank tomorrow morning. Do I hear eleven thousand, three hundred and five dollars?" Martha asked.

All three of the women shook their heads.

Tyler slung his coat over his shoulder. The crowd parted for him to stroll back to Julia and kneel before her. "I am your slave, darlin'. Shall we stay at this party, my lady, or do you have other plans?"

"We'll stay for a while. Sit right here and hold my hand," she said.

Larissa moved down and he squeezed in between them. "Are you sure that's all you want me to hold?"

"For now. We'll talk about anything else later when all these women around me stop drooling," she laughed.

Susanne faked a swoon. "Hot damn! I knew I should've outbid her."

That brought a few chuckles. Martha went on. "Now our own Whit is up for sale. He's got good taste in art and I hear he's a lady's man when the lights go out."

Whit blushed and went to stand beside her. "Tyler is a hard act to follow but remember not every book can be judged by the cover."

"One thousand?" Martha said.

"How long do we own these slaves?" Susanne asked.

"The length of this party. He can't flirt with another woman until my fundraiser is over, which is the stroke of midnight. After that if you haven't lassoed him, he's free to go home without you," Martha said.

The bidding started and ended at eight thousand five hundred with Susanne owning Whit.

He followed Tyler's example and told Susanne that he was her humble slave for the next several hours. Did she want a glass of wine or a chocolate covered strawberry?

She sent him to the bar for a Grey Goose martini and a plate of food.

"Ahh, our next slave is just arriving. Better late than never, I suppose," Martha said. "Come on up here.

Don't be shy. We've already gotten ten thousand for the Italian, eleven and some change for the sexy Tyler, and more than eight for our witty Whit. I expect you'll bring a dollar ninety-eight at least," she teased.

"Well, damn," Julia swore.

"What?" Larissa asked.

"I've spent my money and now I wish I'd waited."

"Why?"

"Hayes Radner just walked in. That's who Martha is putting up on the slave block now."

"Okay, girls, who'll give me a thousand dollar bid for Hayes?" Martha asked.

Susanne moaned. "Damn it, Martha. I didn't think he was coming tonight."

"Two thousand," the brunette said.

"Three," a blonde yelled.

"Someone want to raise it to four?"

"Five," the brunette said.

"Six," the blonde yelled.

"Well, now, we've got a serious bidding war, Hayes. Looks like either Molly or Emma is going to own your for the evening. You got a choice?"

"No, I don't. What's the rules and when does the evening end?" Hayes asked.

"Rules are that the evening ends at the stroke of midnight. You can't flirt with another woman until after that. When the party is over, it's up to the two of you if it goes on or stops," Martha said.

"Ten thousand," Larissa said.

Good God Almighty, why did I do that? I didn't even intend to donate to the fund tonight. I figured Mother would take care of it.

"Looks like a third party has entered the race so don't be choosing between Molly and Emma," Martha said.

"Eleven," Molly yelled.

"Eleven thousand, six hundred and I'm not bidding a dollar higher. That's all I brought and if I use it all, I don't get that new pair of shoes I want," Emma said.

"Twelve," Larissa said. She was in the race and she was going to own Hayes Radner. It was small compensation for him trying to own her Honky Tonk, but it would be sweet revenge. To own him for three whole hours and he couldn't flirt with a single woman in the ball room. She would make a lot of art students very happy and hopefully Hayes Radner just as unhappy.

"Twelve five," Molly said.

"It's for the arts and tax deductible," Julia whispered.

"Fifteen," Larissa said.

"You can have him, honey. Ain't no man worth more than that for one evening," Emma laughed.

"Do I have anything higher than fifteen for Hayes Radner?" Martha asked. "Okay, going, going… gone! Will the voice in the middle of the women's side come forward and claim your slave. We can't see who's been bidding or I'd send him over to you on his hands and knees for that kind of donation."

Larissa stood up and the crowd parted.

Hayes couldn't believe his eyes when she started toward him. His mouth went as dry as if he'd been sucking on an alum lollipop. He blinked several times. Was it really Larissa? Or maybe just someone who looked enough like her to be her twin? He'd know if he could touch even her little finger. Sparks only danced when he touched Larissa.

"Ladies and gentlemen, it looks like our high bidder was Ruth Lawson. She might not look like her mother but she sure knows a hunk of good lookin' man when she sees it. Thank you, Ruth, for your donation and make him work for every dime of the money," Martha said.

"Oh, I plan on it," Larissa said. "Hello, Hayes."

"Hello, Ruth Lawson," he said curtly. So that was the reason he couldn't find out jack shit about the woman. She was a different person in Mingus, just like he was in Palo Pinto. Ruth Lawson? Where in the hell had he heard that name?

From my mother! She's been trying to fix me up with Doreen's daughter, Ruth, for at least five years. Well, get ready to drop in your first dead faint, Mother! Because Ruth Lawson is the tart, your words not mine, who called you a bitch.

"I believe I own you for this evening." She reached up and untied his bow tie and led him toward the door with it. The vibes between them hummed fairly well proving that Ruth and Hayes could produce as many sparks as Hank and Larissa.

The crowd clapped and whistled as she led him out into the flower gardens in the backyard. She heard Doreen tell Rupert that Hayes was the son of her friend that she'd been trying to get Larissa to meet for years.

"It must be fate," Doreen said.

If you only knew how much fate, you wouldn't believe it, Larissa thought.

The next man went on the block and the crowd's attention turned toward him. Larissa dropped the tie and sat down on a white cast iron bench. The rain had stopped and stars glittered around a big round moon hanging in the dark sky. The aroma of roses mixed with fresh rain and wet grass surrounded her. Water droplets hung on rose buds, and full blown roses were heavy with the moisture.

"That bench is wet," Hayes said.

"So my dress will get wet and I'll have the perfect excuse to go back to my hotel," she said.

Hayes sat down. "Sounds like a winning plan to me. So you are Ruth Lawson. The Ruth Lawson. That is so damn funny," he said.

"Why? And how many are there in the world that you would say *the* Ruth Lawson?"

"Because my mother has been trying to fix me up with you for years."

"You got to be shittin' me!" Larissa exclaimed.

"Doreen Lawson is my mother's friend. They've traveled the same circles for years, along with Martha."

"So tell me are you Hank or Hayes?" she asked.

"Are you Ruth or Larissa? And where did the Morley come from?"

"I'm Larissa. Mother told me my biological father's name was Morley. She didn't tell me that it was a nickname and that his real name is Larry Morleo. I'm still angry at you so don't try to change the subject."

"I'm angry with you too, so that makes us even."

"What have you got to be angry about?" She crossed her arms and glared at him.

"Same thing you do. You are Ruth Lawson and you didn't tell me. So I'm Hayes Radner and I didn't tell you. What's the difference?"

She shook her head emphatically and poked him in the arm with her forefinger. "That does not make us even. I wasn't trying to find out about you so I could undermine you and buy your business. My name might have been different but I'm still the same person. You are Hayes Radner now, not Hank Wells."

"You were trying to find out about me?" He removed her finger and held on to her hand, the warmth shooting desire through his body like an IV of pure vodka.

"Sure. I don't let any man get under my skin without finding out who he is. There's too much at stake."

"Your Honky Tonk?" He frowned.

"No, the Ruth Lawson stuff, which isn't nearly as important as my Honky Tonk. Too many men have hit on me with dollar signs in their eyes instead of love. I always investigate someone I'm interested in. You investigated me so don't be acting all innocent." She pulled her hand away. Another minute and she'd be pushing him backwards off the bench into the wet grass and having sex with him under the rose bushes. Thorns in her hind end didn't even sound like a bad trade for a romp in the cool wet grass with Hank.

"What is the Ruth Lawson stuff? You've really been to the Café de la Paix, haven't you? And the islands? All those places we laughed about, you've been there, haven't you? You were playing poor and laughing at me."

"The Ruth stuff is the same as the Hayes stuff and yes I've been to those places, but no, I was not laughing at you. I wasn't playing poor. I just wasn't claiming to be rich. Seems you were in the same place."

"I told you more than you did me," he said.

"Which still doesn't make up for the fact that you were Hayes. So don't take that attitude with me," she said.

"I'm not happy anymore," he said bluntly.

"Well, don't blame me. I didn't do it."

"Yes, you did," he protested.

"I won't carry the burden for that. You did it to your-self. You could have 'fessed up anytime. Like at the lake when we were in the water?"

He grimaced. "If it's any consolation, I wanted to tell you. I almost did that day at the house when we were painting but Sharlene arrived before I could tell you. What do we do now, Larissa?"

"Well, if you are Hayes, you can go to hell. If you are Hank, I'm starving and those finger sandwiches in there ain't going to do a thing to whet my appetite." She didn't tell him that it would take more than physical food to satisfy the longing in her heart.

"I'm your slave until midnight," he said.

"Then use your cell phone and call us a cab. Where is a good place to buy some boiled crawdads and Cajun rice?"

"I know just the place." He felt as if he'd just been given a second chance to get into heaven's doors.

And this time he wasn't going to blow it.

Chapter 14

"Y'ALL BEEN TO A WEDDING?" THE WAITRESS ASKED.

"A fundraiser," Hank said.

She pointed at Larissa and said, "I figured you for the maid of honor." She moved her finger to Hank, "And you for the best man. Guess I lost that dollar bet."

"What'd the other party think we were?" Larissa asked.

"Just plain old rich folks."

"Why'd you think we were part of a wedding party?" Hank asked.

The waitress pushed a strand of brown hair up under her cap. "Because folks that rich don't come in here, especially dressed up like y'all are. You're too old to be out for a prom and besides, the season ain't right. If you were at a fancy fundraiser then she was right and I was wrong and that means I'm out a buck."

"I'm sorry." Larissa opened her purse and put a twenty in the waitress' hand. "Pay off the bet and keep the rest for thinking we'd been to a wedding. I like that better than being rich."

"Thank you!" The waitress beamed.

Larissa wondered if she was a winner or a loser that evening. She glanced at the menu and folded it. The café sat between two empty warehouse buildings in a little weathered shack. The sign declaring it to be Crawdad Heaven swung from the ceiling of the porch. It was painted in stenciled letters with a crawdad wearing a halo at the end of the wording. The place was about the size of the Honky Tonk with booths along three sides and tables in the middle. Fishy aromas wafted through the kitchen into the dining room and she inhaled deeply.

"It doesn't take you long to make up your mind," Hank said.

"I know what I want," she answered. She looked around at the fish nets hanging from the walls and ceiling with sea shells thrown haphazardly into them.

He looked across the table. "In all things?"

"That's right."

"Want to expound upon that while we wait on our drinks?"

"Nothing to discuss. If you are Hank, you know what I want. If you are Hayes you know how important it is to me. This is a neat place. I wonder if the ladies at home would learn to cook crawdads. If they would I'd put in one just like this in Mingus. Any one of those old empty buildings would do to start. I'd finance it and we could give the Smokestack some competition. I'd best stop thinking about Larissa and Mingus. Ruth Lawson bought you so I'd better get into character."

He reached across the table and laid his hand over hers. "I'll always be Hank to you."

She shook it off and looked around the restaurant. "It's not the Brasserie Bofinger, is it?"

"No, but then I doubt the Brasserie Bofinger would serve crawdads. You want to go to Italy? We can be there in that restaurant tomorrow. I'll call the airline and book a flight. We can go just as we are and buy what we need there. Did you bring your passport?"

"No, I did not and I'm not interested in an impulsive flight with you. You broke my heart but it didn't kill me so I must be a stronger woman for the pain of it," she said.

"I'm so sorry, Larissa. Please forgive me," he said.

The waitress returned with two large glasses of iced tea and took their order for a bucket of crawfish with all the sides. The tea tasted better to Larissa than the wine she'd had at Martha's house.

Guess I've really made the change from Ruth to Larissa when I'd rather have a sweet tea as expensive wine, and jeans and boots as this gorgeous dress. I wonder where Hank is in his double life tonight. He said he'd always be Hank to me. What does that mean?

"What are you thinking about?" he asked.

"Why do you ask?"

"There's a faraway look you get in your eyes when you are into the deep thought. You had it," he answered.

"I was thinking about Ruth. That's who bought Hayes so that's who I should be tonight."

"And who is Ruth? I haven't met her. Is she your only alter ego or do you have many?" he asked.

"Only one alter ego and I'd forgotten about her until I came down here with Mother."

"Tell me about Ruth," he said.

"She's my opposite. Refined. Quiet. Well read. Artsy-fartsy. Loves the little sidewalk cafés in Paris and gelato in Italy. She wouldn't be comfortable in the Honky Tonk and that's why I'd forgotten about her."

"Tell me about her when she lived in Perry," he pushed.

"We were the quiet rich folks," she said.

"What's that mean?"

"Grandfather wasn't on every board in the town of Perry. He didn't run for county offices or wasn't on the board at the college in Stillwater. He made a bunch of money and then retired young to enjoy a simple country life. Everyone knew I lived out in the country in a fancy house. But after a while they thought my nanny was my real mother and that I lived there because my mother worked there. It was confusing because my mother told me my father's name was Morley and all the other kids went by their father's last name. But my mother, my grandfather, my grandmother, and I all had the same name and they told me my father had left my mother when I was a tiny baby."

She hesitated.

"Go on," he said.

"I existed and then one day I wanted to live. I can't explain it but I went on a scavenger hunt to find myself and wound up in Mingus. I went to places where my name didn't matter. I could be Betty Boop and no one cared. It didn't matter if I was rich or poor or if my name was Lawson or Morley. I started using my first name rather than my middle one and I liked who I was when I was Larissa. By the time I met you, I wasn't leading a double life. I *was* Larissa Morley."

He reached across the table and laid his hand on hers. "I know that."

"But you were living a double life. You were there on a mission and that was to break me down so I'd sell the Honky Tonk. You betrayed my trust and I don't give that to every beggar off the street."

He withdrew his hand. "I'm sorry. That's all I've got, Larissa. I can't undo it or redo it. I made a mistake in not telling you who I was but I can't turn back the clock."

"Why did you want my beer joint anyway?"

"I didn't. Mother did. It's taken two weeks, a damn good detective, and a lot of phone calls but I've got it pieced together. Mother and Dad were married before she ever knew a thing about Ruby Lee…"

She butted in. "What does Henry and your mother have to do with Ruby Lee?"

"Dad was in love with Ruby Lee. He'd met her at a cattle sale in Dallas. He was there to buy and she was working a second job as a bartender at the sale. They both fell hard and the heat between them lit up half the state of Texas. Her aunt died not long after they'd met and Ruby decided to build a beer joint in Mingus. She loved bartending more than office work and Mingus fit the bill for everything. It was right over the line into Palo Pinto County which was wet and Erath was dry. Dad wasn't very far away so they could see each other all they wanted. Dad was all for her moving close to him, even wanted her to move to the ranch and marry him. But the proposal had a condition. She had to give up bartending and not build a beer joint."

Larissa frowned. "Why? She was a bartender when he met her. You don't change people."

"Think back to the sixties. Women worked outside the home but respectable ones didn't operate a beer joint every night. Dad had a big ranch and lots of money and his pride got in the way. He didn't want folks to say his wife had to run a two-bit beer joint. She refused to marry him unless he let her do what she wanted. She built the

Honky Tonk. Then he's at another cattle sale in Dallas and one of his friends invites him to a party with him and his wife. He meets my mother who, in her words, had never seen so much man in a pair of boots. A few weeks later they flew to Las Vegas for a weekend of fun and they got married on a fluke. He told her about Ruby Lee on the way home. He says it was to clear the air so they could start off fresh."

Larissa whistled through her teeth. "Not a good choice."

He nodded. "Mother refused to give up her company and friends in Dallas. Can't you just see her on a ranch with cows and chickens? She wanted Dad to leave the ranch and go to work for her in the corporation. He'd have died within a year in the big city. Mother was jealous of Ruby Lee and afraid that Dad would go back to her since he and Mother were only together on weekends and you've got to remember how close Ruby Lee was every night of the week. So Mother got it in her head that she'd buy the Honky Tonk and Ruby Lee could go elsewhere. Ruby Lee laughed at her. It became an obsession and it's never ended. The amusement park was a ruse to rope me into the idea. Mother wanted it. She had the financial investors to back her so I went after it. I had no idea that Ruby Lee had played a part in Dad's past until this summer."

Larissa shrugged. "I see. Life does get tangled up like a fly in a spiderweb, don't it?"

"Yes, it does."

She looked across the table at him, straight into those whiskey colored eyes that she'd been so attracted to from the beginning. "I'm Larissa. Who are you going to be when you grow up?"

"I'm thirty-two years old. I guess I am grown up," he said.

"Not until you let one of you come out and play, and tell the other one to take his toys and go home."

He tested the waters. "Which one would you want to come out and play?"

"Honey, that's your decision. Talk to your heart. Not me or your mother or Henry can make that decision. Until you do, you're going to be miserable. I'm Larissa. I'm not Ruth. Ruth would like Hayes probably when she got to know him. Larissa wouldn't."

"Is that the voice of experience?" he asked.

She smiled. "It is."

The waitress arrived with a galvanized bucket of crawdads and poured them out in the middle of the oil cloth covered table. She tied a kitchen towel around Larissa's neck and repeated the process with Hank. "That's to protect your fancy duds."

"Does everyone get this treatment?" Larissa asked.

"Oh, yeah. We protect grease stained T-shirts just as much as we do tuxedos. We just get more of the T-shirts than we do tuxes. I'll be right back with your corn and potatoes."

Larissa picked up a crawfish, turned it over, and peeled the hard shell away from the white tail meat. She dipped it in red sauce and popped it into her mouth. "Mmmm," she muttered.

"Good?" He followed her example.

"Better than New Orleans. You ever ate them down there?"

"Never ate them at all but you are right, they are right tasty. Like big shrimp with more flavor," he said.

"You live close to this little place and you've never visited it?" she asked.

"One of the secretaries in the office pool is from southern Louisiana and discovered it. She was singing its praises last week," Hank answered.

The waitress brought a platter of corn on the cob and boiled potatoes. She picked up a pitcher from a nearby workstation and refilled their tea. "Anything else for you folks?"

Larissa shook her head.

"Then enjoy your meal." She quickly headed to a table where two new customers were seating themselves.

Larissa peeled, popped, chewed, and had another ready by the time she'd swallowed. She wiped her hands on the bright blue towel and buttered two ears of corn while she chewed that bite. She handed one to Hank who'd barely gotten the hang of peeling the tails.

"Try the corn while it's hot. They boil it and the potatoes in the same pot as the crawdads. It's wonderful." She held the corn in her hands and chewed her way around the side like a squirrel.

He did the same. "This is better than finger food at Martha's for sure."

"Glad I didn't let Emma or Holly outbid me?" she asked.

"I might have gotten more than crawdads from either of them," he answered.

She shot him a dirty look. "And what's that supposed to mean?"

He shrugged. "That I don't know what we are doing here. You have just as much of a two-people personality as I do. You were so mad at me at the town meeting that you were steaming hot and then you write a check for

fifteen thousand dollars for a few hours of my time after
you refuse to meet me for a talk. You don't want to be
Ruth Lawson but you were acting like her when you left
Holly and Emma in the dust of your dollars. That proved
to them that you were the daughter of the rich Doreen
Lawson. Larissa Morley wouldn't have done that. She
would have started the bidding at a dime or maybe even
a penny and had something to say about my sorry ass
not being worth anymore than that. She might have even
thrown something at me before she spit in my eye and
told me to enjoy my night with either Holly or Emma or
both of them. I liked her better than Ruth. And you are
sending mixed signals."

She wiped her hands and untied the towel. "And I
like Hank better than Hayes. From now on you can call
me Abe."

"Why's that?"

She stood up. "Because I'm freeing you. You are no
longer a slave but a free man to go where you please and
do what you want. Finish your dinner. I'm going home.
You are free to finish out the evening with Emma or
Holly or both of them on my dollar and tell them they
don't have to send a thank-you note."

He thought she was teasing until she walked up to
the front desk and talked to the waitress. In less than a
minute she was out the door, into a cab, and gone. He
started to run after her but the cab was gone before he
could wipe his hands and stand up. He sat down with a
sigh and looked at all the food before him. He was still
hungry and he'd have to pay for the dinner so he might
as well eat. She would be at the hotel or she'd drive back
to Mingus. Either way, she still had a cell phone. And

these days she was picking it up instead of letting it play the first part of "My Give a Damn's Busted."

He chuckled. Larissa did have a temper and it had surfaced. He was glad. He didn't like Ruth anyway. Granted, she was knock-down gorgeous in that red dress with her hair swept up on top of her head and she'd put an extra beat in Hayes' heart and made his pulse race. But she wasn't his Larissa, the woman he liked in cutoff blue jeans with a paintbrush in her hands or else jeans and a hay hook in both hands. Oh, sure, he'd have the same reaction if he saw her all dolled up in a dress and high heeled shoes as Hayes did. They were both men who appreciated beautiful women. Hayes would never look twice at Larissa. It would be Ruth that took his eye.

Hank had fallen for the impish woman with a foggy past. Now that he knew where she came from and what she really was doing in Mingus, he admired her even more.

Now the problem lying before him was deciding who the man was eating crawdads and corn with his fingers.

In the wake of Hurricane Larissa, he made a decision as he slowly peeled crawdads. He was Hank Wells, not Hayes Radner.

———

Larissa was sitting in the middle of her king-sized bed, eating a hamburger and fries from room service when her cell phone rang. She checked caller ID before she answered it. If it was Hayes or Hank, she wasn't answering it. She'd had enough of both of them for one night.

"Hello, Mother," she said.

"I'm outside your door. Can I come in?"

"Sure. I'm on my way." She pushed her food to one side, slid off the bed, and swung open the door.

Her mother swept into the room in a navy blue silk robe over matching pajamas. "What are you doing home so early?"

"How did you know I was home?" Larissa asked.

"Hayes came back to the party without you. I made excuses and Rupert brought me back to the hotel. What happened?"

"I'm having supper. Crawl up here on the bed and get comfortable. I'll tell you all about it. Does Rupert mind you leaving him alone?" Larissa asked.

Doreen shook her head. "He's fine."

"Tell me before I begin what Hayes did when he came back to the party."

"He put a bid on Martha's painting that very few people could think about outdoing. When a couple of women tried to talk to him, he said that he had been bought for the night and the rules were that he couldn't flirt. Martha laughed and said she was going to put him between a rock and a hard spot. He wasn't allowed to flirt but the rules didn't say anything about the losers flirting with him. When we left Emma and Holly were being absolutely shameless."

Larissa turned green and laid the remains of the burger and fries on the bedside table. "Those bitches. I might scratch their eyes out yet. What will he do with the painting?"

Doreen shook her head. "You can get mad at them if you want but it's useless. There will always be a bitch on the sidelines waiting to see if you are willing to fight for your man. It's up to you to keep them in their place. As far as the painting, he'll probably give it to his mother. She loves that kind of art. She and Martha were into that stuff way back when we were young and in college."

"Tell me about his mother," Larissa said.

"You were going to tell me about Hayes. It was pretty damn evident that you knew him or else you wouldn't have bid so high. When you left with him, I couldn't wait to tell Victoria that our children had finally gotten together. She was as excited as I was and wanted me to point you out to her but you were already gone."

Larissa giggled. "You go first. My story might keep you from telling me everything you know about his mother."

Doreen reached across her and picked up a cold French fry. "If you aren't going to finish that, hand it over to me. Fundraiser food isn't worth a shit, is it?"

Larissa giggled louder. "One weekend in Texas and Oklahoma and your accent and dirty words are back."

"It's what Rupert loves about me so I don't try to cover it up anymore."

"Talk to me about Victoria while you eat," Larissa said.

"Martha, Victoria, and I have been friends for more than thirty years. Back before my folks relocated to Perry we were in the same circles in this area. Then Daddy retired and wanted a quiet life so we went to Oklahoma and they stayed here. But once a year when we were little girls, they'd come to Perry for a week at the beginning of the summer. And Mother would bring me to Dallas for a week toward the end of the summer to shop for school clothes and play with them. Now skip ahead when we were in our twenties. Victoria had just finished college and met a cowboy named Henry who is Hayes' father. He was ten years older than her and sexy as hell. Look at Hayes and you'll understand. He's Henry at that age. Like they say in the love stories, he swept her off her feet. They married while they were in Vegas and about half-looped and she got pregnant right away. It was a nightmare pregnancy and divorce. Probably the catalyst for why I didn't want to marry your father or have you. Anyway, Martha and I got her through the bad times." Doreen stopped long enough to chew up a few more cold fries.

"Why was it so bad?" Larissa asked.

"Henry was in love with another woman. A low-class bartender and what do you grow up to be? A bartender? I just don't have the heart to tell her that bit of news even though she and Martha and I've shared everything all our lives."

Larissa took another bite of her burger. "Don't the world turn around? When are you going to tell Victoria that I own a beer joint?"

Doreen set her jaw in anger. "I do not intend to. Damn, Ruth. If she knew that she'd forbid Hayes from ever seeing you again. You are off doing charity work in a foreign country for all she knows."

Larissa's brown eyes widened. "You lied to her? And what gives her the right to tell Hayes that he can't see anyone? He's a grown man and he can make up his own mind about his love life. Does she think that she's God Almighty or something?" Larissa ranted.

"No, she told someone else that's what she'd heard and I didn't correct her. Get on the phone and tell room service to bring up three more of those burger dinners. I'll take one to Rupert. I know he's probably hungry too. And Victoria doesn't think she's God, honey. In her opinion she's far above God."

Larissa picked up the hotel phone and made the order. "So why was she mad at Henry? Hadn't he gotten over the bartender love thing?"

"Evidently on the flight home from the honeymoon he said that he wanted to clear the air and tell her about Ruby Lee. Don't that sound like a hick hooker's name? He said that he would always love Victoria but he wanted to be honest. Hell, he should've kept his mouth shut and moved to Dallas. He could be president of the company now," Doreen said.

"She really is high on herself, isn't she?" Larissa shook her head slowly.

"Victoria has always gone after what she wants. She wanted Henry and she got him but she should have waited. Another month and she'd have had him out of her system and there wouldn't have been a marriage or a baby. Then she wouldn't have had to raise a son by herself or go through that messy divorce."

"Okay, now it's my turn," Larissa said. "Remember yesterday when you said that I looked sad and only a man could do that to a woman? Well, you were right." Larissa went on to tell the whole story from the time she first hiked a hip onto a bar stool in the Honky Tonk, through the story of Cathy and her trials until she and Travis finally got together. Then she went backwards and told her mother what she knew about Ruby Lee, had found out about Henry, and that Hayes and Hank were two men in the same body.

"And I fell for Hank, the man who is Henry's son and works on a ranch. I do not like Hayes Radner. He's a son-of-a-bitch in every way."

Doreen gasped. "My God! I just made the connection. She called me and told me about the bartender at the same beer joint Ruby Lee built. That's your Honky Tonk, isn't it?"

Larissa nodded. "It is."

Doreen broke out into wicked laughter and couldn't control it. She fell backwards on the bed and put a pillow over her head but that only intensified the picture she had in her mind. Finally she threw the pillow on the floor and sat up. Her mascara had run down her cheeks in long black streaks and her lipstick was smeared.

"You called Victoria a bitch?" she asked between hiccups.

"Actually I called Hayes a bastard and she told me not to call him that. So I said then he was a son-of-a-bitch and told her that she couldn't argue with it," Larissa said.

"I can't wait until Hayes introduces you to her as Ruth Lawson at brunch tomorrow morning," Doreen said.

Larissa cut her eyes around at her mother. "What brunch?"

"I invited them to brunch with us here at the hotel before we leave. Martha and Julia, Victoria and Hayes, Rupert, you, and me."

Larissa slowly shook her head. "Tell Martha I hope my money helped. Tell Julia it was nice to meet her. Tell Victoria she's still a bitch. I'm going home first thing in the morning."

"Oh, no you are not. You might not be Ruth Lawson anymore and I'm not sure how she'd handle this situation but I know how the new Larissa would. She wouldn't run from the enemy. She'd stand up and fight and you will make that brunch. There's our room service. I'll just tell him to take it down the hall to our room."

Doreen was out the door before Larissa could argue.

Chapter 15

LARISSA THREW HER GARMENT BAG OVER HER SHOULDER AND wheeled her suitcase down to the lobby. She checked out of the hotel, gave the valet her ticket, and waited for her car. She'd wrestled with the brunch idea all night and had dark circles under her eyes to prove it. They could eat pancakes or cow patties and discuss the fundraiser or religion. She was like Rhett Butler: frankly, she didn't give a damn. She was going home.

"Is it set in stone?" Rupert asked so close to her that she jumped.

"What?"

"Your decision to leave without going to the brunch? Your mother stayed up half the night telling me about your story. You are a remarkable woman, Larissa."

"Thank you," she said. "Tell Mother to call me after the brunch."

"Why don't you stay and see the fireworks for yourself?"

"Don't want to. One question before I go. Where were you raised?"

"New York City until I was a teenager. Then my Italian mother took me back to her mother country when my father died. I loved it from the first day."

"I thought your accent had a little bit of pure old American in it. Well, good-bye Rupert. I'm glad you are marrying my mother. I'll see y'all at the wedding."

"Sure you won't change your mind?"

She shook her head.

The valet pulled her car under the awning and put her bags into the car. She tipped him and he held the door for her. She slid in behind the wheel and started the engine. He slammed the door shut.

She could not make herself shift from park to drive. Finally, she shut off the engine and got out. "Please park it again. I'll need it in an hour or less."

Rupert smiled and held out his arm. He looked right dapper in his khaki slacks and three button knit shirt. "I'm proud of you."

"Why?"

"You figure it out," he said.

"What were you doing out here anyway?"

"I go for an early morning walk every day. I was just returning from a few laps around the hotel grounds. At home, there's a hiking trail on my estate. Let's get a cup of coffee while we wait on the rest of the party. Your mother will be down shortly. I phoned her before I saw you about to run away."

Larissa bristled. "I wasn't running. I just wasn't being railroaded into another fight with the Radner Corporation. I'm sick of those people. I could have been driving home this beautiful fall morning instead of waiting for the first bomb of World War III to land. Have you alerted the staff that they'd better bend over, put their head between their legs, and kiss their ass good-bye when Victoria Radner breezes through the doors and sees me?"

Rupert laughed down deep in his chest. "If she starts firing I'll be your bodyguard. If you see a gun, head for the elevator. I heard the glass is bulletproof."

She grinned. "Reckon we ought to evacuate the upper floors? She might bring down the whole hotel like an implosion."

"Might not be a bad idea. Would you look at that? Doreen is coming down the elevator and they are arriving. Leave it to your mother to make a grand entrance."

Her heart skipped a beat then took off like a Russian race horse let loose from the chute when she saw Hank. He wore tight jeans, a chambray shirt with two buttons undone at the top, boots, and a big silver buckle. She hadn't seen him looking like that since the night he left her place after a full day of painting. She'd seen Hayes, but not Hank, and she wanted to run across the lobby and hug him so tight that she could feel their hearts beating in unison.

Victoria was beautiful in a casual pant set the color of her eyes. And Martha was the eccentric artist in a billowing tie-dyed gauzy skirt and matching top bloused with a wide sparkling gold belt. Doreen met them and gave each a kiss on the cheek. She was the pretty one with her red hair and plain little green dress with matching sandals.

Larissa held her breath as they drew near.

Rupert reached across the table and squeezed her hand for support, then stood and greeted the guests. "We got here early so we're having coffee."

"What the hell?" Victoria said.

"Hello, Larissa." Hank smiled.

"Hank." She nodded.

"It appears that our children got together on their own without any help from us," Doreen said. "I think you've met my daughter Ruth. Only she's changed her name and her lifestyle and is now Larissa. I'm learning to like Larissa even better than Ruth. Hello, Hayes. I haven't seen since you were a little boy. You grew up to be one handsome man. You should be proud of him, Victoria."

"I'm very proud of Hayes. I'm not so sure about this cowboy. Now would someone tell me why no one has explained this to me?" She pointed at Larissa.

"I guess I should've brought her around on our trips. Then you would have known who you were dealing with and wouldn't have tried to talk her out of her beer joint. But back when we were running around we didn't have much time for kids, did we?" Doreen laughed.

"It's not funny," Victoria snapped.

"Someone has to clue me in. I feel like I'm in the eye of a tornado and there's debris flying all around me. Wow! That's a wonderful idea for a painting. I'll have to work on it this afternoon. I'll call it 'Brunch before Disaster,'" Martha said.

"May I sit beside you?" he asked Larissa.

"Suit yourself," she said.

"Aha, the storm grows wilder. I see lots of red and black," Martha said as Rupert pulled out a chair beside Doreen for her. "Julia sends regrets. She and Tyler both had a hangover this morning."

Hank seated his mother and then settled between the two women. He could feel the wind from the emotional ice storm and it was chilly enough to keep ice cream rock solid for a month.

"Explain right now!" Victoria turned to Hank.

"I'd love to tell you all about this woman. Larissa is Ruth Lawson all grown up. I didn't know that since she's changed her name to Larissa Morley. Of course she thought I was Hank Wells. What would you like to know about her that you don't already?"

"I hate that name—Hank Wells. I should have never let your father talk me into naming you Henry or giving you both our last names, either. You should have been Hayes Radner like your grandfather. But no, he had to have it his way or else. So that's why you got all of it. Henry Hayes Radner Wells. I may go to the courthouse tomorrow and take the first and last ones off."

"Or the two middle ones," he said.

"I'm not getting into this with you in public and I'm not ruining Doreen's last day here," she said.

"When was the last time you saw Ruth?" Doreen asked.

"Probably when she was five or six and you brought her to Dallas for a weekend. Remember she got sick and spent the whole time after that first night in the room with her nanny. We'd planned on taking the children to the museums that day. I left Hayes at home since Ruth couldn't go," Victoria said.

Doreen smiled. "And you didn't recognize her? She hasn't changed."

"She damn sure has. She was a little brown-eyed girl who hid behind her nanny's skirt tails. Now she's mean as a snake," Victoria said.

The waitress brought a carafe of coffee and four more cups, took their orders, and left them to their battle.

"Thank you. I like that description. Just don't you forget it," Larissa said.

"She called me a bitch," Victoria snapped.

Martha poured coffee for everyone. "She got that part right. You are a bitch. Especially when you don't get your way."

"I'll deal with you later. You're supposed to be on my side," Victoria said.

Martha sipped the coffee. "Hot damn! That tastes good. I hate weak coffee. You might as well be drinking lukewarm piss as weak coffee. And I am on your side! But that don't keep you from being a bitch when you can't have your way."

"I bought that damned painting and paid twice what it was worth and you treat me like this in front of friends." Victoria pouted.

"You got a damn good deal on that art and you didn't buy it, Hayes did. Rupert would have paid three times its worth if Doreen had wanted it but she never learned to appreciate good art. She thinks a picture of a rocking chair on a front porch with a bucket of daisies on it is good art. God, anyone with a paint-by-number kit could do that kind of shit," Martha said.

Larissa wished she had been invited along when her mother went to visit her Texas friends all those years if they behaved this way all the time. They were all a hoot. Even Victoria who she'd previously tagged as colder'n a three-day-old corpse was nothing but a petulant little girl when she was with Martha and Doreen.

She poked Hank on the arm and wished she hadn't touched him. Vibes already had her humming. The touch had her nerves practically singing.

"So are you Hayes or Hank today?" she whispered.

Victoria bent forward and glared at Larissa. "He's Hank! Can't you tell? Are you blind as well as stupid?"

"And what would make me stupid?" Larissa shot back.

"You could have made a fortune on that shitty beer joint. I offered you a million plus for it. Anyone who'd hang on to a shack like that for sentimental reasons is stupid," she said.

"Guess that makes you even more stupid than me and still a bitch," Larissa said.

Victoria narrowed her eyes.

Larissa went on without skipping a beat, "Way I see it is you offered me fifty times what the place and land is worth in Mingus just for revenge on your ex-husband so that makes you pretty dumb and pathetic to boot. Add that to the bitchy nature and honey, you wouldn't have a snowball's chance in hell with any of the cowboys who come into my beer joint. If you'd change a little you might rope Henry into a dance or two even at your age."

"Ouch!" Doreen said.

Victoria shot daggers through her son and into Larissa's smart mouth. "At my age? I'm only a year older than your mother!"

"Try lookin' in a mirror. Bitterness sours the soul and ruins the countenance," Larissa said. They weren't her words but her nanny's; however, they fit the situation well.

The waitress set a hot platter of pancakes surrounded by strawberries and covered with warm maple syrup in front of each person. "Enjoy your brunch," she said.

"I can't eat a bite," Victoria said.

"Then pass yours over here. I'll eat them. I'm starving. Next time I do a fundraiser I'm having barbecue and potato salad catered in. I don't give a shit if someone drops a hot wing on their Versace," Martha said.

"You touch my plate and I'll put this fork in your greedy little paws. I'll try to eat a few bites but I'm still so mad I could take on the Yankees," Victoria said.

"Ball team or soldiers?" Larissa asked.

"Well, I'm not talking about a measly ball team."

Hank put up his palms. "Truce. At least until we get through eating. Martha, darling, was the fundraiser a success? I brought in fifteen grand and bought the painting. How much did you raise last night?"

"Half a mil," Martha said.

"With or without my money for the painting?" Victoria quipped.

Martha pointed her fork at Victoria. "Total. Eat or I'm going to steal your pancakes."

Victoria forked a small bite into her mouth and turned to Hank. "Why did you wear those abominable clothes?"

"You must have loved a cowboy or you wouldn't have married Henry. There's not a man alive that's more cowboy than he is," Larissa said.

She wished she would have bitten her tongue off rather than smarting off again to Victoria, especially when everyone around the table would think she was fighting for Hank. But put Hayes in cowboy boots and suddenly she went all mushy and defensive. Damn it all, tomorrow morning he'd be back in a three-piece suit trying to ruin another small town. He was like his mother and didn't need her to buy him a suit of armor to keep his mother from destroying his oversized ego.

Hank bit back the grin and stuffed pancakes into his mouth. Larissa mustn't hate him too bad if she was willing to take up for him.

"Henry was a mistake," Victoria said.

"If it was a mistake then let it go and move on. Thirty years is a long time to carry around a chip on your shoulder over a woman who's been dead for years now.

Might as well hang an albatross around your neck and run around smelling like shit all day," Larissa said.

"From the mouths of babes," Martha said.

"She's right," Doreen said.

"Oh, hush, both of you. I would expect you to take my side. How was I to know this spitfire hellcat was Doreen's daughter?" Victoria turned toward Hank. "How about you? Are you going to wear that to the office tomorrow?"

He shrugged.

"Don't come to work if you plan on it. I'll fire you on the spot. When you are in my presence you are Hayes Radner, not Hank Wells," she said.

He shrugged again. "I guess Dad could always use help this winter."

"Don't you threaten me," Victoria said.

His eyes flashed anger when he looked at her. "Right back at you, Mother."

Not a voice had been raised and a passerby would have thought they were having a nice family brunch before splitting up and heading in different directions. But the tension was so thick a sharp machete would have had trouble slicing through it.

"Okay, enough airing dirty laundry. We always have one lunch when we say what's on our minds. We've done it and now it's time for us all to be civil," Doreen said. "Are you both coming to Italy for my wedding next month?"

"I wouldn't miss it," Martha said hurriedly. "I may stay a month."

"You are welcome," Rupert said. "We'll be gone most of that time on our honeymoon. Just make yourself at home and visit all the art galleries you can fit into your schedule. The staff will be there to take care of whatever you need."

Victoria pushed the rest of her pancakes across the table to Martha. "I may be able to get away for a week."

Doreen clapped her hands. "Then make it the week before the wedding. You'll both have to be fitted."

"For what?" Martha almost choked.

"Dresses for the wedding. You'll both stand up with me."

"Dear God, a bride's maid at fifty-one. That's a ghastly thought," Martha said. "If you put me in apricot ruffles and make me carry a parasol I will hate you forever. Hell, I might do one better and puke on the dress."

"I was thinking a black and white wedding would be nice. Will you be coming with Ru... I mean, Larissa?" Doreen asked Hank.

His face lit up.

A smile tickled Larissa's wide lips but she firmed up her mouth and refused to let it materialize. He would not be going with her. No siree! He'd shot that idea down like a bird out of a tree when he betrayed her trust in him. Hayes Radner could go with his mommy dearest.

"I'm invited?" he asked.

"Sure, come with your mother."

He groaned. "Do I have to?"

"No, you don't," Victoria said. "I refuse to ride on a plane with you if you wear cowboy boots and a hat."

"You are still invited," Doreen said.

Victoria stuck her tongue out at her.

Larissa spewed coffee across the table, spraying the front of Rupert's white shirt. "You are acting like children. Boy, I had the whole bunch of you pegged wrong.

I thought you were all stiff-necked aristocrats and you are nothing but pissy teenage girls."

Victoria tilted her head up and looked down her nose at Larissa. "I am a stiff-necked aristocrat and I do not like you. It's only with Martha and Doreen that I'm like this. They and you bring out the very worst in me."

"Well, butter my fat ass and call me a croissant. Don't you lay the blame on us. You always were the worst of the bunch of us," Martha said.

"Ladies. Rupert. Hank. It's been an education. Thank you for talking me into staying, Rupert. I've got to get on the road toward home. Mother, walk me out to my car." Larissa stood up.

"I'll walk you out," Hank offered.

"No, you stay here and keep your mother in line. I'll go with her," Doreen said.

Hank set his mouth in a firm line. "Keep my mother in line? That's an impossible job. I'd rather walk Larissa to her car."

Larissa wore jeans and a tank top that morning. Her hair was down and she had on very little makeup. He could almost taste the sweetness of a lingering kiss.

"It's a big job, always has been. But you're Henry's son and you can do it. And I've still got a few things to say to Larissa before I let her go. Come on, my child. We've got a lot to talk about and a very short distance."

Larissa looped her arm in Doreen's. It was the first time Doreen had referred to her as her child and it felt good.

When they were halfway across the lobby, she asked, "Why did you change your mind?"

"About what?"

"Me? Telling me about my father. Accepting my Honky Tonk lifestyle."

"I'm in love. Thank Rupert for all of it."

"Why Rupert? You've always gone for young men."

"I'm fifty this year and this is the first time in my entire life that someone needs me to be happy. It's intoxicating to think that someone actually needs me. Not that I need them or that they are providing for my every whim. I'm needed. My parents didn't need me to be happy. None of the men in my life needed me. Hell, Larissa, you didn't even need me. Rupert does. He says without me he's only half a man. I'm happy with him. I've found my soul mate. But don't get too comfortable in that mud you live in, darlin', because I'd still do anything to shake you out of it. Telling you about your father was something that needed to be done. Do with it what you will but I don't want to know about it. Promise me that much?"

"I promise. You're not going to shake me out of my Honky Tonk or my turquoise house, Mother."

"And you saying that isn't going to make me stop trying. You won't back out of coming to Italy for the wedding, will you?"

"I promise I'll be there. Why there, though? Why not in Perry?"

"Because my home is in Italy and that's where I want to be married. Now give that handsome young valet your ticket and call me when you get home. This has been a wonderful weekend. I love the fact that my daughter got the best of Victoria Radner. I've been trying for years and couldn't get the job done." She smiled.

Larissa kissed her on the cheek. "I'm glad I came. It was worth the fifteen grand."

Janice, Betty, and Linda were at her house before she had time to call Stallone inside and give him a handful of treats. Janice brought a pound cake and frozen peaches. Betty set about making a pot of coffee and Linda helped carry in the last of her bags.

"Were any of you at the Tonk the last couple of nights? Did Sharlene do all right by herself? What's happened in town?" She bombarded them with questions after she threw her bags in her bedroom.

"One thing at a time. You want whipped cream or ice cream on your peach shortcake?" Janice asked.

"Ice cream."

"We were at the Honky Tonk both nights. Sharlene did just fine. She got busy once and Tessa helped out behind the bar. She filled beer jars and Sharlene made drinks. Not much happens in Mingus in a year's time, so nothing happened in two days, darlin'." Janice topped the peaches with ice cream.

"So Tessa and Luther?"

"Are still in love and fighting it. Like I said, two days ain't two years," Janice said.

She dipped into the ice cream and peaches. "I feel like I've been gone two years."

"Then you are truly at home in Mingus. If you miss this place it has to be home," Linda said.

"Hey, hey, where are y'all?" Sharlene called from the door. "I was out in the backyard and saw your car go by the Honky Tonk so I came right over. Someday I'm going to buy a fancy little car like that and go to big old fancy fundraisers in Dallas. How did it go? One of my co-workers covered it for the newspaper said it was a riot. That the artist decided to have a slave auction and sold off the men. The story is going to hit the paper on Monday. Tell me what happened before it does so I can gloat next time I see her. I hope there's more of that shortcake or else you're all going to have my spoon in your bowls."

"There's plenty," Janice finally slipped a word in when Sharlene had to suck up a lung full of air.

"Well hot damn! That means I get all I want. Sit still. I'll help myself while Larissa tells us about the party. Did one sorry sumbitch really bring fifteen grand? What fool gave out that kind of money for a man? Hells bells, the best of the lot wouldn't be worth a third of that on a good day and the worst, well, shit, a dollar ninety-eight wouldn't buy their sorry asses."

"That would be me," Larissa said.

The three older women stopped eating and stared at her.

Sharlene set off on another river of words. "God, this is good. Did you make this pound cake from scratch? I'm going to learn to cook one of these days. Momma said the only way to catch a man was to learn to cook and I wasn't too damned interested in any of the men in Corn, Oklahoma, so I wasn't too… what did you say, Larissa?" she asked when Larissa's answer sunk in.

"I said the fool who gave fifteen grand for the sorry ass man was me," Larissa answered.

Sharlene stared at her like she had two heads and both of them were sprouting devil horns. "Was the check hot?"

"No, it was good."

"Was the man hot? Good God, did Martha auction off someone like Blake Shelton or Josh Turner?" She named two young country music artists.

"No, I paid fifteen large for Hank Wells."

Janice gasped. "You didn't!"

"I did. I bought him and he had to be my slave," Larissa said.

"I expect you'd better talk while Sharlene is speechless," Linda said.

Larissa licked the last remnants of peach juice from her spoon. "It's a hell of a long story."

"I've got until opening time tomorrow night," Sharlene whispered.

"We've got until night church starts. That's four hours. You better get started," Betty said. "I'll pour the coffee and we'll go to the living room. Get comfortable, girls. I think this one might be even better than the gossip session of the Sunday school ladies after the town meeting."

"Trust me, it is," Larissa said.

Chapter 16

LARISSA AWOKE TO THE HUM OF VOICES. SHE PUT A PILLOW over her head and convinced herself that she'd left the television on the night before. It could play on and she'd go right back to sleep. She shut her eyes tightly and imagined a black wall but suddenly it was filled with pictures of Hank. A woman damn sure couldn't sleep with those images. So she forced herself to count fluffy sheep jumping over a white picket fence. She got to three before the shepherd popped his head around the end of the fence. And he was Hank in a shepherd's robe that was open halfway to his waist. Her imagination started thinking about how easy it would be to pull that string around his waist and let the wind do the rest.

She'd already given up on time-honored recipes for insomnia when Stallone jumped up on the bed. His breath smelled of fresh cat food and he settled down right beside her nose to wash his tail end. She remembered distinctly putting him out the night before because she had to do it twice. It had been raining and he dashed back inside the warm, dry house before she could shut the door.

She sat up and got a whiff of coffee aroma from the kitchen. The ladies never came before noon and she hadn't told Sharlene where to find the hidden key. Only the ladies and Luther knew that it was under a rock in the flower bed. She checked the clock. Eight thirty. That meant she'd had less than six hours of sleep. Whoever had let the cat inside and was talking on her porch had better have a damn good reason to wake her up.

She didn't bother with a robe but plowed through the kitchen and living room, out the open door, and onto the porch. "Luther, what in the devil are you doing talking to yourself on my porch at this ungodly hour of the morning? Go to work and let me get some sleep."

He was sitting on the porch step with a cup of coffee in his hand and a pitiful look on his big round face. "Me and Tessa had us a big fight. I don't want to go to work and face her."

She popped her hands on her hips. "Whose fault was it?"

He hung his big round head and looked sheepish. "Mine?"

She sighed. "I'll get a cup of coffee and you can tell me all about it."

"Don't need to. I been here an hour. Made coffee and me and Stallone visited for a while. I got to get me a cat. They're right good listeners and they don't tell a man to do something stupid like ignore the problem and it'll go away," he said.

Larissa yawned. "Well, if you and the tomcat have it all worked out, I'm going back to bed."

Luther held up a hand. "Wait a minute. I didn't say that. Stallone got to whining for food so I let him in and fed him."

Larissa must've been even more exhausted than she'd realized. She hadn't even heard Luther and he didn't move like a twinkle-toed fairy. "Okay, then I'll get a cup of coffee and you can finish telling me what's happened before you go to work."

"Naw, I'm going to work and me and Tessa going to get this all settled before it eats a hole in my heart. I couldn't even sleep last night for it. I don't have to be to work until noon every day but I can't wait that long to get it done," he said.

"But that's not fair. You wake me up, let my cat in the house, and I don't get to hear the story. Will you tell me tonight before we open the Tonk?"

"I'll tell you," a voice said to her right.

She whipped around to see Hank sitting in one of her newly painted bright orange rocking chairs. She blinked a dozen times but the apparition did not go away like it did when she opened her eyes in the bedroom. He wasn't a shepherd but his shirt was undone almost to the waist.

"What are you doing here?" she asked.

Luther shook Hank's hand and lumbered out across the yard to a company truck. "I'm going to work now. Hank, if you see that rascal Hayes, you tell him to keep the hell out of the Honky Tonk. I'll still wipe up the parking lot with his sorry ass if I ever see him again."

"I can do that but I don't think he's got the balls to show his face in Mingus again," Hank said.

Larissa melted into the other rocker before her legs completely failed her and she fell on her face out in the yard. "I asked you a question."

"I'm sitting on your porch pretending that road out there is the ocean and I'm in a beach house that is supposed to look like this. If I threw some hay up on the roof, it would help the effect even more. Seriously, it don't look as bad as I thought it would all painted up like one of those doll houses you buy little girls at Christmas," he said.

His boots were worn down at the heels, his jeans faded, and his straw hat stained. It was Hank, all right, and he looked very, very fine. The devil in blue jeans on her front porch. But was it Hayes in cowboy clothes? That fool man couldn't be trusted at all, period, A-damn-men, and he might don Hank's clothes just to get even with her.

"What are you doing in Mingus on a Wednesday? I could understand a Saturday but this is the middle of the week. Aren't you supposed to be behind a big desk in a corner office of Radner Corporation?" she asked.

He started at her bare toes and slowly made his way up her legs to the knit nightshirt stopping at knee level, on up to a picture of Betty Boop on the front, and then to her face. Lips begging for the first morning kiss even though she'd still taste like sleep. Eyes that he could fall into forever. Hair mussed from the pillow. A very faint smell of smoke still in it which said she'd been too tired to shower after work. So that meant she'd had a busy night at the Honky Tonk.

His eyes were on a journey and every inch they traveled set another bit of her skin on fire. She wanted him to look at the cat, at the pretend ocean again, anything at all but at her. When he reached her hair her scalp tingled.

"Are you going to stare at me or answer me?" she snapped. If he touched her she would burst into flames.

"I quit my job and Dad put me to work permanently at the ranch," he said.

"Why?" Her insides quivered.

Hank was home.

He would be living on the ranch.

"Hayes and I had this big fight. I won."

"Oh?" she said.

He'd put Hayes to flight. She should be jumping for joy but down in the depths of her soul, she knew the other shoe could drop any time. There was always the possibility that things would be great for a few weeks, then he would get restless and the shoe was only dangling by a thin string. She couldn't go through the pain again. Garth Brooks sang a song where he said he could've missed the pain but he would have had to miss the dance. Well, Larissa had danced and had the pain. Her heart couldn't take a repeat performance and keep beating.

"What happens when you have another big fight because Hayes has gotten restless at the ranch and wants to go home to his fancy apartment and go to parties where his cute little ass brings fifteen grand on the auction block?" she asked.

"Then I'll win again. I'm stronger than he is and I'm finally doing what I should've been doing for years. I'm going to refill my coffee cup. You want one?"

"Yes, I would," she said.

She drew her feet up into the chair, stretched her nightshirt down to cover her toes, and wrapped her arms around her knees. Her hair billowed out around her face when she plopped it forward resting her chin on her knees. Her sweet little world she'd found with a plastic headed thumbtack had just been blown to smithereens. A Hiroshima-type bomb couldn't have done a better job. Hank was going to be a full-time rancher and Luther had even made friends with him again. Sunday morning she was driving to Perry and pulling that map down again. Surely she didn't belong in Mingus anymore.

"Here you go," he said.

She brushed her hair back and reached for the mug. "Thank you."

Using one finger he tucked a strand behind her ear. "You missed one."

His touch was as soft as a butterfly kiss. How could something that gentle feel like dynamite exploding in her heart? "Now I know what you are doing in Palo Pinto County. Tell me what you are doing in Mingus and on my porch."

"Waiting for you to wake up so we can talk," he said.

"There's nothing to talk about."

"Yes, there is. At least you didn't come out here throwing rocks and threatening me with a restraining order is a good start. We'll build on that. It's enough for one day. I'm here and I'm not leaving," he said softly.

"You going to live on my porch forever? If you got a dumb ass notion like that, darlin', then I might have to think about a restraining order or else talk to Henry about committing you."

Hank chuckled. "You know what I mean, Larissa. I'm back in the area and I'm here to stay. Get used to seeing me around."

"You'll get bored," she said.

"Can't. This summer when I was here Dad said that he was ready to retire. He'd sell the ranch and put part of the money into a trust fund for me or else he'd give me the ranch. I had a year to think about it. It took less than a month to figure out where I really want to be. So

I can't leave. Besides, Mother is one pissed off woman. I'm not sure I could crawl back into her good graces."

"You'll hate it in a year."

"You've been here almost a year. Do you hate it?"

"Hell, no!"

He set the empty cup on the porch and rose up from the rocker, reminding her of the day at the lake. That hot afternoon she'd likened him to a Greek god with water sluicing over his muscular body. That fall morning he stretched and became a flesh and blood mortal that she liked even better than the mythological god from the past, but she wasn't falling into a relationship with him again. She still didn't trust him, not even if he did just make a big declaration about being a rancher and putting Hayes Radner on the run.

"I rest my case. Thanks for the coffee and the visit. I got to get on down to Stephenville. Dad needs a tractor part and that's the only place that's got one available right now," he said.

She sipped the coffee. "That is a crock of shit. Mineral Wells is a hell of a lot closer than Stephenville and I bet they've got tractor parts."

"You'd have to see the tractor. Mineral Wells doesn't have any antique tractor parts dealers. There's an old feller in Stephenville who has a tractor graveyard. When Dad needs a part he can find it there. Want to come along?"

She shook her head. "I'm going back to bed."

He leaned down and kissed the top of her head. "Sleep tight. Don't let the bedbugs bite."

She left half a cup of coffee on the porch and went straight back to bed. But she couldn't sleep. Everything that had happened from the time they'd been introduced by a deer to that morning played through her mind like a television movie. There he was with the hot Texas summer wind blowing his shirt out while he cussed and ranted about the damn deer; on the bar stool in the Honky Tonk; dancing with her; baling hay; painting the house. Trust building with each passing day only to be broken like a thin crystal wine glass when it hits a concrete floor.

Finally she threw the pillow at the wall and jumped out of bed. She stormed into the kitchen and ate three chocolate chip cookies. That didn't help so she drank milk straight from the jug and still felt restless. She made a circle through the house. From her bedroom, through the kitchen where she picked up another one of Linda's chocolate chip cookies from the table and ate it as she paced, through the living room, the spare bedroom, short hall, and back to her bedroom. Twenty minutes and dozens of rounds later she fell back on the sofa.

She would not run away. And she wasn't putting a tack on a map again. It had worked the first time but she wasn't pulling up roots and leaving her home. Hank Wells wasn't making her sell out any more than Hayes Radner had

The clock said it was ten o'clock and it was Wednesday. That meant the ladies would be out of town doing their shopping and having their hair done. The garden had stopped producing and she'd pulled up all the plants so she couldn't spend the rest of the day playing in the dirt. Sharlene would still be asleep. And she wanted to talk. She called her mother but got the answering machine. She hung up without leaving a message.

"Merle," she said aloud. She'd never been to Merle's place but she had a general idea of where she lived. She jerked her nightshirt over her head on the way to the bathroom, took a quick shower, dressed in jeans and a T-shirt, and grabbed her keys and purse on the way out the door.

The mailbox had M-rle Ave-y written on it in black block letters that could be purchased at any hardware store. A "No Trespassing" sign hung on both sides of the fence leading the way up to the house. None of the letters were missing on those signs. She turned across a cattle guard and drove slowly through the pecan tree-lined lane. The house was a long, low ranch house set at the back side of a circular driveway. The flower beds were a blaze of fall colors with yellow, bronze, and gold mums, bright pink and red roses still putting out blooms, dianthus in all shades of bright colors, and rose moss creeping along the edges. It reminded Larissa of the flower beds in Perry. Their gardener took great pains and delight in his flowers and she'd always loved them every season of the year.

She stood beside the car and made a decision never to sell the Perry house. Too many people would be affected if she did—Rosa, the housekeeper, who'd been there at least thirty years; Manny, the gardener; Cleo, the cook; and Lanson, who took care of the garage and all the vehicles in it as well as the pool in the summertime. Four people who'd taken care of her, along with Nanny, and had been there since her grandparents moved into the house. They'd helped raise Larissa. They'd been there when Nanny died. They'd always welcomed Doreen home. They lived in two apartments in a wing off to one side of the place. Rosa and Manny in one; Cleo and Lanson in the other.

"Are you going to come in or stand out there and stare at the flowers all day?" Merle yelled from the door.

Larissa looked up and smiled. "Good morning. They are beautiful. Who is your gardener?"

Merle stepped out onto the porch. "Me. Old southern women are supposed to grow flowers. I put the flower beds in when Ruby Lee died as a memorial to her. Seemed a waste to take flowers to the grave to lie there and die. She was a live wire, not a wallflower, so I planted flowers and when I get lonesome for her, I come out here and sit on that bench and we talk. What in the hell are you doing up and about at this time of morning after the night you had at the Honky Tonk?"

Larissa stopped at the bottom of the porch steps. "What do you do in the winter?"

"I plant pansies and that purple shit that looks like overgrown cabbages. I reckon she don't care what it looks like as long as I don't forget to tell her everything that happens. I've got lunch ready. Made soup today. We'll eat early today. Come on in. You can answer my question while we eat." Merle held the door for her.

"That sounds wonderful, and is that bread I smell?"

"Cornbread to go with the soup. I whipped up some cinnamon rolls for dessert."

"Who else are you expecting?"

"I got up this morning with a feeling that someone would be coming by. Thought it might be Angel. She still might run through sometime today. She often does.

It's closer to come out here than to drive all the way back to the ranch and besides, Garrett's noon and hers is two different things." Merle led the way through the small foyer into a great room that housed living room, dining room, and kitchen.

"Love your house. Want to sell it?" Larissa asked.

"Hell no! Had it built when we came to Mingus exactly the way I wanted and I ain't changed my mind about what I want far as a house goes in all these years. Honey, terrorists couldn't blow my old ass out of it. I'll show you the rest of it after we eat."

"What can I do to help?" Larissa asked.

"Bowls are on the bar with the cornbread. Soup is on the stove. Don't need to do anything but help yourself. We'll eat in here at the kitchen table since there's only two of us. It's cozier. Now tell me what brings you to my house today?" Merle picked up a bowl, crumbled cornbread in the bottom, and carried it to the stove, where she filled it.

Larissa did the same. "Tea in the fridge?"

"Yes, it is. Ice in the door. Make us both one," Merle said.

Larissa blew on a spoonful of hot vegetable soup before she put it in her mouth. "Good," she muttered.

"Picante sauce."

Larissa's eyes asked the question.

"That's the secret. Half a cup of picante sauce. It spices it up and puts a little fire into it. I'm always glad for company but why are you here, Larissa?"

"I woke up to find Luther and Hank both on my porch this morning."

"Luther is fighting with Tessa. She wants to ask you if she can work the bar a couple of nights a week to make some extra Christmas money. She helped Sharlene the other night and she's damn good. Luther don't want her to work in a bar."

"Well, that's a double standard. He works for me," Larissa said.

"Yes, it is and they'll work it out. Luther is still carrying around baggage about his ex-wife and that driller that she had an affair with. He's got to let it go and realize Tessa isn't that piece of trash. She's a good woman. I'm sure Luther wanted you to tell him he was right and to ask you to not hire Tessa. Now what in the hell was Hank doing there?"

Larissa tipped up the tea. "He said he and Hayes had a fight and he won. He says he wants to be Hank on a full-time basis. Henry is giving him the ranch and he's going to be a rancher."

"You got a problem with that?" Merle asked.

"He'll get bored. He's used to the fast life."

"Did you? Mingus is a little smaller than Cairo or London or even Stockholm. They're a hell of a lot more exciting than Dallas, Texas, and you lived in all of them before you moved here. It sounds to me like you and Luther got a lot in common."

"What?" Larissa was dumbfounded. She'd expected Merle to offer to have Hank killed like she had an old boyfriend of Cathy's back in the days when Cathy owned the Tonk.

"Luther's judging and so are you. Maybe not for the same reasons. You didn't know Hayes except for a day, hell, for less than an hour. How do you know that he wasn't dissatisfied with Dallas before he ever met you or came to Mingus this last time?"

"Are you telling me to pick up where we left off?"

"Hell no! You got to start all over if you are interested in that cowboy. Toss the past out the window and start from scratch. Just like me when I make a mess of a shirt. I can't very well put a patch on the design and expect to sell the damn thing. I have to throw it in the trash can, pick up a piece of material, and build another shirt. That's what you've got to do *if* you are interested," Merle said.

"What about trust?"

"That's why you start over. That trust is gone. You never could trust Hayes. Now you got to see if you can trust Hank. And that's already a bit shaky so don't get in a hurry. Give it time. Build a good solid foundation. You can't put up a house without a foundation that'll weather cold, hot, and everything in between. Learn to be his friend and let him be yours. Then go from there."

Larissa smiled. "How'd you get so smart?"

"Old age."

"You? Don't give *me* that line of shit. Merle Avery is ageless."

"For that you get two cinnamon rolls."

The Honky Tonk was full five minutes after the doors opened. Wednesday night used to be the slowest night of the week. Not so, anymore. Three-for-a-quarter songs about cheatin' and drinkin', cold beer, good mixed drinks, and a bouncer who kept things from getting out of hand kept people waiting in the parking lot for someone to leave.

"Need some help?" Tessa asked. She was a tall brunette with green eyes and a splash of freckles across her nose. Black plastic framed glasses perched on her nose that was just slightly too large for her face. Tight jeans stretched across a bottom that was wider than her top half. She had a ready smile and a quick wit.

Larissa thought about it for less than a minute before she nodded. Luther might get mad but he could get glad in the same britches. She did need help and she'd already had it from a damn fine source that Tessa could do the work.

"I pay minimum wage and you keep your tips. You run the beer handles, Tessa. Sharlene, you move up to mixed drinks. I'm going to work the bar and do buckets. Anyone gets in a bind, holler and I'll help whoever needs it," Larissa said.

"Fair enough," Tessa said.

"Luther going to quit because of this?" Sharlene asked.

"That's Luther's problem," Larissa said.

"We had us a talk. He's fine with it now," Tessa said. "But I'm glad you hired me without asking. I hear that Hank Wells is back in town. What do you think of that?"

"Hey, can I get a bucket of longneck Coors?" A customer asked from the far end of the bar.

Larissa grabbed a galvanized milk bucket, shoved six bottles of beer into it, and added two scoops of ice. She carried to the end of the bar and set it in front of the man.

"You got a Wednesday special on this, right?" he teased.

"Sure I do. On Wednesday you get it for twice the amount you pay on Tuesday," she shot back at him.

"That the price for drinkin' instead of listenin' to preachin' on a church night?" he asked.

"You got a guilty conscience?"

"Not me!" He handed her a twenty-dollar bill.

She made change and counted it back to him.

"Want to dance? I see you got lots of help and no wedding ring."

"Don't dance with customers," she said.

"Too bad. I'm a damn fine dancer."

Hank slid onto a bar stool. "I know one customer you danced with once upon a time."

"Yes, and look what it got me," she said. Her crazy heart was acting like her fat cells when they found a hidden candy bar. Over the top with excitement and couldn't wait to get the paper off and taste the sweetness.

"What did it get you? Sharlene, could I get a martini?" Hank raised his voice but didn't take his eyes off Larissa's face. If fate would let him, he would be content to sit on that bar stool the rest of his life, sinking into the depths of her brown eyes.

"It got me in a mess and I thought Hayes was gone."

"He is."

She nodded toward Sharlene who was heading toward the mixed drink table. "Martini?"

"Hank likes them too. Especially the ones that he gets in the Honky Tonk. They're almost as good as the owner is beautiful."

"Flattery will get you nowhere," she said.

"I'm not uttering words of flattery, ma'am. I'm speaking the pure gospel truth."

Sharlene looked at Larissa before she even made the martini. At her nod she put it together and set it in front of Hank. "What are you doing here?"

"I been answerin' that question all day. I'm here for a drink and a little conversation with the customers, to listen to some good old country music and watch the dancin'. I'd ask the pretty boss to dance with me but she told that other man that she don't dance with customers. I guess that's what I am tonight so that's what I'm doing here," he said.

"I need help," Tessa called.

"Enjoy the martini." Larissa left Hank on the bar stool and went to help draw a dozen beers.

"What happened?" Sharlene whispered out the side of her mouth. "I figured you'd shoot him on the spot if he ever showed his face in the Tonk again."

"I'll tell you the whole story after we close tonight," Larissa promised.

"That's five and a half hours from now. I can't wait that long."

"Short version then. He's moved back permanently. Showed up on my porch this morning. More later."

"That'll keep me until we close," Sharlene said seriously.

Chapter 17

LARISSA DIDN'T WANT TO WAKE UP. SHE PEEKED AT THE clock to find that it was noon. Stallone was stretched out on the pillow next to her, his eyes wide open and set on her face. Voices carried from the porch into the house for the second morning.

"Shit!" Larissa moaned. Two mornings in a row was too damn much. The smell of coffee reached her nose and she threw back the sheets. She padded barefoot to the kitchen, poured a cup, and sat down at the table. Luther and Hank needed to find a new place to take their morning break or she was going to put a quart jar on the porch and charge them to sit in her orange rocking chairs. For two men who hated the colors she'd picked out they were damn sure making themselves at home there.

She cocked her head to one side and strained her hearing. That wasn't Luther's voice or Hank's. One of them was a woman's and the other was deep and slow. The masculine one asked a question and the woman talked… and talked… and talked.

"Sharlene!" Larissa said.

Stallone went to the door and meowed pitifully. He reared up on his hind legs toward the doorknob and looked back over his shoulder frantically.

"Okay, okay. I can see you are trying to cross your legs," she griped. She opened the door and he made a beeline to the edge of the porch, dug a hole, and squatted.

"Guess he was in a hurry," the deep voice said with a laugh.

"When you gotta go, you gotta go. Come on out here, Larissa. We won't have many more mornings this nice. Sun is out and the birds are chirpin'," Sharlene called out.

She carried her cup of coffee to the porch. Sharlene occupied one rocker and Henry the other.

He got up and motioned for her to sit. "I'll take the porch step."

"Keep your seat. I'll take the step," she said.

"I ain't arguing with you. I don't have much trouble gettin' down but the gettin' up is a different matter."

Sharlene's kinky red hair was pulled up into a frenzied ponytail. Her paint splotched jeans were faded at the knees and her shirt had been red at one time but was almost pink. She wore her work boots with scuffed toes and worn-down heels.

"I used the key you told me about last night and went on and made coffee since you was still asleep. Stallone was hungry so I fed him," she said.

Larissa looked at Henry.

"I was here before her. Had to run down to Stephenville for another tractor part. Ought to sell the damn things to the man for the tractor cemetery and let him make a few bucks on what parts are good. But I've got a sentimental vein in my heart for old things. Can't bear to get rid of them long as there's parts to fix them. Ever hear that quote about a broke give-a-shit?"

Larissa shook her head.

"If your give-a-shit has a crack, you can fix it; if it's plumb broke you might as well throw it out."

"Kind of like the song by Jo Dee Messina," Larissa said.

"Yep, she probably got the idea from that old saying," Henry said.

Sharlene fidgeted with the chair arms. "Guess I better come right on out with it. It's all bottled up inside of me and makin' me nervous as hell. My paycheck came in the mail this morning. I got my pink slip and a letter. It said they'd give me a very good recommendation for another job but they were cutting back staff again. Last come, first to go type thing. So I'm out of a job at the newspaper. Is that going to be a problem?"

"Not for me. You making enough at the Tonk to live on?" Larissa asked.

"Without rent or utilities and since my car is paid for, I am."

"How much are you savin'?" Henry asked.

"That's a different matter, but I don't have to have a big savings account. If I've got a roof, a place to work, and something to eat, I can be happy," Sharlene said.

"You got a dollar an hour raise starting tonight since you are definitely full time now. What are you going to do during daylight hours?"

Sharlene flashed them a big smile. "Write a book. Please don't think I'm crazy. It's been keeping me awake at night just thinkin' about it. I've already got it named and I think it'll be a best seller."

"I think that's a great idea," Larissa said.

Sharlene wiped her forehead dramatically. "You don't think it's a waste of time?"

Henry reached across the distance separating the chairs and patted her arm. "You write that book.

Whatever is laid on your heart, you do it and you won't have a bunch of regrets later down the road."

"Will you talk to me about Palo Pinto County and Ruby Lee?"

A shiver crawled down Larissa's spine. "Why would you ask that?"

"My book is going to be fiction but Ruby Lee is the inspiration for it."

"I would love to talk to you about Ruby anytime. You just come on up to the ranch and we'll sit on the porch and I'll tell you lots of stories on that pretty lady," Henry said.

"Thank you. I appreciate that, Henry. Larissa, before you let the cat out we were talkin' about this house. Henry says that he hasn't ever seen anything like it," Sharlene said.

"Hank told me all about it but I deliberately come down here today myself so I could take a look at it. It ain't as gawd awful as he said it was but it don't miss it by much."

Sharlene shook her finger at him. "I love it. I wanted to paint the Honky Tonk this color but Larissa wouldn't let me. You'd think I'd be disfiguring a damn shrine the way she looked at me. So since I couldn't paint the beer joint I painted my kitchen table and chairs and every little side table in the apartment a different color. Y'all want to go home with me and see it right now?"

Henry shook his head emphatically. "No, ma'am. This is enough for my tired old eyes for one day."

"Old, my ass. What are you, fifty-two?" Larissa said.

"Sixty-two this past month. I'm helping Hank get his ranchin' legs steady under him for the next year and then I'm retiring."

"What will you do when you retire? Ranchers and farmers don't retire. I come from that kind of country up in Corn, Oklahoma. And I ain't never known a rancher or a farmer to retire. They just keep on doin' what they do until the day they drop dead," Sharlene said.

"That's what I plan on doin' too. Hank will have the ranch and I'm givin' him the house in a year. I'm going to get a smaller one built out in the north forty and help him wherever I can. But I'll be finished making big decisions and worrying about whether it'll be a good year."

Sharlene stood up. "Well, I got to go. Thanks for the raise, Larissa."

"You earned it."

"You saying that means as much to me as the raise. Henry, I'll be up to the ranch in a few days. Write down a few notes so you don't forget anything," Sharlene said.

"Honey, where Ruby Lee is concerned, I remember everything in perfect detail. You just come on anytime. I can always take a break and talk to you about her."

She took time to pet Stallone on the way to her car and waved as she pulled out onto the road and headed back south toward the Honky Tonk.

Henry took a sip of coffee and set his cup on the porch. "The beer joint still looks the same. I'm glad you ain't changed anything about it. I hear it's got to be a right popular place and Luther has to count heads to make sure y'all don't get too many at one time in there."

Larissa moved from the porch step to the empty rocking chair.

"I didn't just come up here and sit in your chair so I could see the house," he said.

"I know," Larissa whispered.

"I'm in the same boat you are, lassy. I don't know if he's made this decision on a whim or if he's thought it out. Ranchin' is tough business. It's hard on the body and the mind. That's why I'm givin' him a year before I turn it over to him lock, stock, and barrel. Will you give him the same amount of time?"

She'd been thinking about Sharlene being at the ranch with Hank and trying to get past a little jolt of jealousy while she listened with one ear to what Henry said. When he asked the question, she came back to the moment with a jolt.

"Why are you asking that?"

"One year, Larissa. In that amount of time we'll see if he's Hayes or Hank. This is my dream. That my son would come home to the ranch that I love but I'm afraid to believe it. He's here partly because of you. You got every right to tell him to go straight to hell, the way he done you. If he was a kid I'd take him out to the wood shed and use a switch on him for it, but he ain't. I'm afraid if you tell him all his chances are gone he'll go back to Dallas. If I have him a year then he'll put down roots."

"Merle says I have to start all over again from scratch if I'm interested in him. That I have to go slow and give it time," Larissa said.

Henry pulled a red bandana from the bib pocket of his striped overalls and wiped sweat from his forehead. "Merle is a smart woman. Always has been. Tried to talk sense to me when we were all younger. I wouldn't listen."

Larissa stuck her hand out. "One year."

He shook it firmly. "If he ain't took root by then, I'll let him go."

—✺—

Larissa was dang glad for Tessa and Sharlene on Saturday night. It had always been the busiest night of the week but that night had been a record breaker. The place filled up more than three times as people came and went and Luther let more in. Not once all night had the number dropped below full capacity. She'd sold enough beer and drinks to float the *Titanic* by two am when Luther unplugged the jukebox and called out that the place was closed.

The cash register was overflowing. Tessa and Sharlene were both dancing jigs when they counted their tips. Larissa decided to get a bank deposit ready even though she was dog tired. Tessa and Sharlene pitched in, counting the bills and rolling the change. It was three o'clock when she finally locked the money into the trunk of her car and drove home.

Stallone didn't rush out from under the kitchen porch to rub against her legs like usual and there was a light on in her kitchen. Neither was unusual since she often forgot to turn off lights and the cat could be out chasing field mice or else sleeping high up in a tree on a limb.

She tossed her purse on the sofa and went straight to the kitchen. She planned to eat a bowl of cereal, forfeit her shower, and go to bed smelling like she was the lone survivor of a forest fire.

"Hello. Was it a tough night?" Hank said from the kitchen stove.

She jumped like she'd been caught naked on Main Street at high noon. "You scared the shit out of me."

"Sorry. I couldn't sleep so I got up and drove down here. I was going to sit on the porch and wait for you but you still hide the key in the same place. You want your eggs fried or scrambled? Bacon is cooked. Biscuits will be out of the oven in five minutes," he said.

I said we'd go slow, remember? Slow my ass. How does one go slow with that much testosterone in a room the size of this kitchen? I'm too tired to chew but I bet I could wrangle up enough energy to jerk them jeans off his sexy butt.

"Fried. Easy over. I'm going to take a quick shower and get the smoke off me."

"Better hurry. Cold fried eggs are horrible."

She threw all her clothes on the floor, stepped into the tub, and pulled the shower curtain, then adjusted the water and asked herself what in the hell was she doing? She should parade out into the kitchen and tell him to take his fried eggs and shove them up his lying ass. But she was hungry and it smelled so good. She'd eat before she sent him packing with orders to never cook her breakfast at three in the morning again.

She shampooed and let the hot water rinse her hair and untie the knots in her back muscles at the same time. When she finished, she wrapped a towel around her head and pulled on a terry bath robe.

"Perfect timing. Biscuits just came out of the oven. I buttered them already and the last three eggs are fried. Have a seat and I'll pour coffee for us," he said hoarsely. The woman was even sexy in a bathrobe and a towel turban. He didn't care if her name was Ruth, Larissa, or Miss Piggy.

She didn't wait for coffee but slid three eggs, half a pound of bacon, and a pile of hash browned potatoes onto her plate. He could cook, paint, and haul hay, plus he could dance and was damn good in the bedroom department. That should be the first block of the foundation of a new and better relationship. But that could be her hormones talking and not her common sense.

"So?"

"Wonderful," she said around a mouthful of flaky, buttered biscuit.

"I don't mean the food. Do I get a second chance?"

She stopped and met his stare across the table. "I'm never quitting my job at the Honky Tonk, Hank. You sure you want a second chance?"

"Did I ask you to leave the Tonk?"

"You are Henry's son," she reminded him.

"And I can learn by his mistakes, can't I?"

"I just wanted to make that clear from right now at the beginning, Hank. Anyone takes me, they take my beer joint."

"I don't care about you being a barmaid," he said.

"Okay, then let's take things very slow and see where they end up. I don't want to rush anything."

"Deal," he said. "I was wondering if after breakfast you would like to go do something very slow."

"I mean it, Hank. No sex."

He raised both dark eyebrows. "Ever?"

"Six months, at least. I said slow. I didn't say never. If we're ever going to build anything from the ashes of a failed relationship, it cannot be rushed."

"I can live with that. But what I was talking about had nothing to do with sex. I am glad that you thought it did because now I know the rule. Got any more?"

"I'll think about it and get back to you. What were *you* talking about?"

He handed her another biscuit. "I've got an old quilt behind the seat of my truck. I know a place up on a rise on the ranch that is a wonderful spot to watch the sun rise. You don't get to see something like that in your line of work very often."

"Okay," she said.

"Thank you." He reached across the table and wiped a bit of butter from the edge of her mouth with his napkin.

Six months! I made the damn rule. Now I'll have to live with it, she thought.

Up in the northern part of Palo Pinto County the land has more rolling hills and curves than in the southern part. She could see little in the darkness but when he drove past the ranch house she realized they were on his land. The ride from there was bumpy at best and made her glad she'd taken time to empty her bladder before she left the house.

Finally, when she thought he was going to drive all the way to the Rio Grande into Mexico through mesquite-covered back country he stopped. He opened his door and the lights came on inside the truck. She looked out across the land but all she could see were short black blobs that were mesquite trees in the process of shedding a few of their leaves.

"We are here." He opened the door for her.

She crawled out and squinted through the darkness, not recognizing a single thing. No oil wells. No barns. No windmills. Just dark night, mesquite trees, and a few hills. "Where is here? It seems to me like you went to the end of the world and made a right."

"We are at the back side of the ranch. There's a fence straight ahead of us that separates our land from the neighbor's. He raises Longhorns. We raise Angus. Got to have good fences. We're going up to the top of that rise." He threw the quilt over his shoulder and picked up a sack.

"This way?" She began to pick her way among the cow tongue cactus and tall weeds. "If I get chiggers, I'm going to pitch a fit."

"I'll check you for ticks when we get home," he laughed.

"That's not original. Brad Paisley put that song out a couple of years ago."

He grabbed her hand with his free one. "Who do you suppose gave him the idea?"

"Are you lyin' to me again?" she asked.

"Yes, I am, but I will be glad to check you for ticks any time you need me to."

"I will remember that offer, Mr. Wells," she said.

"You do that, Miz Morley."

The rise didn't look nearly so steep or so high back at the truck. But when they reached the top she was panting. "I hope there's water in that sack."

"Not water. Beer," he said.

"Even better."

He let go of her hand and spread the quilt out. He pulled a six-pack from the sack along with a box of doughnuts and set them off to one side.

She sat down cross-legged and screwed the top off a bottle. "Beer and doughnuts after that big breakfast at my house?"

He stretched out on the quilt beside her. "Doughnuts are for breakfast after we watch the sun come up."

The beer wasn't as cold as the ones in the Honky Tonk but then it'd been sitting in his truck for a couple of hours. It was wet and it tasted good after the climb up the rise that was really only a foot shorter than Mt. Everest. "What would you have done if I'd said no?"

"Drank all the beers and ate all the doughnuts and wished you were here with me. Stretch out and look that way." He pointed toward the east. "It'll be a couple of hours but you'll be pointed in the right direction. I'll wake you up if you fall asleep."

She held up the beer. She couldn't very well drink it lying on her stomach facing the east.

He took it from her and took a long swig. "We'll share."

Putting her mouth where his had been brought up a very vivid visual of shared kisses. She handed it back to him and flopped down on her stomach. "Damn!"

"Did you hit a rock?" he asked with concern in his tone.

"No, I ate too much. My stomach is too full to lie on the hard ground." She readjusted her weight to get more comfortable. "Got a pillow?"

He patted his arm. "Right here."

"No thank you."

"Don't trust yourself?" he taunted.

She tucked her chin into her chest and looked up at him. "Stretch it out, cowboy."

"We still talking about my arm?" he teased.

"Honey, that's all we're going to talk about for a long time."

He flipped over on his back and stretched his arm out. She lay on her side, facing him, curled up so close that he could feel the warmth yet not touching anything but his arm with her cheek. "You promise to wake me if I fall asleep? I'd be awful mad if I climbed this mountain and missed the sight."

"This barely qualifies as a hill. It's not a real mountain."

"Depends on whether you are climbing it or lookin' at it." She shut her eyes and in three minutes was asleep. Her snores sounded like the deep purrs of a satisfied kitten.

The moon didn't offer much light but combined with his memory and his imagination, it was enough. He looked his fill of her while she slept. Dark hair tied back in a ponytail. Jet-black eyelashes fanned out on her high cheekbones. And lips that begged for him to lean forward and kiss them. But he didn't dare. She said they had to go slow and that might mean no kisses for a month or two. He'd never been a patient man but he'd learn.

A coyote howling in the distance awoke her when the sun was peeking over the horizon. It was a glowing line of orange waking up a whole new world. She was snuggled up close to Hank and he was sound asleep. She took advantage of the moment and stared at his dark hair, feathered back but a little longer than it had been the day of the town meeting. Dark eyelashes resting on his cheeks. A mouth that wasn't full enough to be feminine but not thin enough to be hard. And a body made to cradle a woman's body next to his.

"Hey, you'd better wake up, cowboy, or we'll miss the big show," she whispered in his ear.

He opened his eyes and smiled. "Would you look at that?"

"Beautiful, ain't it?" she said.

"Like all beauty, it's worth the wait."

She smiled. "Is that a pickup line?"

"Nope. It's the truth. Shhh. No more talking. Just prop up on your elbows like this and watch it happen," he said.

She flipped over on her stomach and watched the new day. One with no marks on the page and that didn't care what yesterday had brought or tomorrow had to offer. It was just there for one turn around the earth and then it started all over again.

One day at a time.

That's all anyone ever got, no matter what their names were.

Chapter 18

HENRY LEANED ON THE CORRAL FENCE, ONE FOOT HIKED up on the bottom rail and his elbows on the top one. "This is my favorite day of the year. It's what a ranch is supposed to sound like."

Larissa didn't hear anything but the bawling of cows, a few yapping hounds, and the clattering engine of a big yellow school bus throwing up dust as it came down the lane. Hank had invited her to a rodeo one of the first times she'd met him and Henry had insisted her first one be at the ranch.

She'd arrived thirty minutes early and found Henry waiting by the fence. He was dressed in a western shirt with a red bandana around his neck, a straw hat perched on his head, and spurs on his boots that jangled when he moved. She wondered if he was going to ride bulls or broncs at his age.

"Why would a bus be coming down here? Did you invite the kids to come to the rodeo?"

"No, the kids are the rodeo," he said.

She thought she'd heard him wrong and frowned. "How's that again?"

"This is the most important rodeo in the whole state. I invite the kindergarten children out here for a play day rodeo in September every year. It's good for them but it's better for me. I look forward to it all year long," Henry said.

"And how many kids are there?" She remembered her kindergarten class. Twenty-four students were in her room and there were four different classes. They all had recess at the same time and the playground was a war zone.

"Palo Pinto has a little school. Only has about ninety kids in the whole thing," he said.

"Kindergarten through twelve?" She did the math in her head and that was only seven kids to the class.

"No, just through the sixth grade. They told me they'd be bringing an even dozen today. The teacher is driving the bus so that'll make thirteen. That's a perfect number."

"All day?" Larissa asked.

"Yeah, it sure ain't long enough, is it?"

She turned to look at the bus coming to a stop between her and the house. It sounded like eternity to her.

"Why's a ranch supposed to sound like a kids' rodeo?" she asked as the doors of the bus folded back.

"Lot of land should grow kids as well as cows. Where in the devil is Hank? He's supposed to be here to welcome them with me."

Hank rounded the front end of the bus just as the teacher stepped off. "Hello, Mr. Wells. I am Haley Smith. I've got twelve cowpokes here for a rodeo today. Are you ready for them?"

She was the same height as Larissa. Her blond hair was pulled back in a ponytail with a bandana tied around it. Her pearl snapped shirt was tucked into tight jeans and matched mustard colored round-toed cowboy boots. She carried twenty more pounds than Larissa and most of it was hips and thighs. Brown eyes lit up like twinkling Christmas tree lights when she saw Hank.

"Well, bring them bull riders and ropers on out here so I can meet them," Henry said.

She motioned and twelve children came off the bus in single file. Most of them had a sparkle in their eyes but one little girl hung back and eyed the fence as if it were the biggest hurdle she'd ever come up against.

"I've got eight cowboys and four cowgirls today," she said.

"There's four of us so I reckon that'll be three for each," Henry said.

Larissa's hands started to sweat. She'd never been responsible for three kids in her entire life. She looked across at Hank in time to catch him lower one eyelid in a wink.

"We'll do competition bull riding, some roping, and barrel racing this morning. Then we'll have some lunch up at the cookhouse. Miz Oma is making hot dogs and chocolate cake. After we eat and have a little recess, we're going to get real serious and do some mutton bustin'," Henry said.

"Yeah!" Eleven shouts went up.

The little girl shrunk back against the bus and stuck her thumb in her mouth. When she felt Larissa looking at her she jerked it out with a pop and wiped it off on her hip pocket.

"Okay, then Mitchell, Levi, and Josh, you are with Mr. Wells."

"Ah, man, Miss Haley, I wanted to partner up with Austin today," Mitchell whined.

"Not today. Austin, Ross, and Forest with…" She looked right at Hank.

"Hi, kids, I'm Hank. Looks like if we divide by threes we're going to end up with a girl in the crowd. Why don't me and Dad each take four boys and you ladies take two girls each?"

"That sounds like a plan, Hank." The teacher's eyes left no doubt that she was very interested in the cowboy standing not five feet from her.

"I can take all four girls and that way Miz Smith can be free to rotate among them," Larissa offered.

Damn! Why did I say that? She looks like she would drop her tight fittin' jeans and fall on her back if he touched her with his little finger, so why did I just give her a chance to flirt anytime she wants? Besides, I don't want to be responsible for one kid, much less four little girls all day long. Sharlene is going to get a kick out of this story.

"That's awful nice of you. You'd be Hank's sister, right?"

"I want Austin with my group," Mitchell whined.

Haley was drawn away from Larissa to settle that issue. "That isn't happening. You two get into enough trouble when you are separated. Austin will stay with Hank, along with Ross, Forrest, and Joe. Bobby Dean, you go with Mr. Wells. Miz Wells, you get the twins, Ruby Jane, and Garnet plus Natalie and Brenda. I'll tag along with Hank's group for the first go-around. What are we doing first, Mr. Wells?"

"You can all call me Henry." He grinned. "First rattle out of the chute is bull ridin'. I got the bull all primed and ready. He's a mean one and it'll take a big man to stay on him for eight seconds."

"Or girl," Garnet said. She and Ruby Jane were definitely identical twins. They had the same black hair pulled back in a ponytail, the same slightly toasted skin that said one of their parents was part Hispanic. But Garnet had a confidence about her that Ruby Jane lacked.

Henry tipped his hat at her. "Yes, ma'am. Might be that one of you girls will outride these ornery boys."

"I will," Garnet said. "Put me on that bull and I'll stick to him like I was stuck to his sorry old hide with glue."

"Her dad rides," Haley informed everyone.

Henry put a hand on Mitchell's shoulder. "Sounds like she knows the language and you boys are going to have a tough time with her competing. Okay, my guys, follow me. We'll open the chute and get the bull out so everyone can have a turn. Rest of you cowboys and cowgirls have a seat on the hay bales. And remember the folks in the stands are just as important as the ones doin' the performin' so let's clap and holler for every one of them."

Small square bales of hay had been arranged in a circle around the four sides of the corral. Hay had been strewn in the middle and two small chutes thrown up out of plywood at the far end. Mitchell, Levi, Josh, and Bobby Dean followed Henry to one chute and stood to the side.

"Surely there's not a real bull in there," Larissa mumbled.

Ruby Jane reached up and grabbed her hand in a tight squeeze. "I'm afraid of them things. Garnet, she ain't afraid. But I am. We ain't goin' to have to touch a real bull, are we?"

"Well, for this time around all we have to do is watch," Larissa told her.

She kept a tight grip on Larissa's hand. "Will you sit by me?"

"Yes, I will."

The other three little girls ran on ahead and settled on seats on the other side away from Hank and his boys who were bouncing around like rubber balls.

"I betcha Mitchell falls on his ass," Garnet said.

"Shhh. Don't you say that word or Miz Haley will put you on the bus. She said if you said another bad word, you wouldn't get to ride in the rodeo," Ruby Jane said.

"Well, shit!" Garnet muttered.

Larissa laid a finger over her lips. "I'm bettin' that you beat every one of those boys over there. But you've got to be careful and not say bad words. Wouldn't it be awful if they won because you were in the bus and couldn't ride? Tell me those boys' names again."

Brenda pointed. "That's Mitchell. Him and Garnet get into the most trouble. Garnet says bad words and Mitchell won't be still. That's Levi. He's all right but he picks his nose. That's Josh. He's smart and can already read. And that other one is Bobby Dean."

"What does Bobby Dean do, Garnet?" Larissa asked.

"He's a big baby. He can't even tie his shoes. He's goin' to fall off the bull in one second."

"He is not a big baby," Ruby Jane said.

"He is too and so are you."

"Am not."

Larissa rolled her eyes at the cloudless blue sky. A whole day of this and she'd be ready to give the Honky Tonk to Victoria Radner, lock, stock, and barrel and light a shuck to Egypt to live the rest of her life as a nomad in tents with no possibility of ever clapping eyes on a man. That way she'd never have to worry about children.

Henry got everyone's attention by clapping his hands. "Okay, listen up. This is a mean bull. I worked him over real good before y'all got here and told him to buck his hardest. Hank will have to leave his rodeo crew with Miz Haley for a little while and come help corral this wicked critter."

Hank left the teacher with two little boys on either side. When he reached the corral door he opened it up and jumped back in mock horror. "It's black and mean and ready to ride. Okay, bully bull, come on out and we'll see who's boss. I've got some mean hombres here ready to tame you."

Henry smiled brighter than Larissa had ever seen.

Ruby Jane's hand relaxed when they pulled the bull from the chute by the horns. The meanest black bull in all of Palo Pinto County had started out life as a tractor tire. Henry had used a box cutter to turn him into a proper bull and then tied him to a wooden framework with ropes. The whole thing resembled a homemade rocking horse that Larissa had when she was a little girl. Only the one she'd gotten for Christmas that year was a brown and white plastic horse on a metal frame. Henry had attached one long rope to the front right corner of the bull and one to the back left. Henry grabbed one rope and Hank the other and began to jerk the bull from side to side.

"See how mean he is. I call him El Diablo. There ain't been a kindergartner this year that's been able to stay on him for eight seconds. You got the stopwatch, Hank?"

Hank made a show of pulling it from his pocket. "Right here."

"I'll ride 'im first," Garnet said.

Ruby Jane let out a whoosh of air. "It ain't a real bull. It won't bite me."

"No, it won't and you're going to show them boys that you aren't a big baby. You're going to ride that thing longer than anyone else," Larissa whispered softly into her ear.

She nodded seriously.

"Okay, first up is old Cowboy Mitchell," Henry shouted. "Mount up, cowboy. Here, put this glove on and settle your hat down real good. Remember the rules. One hand up and it can't touch the bull or the ride is over."

"I reckon I'm going to need some help with this stopwatch," Hank said.

"I'll do it," Haley yelled. "You boys sit right here. Larissa, if you see them acting up you tell me when the ride is over and they won't get a turn."

"Can we holler?"

"Of course you can. It's a rodeo," Haley said.

Mitchell picked up a handful of straw and rubbed it on his hands before he put the glove on. Hank hoisted him up on the bull and he wrapped the rope around his gloved hand three times, held up his other hand, and nodded at Hank.

The yelling began with three boys beside the chute, four across the arena, and three little girls shrieking from Larissa's corner. Ruby Jane watched quietly, her eyes narrowed and her chin tucked into her chest.

Haley pushed the button on the stopwatch and the ride began with Henry yanking the bull one way and

Hank the other. Six seconds later Mitchell slid off the side and bit the dust. Haley held up six fingers.

Mitchell knocked the dust from his hat by hitting it against his leg. "It was a mean old critter."

"Good ride!" Henry told him.

"I'll go next," Levi said.

He lasted five seconds and Mitchell beamed.

Josh mounted up for the third ride and the kids all began to scream and holler for him to hang on tight. He tied Mitchell's score. Bobby Dean was a scrawny little blond-haired boy with big green eyes and thick glasses. His jeans were clean and ironed with a crease down the legs but were an inch too short. His knit shirt was a size too big and his boots flopped slightly on his feet when he walked out to the bull.

"He gets meaner and meaner. It'll take a big man to tame him this time, Bobby Dean. You up for the ride?" Henry asked.

The little boy swallowed hard and nodded. He didn't rub dirt or straw on his hands but put the glove on and wrapped the rope around it three times counting carefully as he did so he'd get it right.

"You ain't got a hat. Man can't ride a bull without a hat," Henry said. He opened a wooden feed bin beside the chute and brought out a straw hat to settle on Bobby Dean's head. "You stay on that mean critter for eight seconds, son, and that hat belongs to you," Henry whispered.

The corners of the little boy's mouth turned up in a shy smile. He nodded at Hank and the ride began. Henry pulled and Hank yanked and Bobby Dean held on. The crowd roared. Henry pulled harder. The bull bucked one way and then the other and the crowd screamed even louder.

"That's it! Eight seconds!" Haley yelled.

Ruby Jane danced around Larissa screaming, "He done it. He beated Mitchell."

Henry darted around the bull like he was afraid for his life and finally reached up to rescue Bobby Dean. "Whew, man, I thought that thing was going to keep you and not let me get you off his back. You really tamed that bull, Bobby Dean. I reckon you'll grow up to be a cowboy rancher for sure."

"Yes, sir. Can I really keep the hat?"

"You can. You earned it. That was a big job you just did. Means you got the right to wear a cowboy hat like a real man. Everyone who can stay on this bull for eight seconds today gets a hat. You'll have to work hard as Bobby Dean to get one. So far, he's the cowboy of the day," Henry said.

Mitchell slapped his hat against his leg and crossed his arms over his chest. "Can I try again?"

"No, but you might win something for mutton busting this afternoon, or else lassoing later on today," Haley said.

He looked like a Halloween pumpkin with a big snaggle-toothed grin. "I'll whip you on the mutton, Bobby Dean."

The little boy tipped the brim of his hat. "You'll have to work hard. I stayed on that bull and I can stay on the back of a sheep."

"Girls next or boys?" Henry asked.

"Boys!" a yell went up.

"Girls!" Garnet yelled.

"What do you say, guys? Cowboys are tough but they are respectful of the women, aren't they?" Henry asked.

It was then that Larissa realized the value of the rodeo. It wasn't to come to a ranch and have a play day. Henry was teaching them lessons and they thought they were there for fun.

"Boys!" Austin yelled.

"Girls!" Garnet shook her fist at him.

"Charm is part of a cowboy's way," Henry said.

"And a cowgirl's," Larissa said.

"Well, shucks, go on and let the girls ride. It'll be over real quick when they get on the bull anyway," Austin said.

Henry chuckled. "Okay then, ladies, who is first?"

"Me." Garnet started toward the bull.

"I think Ruby Jane is first," Larissa said.

Ruby Jane hung back. "Me?"

Larissa pulled her up to her side and laid a hand on each shoulder. "Sure. Bobby Dean tamed that bull down. If you ride him now he won't be nearly as mean as when Garnet gets through spurring him and making him mad."

Garnet stuck out her lower lip. "But I want to go."

"Ah, let Ruby Jane go. She'll fall off in one second," Brenda said.

"Bet I won't." Ruby Jane marched out to the bull and spit on her hands. She rubbed them together and slipped the glove on. She nodded at Henry who sat her on the bull, wrapped the rope three times, and looked at the bin where the hats were kept.

Henry picked out a pink hat and put it on her head. "Is this cowgirl ready to show this old bull who's the boss?"

"My name is Ruby Jane and I can ride anything my sister can," she said with a lisp.

Henry's smile got even bigger.

Larissa saw him wink at Hank. The ride began and the crowd cheered her on. Henry pulled and Hank yanked. The way they hollered and yelled about it being a tough old bull convinced every kid there that Ruby Jane was riding for her life.

"Eight seconds! Bring out the rodeo clowns to get her off this critter," Haley yelled.

Hank danced and twirled around, acting like the bull was biting at his rear end and trying to gore him. He finally grabbed Ruby Jane and ran back to the gaggle of giggling girls to set her beside Larissa.

"Your turn," Ruby Jane said to Garnet.

"If I don't win one of them pink hats, can I wear yours sometimes?" Garnet asked.

"Yes, you can. But I bet you get one when you ride the sheep. I'm afraid of them," Ruby Jane said.

Garnet made it seven seconds before she bit the straw. Natalie barely got five and Brenda tied Garnet. They were content to have stayed on long enough to match the boys. The remaining four boys had their ride and the kids all yelled encouragement but none of them made it the full eight seconds.

Next up was the barrel racing contest. Henry set up galvanized milk buckets upside down in a long line down the middle of the area. Then he set a plastic glass full of water on each bucket.

"I'm going to show you how it's done," Henry said. "You got to weave in among these barrels without knocking over a single glass of water. Miz Haley is going to keep score. Water spilling is a minus one. I got a prize for any of the kids who make it all the way to the end without spilling a drop." Henry picked up a hoe with a sock attached to the business end. "This here is old Buster. I've ridden him a good many years at this rodeo and he's a right fine barrel racing horse. I know you kiddos have got smaller horses and you ain't rode them before. But I'm a stick horse whisperer and we had us a conversation before I took them out of their stick horse stalls today, so they ain't going to act up. Okay, can I get some yelling out there so old Buster will do his best barrel racing ever?"

The kids yelled loud enough to noise pollute the whole northern side of Palo Pinto County.

Henry slung a leg over the hoe and nodded at Haley, who clicked the stopwatch. He slapped the back of the hoe and took off like lightning, weaving between the buckets. When he reached the end he patted his horse and looked back at Haley who gave him a thumbs-up and wrote down his time.

"Okay, kids, go choose your ponies," Hank said.

There were ten brown ponies with stuffed toy horse heads on brown sticks. Two purple ones and four pink ones. The boys grabbed the brown ones. Natalie, Brenda, and Garnet laid claim to pink ones and Ruby Jane slipped a purple one out of the cardboard box with "horse stall" written on the front in lopsided letters.

"Who's first?" Henry asked.

"Girls," the boys grumbled.

"That's right gentlemanly of you guys," Henry said.

"Okay, Garnet, let's see what you've got."

She whispered in her pony's ear, slapped his skinny back, and off they went. Her mount slapped a bucket with his hind leg once and a little water spilled out on top of the bucket but she made it to the end without another mistake. Haley gave her a thumbs-up sign and wrote down the time.

When the rides were finished Garnet had a pink bandana tied around her neck and Bobby Dean had a red one.

Next up on the agenda was roping. Henry amazed them with a few tricks before he told them the rules of the game. He rolled a stick horse set into an old rusted milk bucket filled with concrete out into the middle of the arena. "This is one ornery bronc. He's been runnin' wild out in the mesquite. His momma never did bring him up to the house so he don't know anything about bridles or reins. So we've got to lasso him and bring him to the corral so I can teach him to be a good horse. I'll make a loop in the rope and you've got to ride your horse all around him. Get him kind of dizzy so he don't know what's comin', like this." Henry dashed around and moved in close enough to drop the loop around the stick horse.

"Who's going first?" Haley asked.

Ruby Jane raised her hand and mounted her stick horse.

"Can I ride the mutton first?" Austin asked.

"I'm giving points for good behavior. Remember, I've got eyes in the back of my head. So whoever has the best behavior gets to go first at the mutton busting," Haley told them.

"Ready," Ruby Jane said and galloped around the bronc four times before she slung her rope and lassoed him.

"Good job," Larissa yelled and clapped.

When they'd all had a turn Henry opened up a bag and pulled out a silver star to pin on their shirts. "I think everyone got that pony lassoed to bring into the corral for me to tame so everyone gets a star. And now it's time for a bunch of rodeo stars to get on up to the cookhouse and eat hot dogs. I got any kids that might be hungry after a hard mornin's work?"

Twelve hands went up with shouts. Ruby Jane kept hold of Larissa's hand while the rest of the class took off toward the house in a dead run. Haley hung back with Hank and Henry fell into place beside Larissa.

"You look mighty fine in that pink cowboy hat," Henry told Ruby Jane.

"It's a cowgirl hat," she giggled.

He grinned. "Yes, ma'am, it surely is."

Hank would have much rather been next to Larissa. He put a little more speed into his step but Haley kept pace.

"So are you and your sister just visiting the ranch or do you live here permanently? I'm new at the Palo Pinto School and this is my first time out here. The principal said this is a yearly event and to tell the truth I wasn't looking forward to it. But your dad has been so good with the kids. Bobby Dean and Ruby Jane might come out of their shells because of today. How did he know?"

"He's good that way but…" Hank had it on the tip of his tongue to tell her that Larissa was not his sister.

Natalie ran up and grabbed the teacher's leg. "Miz Haley, I got to go to the bathroom and I don't know where it is."

"I'll take her," Larissa said.

"Thank you, Miz Wells. I never did get your first name."

"Larissa," she said as Natalie drug her off toward the front door. "And I'm not Miz Wells."

"Oh, okay." Haley blushed and turned to Hank as they walked up on the porch together. "I'm not usually this forward but I'm a very good cook and I'd like to invite you to dinner at my house one day next week. Call it a thank you for what all you are doing today."

Kids surrounded them and Henry slung open the door. "Do you hear that?"

Every sound stopped and they looked up at him.

"I think that might be, why yes, it is," he said.

The dinner bell clanked loudly.

They all shouted and high-fived one another.

Larissa and Natalie came out of the bathroom while everyone was lining up for Miss Haley to hand them a wet-wipe to clean their hands before they ate. Oma had set up two card tables at either end of the long dining room table so they could all sit together. She went around the table asking each child their name and visiting with them. Then she grabbed Hank's arm and pulled him into the kitchen to help her.

"You are about to ruin everything," she hissed as she put chili and cheese on top of a hot dog in a bun.

He frowned. "What are you talking about?"

"Flirtin' with that schoolteacher right under Miss Larissa's nose. She ain't blind or stupid. She can see what's goin' on. You want her to trust you? Well, you better do different than you been doin' today. Not that it's a bit of my business but I see what I see and I ain't one to keep my mouth shut. You ain't goin' to win her over by making her jealous. You got to win her by showing her that she's the only one."

Hank's temper flared. "I wasn't doing anything but being a good host. Larissa will understand."

"If you think that, you got brain fever. Take this plate out to that little boy with the big thick glasses. He needs some help on his ego building so he gets first plate and he already told me what he wants on his hot dog," she said.

"That's Bobby Dean and Dad saw the same thing. But Oma, I wasn't flirting."

"Who are you trying to convince? Me or you?" she asked.

"Hello, you need some help? I'm just standing in there with nothing to do. Mr. Wells is entertaining the kids with a story about the old chuckwagon days. He's sure got a way with children. Are you his only child then?" Haley asked.

"Yes, I am his only child." He picked up a plate and hurried past Haley.

"You can carry these chips out there." Oma handed her a basket filled with individual bags of chips.

"I can do that, ma'am," Haley said. "So what does Larissa…"

Larissa came around the corner. "Did someone mention my name?"

"Yes, I'm sorry I thought you were Henry's daughter. What is your job on the ranch?"

Larissa smiled. "Oma, do I have a job title?"

"Lord no!" Oma exclaimed.

Haley took the chips to the table and passed out a bag to each student.

"Got anymore ready?" Hank joined them.

"Two. Start on the left of Bobby Dean. Deliver these two and get two more orders." Oma handed him two paper plates.

"Here, I'll fix Ruby Jane's and Garnet's and take theirs out to them. I heard their orders. Nothing but ketchup and wieners," Larissa said.

Haley returned to the kitchen area and asked, "So is she just a friend of the family?"

"Larissa is a lot more than that," Oma said.

"I keep hearing my name. I need two with mustard only," Larissa said.

"I want to know where you fit in here. I asked Hank to dinner at my house one day next week to thank him for today," Haley said.

"And what did he say?" Larissa asked.

Hank returned for two more plates. "I didn't say anything because of the circus going on around us. Miss Haley, I thank you for the invitation but I'm involved with someone right now that I'm pretty serious about."

"Fair enough, but if you are ever uninvolved please give me a call. The invitation stands. Now what else can I do, Oma?"

Oma pointed. "Juice packs all lined up on that tray. Several different flavors for them to choose from. After they finish eating all the hot dogs they can hold we've got chocolate chip cookies and chocolate cake."

Haley picked up the tray and said, "You never did answer me about what it is you do on the ranch?"

"She's that person I'm involved with," Hank said.

"Oops! Well, this is awkward." Haley giggled and darted to the dining room table.

"Why'd you do that?" Larissa asked.

"I'd like to stand up on the roof and shout it," Hank said.

"Don't you dare!"

"Why? You got someone else you are having dinner with this week?"

"Maybe!"

Hank stood perfectly still. His heart stopped and then only beat at half speed. His stomach tied itself into a pretzel. It had never entered his mind that she might have fallen for someone else between the town meeting and the time they met again in Dallas.

"Who?" he growled.

"Jealous?" she asked.

"As hell."

"Good. Now you know how I felt when I had to sit across the rodeo arena and watch you two flirt."

"Who are you having dinner with? And I wasn't flirting."

"But you weren't making her stop when she was," Larissa said.

"I didn't know she was flirting. I thought she was just being nice because we are hosting the play day," he whispered.

"Being nice doesn't involve batting eyelashes," Larissa said.

"See. I told you," Oma said.

"Who are you having dinner with?" he asked.

"Probably Stallone or Luther," she said.

He swallowed hard. "That's not funny."

"Neither was this morning."

"Are we fighting?" he asked.

"Hell yeah."

Oma giggled behind them. "Fight all you want but keep your voices down. Them kids don't need to hear anything but a good time today. When you get finished fightin' go somewhere and make up."

"You are right, Oma. We've got jobs to do. We'll finish this later." Larissa went back to the table to see if her girls needed anything.

After dinner the children had thirty minutes of free time to climb fences and pet the sheep or a horse that Henry brought from the barn.

"Can we ride her?" Garnet asked.

"Sure you can." Henry set her up in the saddle and led the horse around the yard. When he brought her back a line had formed with Ruby Jane at the front. Everyone had a turn around the yard and then he took them all back to the area where he'd set up for the mutton ride. He'd chosen two big woolly sheep from his stock and put them in the arena. Then he turned two kids at a time into the pen. Their job was to work together to catch one of the animals and stay on it eight seconds. Each team had five minutes and the bull was tame compared to the sheep.

Larissa held her sides and laughed until tears messed up her makeup watching the first two little boys try to ride the sheep. If they were all as funny as the first two she wouldn't be able to work that night for aching ribs.

She felt Hank's presence behind her before she even looked over her shoulder to find him close enough she could see individual eyelashes.

"How many of them do you want?" he asked.

"Stallone would get really mad if I brought a sheep into the house."

Hank touched her arm. "I'm talking about little boys."

"Well, I'll take Bobby Dean and Ross. The rest can go on home with the teacher."

Hank slipped an arm around her waist and buried his face in her hair. "How many of your own do you want?"

"One at a time." She got tickled all over again when it was Ross and Joe's turn in the sheep pen. They chased. They mounted. They fell on their hind ends. They fell on their faces. They yelled when the sheep went for a corner and refused to move.

"How many times?" Hank asked.

"On days like this, a dozen. When they have colic and all those gawd awful things that babies have, none," she said.

"Okay, two ladies now," Henry said.

Garnet grabbed her twin sister's hand and two dark ponytails bobbed out into the middle of the pen.

"We'll double team that sorry ass critter," Garnet said.

"I'm afraid and Miss Haley is going to be mad if she hears you," Ruby Jane whispered.

"Don't tell. I'll help you ride this dumb ass sheep if you don't tell on me."

Ruby nodded.

Garnet grabbed a sheep by the neck and motioned for Ruby Jane to get on its back. Ruby Jane did and Garnet let go. The sheep took off in a run around the arena. It didn't buck like the bull or kick or squirm. It just ran and bahhhhed. Ruby Jane leaned forward and held on to the rope tied around the sheep's middle. While she rode, Garnet chased down her animal and mounted. No amount of yelling did a bit of good. It refused to move.

"You sorry piece of shh… sugar," Garnet said.

The sheep put its head down and Garnet landed on her bottom. She hopped up and remounted. "Either you move or Mr. Henry is going to butcher you and we're going to eat you for supper," she yelled above the noise.

The sheep took off like a shot and overtook the one Ruby Jane was still hanging on to as if her life depended on it.

"I might name the first one Garnet," Larissa said.

Hank grinned. "So there might be a first one? I thought Ruby Jane had you wrapped up tight around her little finger."

"I *should* name a little girl Ruby. Maybe I'll have a boy first and I'll name him Ruby."

"Good God, you will not!"

"God isn't just good. God is great. Beer is good. People are crazy. If you don't believe me, ask Billy Currington. He sings that song," she said. Anything to get her mind off having children. She and Hank had a long way to go to see if they were compatible. She'd never bring a child into the world unless she was one hundred percent sure that it would have both a mother and a father. She'd been down the single parent, no parent road. It was a very bumpy ride.

Garnet and Forrest won the prizes for the mutton busting. Henry gave them each a certificate to the western wear store in Mineral Wells for a new pair of boots.

"And now, for the rodeo finale," he said above the din.

The children gathered around him and got quiet. "There's a party set up in the backyard where we'll have our rodeo dance. A good rodeo ain't worth much if the folks who rode and the folks who watched can't finish off with a dance. Miss Garnet, will you do me the honor of the first dance when we get there?"

She stretched her neck so she could see all the way to his face. "You know how to line dance?"

"I can try," Henry said seriously.

"Then you can have the first dance. Come on, girls. Let's go to the bathroom and fix our hair. We're goin' to a dance." All four of them disappeared across the yard in a flurry of giggles and into the house.

"Ah shucks!" Mitchell kicked at the straw.

Henry stooped down and put a hand on the boy's shoulder. "What's the matter, son?"

"I got whupped on the bull and the barrel racing and I wanted a new pair of boots. And now I got to dance with a dumb old girl?" he said.

"How about you?" Larissa whispered to Hank. "You got to dance with a dumb old girl?"

"I was hoping that I might get to dance with the prettiest one here." His warm breath caressed her earlobe and sent shivers up her spine.

Henry chuckled. "Mitch, my boy, do you know how to dance?"

"Daddy's been teachin' me."

"Well, I bet any one of them girls will be honored to dance with you," Henry said.

"Garnet's the only one I like." Mitch blushed.

"Then I'll give you the first dance with her and I'll see to it that it's a two-step. Is that what your daddy's been teachin' you?" Henry remembered when Hank was about that size and he'd taken him to a sale barn dance.

Mitch nodded.

The dancing amused Larissa even more than the mutton busting. The girls came out of the bathroom with their faces wet and glowing and handprints on their jeans where they'd used them to dry rather than the hand towel.

"Okay, first song is a slow one. Sorry Garnet, we'll have to do that line dance later," Henry said.

"We've only got four girls so you boys better get up your courage. Big old dudes like you that ain't afraid of my bull or the sheep ought to be able to ask a girl to dance," Henry said.

Bobby Dean was the first one on his feet. He crossed the yard from the chairs set up on the back to the porch and held out his hand to Ruby. "Miss Ruby Jane Torres, would you dance with me?"

She put her hand in his and he led her to the middle of the yard. Henry raced over to the CD player and pushed a button. Garth Brooks' song "The Dance" played and Bobby put one hand on Ruby's shoulder, pushed his glasses up on his nose with the other, and then slipped it around her waist. She put a hand on his shoulder and hooked her other one in a belt loop at his back like she'd seen her mother do when she danced with her father in the kitchen. It might not have been the best two-stepping Larissa had ever seen but it was the most animated. They didn't listen to the music but barely moved their feet as they looked everywhere but at each other.

"I guess the rest of you boys are too tired to dance?" Henry called out. "Well, I guess me and Hank is about to beat y'all's time with this group of pretty young fillies."

Mitchell jumped up and held his hand out to Garnet. "May I have this dance?"

"You step on my toes and I'll kick you in the shins," she said.

Austin stepped up to ask Natalie and Joe shyly came forward to ask Brenda. The other four boys sighed in relief. When that song ended a fast one began and all twelve of them formed a line dance to the fast country music. They slapped their heels and the whole yard rang with their laughter.

"That's what a ranch is supposed to sound like," Henry said.

Larissa understood exactly what he meant and how lonely it must have been every year when Hank went back to Dallas. Henry was so good with the children that he should have had a whole yard full of ornery boys with a couple of girls tossed in just for fun.

The dance was over all too soon and the children yelled good-bye to Henry, Oma, Hank, and Larissa from the school bus windows until they couldn't see the ranch house anymore.

Larissa stepped out of Hank's embrace and said, "I've got to go too. Sharlene and I've got a bank statement to balance and the beer and pretzel guys both come by about five on Monday to restock."

She didn't want to leave. She'd rather sit in the dining room with Oma and the guys and talk about the fun they'd had with the children. She'd rather go out to the barn and make up with Hank for the minor spat they'd had about the schoolteacher. Anything but leave the ranch.

"I'll walk you to your car," Hank said.

Oma poked Henry in the ribs and he winked at her.

He slipped her hand into his. "Someday I'll take you to a real rodeo with real bulls, bronc riders, and barrel racers."

"It wouldn't be a bit more fun than this one. I loved it all."

"Even the jealousy?" he asked.

"Even that." She smiled. "You comin' into town tonight?"

"Will you save me a dance?"

"Don't dance with customers," she said.

He kissed her forehead. "Think I'll ever be more than that in the Honky Tonk?"

"Long as you don't go to dinner at Miss Haley's house you might have a fightin' chance. But if you do I'm going to kick you in the shins."

She parked in the lot at the Honky Tonk and was about to open the door when her cell phone rang. She didn't even look at caller ID because she was sure it was Hank.

"Hello, cowboy," she said.

"Well, hello to you, but I'm no cowboy. Who were you expecting?" Doreen asked.

"Hank. I just left a kiddy day rodeo at his ranch and…"

"Hank is back on the ranch? What happened? I know Victoria was angry with him but I didn't know he'd gone to Henry's. Tell me all about it and then I'll tell you my news."

"He came back. He wants to see me again. I'm not sure if he'll stay because I'm afraid he'll get bored. Your turn."

"Oh, no! That's not going to do. I've saved an hour for this phone call and my news takes five minutes. So talk and start at the beginning," Doreen said.

"Okay, in the beginning God made dirt and Henry bought some of it," Larissa said.

"You don't have to go back that far. Start with when you got home from the benefit. How long until Hank was there?"

"Okay. Once upon a time a Honky Tonk angel was sleeping when she heard voices on her front porch," Larissa went on to tell Doreen the whole story. "And now I've got to get to the Honky Tonk because the beer man is coming to restock. Your news?"

"Rupert and I got married this morning. His mother died last week and it wouldn't be proper to have a big wedding so soon after a funeral. I would have called you but you didn't know the lady. I'd only met her once. She was in a care facility and didn't even know Rupert most days. Anyway, we just had a civil ceremony. However, I'm calling Martha and Victoria and telling them they can do a reception next month. None of you will have to fly over here after all. But you all know you are welcome any time you want to come see us. We're going to honeymoon on an island that he owns for a couple of weeks and then do some sightseeing. After that we'll be in Dallas for the week that you'd planned to be in Italy."

"Wow! Congratulations, Mother. And tell Rupert I'm glad to have him in the family," Larissa said.

"Thank you. I'll make plans at the Hyatt for you. Would you like to bring your friend Sharlene? We could plan the reception on Sunday night so you could both be away from your beer joint."

"Yes, I would and thank you for thinking of her. She'll squeal and talk my ears deaf."

"What?"

"Sharlene talks too much. Especially when she is nervous."

Doreen laughed. "So does Victoria."

"The great Victoria Radner has a fault?"

"Oh, yes, sweetheart. When you get to know her, you'll be amazed at how many she has. I'm not telling you anymore though or she'll tell you all about mine."

"The great Doreen Lawson has a fault?" Larissa giggled.

"Lady Doreen Jovani now," she said.

"Well, la-tee-damn-dah," Larissa said.

"And Lady Doreen does have a fault or two that she'd just as soon her daughter didn't know about," Doreen said.

"Now you've got my curiosity piqued," Larissa said.

"Does Lady Doreen's daughter have anything she doesn't want her mother to know about? That the tabloids in Italy or England might find amusing?"

"Aside from the fact that she owns and operates a beer joint down in Texas, United States of Wonderful America, I can't think of a thing," she said.

Doreen laughed. "I'll see you in a few weeks. And don't forget a single detail about what all happens with your cowboy."

"You got it," Larissa said and flipped the phone shut.

She went in the Honky Tonk door to find Sharlene mopping the floor. "Put that down and open us a beer. You've got to hear about my day."

Chapter 19

THE NIGHT AIR WAS BRISK HERALDING THE END OF A LONG Texas summer and the beginning of fall. Larissa inhaled deeply several times from the garage to the Honky Tonk. Her cell phone vibrated in her hip pocket and she smiled. Hank had gotten into the habit of calling every night right before she opened the beer joint doors. Brisk air. Secrets out in the open. Nothing could possibly go wrong.

"Hello," she said.

"How are you liking this football weather?" he asked.

"Love it. Did you play in high school?"

"Not me. I was the computer geek."

"You promised never to lie to me again," she said.

"And I'm not."

"I can't even begin to picture you as a computer geek. You look like a football player. You coming into town tonight?"

"I'm too tired to drive to the end of the lane. Much as I'd love to see you, darlin', I'd be a danger to anyone on the road including myself," he answered.

"Then Sharlene and I'll see you in Dallas tomorrow?"

"My pickup has plenty of room if you women don't take your entire closets, we could all go together. There'll be half the backseat to put luggage."

"Then we'd be glad to go with you. We'll be ready at noon."

She heard him yawn. "Go snore in front of the television with Henry until bedtime."

"Goodnight, Larissa."

"Goodnight."

She flipped the phone shut and went into the Honky Tonk to Jo Dee Messina's voice coming from the jukebox declaring that her give a damn was busted. Sharlene was pouring pretzels and peanuts in bowls.

"You got a reason for playing this song?" Larissa asked.

"Yep, because my give a damn is busted. Not cracked. Busted wide open and there ain't no pieces to fix it," Sharlene said.

"Why's that?" Larissa asked.

"I had this boyfriend up in Corn, Oklahoma. We dated in high school and then I went into the service and he stayed home to farm with his dad."

"And?"

"He got married today. I just got off the phone with his sister."

"If you loved the man, why didn't you go to Corn and try to talk him out of marrying another woman?"

"I thought maybe someday he'd leave Corn and ride his white horse to find me and we'd ride off into the sunset. But it wouldn't be to Corn. I don't want to live there ever again. Visiting for holidays is fine. Living there is another matter."

Larissa spaced the bowls of pretzels and peanuts down the bar. "You grew in different directions. He stayed and grew roots in farming. You've spread your wings. He couldn't wait forever and he couldn't fly."

"Makes sense. And I don't even know why it bothers me because if I'd loved him I'd be in Corn, not Mingus.

It's just like another door has closed and I wasn't ready for it," Sharlene said.

"Love shouldn't be a backup plan, honey."

Sharlene sighed. "I didn't even realize that's what it was until now. Is your give-a-damn coming around tonight?"

"No, but we are going to ride to Dallas with him tomorrow. You'll be ready at noon?"

"I surely will. Maybe I'll find a new backup plan amongst the rich and shameful," she teased. Her smile returned and her green eyes sparkled. "Maybe that Whit you told me about. I like that name. It sounds like a man who'd be on the cover of a big thick romance book. I can picture him wearing nothing but a Scottish kilt, his broad chest rippling with muscles as he pulls a red-haired vixen to him."

"Good lord, Sharlene. You really should write books."

"Hello, ladies," Luther said. "Parking lot is already filling up. Ten minutes until opening. Y'all ready for the stampede?" He made his way across the dance floor to the bar, picked up a red and white cooler, and shoved six cold Cokes in it and added a scoop of ice.

"How's things with you and Tessa?" Sharlene asked.

Luther shook his big head and exhaled loudly. "I love that woman but God Himself don't know why. She's independent and a band of angels couldn't change her mind once it's made up."

"And you are griping why?" Sharlene asked.

"Big old man like me likes to feel like his woman needs him."

Sharlene reached over and patted him on the shoulder. "Honey, Tessa doesn't need protection. She needs someone to love her for who she is. She can protect herself." She opened the cash register and handed him a dollar. "Go get the band fired up so the folks will come in to music and get busy working up a thirst. Play something fast and twangy."

Luther slid the cooler under his chair beside the door and fed the dollar into the jukebox. At exactly eight o'clock he opened the doors and let the customers file inside. In five minutes he'd counted one hundred. When the last song the house paid for finished the dance floor was full, tables were claimed, pool tables staked out, and he was past the second hundred on the count. Tessa was behind the bar drawing beers. Sharlene was taking care of mixed drinks. Larissa worked up and down the bar.

"Where's Hank? Haven't seen him all week. He's usually here on Saturday night at least," Tessa asked.

"He's finding out that ranching isn't a nine to five and then go home job," Larissa said.

"You okay with that?"

"It's who Hank is. Whether I'm okay with it or not doesn't change the way it is."

Sharlene filled six Mason jars with beer and set them on a tray. "Good answer, Larissa. I needed to hear that tonight."

"Hey, lady. I'll buy you a drink if you'll dance with me," Justin said from the end of the bar.

"Where did you come from? I haven't seen you in months," Larissa said.

"Hurt my back and they put me on the desk. I only got to make this run because they needed an emergency haul. Got a place out back I can call mine after hours tonight?"

"You got it. I'll write you up for your same old space. Sorry about your back."

"Me too. It kept me home and me and the girlfriend found out that we didn't do so well on a twenty-four-seven basis. We did better when I was gone most of the week and there was always the drama of the parting and the joy of the homecoming. We broke up so now I'm free. You want to run away with me tonight and live in the big city of Houston?" he teased.

"Not me," Larissa said.

"She's got a feller. I might run away with you," Sharlene said.

Justin looked her up and down. "You get serious about that, Red, and we'll talk. But don't tease a poor old crippled truck driver. Want to dance?"

"Don't dance with customers," Sharlene said.

"Lord, Larissa, do you have to train them all to be just like you?" Justin asked.

"Kinda happens that way," Tessa said. "Don't bother asking me. I can't go. I've got my brand on the bouncer."

Justin raised an eyebrow. "Luther?"

"That's right."

He looked from Tessa to Larissa. "And which one of these cowboys belong to you?"

"None of them."

"Yet," Sharlene laughed.

"Which one wants to belong to you?"

Sharlene swept her hand in a gesture to include the whole bar. "All of them, but Hank Wells is the one who could win the brass ring."

Justin's brow wrinkled as he thought. "That was the cowboy who came in here last time I was able to drive. The one you'd had a wreck with?"

Larissa nodded. "That's the one."

"Well, damn. My timing ain't never right. You was ready and I had to go and hurt my back. Ain't that the luck," Justin grumbled.

"Stop your whining and go find someone else to dance with. There's a whole beer joint full of women who'd love to run away with you," Larissa said.

"Yeah, but the best one of the lot is already taken. I can see it in your eyes," he said.

―――᷇᷆――᷆

Larissa pulled on a silky dress in a color called liquid pewter that barely skimmed her knees. It had a scoop neckline and long fitted sleeves and she'd chosen silver high-heeled pumps, a silver necklace with a black onyx drop, and matching earrings. She was checking her reflection in the bathroom mirror when Sharlene knocked on her hotel room door.

When she slung it open Sharlene breezed inside. She wore a bronze dress that flowed from a fitted waistline with a ruffled hemline. She'd chosen the same color shoes and jewelry and had scrunched her hair into a mass of shoulder-length curls.

"Whew! You look like a magazine cover." She gave Larissa the toe-to-head inspection.

"Me? You're the single girl who's going to knock 'em dead this afternoon. I thought we weren't supposed to outdo the bride. You might be in trouble." Larissa picked up her purse and they headed toward the elevator doors just down the hallway.

"So have you heard from your mother?" Sharlene asked as they waited for the elevator.

"She called when they got to Victoria's house last night. Nothing doing but they had to stay there rather than the hotel so that's where they are. I'd rather sleep in an outhouse. That woman would poison me and declare I'd died of natural causes in my sleep."

Sharlene shivered. "I'll take crackers in my purse."

"I'm surprised I'm even invited to the reception," Larissa said.

Sharlene pursed her lips and frowned. "Seriously, what do you expect? You run the Honky Tonk, the very place that she hates, you refuse to sell it to her so she can burn it to the ground, and then you call her a bitch. And now you've stolen her son. She may be buying voodoo dolls with black hair, poking pins in them, and chanting ancient curses."

"That sounds more like Martha. She's the artistic, eccentric among the three."

The elevator doors opened and there was Hank.

"Ladies," he said.

"We didn't expect you to come up to escort us down," Sharlene said.

Larissa was glad that Sharlene was a talker because she wanted to look, not talk. He wore a black western cut suit, polished boots, white shirt and tie, and his hair cut and brushed back. The sparks became a blaze that only one thing could put out. And they couldn't go back to the hotel room. They had a reception to attend.

Sharlene stepped inside the elevator and Larissa followed.

He pushed the button and the doors closed. "You ladies are both beautiful."

"Well, you don't look so shabby yourself," Larissa said.

He reached across the few inches of space separating them and squeezed her hand. "I'm glad you are going with me."

"Why?" Sharlene asked.

"I haven't seen Mother since I told her I was quitting Radner and moving home to the ranch. She's called a couple of times but it was to wrap up business. It'll be easier if you are there beside me."

"Man, I wouldn't want to be in your shoes. First time I went home after basic training, my dad wouldn't even speak to me for two days. He was so mad when I left for the service. In his world men shouldn't go fight in wars and women damn sure ain't supposed to do such an abominable thing. It's awkward at best, heart wrenching at the worst," Sharlene said.

Hank stepped aside and let them out of the elevator first. "What did you do?"

"Wore him down. I made sure I was in the barn when he was. I took his lunch to the field. I baled hay with him. Pretty soon he had to talk to me," Sharlene said.

"If he's against women in the military, how does he feel about you living in the back of a beer joint and working there?" Larissa asked.

"I haven't told him," Sharlene said. "Might not ever tell him. He doesn't even agree with women working outside the home. He can barely swallow me living alone and working at a newspaper. The bar idea might give him a stroke."

Hank's truck waited under the awning. He helped Sharlene get settled in the backseat and then opened the passenger door for Larissa. He'd seriously considered hiring a limo just so he wouldn't have to drive and could sit in the backseat with the two women, but that wasn't who he was anymore. He was a rancher who'd traded his BMW in on a Chevy Silverado extended cab truck. And if his mother didn't want to forgive him, then he'd simply have to wear her down like Sharlene had done with her father.

They were greeted at the door by Martha, who air-kissed Larissa and Hank. She wore a flowing caftan in a splash of oranges and browns, clunky jewelry, and sandals. Toenails that had been done in bright orange peeked out sporadically.

"I'm so glad to see you two. Hayes, you look more like your father every day. And this is?" She turned to Sharlene.

"I'm Sharlene. I work at the Honky Tonk for Larissa. You must be Martha. I've heard so much about you and your art," Sharlene said.

Martha smiled. "And I'm sure every word of it was wonderful. Come on. I'm sure Larissa Ruth is dying to see her mother. Doreen is so happy and Rupert, well, darlins, if I wasn't such a good friend, I'd take him away from her. I can't wait until Victoria sees Sharlene."

"Why?" Sharlene whispered to Larissa.

"You'll see."

"Larissa Ruth." Doreen hurried toward them and wrapped her daughter up in a tight embrace.

"Just Larissa, Mother," she said.

"Can't do it. You were Ruth too many years. I'll have to ease into the first name so bear with me. And this is… oh, my lord."

Sharlene and Doreen eyed each other and then giggled.

"Now I understand," Sharlene said.

They were the same height, had the same red kinky hair and face shape.

"Did you ever play the Annie part in a school play?" Doreen asked.

"Yes, ma'am. Did you?"

Doreen nodded.

"Hayes?" Victoria crossed the room. "You look just like Henry back when he was younger in that suit and boots."

He kissed her on the cheek. "Mother."

"You are not forgiven," she said.

"When you stop calling me Hayes and start calling me Hank, I'll know you've had a change of heart."

"Don't hold your breath," she said. "Dear God, Doreen. You didn't tell me you'd given birth to two daughters. You have kept a secret from your best friend, haven't you?"

"She's not mine," Doreen said.

"Unbelievable. Who are you?" Victoria asked.

She extended her hand. "I'm Sharlene and I work for Larissa at the Honky Tonk."

Victoria shook it and blinked several times. "Where are you from?"

"Corn, Oklahoma, originally."

"Well, it's amazing. Everyone here will think you are the daughter."

"It *is* a little eerie," Sharlene said.

"You all go on and visit with Doreen and Rupert and mingle among the guests." Victoria looked at Hank. "I'm expecting you for a visit tonight, *alone*. Informal. In the library at eight."

"I'll be there," he said.

Emma grabbed Hank on the right and Holly looped her arm through his on the left side. "We've got a corner all saved. We're dying to know why you left Radner. Are you crazy? Working on a ranch when you could be the next in line for one of the biggest corporations in Texas?"

He shook them off and took a step closer to Larissa who was talking to her mother. "I'd like you to meet Larissa Morley."

"You are the woman who paid all that money for him and then sent him back to the party, aren't you?" Emma said.

Larissa told Doreen that she'd catch up with her later and turned around to face the women and Hank. "Yes, I am. And you were the ones who were bidding against me?"

They nodded.

"And we heard you own a beer joint. Is that right?" Holly asked.

"It is," Larissa said.

"Must be a damn good business," Emma said coldly.

"It keeps me from sleeping in the street and out of jail for catfights. You'll have to excuse us now. Sharlene and Hank and I have to go have a word with Rupert." She tucked her arm in Hank's and led him away from the two women.

"You can thank me later," she said.

"For what?"

Sharlene giggled nervously and looked at Hank. "She just saved your sorry ass from those two she-coons. Larissa won that catfight."

Larissa led them to the small group of people standing with Doreen and Rupert. Rupert's eyes lit up when he saw her. He reached out and draped an arm around her shoulders and hugged her up next to him.

"Everyone meet my new daughter? I'm told she looks more like me than she does her mother," he said.

"Well, that one looks like her mother. There's no denying it," a lady said.

"But I'm not," Sharlene said.

"Honey, somewhere down the genetic line you two sprang from the same relative," the woman said.

Doreen whispered to Larissa, "Talk of genetic lines reminds me. I've left a present for you at the hotel. It will be delivered to your room at eight tonight. I know that Victoria is going to have a heart-to-heart with Hank and this will give you a little something to keep you busy this evening."

"What about Sharlene?"

"She's a big girl. She can entertain herself," Doreen said.

<hr />

Hank kissed Larissa hard and passionately outside her hotel room at seven thirty. "I'll be here to pick you up at eleven in the morning."

She didn't doubt that he would be there to take her and Sharlene back to Mingus. She did have a niggling little qualm that Victoria would convince him to come back to Radner. He'd had a month at the ranch again and this time it wasn't vacation time where he helped when he wanted. He was taking on more and more responsibility and Henry was doing less and less. He was lucky if he got to run by the Honky Tonk on Saturday night for a couple of hours. It would be easy to fall back into the lush life that Radner Corporation offered.

She leaned against him and hugged tighter. "I thought you might be my present."

"What present?"

"Mother said she was having a present sent up to my room. I thought maybe she and Victoria cooked up a story to tell me about you needing to be gone this evening and you were my present."

He sighed. "I would have loved to have been your present. What would you have done with me if I had been?"

"What you do with all presents. Unwrap them," she teased.

He moaned.

She stepped back. "Go on and get it over with. I imagine Mother is sending me a bottle of vintage wine from Italy. If I have a headache tomorrow morning and I'm all grouchy on the trip home, you can blame her."

"Next Sunday belongs to me. Don't make plans. We'll go on a fall picnic if it doesn't rain," he said.

"And if it does?"

"Then we'll spend the day in bed," he teased.

One dark eyebrow lifted slightly. "Sleeping?"

"As tired as I've been that's probably the gospel truth of the matter." He hurried to get in the elevator.

Another five minutes and he would have called Victoria to tell her he'd see her the next morning for brunch and the visit. He already knew what she was going to say and he wasn't interested. He'd never worked so hard as he had the past month or been so frustrated because of a woman. But there was peace in the weariness and the aggravation.

His heart wanted Larissa to be there forever and he wanted to fall down on one knee and propose but he couldn't. Not until he'd proven for himself that he was truly a rancher. He couldn't offer her a life until he'd taken care of his own doubts. He drove back to his mother's beautiful estate on the outskirts of Dallas. When he pulled up in the circular driveway in front of the house, Leroy, the butler, came out to greet him and take his keys.

"She's waiting in the library and you are two minutes late," Leroy said.

"Yes, sir," Hank said. If that kiss had led to something more he would have been even later.

"You're late. You know I expect punctuality," Victoria said when he slung open the double doors. She had changed into a royal blue velvet lounging outfit and had taken her hair down.

"I don't work for you anymore," he said.

"But you will always be my son and as such you should be on time."

He poured two fingers of Scotch into a glass and sat down. "How is it that you are so animated and free with your friends and you treat me like an employee?"

She sipped her drink then set it down on the coffee table separating them. They shared a brown leather sofa—one on one end and one on the other, three feet of space between them. Books lined three walls with the fourth one solid glass looking out over the gardens. It was a blaze of fall colors in yellows and oranges at that time of year and kept two full-time gardeners busy five days a week.

"Are you happy up there playing in the dirt?" she asked.

"I am and you didn't answer my question."

"You always did have more of him in you than me. I hate that and I worked so hard to keep you away from that damned ranch. You've got a life here. One of relative ease and you were happy until you went up to that gawdforsaken shit hole. I'll answer your questions. Martha and Doreen have known me since we were kids. I can be like that with them. Carefree like a child. With you, it's different. I can't explain it." She fumbled with the coaster.

"Okay, fair enough. There are things I can't explain either. So fire away. Give me your best speech."

Victoria shook her head. "I don't have a speech. I will offer you your old job back with a substantial raise, the penthouse apartment at the corporation, and a company car until you can get that ugly truck sold. The offer is on the table for exactly five minutes." She looked at her watch.

He shook his head. "No, but thank you."

"What if I'd said forever? That you could come back anytime and it would all be waiting for you?"

"Answer would be the same. I'm in love with Larissa, Mother. I want to spend my life with her. I can't ask her to trust me with her heart until I'm sure I'm trustworthy. I hurt her and I have to go slow when I want to rush in with both feet, my heart, and soul."

Victoria gasped. "You cannot be serious. That girl might be Doreen's child but she's a bartender, for God's sake, Hayes. I cannot have a daughter-in-law who owns a beer joint in Mingus, Texas."

"Maybe not, but I could easily have a wife that does. It'll be your loss if you can't get past that. Good night, Mother," he said.

"Good night, Hayes. I won't change my mind."

"I won't either."

He started up the stairs to his old bedroom and thought that if he was at the ranch, Henry would have said, "Good night, son."

Chapter 20

LARISSA HAD TWENTY MINUTES BEFORE HER FANCY BOTTLE OF imported wine would arrive at the door. She made a trip through the restroom and went back down the elevator to the bar in the lobby. Only one other person was at the bar and he was sitting at the far end. She ordered a Coors and carried it to the lounge where she sat on a long modern sofa and watched the people.

The man at the bar picked up his beer and sat down beside her. "Are you Larissa Morley?"

Her spine felt as if someone was drizzling cold water down it. "How did you know my name?"

"I think I would have known you without knowing your name. You are the absolute image of my mother," he said.

So there was another double in the world. Sharlene looked like Doreen. And now this man thought she looked like his mother. It was a stupid pickup line and she had it on the end of her tongue to tell him so.

"I'm Larry Morleo. I understand that you are my daughter. I was waiting until eight o'clock to knock on your door, just like your mother said for me to do. But when I saw you at the bar, I knew it had to be you. You look so much like Elvira Turnbull Morleo that it's uncanny."

Larissa couldn't speak. Words would not come. She thought she'd have a full-blown stroke before she finally whispered. "My mother found you?"

He nodded. "Last week. She called and told me the whole story."

She stared.

He did the same.

"You don't look a thing like I pictured you all these years," she said.

"How did you picture me?"

"Oh, ten feet tall, bulletproof, a sorry bastard part of the time for leaving me and Mother when I was tiny. A knight or a king some of the time, a rodeo cowboy on occasion."

He smiled. His face was the same shape as Larissa's. He had the same dark brown eyes with heavy lashes. His hair was sprinkled with gray in the temples. He was tall and carried himself like he'd been in the military.

"I didn't know about you. If I had I wouldn't have left you," he said.

"Where do you live?"

"Abilene. I went to Oklahoma State University on a scholarship. All my family is from Abilene. I'm retired from the Air Force now and took over a construction business from my father when he retired last year."

"I have grandparents?" She was in awe. She'd pictured having a father, meeting him someday, but not in a hotel lobby with a bottle of Coors in her hand.

He nodded. "And cousins, aunts, uncles. Too many to name or count."

"Brothers or sisters?"

He shook his head. "My wife wasn't able to have children."

"How does she feel about this?" Larissa asked.

"Well, let me tell you how it happened. We were having supper at our home with my brother and his wife when the phone rang. It was your mother and when we got through with the 'do you remember me' and all that, she hit me with the bomb. I didn't know what to say, to tell the truth. So I told her that yes, I would come over here and see you on this day at this time. When I turned around my wife said, 'Before or after we met?' I didn't know what to say. So she repeated it. 'I know you were talking to a woman who says you have a child. We've been married twenty years. Tell me that it was before that.' So I told them the whole thing."

"You didn't answer my question," Larissa said.

"She would like to meet you but she said I was to come alone this time because we needed time to talk and bond. Are you married? Do I have grandchildren?" His voice sounded almost wistful.

"I'm not married. I own and operate a beer joint called the Honky Tonk in Mingus, Texas. No grandchildren. This is awkward, isn't it?"

He touched her shoulder. "Yes, it is. We're bound by blood and heritage but not by experiences and love yet. Give it time, Larissa. This is our first meeting."

"Thank you. When I was a little girl I played this scene in my head so many times. It changed as I got older. You weren't an astronaut by the time I was seven."

He smiled. "I see you like beer. Your mother hated it."

"Still does. She's a champagne woman. I didn't even realize I liked beer or country music until I moved to Mingus," she said.

"You don't have to work in a beer joint. I'm not a wealthy man but my wife, Mary Beth, and I are very comfortable. You could work for me," he said.

She laughed. "I work in the Honky Tonk because I love it, not because I have to, and besides all that, I own the place as well as work there. Thank you for the offer but I'll stay where I am."

"The offer will be there in six months or six years," he said.

She studied him for a long while before she answered. "How can you say that? I could be a druggie or an alcoholic or I could be lying to you about my beer joint just to fleece you. How can you trust me enough to make that statement?"

"I'm a pretty good judge of character and you are so much like my mother. I can't wait for you two to meet each other. I can't explain it. You'll have to meet her and then you'll understand," Larry said.

"What do we do now?" she asked.

"I suggest we finish these beers and sleep on what we have found out about each other. Maybe we could have breakfast together tomorrow morning? And then if you'll give me your number, I'll call. Or you're going to laugh at this, but Momma still likes to dance and loves country music. Would it make you uncomfortable if we showed up at your Honky Tonk?"

Larissa could hardly believe her ears. "My grandmother in a beer joint? That's hard to envision but bring her and whoever else wants to come dance on over. Monday through Wednesday the old songs are played on the jukebox. Friday and Saturday are new ones. Thursday is a toss-up."

"How do you manage that?"

"Two jukeboxes," she said.

He tipped back the beer and finished the last of it. "I think you and I might be friends."

"I hope so," she said.

"Well, goodnight," he said.

"Goodnight."

She watched him go all the way up in the elevator. She'd met her father. The hotel didn't come crashing down any more than it had when she had to face off with Victoria in the same lobby. He didn't wear a Superman cape but neither was he a homeless drunk. She dug her phone out of her purse and punched in Hank's number, hoping he was finished with his powwow with his mother.

"Hello," he answered immediately.

"Did I interrupt anything with you mother?"

"No, that's over," he said.

"I've got the most amazing news and I want to share it with you and I don't want to do it over the phone and…"

Hank butted in, "Slow down, Larissa. Was the present not a bottle of fancy wine or is it so good that you want to share it with me? I really wanted to see you tonight too."

"It's better than musty old wine from Italy," she said.

"Larissa."

She held the phone away from her ear and looked at it.

"I'm right here," he said.

She looked up to see him standing in front of the elevators. They each took a dozen long strides and she threw herself in his arms and hugged him tightly. "You go first because when I start I won't be able to stop. Let's go get a cup of coffee and talk."

They sat at the same table in the café that they'd been at when Victoria and the rest of the family were there.

He told her about his conversation with his mother and she told him the whole incredible story of her father. When she finished she reached across the table and wrapped both her hands around his.

"Stay with me tonight. I want you to hold me while I fall asleep and be there when I wake up in the morning," she said.

His eyes never left her face as he said, "Lead the way."

Chapter 21

LONG HARD KISSES STARTED IN THE ELEVATOR AND GREW more passionate as they stumbled down the hallway toward her door. She'd only invited him to hold her while she slept but one brush of her hand against his started a chain reaction of heat that went from red-hot fire to blue blazes to white hot by the time he fumbled with the door card, picked her up, carried her inside, and then kicked the door shut with his boot heel.

He peeled her dress down over her hips. She unbuttoned his shirt, fought with the cuff buttons as she tried to take it off, and ended up throwing it against the far wall without ever breaking the kiss. He strung kisses from her neck to her breasts while he unfastened the silver lace bra and sent it flying to land on his shirt.

She gasped when he trailed his finger tips down her ribs to the edge of her underpants. He slowly slid them down to her ankles and picked her up like a new bride. He laid her on the bed and started a whole new session of scorching hot kisses.

"You are so beautiful," he mumbled.

"You'd be beautiful if you'd get out of those jeans and…"

How he could take off his pants without stopping amazed her. When he stretched out naked beside her, she moaned. The touch of his hand brushing against hers in the elevator had sent tingles up and down her spine.

Multiply that by hundreds of square inches of bare skin against hers and it made for a bonfire so big that the flames stretched up to heaven.

She ran her fingertips over his muscular back. "You feel wonderful."

"Turn over and I'll give you a full body massage. There's lotion in the bathroom, right?"

She kissed him passionately one more time and flipped over on her stomach. Cold lotion against hot skin made her shiver.

"I'm sorry, darlin'. I'll heat it up in my hands next time." He straddled her back and began to rub in the lotion. Bare hind end touched leg muscles. Back muscles relaxed at the touch of his hands. Before he finished with the first of the lotion she'd flipped over and pulled him down on top of her.

He pulled the cool sheet up over them. His lips went to hers to taste the cool beer still on her breath. It was a great way to taste beer without drinking it. He'd have to remember that in the future. He nibbled at her lower lip until she opened up and he made love to her mouth with his tongue.

Her back arched against him and she moaned his name. "I've missed you so much, Hank."

"I was crazy with wanting you but I was afraid to rush things. I never want to lose you again, Larissa."

She looked up to see those whiskey colored eyes staring at her with intense passion and she knew that she could trust Hank. In that split second she knew he would never leave her again. She laid a hand on his chest. The chest hair was soft and his heart was racing.

"Please," she murmured.

"So soon. I'm barely getting started and the night is young," he whispered then nibbled on her earlobe.

"Act one doesn't have to last forever. It can be a three act play like the one at the lake," she said softly.

"Well, with that in mind, the actor enters from center stage," he teased.

"The sexy actor with the most beautiful eyes in the world," she said.

He positioned himself above her. "You are wonderful, Larissa Morley."

Act one only lasted a few minutes. When he rolled to one side he wrapped his arms around her pulling close to him. She purred as she stretched out, making sure every bit of naked skin touched a part of him. Bare breasts against soft chest hair. Belly buttons together. Legs stretched out side-by-side with her toes touching his shins.

"Awesome can't begin to describe that," she said breathlessly.

"Round two begins now." He shut his eyes and aimed for her lips, missed and kissed the tip of her nose, readjusted, and the next time hit the target. His hands moved over her body, causing every nerve ending to burn with desire. His body moved as if he had twenty hands and every one of them were intent on pleasing her.

Act two lasted longer than the one before it and had even more intensity. When it came to an end with all the bells and whistles of a thundering performance, Larissa pulled the sheet up over his back and let the whole room light up in lovely golden afterglow. Hot damn! She was in love. It might take them both a year to get around to admitting it aloud but they had time and if they spent it like this every night or even once a week, she didn't care if it took two years.

"Act three?" she asked after a few minutes.

He gathered her up in his arms and kissed her passionately. "Always save the best until last."

"Why?"

"So you'll go to sleep with a smile on your face," he said.

He let his hands go where they wanted. His fingertips created fire from her eyebrows to her toes and back again. Hot sultry kisses followed every touch and had her panting by the time he began that familiar slow rhythm that took her to another world where there were no words. Only feelings that ran so deep that she couldn't imagine living without him, in or out of the bedroom.

She splayed her hands out over his broad muscular back so that she could feel every sensation in her fingertips and palms. The sweat, the ripples, the heat… everything that made him Hank and everything she wanted for the rest of her life.

"Damn!" he said as he collapsed.

"Why damn?" she panted.

"The curtain is closed and the play is over. I wanted it to last longer," he gasped.

"Why? It was perfect," she murmured.

He pulled her close to him and buried his face in her hair. In seconds, they were both asleep.

He awoke to a gorgeous orange sun peeking over the window ledge and lighting up the hotel room. Larissa slept on her side, facing him, still purring like a kitten. Her eyelids danced with movement and he wondered what she dreamed about. He eased off the bed and took a quick shower before dressing. He had to go back to his mother's house to get his things and then pick up the ladies before eleven. He brushed a soft kiss across her lips before he left.

She reached up and put both arms around his neck. "Do you have to go?"

"Yes, I do, darlin'. You've got breakfast in an hour with your father and I've got to go get my things. I'll be back at eleven."

"Not fair," she said huskily without opening her eyes.

"I know, sweetheart," he whispered.

———— ᨯᨯ ————

"You got laid," Sharlene singsonged when she and Larissa met in front of the elevator.

"I don't kiss and tell," Larissa said.

"You don't have to. I was coming into the hotel when you and Hank got on the elevator. And I was in the lobby a while ago when he came down the elevator and had an extra little sling in that cute little ass of his as he crossed the lobby. I had just stepped out and was on my way to wake you up from your sex-drugged sleep when you opened your door. I waited on you and the look on your face says it all."

"I'm old enough to vote, old enough to sell beer, so I guess I'm old enough to have sex if I want to," Larissa said. "You on your way to breakfast?"

"Yep, I've already checked out the menu. I'm having that breakfast bar and I'm going to eat enough to warrant paying that much for it. And I didn't get laid so they're in luck."

Larissa pushed the button when they were inside the elevator. "What does that mean?"

Sharlene rolled her green eyes and frowned. "Sex must've been good."

"Why do you say that?"

"You can't even think, girl. What's the first thing you want in the morning after a night of rumpling the sheets?"

"A shower?"

"And then?"

"I'm starving. Just tell me what you're getting at, Sharlene."

The doors opened and they stepped out. "You want food. I didn't get lucky so I won't clean out the bar. You'll probably make them lose money on your breakfast. I'll know how good it was by how much you eat."

"You are crazy. And there is my breakfast date. Come on, girl. You're fixin' to meet my father." Larissa looped her arm through Sharlene's.

Sharlene stopped in her tracks. "Your who?"

Larissa pulled at her arm until she started to walk. "My father. Hi, this is my friend and my employee Sharlene Waverly. Sharlene, my father Larry Morleo. Shall we find a table?"

"I've already got one and had a pot of coffee brought over. You do drink coffee, don't you?"

"Black as tar and strong as you can get it," she said.

"Just like my mother. I swear it's uncanny." He led them back to a table on the edge of the restaurant away from the noise.

The waitress came right over and asked if they needed menus.

"No, ma'am. We are having buffet," Sharlene said.

"Three buffets then." Larry led the way to the bar and they followed.

Larissa put two plates on her tray. She filled one with pancakes; the other with eggs, sausage, gravy over biscuits, and bacon. Then she added a bowl of fresh fruit and a lemon poppy seed muffin.

"Must've been damn good," Sharlene whispered.

"This is just for act one," she whispered back.

Sharlene moaned. "Hot damn! I want details."

"Not from me."

Larry chose pancakes covered with fruit and whipped cream and was already seated when they returned to the table. "So did you think of any more questions you want to ask me since last night?"

Larissa put a forkful of eggs into her mouth and nodded. When she'd swallowed she said, "You mentioned my grandmother, Elvira. What's my grandfather's name?"

"James Lawrence Morleo, Jr. I'm the third. He's the one with the Hispanic heritage. About a quarter. Mother is a quarter Indian. Now I've got a question for you. Did you finish high school at Perry?"

"Yes, and college at OSU with a degree in business finance. Then I went on a seven-year tour of the world to find myself. Didn't get it done in that length of time so I came back home to Perry, pulled down a map in the library, shut my eyes, turned around three times, and stuck a pin in the map of the whole United States. It landed square in the middle of Mingus, Texas."

He sipped his coffee and smiled. "You even have her voice. I've been to Mingus. What did you think when you went there?"

"That I'd gone to the end of the world, made a left turn, and found hell."

He laughed loudly. "I understand. What kept you there?"

"Sheer determination laced with weariness. I hadn't found myself anywhere else so I decided to give it a try. Now I've got good friends, a good business, and I'm happy," she said.

"How in the world did you finance a seven-year tour? Did you work in all those places you landed?"

She finished her eggs between answers and started on the biscuits and gravy. "Did Mother ever tell you about herself?"

"Just that she was from Perry, Oklahoma, and her retired parents still lived there," he said.

"She was very wealthy. I had a trust fund from my grandfather when he passed away that let me travel. Sometimes I worked. It was never because I had to, but in Italy I got a job at a travel agency and in Egypt I worked at a research laboratory. You got to get to know the people if you think that's where you are supposed to hang your heart," she said.

"I thought it was your hat that you hung," he said.

"That too. But if the heart ain't happy, you might as well toss that hat in the nearest trash heap."

"I see."

"I got a question," Sharlene said.

They both looked at her. "How in the devil did you two wind up at this hotel at the same time?"

Larry looked at Larissa and they both started to talk at once.

"You tell her," Larissa said.

"I've got to get home to work this morning. Here's my card with my cell number on the back. Call me anytime. So you can tell her the story while you two finish your breakfast," Larry said. He motioned for the waitress who brought the ticket. He shoved some bills into the folder and handed it back to her.

"I'll call," Larissa said.

"I'll be waiting," Larry answered and waved as he wheeled a small suitcase across the lobby floor.

"I'm waiting right now. This is huge. This is beyond huge," Sharlene said.

Hank picked them up at eleven and they stopped for a late lunch at the Smokestack on the way. The waitress brought the menus and Sharlene didn't even look at hers.

"I want an order of french fries and a Coke. After that breakfast, I may not eat for a week," she said.

"Well, all I had was yogurt and a bagel at my mother's place so I'm starving," Hank said.

Sharlene giggled.

"What's so funny?"

"Larissa can tell you later. I'm not sure I could without blushing."

He dropped one hand and squeezed her knee. "How much later?"

"Very much later!" Larissa said.

He moved his hand up a few inches.

"Tomorrow," she said.

He moved it a couple more inches.

"Tonight," she said.

The waitress appeared with their drinks and an order pad.

He clasped the menu with both hands again. "Chicken fried steak, fries, Ranch dressing on my salad, save me a piece of coconut pie, and make that double fries."

She looked at Larissa. "Same thing."

"French fries and a Coke," Sharlene said. "Okay, we'll change the subject so neither of us will light up this place like the Fourth of July. What are y'all doing for Thanksgiving? I know it's a whole month from now but I was thinking maybe I'd go home on Wednesday and stay over until Friday morning. I'd only miss one night of work and Tessa might be able to pitch in then."

"If she can't I will," Hank offered.

"Where are you having Thanksgiving?" Larissa asked him.

"At the ranch with you," he said.

"I've always had it at Perry. Why don't you go with me?"

"What is that? A five-hour drive?" he asked.

"Depends on whether you are driving or flying. I'd planned on renting a charter to take me on Thursday morning and bring me back on Friday morning. The Honky Tonk is closed on Thanksgiving and Christmas so I wouldn't miss work," she said.

"I already promised Dad I'd be there with him this year," he said.

Sharlene felt the tension mounting. "Hey, you got six weeks to get that worked out. You can both go home with me to Corn and believe me, after a couple of days there, you'll both love Mingus even more."

Suddenly, Larissa had a burr in her underpants and put a damper on her near perfect previous evening. She tried wiggling it away but it wouldn't budge. She'd have to work on it later because she wanted that sweet feeling back that she'd had when Hank kissed her that morning. She wanted to relive the joy of meeting her father and she damn sure wanted to feel the ecstasy of what she and Hank had shared the night before.

It didn't really matter where she had Thanksgiving. She could eat it on a pallet in the Smokehouse parking lot in the middle of an ice storm. So why did it upset her that Hank hadn't jumped on the bandwagon with her to go to Perry?

Because I'm afraid to ride the rainbow for fear it's going to slap me right off into misery again. If I let him get too close and start making decisions and he gets tired of living a rancher's life, he will leave me behind with the ranch. It's like walking a tightrope with no net and trusting my partner not to push me off on the hard ground. If I'm ever to have a real relationship past the bedroom with this cowboy, I have to trust him.

Chapter 22

It might snow once in every sixth blue moon in north Texas and never before January or February. But that year a cold front blew down from Colorado two days before Thanksgiving. By closing time at the Honky Tonk bare tree limbs and telephone wires were coated with enough ice to make them sparkle when the parking lot lights hit them. Then the snow started in earnest and when it finished a coating of sleet covered that. It wasn't deep but it was deadly, especially on back roads.

On Wednesday morning Sharlene called her parents and told them she'd be home for Christmas, good lord willing and if the creek didn't rise. Merle called Larissa to pout that there was no way she was going to drive south to Angel and Garrett's ranch. Luther couldn't get out of Texas to take Tessa home to meet his family in Ardmore, Oklahoma. Larissa's pilot canceled all chartered flights for the rest of the week.

They opened the Honky Tonk that night. Luther and Tessa were there because Luther drove them in the tow truck. Four of them sat at a table and talked about the unfairness of the weather until ten o'clock. Then Sharlene jumped up and grabbed her cell phone.

"Hello, Merle. You got a turkey in your freezer? You do! Great! I'm having Thanksgiving dinner at the Honky Tonky on Thursday at noon. I'll send Luther for you and turkey and cornbread dressing at noon. Call Tinker and tell him if he can get into town he's welcome to come eat with us," she said.

"Now you call Linda, Betty, and Janice and tell them to bring something to our dinner. There ain't no way their kids are going to get here. They might as well join us. And call Hank. Tell him to bring Henry and Oma," Sharlene said.

"You are a genius," Tessa said. "Get some paper and a pencil. Put me down for pecan pies and sweet potato casserole. We'll push the tables all up together."

"I make the best damn ham in Oklahoma. I'll bring it," Luther said.

Sharlene tossed her phone at Larissa. "Hank first."

She dialed the familiar number. It was on the tenth ring when Hank finally answered. "Larissa, what are you doing calling at this time of night? Aren't you at work?"

"I am but Sharlene has an idea. Since none of us can go home for the holiday we're having Thanksgiving in the Honky Tonk. I know Oma will make dinner there but…" she paused.

"Are you inviting us to your dinner at the Tonk?" he asked.

"I am."

"Let me ask Oma and Dad. Can I get back with you in a few minutes?"

"That'll be fine."

Sharlene reached for the phone. "You call Janice. I'll take Linda and Tessa can call Betty. List is right here." She laid a yellow note pad and pen on the table.

Twenty minutes later the list was growing. Janice offered to bring hot rolls and baked beans and was grateful that she didn't have to do a full fledged meal for two people. Betty said to put her down for pumpkin pies, chocolate cake, and potato casserole. Linda had planned on a big family to-do and had all the paper goods plus decorations and would bring broccoli casserole, green beans, and pumpkin gooey cake.

Hank called back to tell her that Henry said they could put the chains on the four wheel drive truck. And Oma wanted to know what to bring.

"Anything she wants to fix," Larissa said. "Looks like we've got about sixteen lined up right now. It'll be fun. We plan on eating at noon, so start early and drive slow."

"Do I have to leave early and drive slow?" he asked.

"You could stay late and not drive at all," she teased.

"Wooo who!" Tessa raised both arms and did a jig on the dance floor.

Hank laughed. "It'll be nice to spend the day with you."

"Same back at you," Larissa said and flipped the phone shut. "Let's close it up, folks. Ain't no need in sitting here until two and we won't open tomorrow night. Weatherman says it's not going to melt until Friday. Ain't that the shits?"

"If there's anything worse than shit, then that's what it is. But now I'm looking forward to the day at least. I was dreading spending it all alone," Sharlene said.

"You and I would have had bologna sandwiches if nothing else," Larissa said. Her stomach lurched at the thought of putting a bologna sandwich in her mouth. She hoped she wasn't getting the flu right when they'd figured out a way to have a nice family dinner.

"Yuck," Sharlene snarled her nose.

Tessa bundled up in a wool lined denim duster and Luther ushered her out the door. They waved and said they'd have Merle there by noon on Thursday and if the weather got worse to call and they'd make trips in the tow truck to get the rest of the guests.

"You might as well stay here tonight. You can have my bed and I'll take the sofa," Sharlene said. "Ain't no way Hank is going to heat up your bed anyway."

Larissa shook her head. "Thanks, but no thanks. I'll drive very slow. It's not that far and I feel like I'm coming down with the flu. I'm going home and drinking lemon tea until it passes. I sure don't want to give it to you."

Sharlene threw up her arms in a cross. "Get thee behind me, devil woman. I don't want to be sick right here when we've got a wonderful meal all planned out."

Larissa picked up her coat from the back of her chair and started across the dance floor. Everything started spinning and she had to grab the doorjamb to keep from falling on her face.

"You all right?" Sharlene called out.

"Got a head rush when I got up. It's that blasted flu. If I'm sick on Thanksgiving I'm going to cry."

"Go home and get well. If you need anything, call me and I'll make Luther go get it for you. If you don't feel like cooking tomorrow I'll make enough for both of us to contribute to the dinner," Sharlene said.

"I might take you up on it if I don't get to feeling better," Larissa said. Twice on the way to the garage she had another dizzy spell but they were both very brief. She couldn't be sick on her first Thanksgiving with Hank.

The five-minute trip from the Honky Tonk to her house took fifteen minutes with the slick roads and Stallone was meowing at the back door when she pulled up in the driveway.

"Come on in, old boy. I bet you are cold tonight even with that fur coat. I'll fix a litter pan and you can stay in the house but don't expect it every night. Only when it's cold and miserable outside," she said. "Besides, I miss Hank. This once a week crap isn't enough anymore."

Stallone darted into the house as soon as she opened the door and went straight for the heater vent. He lay as close as he could get and the look on his face said he'd died and St. Peter had given him the ticket to get past the Pearly Gates.

Larissa showered, donned a pair of flannel pajamas, and curled up on the sofa with a cup of lemon tea and the remote. She wished it was Saturday night instead of Tuesday. Had it really only been three days since she'd lain in Hank's arms after they'd made love? It seemed like a month.

Her cell phone began playing the first bars of "People Are Crazy." She stuck the remote to her ear and said, "Hello, Mother." When she realized what she'd done she threw the remote down on the sofa and flipped the phone open and said it again.

"I was about to leave a message for you to call me later. What is that horrible song that plays before your message machine comes on?" Doreen asked.

Larissa laughed. She'd forgotten that instead of a message, "My Give a Damn's Busted," played after the fourth ring. "I should change it. I put it on there when Hank and I were never going to see each other again."

"And that has changed for sure?" Doreen asked.

"It has. He's busy in the day and I'm busy at night. That sounds funny, doesn't it? Sounds like I'm a two-bit hooker."

"Well, a beer joint is barely a step up from that," Doreen said. "I was calling to make Christmas plans. Rupert and I will be in the States. You want to come to Perry?"

"I'd love to." Tears welled up in Larissa's eyes and she had to swallow three times to get the orange-sized lump out of her throat.

"Bring Hank with you. Bring Henry if he wants to come along. Just let me know so there will be presents under the Christmas tree for everyone."

"How about Oma?"

Doreen hesitated. "Is that your cat?"

Larissa laughed. "No, it's the cook, dishwasher, surrogate grandma person who keeps the place running for Henry."

"If it's not an animal, it's welcome," Doreen said. "Got to go. Rupert is pouring wine."

"Good-bye, Mother," Larissa said.

"Change that horrid message."

Stallone's purring was the only noise in the house until she pushed the power button on the remote and surfed through the channels until she found a late night movie to watch. There wasn't a bit of sense in going to bed before two thirty. She'd just lie there and try to make sense of the whole situation with Hank and there was no figuring the man out.

"And they say women are hard to understand," she mumbled.

She fell asleep on the sofa and felt wonderful when she awoke the next morning. The lemon tea must have kicked the flu right in its hind end because she had energy and all the dizziness was gone. She dragged down the two cookbooks she'd bought at a garage sale and pored over the gorgeous pictures and recipes.

Finally, she decided on a three-layered banana nut cake like Rosa would be making in Perry. It would at least bring a bit of home to the Thanksgiving table at the Honky Tonk. She checked ingredients and luckily had everything she needed in the house. By mid afternoon it was made and sitting perfectly on a cake stand she'd bought the same day she'd gotten the cookbooks. She put the glass dome on the top and heated up a can of chicken noodle soup. If there were remnants of a flu bug in her system, surely chicken noodle soup would flush it out.

Sharlene called a dozen times to tell her what she was making and keep her up-to-date on the other ladies who were making food in their kitchens. Merle was excited because she said that Ruby Lee's spirit was still in the Honky Tonk and they hadn't had a holiday together since she died. Janice, Linda, and Betty were happy to be in good company. Luther said the ham had his whole house smelling wonderful and that he and Tessa were arguing over whether to chop pecans or leave them whole for the pies.

At nine thirty Oma called to say that she'd be bringing chicken and dumplings and peach cobbler, and to thank her for inviting them. "It's the first time in all the fifty years I've been at the ranch that I don't have to make the big meal. It's quite a treat for me. And I get to be among all you young people too."

"Merle's not so young," Larissa said.

"I met Merle once. I won't tell her you said that," Oma said.

"Thank you," Larissa said.

She flipped her phone shut and pulled Stallone up into her lap and suddenly the thought of dough balls floating in chicken broth gagged her. She threw her hand over her mouth and barely made it to the toilet in time. She felt like she'd thrown up her toenails right along with everything else she'd eaten that day.

Stallone washed his face at the door and waited.

"It's back," she groaned. "I thought we'd kicked it, but it's back in full force." She stood up and everything did a couple of spins before it settled down. She gagged when she brushed her teeth and the cold wash cloth felt icy on her skin. "Please not a fever. I don't want to be sick tomorrow. Nothing about this holiday is working for me. Just don't let me have fever or I won't be able to go for fear I'd be contagious."

Stallone rubbed around her legs and followed her back to the sofa where she went right to sleep and didn't wake until morning. She eased one eyelid open and waited. She moved slightly but her stomach didn't seize up. Very carefully, she stood up and felt wonderful.

"It's got to be something I'm eating at night. Lemon tea! I wonder when I developed an allergy to that. I haven't had it in a couple of years but it looked so good at the supermarket that I bought a box. That has to be the culprit. No more lemon tea, Stallone." She bent over and petted the cat and didn't even feel dizzy when she quickly stood up.

They spread the tables with plastic tablecloths decorated on the edges with pumpkins and turkeys. Each table had a fold-out centerpiece that was either a turkey or a pumpkin and two gingerbread scented candles glowing brightly. Sharlene had strung orange, green, and brown crepe paper from the ceiling and had votive candles strung up and down the bar.

Larissa sat on a bar stool and told all four of the women doing the decorating that the place looked like a kindergarten classroom. "But it is beautiful and I'm glad to be here today."

Merle and Luther came inside and quickly shut the door against the cold north wind. Luther carried an enormous roaster holding a turkey and dressing. The aroma joined with the others and the whole Honky Tonk smelled like a restaurant.

"I think it's all beautiful, no buts about it," Merle said. "Where's Hank and Henry? It's been years since I've seen that tall old cowboy. I'm looking forward to visiting with him about Ruby Lee."

Sharlene hugged her and then handed her a beer. "He's on the way. Should be here any minute. Larissa doesn't want us to notice but she's been watching the door for an hour."

"I have not."

"Have not what?" Hank opened the door, let Oma and Henry inside, and then shut it behind him. "You have not what?"

Sharlene went to take the casserole dish from Henry. "She's been watching for you and getting antsy. You know what that means?"

Hank nodded. "That she's hungry."

"That she's going to throw rocks at you on the playground during recess. I think she might like you,"

Sharlene said. "The curse of the Honky Tonk has struck again."

"It has not," Larissa said right behind her. She walked into Hank's arms and laid her head on his chest. The sound of his heartbeat in her ears was so peaceful that she hated to open her eyes.

Chapter 23

THE SUN CAME OUT LATE FRIDAY AFTERNOON AND THE WIND twisted around to the south. By night the roads were clear enough that pickup trucks could navigate and folks were tired of being homebound. Luther didn't have to count the customers but there were enough people to fill up the dance floors and keep all three bartenders busy most of the time.

Larissa felt Hank's presence before she noticed him skirting a double string of line dancers taking up most of the floor. He claimed a stool at the end of the bar and their eyes met in the middle. He pointed toward the Mason jar she was filling for someone else and she nodded. When she'd finished that order she picked up a pint and pulled the handle marked Coors.

"I wasn't expecting you tonight," she said.

He handed her a five-dollar bill and she made change. "Roads were clear enough to drive on. Ice patches still on the bridges but they have been sanded. Just have to be careful."

"Are you staying in town?"

"Depends on whether I'm asked." His eyes twinkled.

Justin Langley claimed the last two bar stools on Hank's left. "Asked what? I brought someone for you to meet, Larissa. I can't believe you are still around here. What was your name? Hank something? I figured you'd have given up on her by now. Most cowboys only last a few weeks."

"How about you?"

"Justin?" the tall brunette with him asked.

"Ah, honey, you know I like to tease. Larissa, meet my wife, Denise. We got married the day before Thanksgiving and were on our way to Branson, Missouri, for a honeymoon when the snow stopped us. We spent two nights holed up in a motel and now we're back on the road to Branson. The Christmas stuff is all lit up and she loves Christmas, don't you?"

"I do, and it's nice to meet you, Larissa. I'd like a Grey Goose martini."

"Nice to meet you. Your first drinks are on the house. Glad to see that you roped Justin down and I hope you have a long and wonderful marriage," Larissa said.

"Thank you," Denise said.

"Beer?" Larissa asked Justin.

"No, I'll have whatever she's drinking tonight."

She hustled two real martini glasses from under the cabinet, cleaned them until they sparkled, and poured the drinks into them.

"Where's the jars?" Justin asked.

"Denise deserves something fancy if she's going to put up with your sorry hide the rest of her life," Larissa said.

Denise was still smiling as they carried their drinks to a table, removed jackets, and draped them over the back of chairs and hit the dance floor just as a slow Alan Jackson song started.

"And another good man bites the dust," Hank said.

"You better watch your smart mouth or you'll be driving right slow across the bridges tonight," Larissa said.

"Is that an invitation to stay over?" he asked.

"It is," she said.

"Could I get a pitcher of margaritas and one of hurricanes?" a man at the other end of the bar asked.

Larissa nodded and went to work. She set them on a tray when she finished and took his money. When she looked back down the bar, Hank was talking to an older couple who had taken Justin and Denise's places.

"Can I get you something?" she asked without even looking at them.

"Larissa, this is James and Elvira Morleo. They came from over in Abilene," Hank said.

She was so engrossed in Hank that it took a few seconds for what he said to sink in. When it did, she looked across the bar and gasped. Her father had been right. She was looking into the future forty years at the reflection of herself. Her grandmother was about the same height, had black hair sprinkled lightly with gray, and brown eyes. The face shape was the same and although Elvira carried twenty or thirty extra pounds it wasn't hard to imagine her at thirty looking exactly like Larissa.

"Quite a shock, isn't it?" Elvira said.

"Unbelievable," James muttered. He was the same height as Elvira. His hair was gray and his face shape and eyes were like Larry's.

"I think I'll have a Coors in one of those jars. James likes Bud in a bottle. Larry is outside parking the car. This might not be a good time or place but the family wanted to come over here and meet you. They all love country music and dancing. Don't worry about remembering their names. It'll all come with time. Right now we just want to see you," Elvira said.

Sharlene took over the bartending when Larry and his wife walked up to the bar.

"Hello, Larissa."

She nodded.

"This isn't a problem is it?"

She shook her head at thirty or more people filing into the bar, setting up camp at two empty tables. "Not at all. I got to admit, that much family scares me, but it's never a problem."

"Go on and be nice," Sharlene said. "Tessa and I can take care of this for a while."

Larissa's eyes darted toward Hank. "Go with me?" she mouthed.

He finished off his beer and stood up. "I'm Hank Wells. Larissa and I've been seeing each other a few months. You'll be Larry, her father? I've heard a lot about you." He extended his hand.

Larry's handshake was firm and he studied Hank's face as he shook. Finally, he smiled. "I'm glad to meet you, Hank. I'd like to introduce my wife, Mary Beth, to you and Larissa."

She looked from Hank to Larissa. She was about the same height as Sharlene. She had strawberry-blond hair cut chin-length and blue eyes. She was slim built but something about her said that she could take care of herself.

"I'm glad to meet you, Larissa. I'm looking forward to getting to know you better. This probably wasn't a good idea—hitting you at your business with so many of us—but it didn't sound so formidable at home. Forgive us if we've overwhelmed you," Mary Beth said.

"Not at all. It's a pleasure to meet you. Let's go see everyone else," Larissa said as she came through the swinging doors at the end of the bar. Hank met her a few feet before she reached the party of four at the bar and slipped his hand in hers. The support of his touch couldn't be measured in gold, silver, or even time.

She met Larry's brother and sister-in-law, four cousins and their spouses, Elvira's sister, her husband and two of their five kids, plus cousins and spouses with that connection. Names went over the top of her head and faces were a blur.

"It's not often I get this woman out from behind that bar. So if y'all will excuse us I'm going to dance with her," Hank said.

"That's fine, son. I reckon she needs a breather away from all of us for a little bit," James said. "I'm going to the bar for buckets of beer. Anyone want a mixed drink?" He waited a few seconds but got no takers. "I hope you didn't want a sophisticated bunch of relatives, Larissa. We're basically a bunch of rednecks."

"Family could never disappoint me. I'm just happy to get to know you all, and for the record, I'm a beer drinker too," Larissa managed to get out.

Hank led her out to the dance floor and wrapped her up in his arms. "You handled that beautifully."

"I want a beer, maybe a whole six-pack. One day the only relative I have is my mother. The next, just look, and Elvira said this was only the tip of the iceberg."

"Scary, ain't it?"

"As hell. How many relatives do you have?"

"Mother was an only child. Grandfather had a brother and he had a son. They live in Hawaii and I've met him one time. Dad had three brothers, all older than he is and all dead. They had kids but they're scattered six ways to

Sunday. Dad keeps them on the Christmas card list and Oma sends a greeting once a year. Nothing like this for you to have to meet," he said.

"Thank God!"

At midnight she'd danced with her grandfather, her father, and several cousins. They'd told her stories and did their damnedest to pull her into their vast family. When they left she and Hank walked them to the door and introduced her grandparents, Larry, and Mary Beth to Luther. She waved her hand to include the rest. "And these are all relatives too, but I can't remember their names. This is Luther, one of my first friends when I came to Mingus and the best bouncer in the state."

Luther took them all in with one nod. "Pleased to meet you. Come back and visit us anytime."

When the last one filed out the door, she leaned against Hank. "Thank you."

"Things are slowing down. Why don't you let Tessa and Sharlene close up tonight and you go on home. That had to have knocked the sap out of you, but you don't need one of them DNA things to know that that was definitely your blood kin. You are the spittin' image of your grandma and her sister," Luther said.

"Yes, I am. And I think I will go home." She headed back to the bar to tell Sharlene and Tessa. The room did a couple of spins but she got control quickly. She'd had too much all at one time and she hadn't had a thing to eat since lunch. Her blood sugar was probably bottomed out.

She drove home with Hank's headlights in her rearview mirror. Why hadn't she thought about letting Sharlene close up before that night? She could have been spending hours more with Hank.

Since when did anyone or anything mean more to you than your Honky Tonk? The question brought her up short and scared the hell out of her.

Chapter 24

LARISSA SAT ON THE EDGE OF THE BATHTUB. EVERY SECOND that ticked off the clock lasted two hours. Her hands were clammy. Her stomach was tied up like a pretzel. Finally, the second hand made its way around the numbers one last time. She picked up the stick and shut her eyes. She should've called Sharlene to come look for her but she couldn't tell anyone her biggest fear.

She opened one eye a tiny slit but the stick looked fuzzy. There was nothing to do but spring them both open and find out.

"Dear God!" She threw the stick in the trash as if it were evil and threw up in the potty.

She went back to bed, rolled over on her side, and thought about the line on the pregnancy stick. Hank mumbled something in his sleep, slipped one arm under her and one around her, and molded his naked body next to her back.

He nuzzled his face into her hair and slowly opened his eyes. "Have I told you this morning that I love you?"

"I don't think you've ever told me that," she said. He hadn't even said those words six weeks before when they'd had that fabulous three act sex bout in the hotel in Dallas. Lord, that's when it happened! She counted backwards and remembered every single time since then and for the test to be positive it had to have happened at the Hyatt in Dallas.

"Well, I'm telling you right now. I know it's probably too early to say the words but I've wanted to for a long, long time. I love you, Larissa Morley, with my whole heart. Are you crying?"

She nodded. "You know I love you and for the record I've never said those words to another man. I'm just all emotional this morning."

He turned her over to face him and strung kisses down her neck. "I'm in awe."

"Well, get ready to be stunned as well as in awe," she said.

"Are you going to propose to me? I thought you might a week ago after family night at the Honky Tonk but got my hopes dashed when all you did was come home with me at a decent hour," he teased. It felt so good to say the three words to her, to get them off his chest and let her know that he was serious about their relationship and commitment.

"No, I'll leave that job to you. Please don't feel like you have to…"

He jumped out of bed, pulled her up to a sitting position, and dropped down on one knee in front of her. Naked as the day he was born, he took her hand in his and said, "Larissa Morley, will you marry me? We can have a long engagement. I'll wait forever if you'll just give me some hope. You can work at the Honky Tonk and we'll live at the ranch. Or we can live right here in this gawd awful house and I'll commute back and forth to the ranch every day."

Her dark eyelashes couldn't keep the tears back. He had proposed before she told him. She'd never feel like he'd been doing his duty.

He got up off his knees and sat down beside her on the bed. He figured she couldn't say yes because she still didn't trust him and she couldn't hurt his feelings by saying no. He took her hand in his. "Darlin', don't cry. You don't have to give me an answer right now. I'll wait six months and ask you again."

"I can't…" she sobbed.

He hugged her tightly. "I'm sorry I put you in such a spot. I was so excited to hear you say the words and I love you so much."

"I can't tell you because I'm afraid you'll be upset. It was an accident. I promise I didn't do it on purpose," she said.

"Larissa, what in the devil are you talking about? You didn't do what on purpose?"

"The stick is in the trash. I thought I was getting the flu or that I'd eaten something wrong. But the stick is positive and I…" She laid her head on his chest and wept.

"Stick? Positive?" He frowned.

"I'm pregnant."

He jumped up, grabbed her, and danced around the bed. "I love you. I'm not mad and I wouldn't give a damn if you did do it on purpose."

Tears turned to laughter. "Really?"

"Yes, really. When are we getting married?"

"I love you too, Hank Wells. Is tomorrow soon enough? The courthouse isn't open on Sunday."

————

They were married the next morning at the courthouse in Palo Pinto. The court clerk and the janitor served as witnesses to the wedding. She wore an off-white lace dress and new white dress boots that she'd gotten on sale in Dallas when she and her mother went shopping. Hank wore the same western cut suit that he'd worn to Doreen and Rupert's reception.

He picked her up like a new bride and the kisses started when they left the courthouse doors. "I love you, Larissa Wells," he said between kisses so hot that they could have heated up all of Palo Pinto County.

"I love you, Hank Wells. You sure you don't want to stop at a motel between here and the ranch?"

He chuckled as he set her in the passenger's seat. "Honey, there's not even a gas station between here and the ranch. We'll tell Henry, stop by and let Sharlene know the news, and then go anywhere you want, as long as I don't have to share you for a whole week."

"Will Henry be all right at the ranch that long without you?" she asked.

"To get you, Henry would let me leave for a month." He pulled her close to his side. "I can't believe we are married and we're going to have a son."

"Better hope it's a girl because its name is Ruby," she said.

"Victoria?" he said with a frown on his face.

She giggled. "Ruby Victoria. I like it."

"I wasn't asking to use her name. I was thinking about how she'd go up in flames if the baby was a girl and you named her Ruby. Flames won't even begin to describe the inferno she'll set to blazing if you put her name in there with Ruby's."

"Flames? Maybe she'll have red hair like Mother. I don't know which you are happier about, cowboy. Me as a bride or the baby," she said.

He tilted her chin up and kissed her tenderly, yet passionately. "Darlin', we might have a dozen kids or this might be our only chick. I will love whatever we are blessed with. But you will always be number one with me. I keep pinching myself to assure myself that I'm not dreaming and touching you to make sure you aren't going to vanish into a puff of smoke. Have I told you today that you are a stunning bride?"

Tears welled up in her eyes. "You are making me all weepy again."

"You are making me happy."

"I love you," she whispered again.

"That still amazes me after everything we've been through. I love you too."

———∿∿∿———

It was a lovely day for the second week in December. A little nip in the air and all the trees bare of leaves, but the sun was shining brightly when they drove up in the yard at the ranch house. She slid under the steering wheel and got out of the truck on Hank's side. He threw an arm around her shoulders and felt her shiver.

He quickly removed his coat and wrapped it around her. "You are cold."

"Is Henry going to be angry with me?" she asked.

"Hey, what are you two doing all dressed up?" Henry said from the corner of the porch. "You look beautiful in that lacy thing. Don't know that I've seen you in a fancy dress before. What's the occasion? Come on over here and draw up a rocking chair. We ain't going to have very many more nice days. Surprised that we got this one after that snow business a couple of weeks ago, but the weather is fickle in this part of the world. An ice storm don't mean that it won't warm up again."

Larissa sat down in the rocking chair next to him and Hank propped a hip on the side of the same chair. "We got something we need to talk to you about, Henry."

"Okay, sit down and shoot," he said.

"We just came from the courthouse. We got married," Hank said bluntly.

Henry jumped out of the chair and embraced them in a three-way hug. "Well, hot damn! And you done it the right way. I don't even have to wear a monkey suit and go to a weddin'."

"Well, there *is* going to be a reception at the Honky Tonk next week so you'll have to get dressed up for that," Larissa said.

He sat back down in his rocker but he kept a hand on Larissa's arm. "I reckon I can do that. When are you moving to the ranch?"

Hank leaned over and kissed her on the cheek. "I told her that she could live in town and run her Honky Tonk, Dad. I'm not making the same mistake you did."

Henry nodded. "Then you'll be moving to Mingus and coming back and forth. That'll be hard on both of you but if it's what you want, then I understand."

"It's not what I want," Larissa said. "I want to live here and learn new things. I want Oma to teach me how to run this place. I've got a degree in business finance. I can help and I want to be where I can see my husband any time of the day or night."

Henry wiped at his eye with a handkerchief he pulled from his hip pocket. "I couldn't wish for nothin' better. Sharlene going to manage the Honky Tonk for you?

Hell, I don't even care if you see me cry. You've both made me the happiest man in the state of Texas today."

"Sharlene is going to own the Tonk. Hank and I might visit sometime. But I'm making a clean break."

"Well, double hot damn! Let's get a beer and celebrate," Henry shouted.

Larissa shook her head. "I can't have a beer, Henry, or a martini or a drink for the next few months. I'm pregnant."

The few crickets who'd survived the ice storm stopped chirping. The wind stopped blowing. The coyotes fell silent. Not a bawling Angus cow could be heard. The silence was as heavy as concrete.

"My prayers have all been answered," Henry whispered then he shouted. "Oma, come out here and hear the good news!"

—‚‚‚—

The reception was held in the middle of the afternoon on a Sunday. Everyone in town was invited. Doreen and Rupert arrived an hour early. Victoria arrived fifteen minutes late.

Larissa wore her wedding dress, a wide gold wedding band, and a big smile. Hank was dressed in his western suit. Pictures were taken. Merle served punch and Linda, Betty, and Janice took care of the cake and finger foods.

When the parents were all there, Sharlene picked up the microphone from her karaoke machine and said, "Family and friends, we are here to celebrate Larissa finding her cowboy and proving that the Honky Tonk charm worked one final time. Larissa has given me the Honky Tonk and I'm here to stay. Three times is the limit of any genie lamp or magic. Luther is putting money into the jukebox right now for the first bride and groom dance. While they are dancing, cake and punch are being served and the bar is open for anyone who wants something stronger."

Hank led Larissa to the middle of the floor. She wrapped both arms around his neck and nodded at Luther.

"Please tell me he isn't going to play 'My Give a Damn's Busted,'" Hank whispered.

"Well, it damn sure was. Thank goodness it wasn't completely broken. There were a few parts where we could fix it. I had to go to an old give-a-damn graveyard to find the parts," she teased.

"Where is that graveyard just in case I mess up again and need to find a part or two?" Hank asked.

"It's out on the backside of the Lazy R Ranch. Up on a rise," she said.

He tilted up her chin with his fist. His whiskey colored eyes met her dark brown ones and his lips found hers in a lingering kiss.

Garth Brooks sang "To Make You Feel My Love." The lyrics talked about everything he would do to make her feel his love. He sang that he could hold her for a million years and that he'd known it from the moment he'd met her. That there was no doubt where she belonged, that he would go hungry and would crawl down the avenue to make her feel his love. He said that she hadn't seen nothing like him and that he would go to the earth to make her happy and make her dreams come true.

When the song ended, he kissed Larissa passionately. "Do you really feel like that?"

"If I didn't I wouldn't be married to you."

He led her off the dance floor. "I want to buy that CD and play it for you every single night."

Victoria slid off a bar stool and met them at the edge of the floor. "Hank?"

"Mother, I can't believe you called me Hank."

"Would you give me and Larissa a moment?" she asked.

He looked at his new bride and she nodded.

"But only a moment, Mother. I will never share her very well and I won't leave her side very long. I'll get us some punch, darlin'," he said.

Larissa looked at Victoria. "Yes, ma'am?"

"I still don't like you," Victoria said.

"I wasn't expecting a miracle right along with my wedding ring and marriage license. Frankly, I don't give a damn if you like me or not. But I reckon we can call a truce a few times a year for Hank, can't we? And then there's the matter of your grandchild."

"Dear God, so that's the way you roped him in," Victoria said.

"No, he proposed to me before he knew about the baby. If he hadn't I wouldn't have married him. We are in love. It's your choice to be a part of our lives or not. I won't force anything on you," Larissa said.

"You are more like your mother than I thought. She always could put me in my place. Okay, then, I will try." Victoria pouted.

"That's a start," Larissa said.

Henry touched Victoria on the shoulder. "Could I have this dance?"

"My God, Henry. I forgot that you'd be here," she gasped.

He held out a hand. "You're lookin' good, Vic."

To Larissa's surprise she walked into his arms.

Garth began to sing "If Tomorrow Never Comes." Hank crossed the room in a dozen long strides and took Larissa in his arms again.

"What did she say?" he asked.

"Not much but I think everything is going to be just fine." Larissa smiled up at him. "Do you think they are listening to the words to this song?"

"No, but I am," he said. "And I intend to tell you every day and try in every way to prove that you are my only one just like he's saying."

"Have I told you in the last five minutes how much I love you?" she whispered.

"Yes, but I'll never get tired of hearing those words," he said. "Look over there."

Larry was leading Doreen to the dance floor and Rupert had an arm thrown around Mary Beth.

Larissa sighed. "And it all came about because of a thumbtack stuck in the middle of the map of the United States."

THE END

About the Author

Carolyn Brown is an award-winning author with more than forty books published, and she credits her eclectic family for her humor and writing ideas. Her books include the cowboy trilogy *Lucky in Love, One Lucky Cowboy,* and *Getting Lucky,* and in the Honky Tonk series, *I Love This Bar* and *Hell Yeah*. She was born in Texas but grew up in southern Oklahoma where she and her husband, Charles, a retired English teacher, make their home. They have three grown children and enough grandchildren to keep them young.

From

HONKY TONK
CHRISTMAS

A sliver of sunshine poured into the room in a long uneven line through a split in the draperies. Sharlene grabbed a pillow and crammed it over her head. She hadn't had such a hellish hangover since she got home from Iraq. They'd had a party to celebrate her homecoming and they'd really tied one on that night. The next morning her head had been only slightly smaller than a galvanized milk bucket. Her head throbbed with every beat of her heart and she'd sworn she'd never get drunk again. But there she was in a hotel room with the same damn symptoms.

She needed a glass of tomato juice spiked with an egg and lemon and three or four aspirin. Somehow she didn't think raw eggs and tomato juice would be on the free continental breakfast bar in the hotel dining room. She peeked out from under the pillow at the clock. The numbers were blurry but it was nine o'clock. Two hours until checkout. That gave her plenty of time for a shower. Maybe warm water would stop her head from pounding like a son-of-a-bitch.

She and her friends had hit four... or was it five
bars? She didn't remember dancing on any tabletops
or getting into fights. She checked her knuckles and
they were free of bloody scabs. No bruises on her arms
or legs. She wiggled but didn't feel like she'd been
kicked or beaten. Either she didn't start a fight or she
won. She frowned and in the fog of the hangover from
hell she remembered arguing with a man. Then the
helicopters were overhead and she told him that Jonah
was dead.

Then they all left and the man brought her to the hotel.
She sat up so quickly that her head spun around like she
was riding a Tilt-A-Whirl at Six Flags. She was hot and
sweaty, barefoot and her skirt was missing. She was still
wearing panties, a T-shirt, and a bra, so evidently the
man had put her to bed and left.

The newspaper reporter in her instantly asked for
what, when, who, and how. She drew her brow down
and remembered the what. She'd been drunk and passed
out in his truck. The when involved after all the bars
closed. The rest was a blur.

She moaned as she sat up on the edge of the bed
and the night came back in foggy detail. Four of her
girlfriends who'd served with her in Iraq had come to
Weatherford for a reunion weekend. One from Panama
City, Florida; one from Huntington, Pennsylvania;
another from Orange Cove, California; and the fourth
from Savannah, Georgia. Sharlene could only get away
for Sunday so they'd flown into Dallas and saved the
best until she arrived. One beer led to another and that
led to a pitcher of margaritas and then the tequila shots.
She vaguely remembered a tequila sunrise or two in the

mix. Her stomach lurched when she stood up and the room did a couple of lopsided twirls.

She leaned on the dresser until everything was standing upright and her stomach settled down. If she waited for her head to stop pounding she'd be there until hell froze over or three days past eternity—whichever came first.

She held her head with both hands as she stumbled toward the bathroom. Hangovers had been invented in hell for fools who drank too much. Or maybe the angels developed them. A good hangover would keep more people out of hell than a silver-tongued preacher man ever could.

"Holt Jackson! Dear God! That's who brought me home. Lord, he'll think I'm a drunk and a slut."

She'd slept in his arms and had *not* dreamed. Even with a hangover, she knew she hadn't dreamed. She hadn't seen Jonah's eyes the night before and she'd slept for the first time in years without the nightmares. She looked back at the tangled sheets on the king-sized bed and the rush of what might have happened made her even dizzier than the hangover. She grabbed the wall and scanned each corner of the room.

"Did we? I can't remember. Oh, shit! I can't remember anything but getting into his truck," she whispered. She reached for the knob to open the bathroom door: It swung to the inside and there stood Holt Jackson, drying his hands on a white hotel towel. She had to hang onto the knob for support or she would have fallen into his arms.

"Good morning," he said.

She rushed inside, shoved him out, and hung her

head over the toilet. When she finished, she washed her face and brushed her teeth. She heard deep laughter and bristled. Sure, she was in misery, but he had no right to laugh at her unless he was a saint or an angel and had never had a hangover. When she opened the door, he was sitting on the end of the bed putting on his boots and watching cartoons. He ran his fingers through his dark brown hair and green eyes looked at her from beneath thick deep dark eyelashes. His face was square with a slight dimple in his chin and his lips were full.

The anger left and was replaced with remorse. "Sorry about that. I haven't been drunk in many years."

"Not since Iraq, huh?" he said.

She glanced at the bed. "We didn't… did we?"

"You snored and I fell asleep. Didn't mean to but it had been a long day with the moving and then driving to Fort Worth for supper. I apologize. Other than that, nothing happened."

"How did you know about Iraq?" she asked cautiously.

"You tried to convince me that if you could drive an Army jeep to the barracks from something or somewhere named Shalma that you could drive your pink Bug to the hotel," he said.

"That all I said?"

"There was something about sand and helicopters, then you passed out. What did you do over there?" Holt asked.

"My job," she said. "Thanks for taking care of me. I appreciate it. I'm going to take a shower and go home."

"Sure?" he asked.

"My head is throbbing and my stomach isn't too sure about whether it's going to punish me some more, but

I'm sober. Still being drunk wouldn't hurt this bad." She tried to smile.

"Okay, then. I'll see you tomorrow at the building site. Be careful." He waved at the door.

She nodded and threw herself back on the bed.

I LOVE THIS BAR

THIS BAR

BY CAROLYN BROWN

Saddle up, cowboy...

She doesn't need anything but her bar...

Daisy O'Dell has her hands full with hotheads and thirsty ranchers until the day one damn fine cowboy walks in and throws her whole life into turmoil. Jarod McElroy is looking for a cold drink and a moment's peace, but instead he finds one red hot woman. She's just what he needs, if only he can convince her to come out from behind that bar, and come home with him...

Praise for *One Lucky Cowboy:*

"Jam-packed with cat fights, reluctant heroes, spirited old ladies and, of course, a chilling villain, Brown's plot-driven cowboy romance...will earn a spot on your keeper shelf."

—*Romantic Times*, 4 stars

"Sheer fun...filled with down-home humor, realistic characters, and pure romance."

—*Romance Reader at Heart*

978-1-4022-3926-7 • $7.99 US / $8.99 CAN / £4.99 UK

HELL, YEAH

BY CAROLYN BROWN

She's finally found a place that feels like home...

When Cathy O'Dell buys the Honky Tonk, the nights of cowboys and country tunes come together to create the home she's always wanted. Then in walks a ruggedly handsome oil man who tempts her to trade in the happiness she's found at the Honky Tonk for a life on the road with him.

Gorgeous and rich, Travis Henry travels the country unearthing oil wells and then moving on. Then the beautiful blue-eyed new owner of the Honky Tonk beer joint becomes his best friend and so much more. When his job is done in Texas, how is he ever going to hit the road without her?

Praise for Carolyn Brown:

"Carolyn Brown takes her audience by storm... I was mesmerized." —The Romance Studio

"Carolyn Brown creates a bevy of delightful and believable characters." —The Long and Short of It Reviews

---

978-1-4022-3927-4 • $7.99 US / $9.99 CAN / £4.99 UK

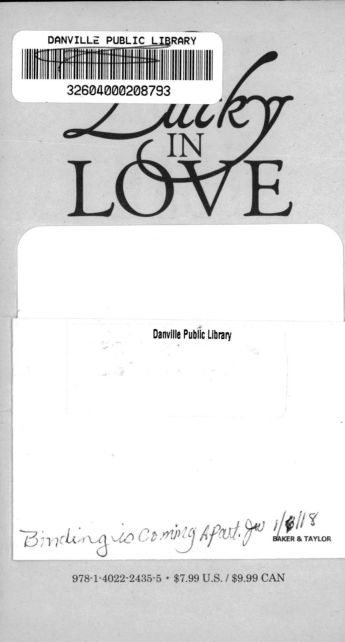

Lucky
IN
LOVE

Binding is coming Apart. Jw 1/8/18

BAKER & TAYLOR

978-1-4022-2435-5 • $7.99 U.S. / $9.99 CAN